"They're not goi[ng] ~~this. I'm not going~~ [to let them.]"

Every word rang with determination, leaving Elena with no doubt that Matt fully intended to do what he promised.

Them. It didn't matter if it was only one person.

This damn town. She should have gotten out when she'd had the chance, should have left it behind her and never looked back.

Matt gently turned her around to face him. "Don't let them do this to you. You're going to make it through this."

It was the tenderness in his voice more than the words themselves that called to Elena, making her raise her head to meet his eyes.

The kindness she saw there, the concern, nearly broke her. She couldn't even remember the last time anyone had looked at her like that, when anyone had so genuinely cared about her feelings.

Then the look in Matt's eyes changed, became more heated, more intense. And out of nowhere, Elena felt her body respond. The emotions that had been churning within her ebbed away, replaced by an incredible sense of warmth that flowed outward to fill every part of her.

This wasn't nostalgia. This wasn't a remembered emotion. It was real, and it was more powerful than anything she remembered…

Every word rang with determination. Leaving Nicos
with no doubt that what Truly intended to do what he
promised.

Then it either made sense or the person—

This made sense. She should have acted on it when
she'd had the chance. Should have left it behind her
and never looked back.

Shan't really make her promise to face him? How's
or them do this to anyone. You're going to make it
through this...

all was the tenderness in his voice, more than the words
themselves, that called to Elena, making her raise her
head to meet his eyes.

The kindness she saw there did something deeply
broke her. She couldn't even remember the last time
anyone had looked at her like that, when anyone had
so genuinely cared about her feelings.

When she took in Matt's eyes changed, became more
darker, more intense. And all at nowhere, Elena
felt her body respond. The emotions that had been
churning within her ebbed away, replaced by an
incredible sense of vulnerability, flowed outward in all
every part of her.

This wasn't anticipate. This wasn't a temperamental
emotion. It was real, and it was more powerful than
anything she'd known.

HER COWBOY
AVENGER

BY
KERRY CONNOR

First published in Great Britain 2013
by Mills & Boon, an imprint of Harlequin (UK) Limited,
Eton House, 18-24 Paradise Road, Richmond, Surrey TW9 1SR

© Kerry Connor 2012

ISBN: 978 0 263 90634 9
ebook ISBN: 978 1 472 01199 2

46-0613

Harlequin (UK) policy is to use papers that are natural, renewable and recyclable products and made from wood grown in sustainable forests. The logging and manufacturing processes conform to the legal environmental regulations of the country of origin.

Printed and bound in Spain
by Blackprint CPI, Barcelona

A lifelong mystery reader, **Kerry Connor** first discovered romance suspense by reading Mills & Boon Intrigue books and is thrilled to be writing for the line. Kerry lives and writes in New York.

To The Old Book Barn in Forsyth, Illinois, where I first
discovered Intrigue and so many wonderful books.

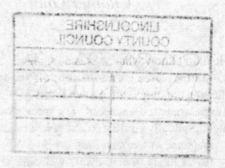

Chapter One

He didn't know what he was doing here.

Matt Alvarez eased his foot off the gas pedal as the sign announcing the town limits of Western Bluff, Texas, appeared up ahead. The truck slowly decelerated, gradually coming to a stop just before the sign.

Welcome to Western Bluff.

It was likely to be the only welcome he received in this town. It hadn't been a particularly friendly place the first time he'd been here, and he wasn't counting on that having changed much. When he'd left eight years ago, no one had bothered telling him goodbye, and he doubted there were many who'd remember him all these years later.

No, there was only one person he could count on remembering him. The person who'd reached out and brought him back after all this time.

From what he could see, the town up ahead looked the same. Short, square buildings were lined up along what passed for a Main Street. Around it stretched the dry desert landscape as far as the eye could see.

It wasn't too late to turn back. It sure as heck would make a lot more sense than driving all the way from New Mexico to this dusty West Texas town in the middle of nowhere, all because of a newspaper article he'd received in the mail.

That article lay heavily in the front pocket of his shirt, tucked in the envelope it had arrived in. He didn't know for sure who'd sent it; there hadn't been a return address. But there was only one person he could imagine sending it. He just couldn't understand why. For help, he supposed. If the story in the article was true, she could probably use it.

That didn't explain why she would have sent it to him of all people, nor why he had come.

He'd been asking himself that last one from the moment he'd climbed into the truck and during every stretch of the drive.

Now he was finally here, and he still didn't have an answer.

Whatever the reason, he couldn't sit there in the middle of the highway forever. The road was clear enough—he didn't see anyone coming up behind him in the rearview mirror—probably not a surprise given the size of the town up ahead. Few people would have a reason to pass through this out-of-the-way place.

But here he was nonetheless.

With a sigh, he moved his foot to the accelerator and put the truck back into motion.

He slowly drove into town, taking in his surroundings as he passed along the main drag. Just as he'd expected, an up-close inspection revealed it really hadn't changed at all. The buildings were all the same, with no signs of any new ones having been built and no alterations on the existing ones as far as he could tell. He still recognized the names of some of the businesses—the lawyer's office, the bank, the Realtor. It was almost as if he'd never left, he realized as an uncomfortable feeling slid down his spine, with the town preserved exactly as it had been the last time he'd been here.

He didn't see many people around, which was kind of odd for two o'clock in the afternoon in any town. But then, it wasn't as though there were that many people in this town to begin with, and he supposed most were at work. There were only a few pedestrians on the sidewalks. He couldn't help but search out the faces of those he did see, even before he realized he was doing it, looking for anyone who appeared familiar.

Or a particular someone, he had to acknowledge, even though the idea gave him no pleasure.

He started to focus back on the road when he caught sight of a dark blue pickup truck up ahead pulling into a parking space on the street. It had barely come to a stop before the driver's-side door opened. A moment later a lean, unmistakably female body emerged, shoulder-length black hair ruffling slightly in the wind.

And there she was.

Damned if his heart didn't stop in his chest, just for an instant.

He hadn't seen her in eight years, a long enough period of time that he shouldn't have been able to recognize her immediately. Eight years was a long time. People changed. But the moment he caught sight of her, he knew it was her.

Elena Reyes—Elena Weston now, evidently.

The only woman he'd ever believed himself in love with.

A woman who—if there was any truth to the newspaper article in his pocket—was now a murderer.

EVEN BEFORE SHE CLIMBED OUT OF the truck, Elena could feel eyes on her. She would have been surprised if it had been any other way—after all, this was her first trip into town in nearly a week—but in this instance she would have loved to be surprised. She resisted the instinctive urge to glance around and see who was watching her, unwilling to let them know she was uncomfortable with their scrutiny.

Let them look. She didn't have anything to be ashamed of. She hadn't done anything wrong.

It took some effort to remember that as she closed the door of the truck and headed to the grocery store, that oppressive feeling of being watched growing in intensity. Luckily, there'd been a parking space close to the entrance so she wouldn't have to walk far, which was the first bit of luck she'd had in weeks. She made herself keep her head high and her shoulders straight as she walked, refusing to do anything that would make it look like she felt guilty.

Still, when she reached the door she paused on the threshold for the briefest of moments and took a deep breath to prepare herself before stepping inside.

As soon as she did, she wasted no time, quickly picking up a basket from inside the door and heading down the nearest aisle. It took less than ten seconds before she felt the air inside the store change, the shift as noticeable as a sudden chill wind blowing in her wake. The light buzz of conversation in the space evaporated, replaced by an eerie stillness that seemed to fill the store.

She wanted to believe it was her imagination. She knew better than to think it was.

She knew how judgmental this town could be, knew what it was like to have people look at her a certain way because of who she was. She'd grown up enduring those looks. But there was a big difference between being the daughter of Ed Reyes, the town drunk, and having everyone believe she'd killed her husband.

As she moved through the aisles, a few people turned rather sharply away as she approached. Several others openly stared. Glared, was more like it. Elena did her best to avoid eye contact. Lord knew she didn't exactly have the energy to deal with outright hostility. Still, she couldn't help but see them out of the corner of her eye and place names to the faces. Connie Raymond, who worked at the local beauty parlor. Delia Hart, whose son had worked for Bobby last summer.

No one said a word to her. No one had to. She knew exactly what they were thinking.

Murderer.

She'd known coming into town would be an ordeal, but there'd been no way around it. She was completely out of supplies, and if she didn't want to starve she was going to have to come and buy groceries. There was no one around to do it for her. The few ranch hands Bobby had still had around had quit, having no interest in working for her, most of them likely knowing she had no way of paying them anyway. Joann Bloom, the cook who'd worked for the Westons for years, had left, as well. She'd said her husband was making her quit, but Elena figured Joann hadn't fought the order too hard, if she had at all. Joann's loyalty had to be with the Westons. Even if Elena could pay her, Joann wouldn't want to keep working for the person accused of killing the last of them.

So it was just Elena, rambling around in the old ranch house with the walls rapidly closing in around her, trying to figure a way out of this mess, wondering what she was going to do. Until the need for supplies had finally forced her into town.

Now though, feeling the stares of half the people around her and the cold shoulders of the others, she couldn't help but wonder if starvation wouldn't have been the better option.

As she rounded the corner to the dairy section, she suddenly found herself facing Cassie Gerard, whose husband, Travis, was Bobby's closest friend—and one of the deputies determined to prove Elena's guilt. Cassie stood in front of the milk cooler, looking toward Elena as if she'd known she was coming.

Their eyes met. Elena froze, uncertain what to say. They'd never exactly been best friends, had only been thrown together because their husbands were, but they'd socialized for years, had dinner at each other's homes, spent holidays together. Yet Cassie stared at her, her expression completely blank, as though she didn't know her at all.

Finally, Elena tried to muster a smile.

Before she could manage it, Cassie turned on her heel and pointedly walked away.

Everything inside Elena deflated like a punctured balloon.

These were people she'd known for years. Her neighbors. They knew her. They knew she wasn't a murderer. At least they should.

But their responses proved they didn't.

Figuring she had enough in her basket to make do for a while, she made her way back to the front of the store. There was no one in line to check out when she got there. Moving to the counter, she quickly unloaded the basket, then set it aside in the stack on the floor.

Only when she straightened did she realize the cashier—Candice Dobson, a local girl Elena had known practically the girl's whole life—hadn't made a move to begin ringing her up. She stood frozen, simply staring at Elena, eyes wide, as if she didn't know what to do.

"Is there a problem?" Elena asked, keeping her tone as pleasant and neutral as possible.

Uncertainty etched across her face, Candice glanced over her shoulder.

Elena followed her gaze. Jacob Higgs, the store manager, stood in the doorway of his office, arms folded over his chest, staring at her.

Finally, he nodded once.

Candice immediately began grabbing Elena's purchases and ringing them up, her motions jerky as she moved as quickly as possible.

Elena never took her eyes from Jacob. She nearly had the ridiculous urge to thank him. But for what? For doing what he was supposed to do and not refusing to serve her? Not to mention, there wasn't the slightest hint of kindness in his hard face as he continued staring at her. Whatever his reasons for not blocking her purchases, it hadn't been to be nice.

Heck, he probably wanted to make sure she didn't drop dead before she could stand trial.

I haven't even been arrested! she wanted to yell, but it was clear she'd be wasting her breath. Nobody here wanted to hear it. They probably thought it was only a matter of time.

It was an opinion she shared much of the time, she acknowledged, her stomach clenching with fear. Sheriff

Bremer had made no secret of the fact he thought she was guilty and was doing everything he could to prove it. The only company she'd had at the house during the past week had been him and his men as they'd searched the house, not bothering to be gentle as they'd tossed all her possessions here and there in an attempt to find evidence. They hadn't, but Elena knew better than to think that would mean they'd stop trying.

Candice finally finished ringing her up. "Twenty-three fifty." She announced the total without looking up, focusing on bagging Elena's purchases. Once she was done, she extended her hand for Elena's money, quickly making change and handing it back to her.

"Thank you," Elena said politely as she accepted it.

Candice didn't say anything, simply lowering her head and not looking at Elena any longer.

Cheeks burning, Elena picked up the two bags and headed to the exit.

Once outside, she began to fumble in her purse for her keys, more than ready to get out of here as quickly as possible. Her attention on juggling the bags in her arms, it wasn't until she was almost to her truck that she noticed something was wrong. The truck was leaning oddly on one side. She glanced down.

The front tire was flat.

No, she realized, her gaze shifting. Both the front and back tires on this side were flat.

She skidded to a stop, clutching the bags in her arms, her heart suddenly pounding in her chest as she came to the inescapable conclusion.

Someone had slashed the tires.

Part of her immediately tried to reject the idea, not

wanting to believe it, not wanting to believe someone she knew could do such a thing.

But it was the only explanation. Two tires on the same side of a truck didn't just go flat on their own. No, this was deliberate. Someone had done this, purposely, maliciously, to hurt her. Someone she knew. A neighbor. Someone she might have once considered a friend.

Tears of frustration suddenly burned the back of her eyes. She did everything she could to hold them at bay, not about to let a single person in this town know they'd driven her to that and grant them the satisfaction. The mere thought of the smug, vengeful expressions that would no doubt greet her tears was enough to make them dry up.

Unable to bear the sight of her flattened tires, she started to back away, only to immediately collide with something. Big hands closed around her upper arms. A man.

Anger surged through her, killing the numbness that had fallen over her. She lunged forward and jerked out of his grip. The cold stares and whispers were bad enough, but damned if she was going to put up with being physically accosted. She whirled around to face her attacker, her mouth opening to tell him exactly what she thought—

The words died, every thought in her head and every trace of anger vanishing as she laid eyes on the man in front of her. She could only stare, unable to fully comprehend what she was seeing.

A single word rose in her mind, like a distant echo spoken by someone else.

Matt.

For an instant, she was twenty again, staring up

into the eyes of the man she loved more than anything she'd ever imagined. The man whose presence sent her heart racing and her stomach clenching whenever he was close. The man who inspired feelings and passions so deep and fierce that everything she'd experienced before that seemed like nothing. The man who filled her thoughts every waking moment and in all of her dreams. The man she didn't believe she would ever be able to live without.

The man who hadn't loved her enough. Or maybe she hadn't loved him enough. She'd spent a great deal of time over the years wondering which it had been. She never had arrived at an answer.

Then she was back in the present. Because the man in front of her wasn't the one she'd loved. This man was older, faint lines worn into the skin around his eyes, his face harder, his body bigger and more muscular. This was Matt Alvarez, with eight more years—years he'd lived without her—on him.

He was still the most beautiful man she'd ever seen. That lustrous black hair, those piercing dark eyes, that magnificent face, somehow even more devastating than the last time she'd seen him.

Of course, the last time she'd seen him she hadn't been looking at his face. She'd been staring at his back as he'd walked away from her.

She'd officially lost her mind. That had to be it. That vaguely unreal feeling she'd been experiencing since Bobby's death, the sense that none of this could be happening, washed over her, stronger than ever. Because there was absolutely no way that Matt Alvarez could be right here, right now.

"Hello, Elena."

And yet he was. Because even eight years later, that voice remained the same.

"Matt" was all she could bring herself to say, her mind still incapable of reconciling the fact that he was actually here in front of her.

"We need to talk."

"About what?" she answered automatically.

"I think you know."

At the moment she was starting to doubt if she knew even her own name. "What are you doing here?"

"That's what we need to talk about." He looked up and glanced around them. "But not here."

Elena repeated his gesture. There were a few people in view on the sidewalk and in nearby vehicles, none of them openly watching her and Matt, though she had no doubt they were. She could only imagine how many others were observing from the windows of the storefronts. Her earlier urge to get out of town and back to the solitude of the ranch as quickly as possible returned with a vengeance. "No," she agreed. "Definitely not here."

"Why don't I give you a ride home? We can talk there."

The offer immediately reminded her of why she couldn't drive herself home. She glanced back at her tires, wincing at the sight. "Did you see who did this?"

"No."

She eyed him doubtfully. For a second, she almost wondered if *he* had done this, but then, she couldn't think of a reason why he would. Of course, she couldn't think of a reason why he was here now, either. None of this made a bit of sense.

"You have a car?" she asked numbly.

"A truck," he said, nodding toward a black pickup parked a short distance down the street. "Come on."

He started to reach for the bags to take them from her. She shook her head, clutching them tighter, needing to hold on to something that was tangible and real.

He motioned for her to proceed in front of him. She hesitated for a moment, unsure. She needed to call someone and figure out about getting new tires. She had one spare, but she would definitely need help getting another. The thought of facing the police right now, of having to deal with this while all the unseen watchers observed and judged from their windows, was suddenly more than she could take. At the moment, she wanted nothing more than to get out of town and back to the relative safety of the ranch.

"All right," she murmured. She had no idea what he was doing here—wasn't quite convinced he wasn't some kind of illusion conjured by her desperate mind, for that matter. But right now he was offering to help her, which made him just about the only person in her world who was.

Chapter Two

"You're going to want to head right," Elena said as Matt started to back out of the parking space.

He agreed with a nod, turning as she directed without looking at her. He didn't let himself, even though it seemed like the only thing he wanted to do.

Fifteen minutes ago he hadn't seen her in years. Now she was here, sitting in his truck. She'd placed her two grocery bags on the seat between them, yet they were hardly much of a buffer. She might as well be pressed up against him, the way he felt her closeness.

He'd thought he would be prepared to see her again, thought he wouldn't feel anything after all these years. It had all been so long ago. She was nothing more than a distant memory to him, and not a particularly good one.

But good God, from the moment he'd found himself face-to-face with her, it all came back, hitting him like a blow square to the chest, the memories as vivid as though they'd happened yesterday.

Elena Reyes.

The prettiest girl he'd thought he'd ever seen. He'd thought he loved her. Whatever he'd felt back then had been the closest thing he'd ever experienced to it. He'd been a dumb kid, feeling things for the first time, *letting* himself feel those things for the first time. Back then, he'd never been able to get her out of his head. The mere sight of her had always made him happier than he'd ever been. Every time she'd smiled at him it had been like someone giving him the best present he'd ever gotten.

She hadn't been smiling the last time he'd seen her, of course. She'd been crying then. Back when she'd told him she didn't love him as much as he loved her. At least that had been the gist of it. And he'd realized he'd been a fool to feel all of those things he thought he had.

She wasn't smiling now, either. There were no tears, but her expression wasn't much brighter, her lips locked in a grim line, her eyes bleak, her features tense.

Damned if she still wasn't the prettiest thing he'd ever seen.

It didn't matter that she wasn't smiling, or that her face showed every bit of the stress she was under. It didn't even matter that it was eight years later and she was no longer the fresh-faced young woman he'd once known. If anything, the extra years had only added to her looks, delivering the full beauty that had only been hinted at when she was twenty. He'd thought she was beautiful then. If only he'd known what she would become.

Damn.

He almost wished she did look worse after all these years. It would certainly make things easier for him. He wouldn't be having this crazy reaction to a woman who really meant nothing to him. The woman who'd taught him just how foolish all those crazy emotions were in the first place.

"Okay, Matt," she said, thankfully pulling him out of his thoughts. "Now what are you doing here?"

Grateful for the reminder of the task at hand, he reached into his pocket and pulled out the envelope. "I got this in the mail," he said, holding it out to her. "Didn't you send it?"

She began to answer even before she took the envelope from him. "No, why would I?"

He could immediately tell she wasn't lying, her confusion too genuine to be faked. "I have no idea. I don't know why anybody else would, either."

"I didn't even know where you were these days," she said, flipping the envelope over and reading the address. "New Mexico?"

"That's right. Somebody around here obviously knew where I was, and I can't think of anyone besides you who would care."

"Neither can I, but it wasn't me." She waved the envelope. "What is this?"

"An article from the local paper about your husband's death."

She went still, staring at the item in her hand as though it contained something toxic and she wanted nothing more than to drop it before it contaminated her further. "Why would somebody send you that?" she whispered.

"I guess they wanted me to know about it," he said reasonably.

"But why? What purpose would that serve?"

"Only reason I could figure was that somebody wanted me to come here." He hesitated, feeling foolish for a slight second before he shoved the feeling away. "Like I said, I figured it was you."

She frowned at him. "Why would *I* send you that?"

Matt shrugged a shoulder, feeling foolish again. "I

thought maybe you needed help and were desperate enough to reach out to me of all people. From the sound of that article, things aren't looking too good for you. Maybe somebody else sent it for the same reason."

"In hopes that you'd help me?" She exhaled sharply, the sound almost like a snort. "Whatever the reason, I doubt it was good."

"What makes you say that?"

"People around here haven't exactly been going out of their way to help me out. As you may have noticed, I'm not Ms. Popularity at the moment."

He couldn't disagree with her there. He wished he'd seen who'd messed with her truck, but he'd been watching the store so closely for her to come out he hadn't been paying attention to anything else. "Has anything else happened besides someone cutting your tires?"

"That's the first outright act against me. Mostly I've been getting a cold shoulder from everyone in town. Almost no one has said a word to me since Bobby's death. Only the police." She shuddered slightly, the gesture making it clear exactly what that experience had been like for her.

He surveyed her out of the corner of his eye, this woman he hadn't seen in eight years, this person who was so familiar, yet different at the same time. She definitely wasn't the girl she'd once been. But could she have really changed enough to become a killer? It was possible. He could believe anyone was capable of killing for any number of reasons, whether out of anger or vengeance or self-defense. Was that what had happened? Had circumstances turned her into a killer? Or had she really become a far different person than the one he'd thought he'd known?

Or was it, as he'd wondered plenty of times after they parted ways, that he'd never really known her at all?

"What happened, Elena?"

She glanced at him, her left eyebrow quirking. "Didn't you read the article?"

"I'd rather hear it from you."

She simply continued to stare at him, remaining silent for a long moment. "What are you even doing here, Matt?" she repeated. "Someone sends you an article about…someone you knew a long time ago and you come all this way from New Mexico? For what?"

Someone you knew a long time ago. That was certainly an interesting way of putting it. He hadn't missed her hesitation before phrasing it that way, and he couldn't help wondering what her first instinct had been to say instead. "Guess I wanted to know why," he answered. "And yeah, I wanted to know if it was true."

"What do you care?"

"Are you saying it is?"

"No, I'm asking what difference it makes to you."

It was still a very good question. "Call it curiosity, I guess. You never struck me as a killer. Guess I wanted to know if a person could change that much."

She lowered her head, her shoulders slumping. "Thank you," she practically whispered.

"For what?"

"For thinking I'm not the killing type. People who've known me a lot longer don't even seem to believe that."

"So you're saying you didn't do it?"

"That's exactly what I'm saying," she said firmly.

"So what happened?"

Elena opened her mouth and took a deep breath, as

though on the verge of beginning, only to raise her hand and point in front of them. "In a minute. We're here."

He saw the turnoff to a ranch up ahead and smoothly guided the truck into the turn. A sign over the end of the driveway declared it the Weston Ranch. From the first glimpse, he could tell it was a big spread, wide-open pastures stretching out into the horizon. It looked like Elena had married well, he noted darkly. Not that he was surprised. He hadn't worked for them, didn't think he'd ever met any of them, but he remembered the Weston name had been big around here.

The driveway eventually ended in front of a large two-story ranch house, a barn not far from it. He could see cattle grazing in the distance in one of the pastures, a sight he knew well. She must have a lot of people working for her to be dealing with a place this size. More important, it meant there were people they were going to have to explain his presence to, something he wasn't sure just how to do.

"How many people do you have working for you right now?"

"At the moment, none."

He couldn't help but glance at her in surprise. She met his eyes and shrugged lightly, a hint of resignation in her dark brown gaze. "Nobody wants to work for a murderer."

"So how are you keeping this place running?"

"The best I can," she said simply.

As soon as he brought the truck to a stop in front of the house, she pushed her door open and climbed out, reaching back in for the bags and taking them before he could offer to help. He followed, unable to help but notice her strong, confident stride as she walked to the house and climbed the steps. She definitely wasn't a girl anymore. She was all woman, exuding a strength and grace he now saw she'd only been starting to develop back then.

Crossing the wide front porch, she opened the door. "Come on back to the kitchen," she said. "I need to get these groceries put away."

He followed her through the house, getting a quick glimpse of the living room as they passed through it. As he'd seen from the outside, it was a big place, but comfortable. Homey. The home she'd shared with her husband, he registered, the thought bothering him more than it should before he brushed the feeling aside.

In the kitchen, she put the bags on the counter and immediately began unloading them, moving some of the items to the refrigerator. There was a big table with plenty of chairs, but he remained standing, leaning against the doorway and watching her move.

Closing the refrigerator and turning away from it, she suddenly noticed him standing there and started. "I'm sorry. I'm not being a very good hostess. Can I get you something to drink?"

He gave his head a terse shake. "I'm fine. You were going to tell me what happened?"

She sighed, then nodded. "That's right. I guess I'm just not sure where to begin."

He wasn't sure he did, either. A lot of it was going to involve her relationship with her husband, a topic he didn't know if he wanted to hear all that much about, no matter how much he needed to. At the same time, he couldn't say why the idea bothered him. Or maybe he was just bothered by the implications of why it would.

"Have to admit I was surprised to find out you were

still in Western Bluff," he said. "Thought you had all those plans of being in the big city. That summer you couldn't wait to get back to school."

"I know," she said softly, without looking at him. "I never intended to stay here, either."

"So what happened?"

She shrugged helplessly. "Things changed. Bobby and I...started seeing each other, and then...things changed," she repeated weakly.

She lapsed into silence, her eyes sliding briefly to his, her discomfort with the topic etched across her face. Clearly, her relationship with her husband was just as awkward for her to talk about as it was for him to listen to.

His gut churned at her words. He'd never met Bobby Weston, not that he could remember anyway. He wished he had, wished he could know the kind of man Elena had been willing to change her life plans for when she hadn't been willing to do the same for him.

But then, he'd just been a ranch hand, offering her an uncertain life on the road. He hadn't had a spread like this to offer her. Maybe if he had, things would have been different. Maybe she would have picked him.

With a jolt of anger at himself for even thinking about it, he did his best to push the thoughts away. What did it matter? It was a long time ago. Things had happened the way they had, and there was no changing them. He had a perfectly good life, and it looked like she had, too—at least up until the point her husband was killed.

"Must have been some guy," Matt said, keeping his tone neutral.

"He was," she said quietly. "At least in the beginning. We started seeing each other…the summer after you left."

The words sent another jolt through him, and again he was irritated by his response. A year was a long time, so why did it feel like a betrayal, like she'd moved on far too quickly? It wasn't as if he'd been a monk in the year after he'd left this place—left her—behind. But then, he hadn't ended up marrying any of the women he'd been involved with, either.

Pulling out one of the chairs from the table, Elena sank into the seat. "We'd known each other, or at least known *of* each other, for years, of course. The town's too small for us not to have. I can't remember us saying two words to each other, though. He was a few years ahead of me in school, a member of one of the town's founding families, and I…wasn't. Our paths never really crossed. Then that summer I was waiting tables at the diner again, and he struck up a conversation with me. It was probably the first time he ever really noticed me. We got to talking, and we actually had some things in common.

"First and foremost, Bobby didn't want to stay in Western Bluff, either, and he wasn't supposed to. I don't know how much you heard about the Westons, or even remember if you did, but Bobby's older brother, Jim Junior, was the one who'd been groomed to take over the ranch. Bobby's father, Big Jim, died about twenty years ago when Bobby was just a boy. Junior was all of eighteen, but he managed to take over and make the ranch his own. He offered to make Bobby a place as he got older, but Bobby wasn't really interested in the ranch. The summer you were here, he had an internship at a company in Houston, so he wasn't in town. He wanted to be in the city as much as I did. The only reason he was back that summer was because Junior said he needed his help and asked Bobby to stick around. Bobby had already graduated but didn't have a job lined up yet, so he agreed."

Elena grimaced, her eyes far away. "That whole summer we talked about how we were going to get out of here. He was going to come to Austin with me when I went back to school." Matt nearly flinched at the words, at the significance of them, but managed not to. "He knew people there so he could try to find a job just as well as he could in Houston. It should have worked out perfectly. But when the summer was over, Junior asked him to stay a little longer, and made a big enough deal about it that Bobby agreed. That's when he asked me to marry him. He wanted to make things permanent, because he said there was no doubt we'd be together. And I said yes."

"How long had you been going out with him before you got married?"

Her eyes flew to his face. He met her gaze and held it. He could tell she didn't like the answer, and suspected he wasn't going to like hearing it, either.

"Three months."

He had no trouble understanding her reaction and did his best to hide his own.

Three months. The same amount of time Matt had been involved with her before they'd parted ways, before she'd refused to make the same commitment to him she'd made to another man just one year later.

"You must have really loved him," he said, instantly hearing the trace of bitterness in his own voice and hating himself for it.

She lowered her eyes. "He was crazy about me, and I—" she swallowed "—was crazy about him."

Matt didn't miss the way her voice faltered before she finished the statement, or how strained it sounded uttering those words. Were they that hard for her to admit? Or was it admitting them to him?

"I'm sure your father must have been thrilled that you got married so fast," he said wryly, remembering the man's reaction to Matt's involvement with his daughter. Ed Reyes had been so protective of his daughter Matt couldn't imagine him thinking anyone was good enough for her. Or maybe Bobby Weston's background had made him a more acceptable prospect than a humble ranch hand.

"He wasn't," she acknowledged with a sardonic smile. "We eloped and didn't tell anyone about it until it was done, and then I went back to school.

"We both thought it would only be a few months until he joined me in Austin. Instead, a few months later we found out the truth about Junior. He hadn't been feeling well, had been going to doctors to get checked out, which is why he needed Bobby's help, though he assured everyone he was fine. But he wasn't. He wasn't just sick, he was dying. He was going fast, and didn't admit it almost until the end. Then he was gone. He wasn't married and didn't have any kids, so Bobby inherited the ranch.

"At first I assumed he'd sell. But Bobby felt like he owed it to Junior to stay and run the ranch. I understood, and felt like I had to support that. His brother had just died, this was his family spread, and he was the last of the Westons. I couldn't exactly argue with him. So when I finished school, I came back, too, and we stayed."

"And you're still here," Matt summarized.

Elena nodded, more than a hint of resignation in the gesture. "Still here."

"Were you happy?"

She looked at him, her gaze steady. "No," she said flatly. "Neither of us were. After the first couple years I did begin to argue that Bobby should sell, but he wouldn't. The thing is, Big Jim was something of a local legend around here, and all his life Bobby heard about how great his father was. And then, after being the second brother, the one who wasn't expected to take over, he suddenly had pretty big shoes to fill, especially since he was the last Weston. It was a lot of pressure. At least he saw it that way, and it changed him. We had some setbacks over the years, some rough times, and Bobby took every one of them personally, as though he was failing his father and his brother. He became obsessed. The ranch was all he ever thought about. He was constantly coming up with plans and schemes to make things work better around here, none of which ever panned out, which only made things worse.

"The night he was killed, we'd had an argument. I'd pretty much had enough. Bobby had this idea to build this new irrigation system, claiming it would make things work a lot smoother around here. Of course, it would also require digging up half the spread and spending every last remaining cent we had. It was complete madness and would do nothing to solve any of the actual problems." She swallowed hard. "I told him if he intended to go through with it, I would have no choice but to leave him. I wasn't going to stand by and watch him destroy himself and what was left of our lives on his obsession with the ranch. He told me to go, because if I couldn't understand how important it was to him, then I didn't really love him anyway.

"I walked out and went for a drive to clear my head. I just needed to think about things for a while. I didn't really go anywhere, didn't think about where I was headed. I just drove until it seemed like I'd gone far enough, turned around and came back. I was gone for about four hours. When I came back, I noticed the door to his study was open and the light was still on. I almost ignored it, just wanting to go to bed and not have another confrontation, but I knew if I did he'd just stay up all night the way he did too much of the time."

Elena sucked in a breath. "That's when I found him. He was lying on his back on the floor. He'd been shot in the chest. I felt for a pulse, but he was already dead. He was still warm though. I don't know how long he'd been there. Maybe if I'd come home earlier, I could have called someone, could have saved him—"

"You can't think like that," Matt said gently. "If you'd come back earlier, the shooter could have killed you, too."

"I know," she admitted softly. "But I wish I could have done something for him. Instead, all I could do was call the police and tell them he'd been killed. Unfortunately, everyone knew that we'd been arguing, and no one else had a reason to kill him, which makes me the prime suspect. The sheriff has made it clear he thinks I'm guilty. I know he'd love to make an arrest. The only thing keeping him from doing it is a lack of physical evidence. The murder weapon was most likely a pistol that belonged to Bobby. He kept it in his gun cabinet. It's been missing since the murder. The killer must have taken it, but the sheriff is convinced I hid it somewhere, which is why he and his men have been by pretty much every other day to search the place.

"In the meantime, the hands quit. We had only a few working for us. I paid them for their work to date, but they knew I couldn't afford to keep them on. At least one made the point that I was probably going to need every penny I had for my defense."

"Sounds like somebody you're better off not having around," Matt noted.

"Most likely," Elena agreed. "But the result is that I have this ranch to run all by myself with nobody to work it, and a whole town that thinks I murdered my husband."

"Surely there have to be others who had issues with your husband, especially if the ranch was having as much trouble as you say it is."

"I've been over the books numerous times over the past week. We're low on funds and have plenty of debts, but these are held by banks and certainly wouldn't be worth killing him over. And while not everybody in town necessarily loved him, I haven't been able to come up with anyone with serious enough issues to want to do him harm. Believe me, I've been racking my brain trying to think of a single possibility."

"What about these hands you had working for you? Weren't any of them around that night? Didn't any of them see anything?"

"No. They'd all gone to town. Bobby had given them the day off."

"Convenient," Matt said. "That strike anybody as odd?"

Elena shrugged. "Not really. Afterward I kind of wondered if he suspected this blowout between us was coming and didn't want anyone around to overhear. It had been building for some time," she admitted.

"Is it possible one of the hands killed him? Maybe they were worried about getting paid?"

"They were all in town at the bar. They have alibis."

Her voice was thick with frustration. He could understand why. The situation certainly didn't look good. But listening to her, he didn't have a doubt in the world that she was telling the truth. She was no murderer. Whatever else might have changed about her over the years, that hadn't. Which meant she needed help. She might not have sent the article to him—he definitely believed her about that, too—but the result was the same.

Before he could say anything, the sound of an engine reached them, drawing their attention toward the front of the house. Someone was coming up the driveway.

Matt glanced back at her. "Expecting company?"

Her heavy frown answered before she did. "No," she said, rising from her chair.

He pushed away from the door frame, ready to follow. "Any idea who it could be?"

"Not really," she said, moving past him. "But if there's one thing I've learned by now, it's bound to be trouble."

Chapter Three

She'd been right, Elena reflected grimly as she watched the two men climb out of the police vehicle they'd parked in front of the house. It was trouble.

Sheriff Walt Bremer climbed out first, heaving himself from behind the driver's seat with a great deal of effort. In his mid-fifties, he was a big man in every way, increasingly around his midsection. He'd always been pleasant enough to Elena and she'd never had any issues with him before. But once he'd zeroed in on her as his prime suspect, he'd turned on her so thoroughly it was hard to believe he'd ever had a kind word for her in the past.

A second, equally familiar man emerged from the passenger seat. Travis Gerard—Cassie's husband, Bobby's best friend since they were boys, and a local deputy. He was thirty, like Bobby had been, a long, lean figure with close-cropped hair and dark eyes. Like Cassie, he was someone she'd socialized with numerous times over the years due to his friendship with Bobby. But their relationship had started out cool and only grown cooler at the same time her marriage had, understandably enough. As Bobby's best friend, she knew he'd been treated to plenty of Bobby's complaining about her over the years, how she wasn't supporting him, how she was too concerned about money. Once he'd actually pulled her aside and tried to play marriage counselor, by telling her she had a responsibility to be there for Bobby. She hadn't been in the mood to explain Bobby's latest bright idea, and hadn't really thought it was any of his business, so her lack of cooperation had likely only lowered his opinion of her. He'd been cold enough toward her when it seemed like she wasn't getting along with Bobby. Unsurprisingly, now that it seemed that she'd killed him, Travis was hellbent on making her pay.

As they approached, she saw that the men's interest wasn't in her, but in the man standing at her side, and she knew immediately why they'd come. Her interaction with Matt in town, and the fact that she'd driven off with him, hadn't gone unnoticed. The sheriff no doubt wanted to know who Matt was—and what he was doing with Elena.

For a second, she felt a flicker of apprehension. She hadn't thought about the outside impact of Matt's presence here. If their prior relationship came out, the fact that he'd come back to town so soon after Bobby's death could look very bad—for both of them.

Before she could begin to sort through the ramifications and how to deal with the issue, the men had reached the house. "Afternoon, Elena," Walt said with a pleasantness that couldn't have been more fake.

She made the immediate decision to go on the offensive. Once again, she couldn't afford to look the slightest bit weak or guilty. "Good afternoon, Sheriff. Travis," she said, nodding to the younger man in turn. She noticed he didn't bother looking at her, his attention fixed on Matt, eyes narrowed with clear suspicion. "I'm glad to see you both."

The briefest flash of surprise crossed across Walt's face. "Oh, you are, are you?"

"Of course. You're here about my truck, right?"

"What about it?"

"Oh, I thought you might be here because someone slashed my tires when I was in town a little while ago."

The sheriff's eyebrows shot sky high. "That's a pretty serious allegation, Elena. You have any proof?"

"Two tires don't just go flat for no reason."

Walt shrugged one shoulder. "Stranger things have happened."

"But I'm sure you'll investigate to find out what really happened, won't you, Sheriff?"

"I'm a little busy trying to solve Bobby's murder at the moment to waste time on a minor nuisance matter. I'm sure that's where you'd prefer my resources to be focused—catching your husband's killer, isn't it, Elena?"

His cloying tone made it sound like he'd caught her in some kind of trap. She simply stared back at him, unyielding. "Of course. I'd like nothing more than for you to catch the actual person responsible for killing Bobby."

Walt's expression turned sardonic, clearly saying he saw what she was implying and he wasn't fooled by her in the least. But when he spoke what he said was, "Aren't you going to introduce us to your friend, Elena?"

She almost started. For a moment, she'd actually managed to forget Matt was even there.

Before she could figure out how to explain Matt's presence and who he was, Matt answered first.

"Mrs. Weston just hired me to help her out around here."

It was all Elena could do not to snap her head toward him in surprise. Instead, she did her best not to let her reaction show, not wanting to tip off the policemen that it was a lie when that would only look more suspicious.

It turned out she didn't need to worry. Walt and Travis never took their eyes off Matt, Walt's expression becoming contemplative, Travis's plainly hostile.

"Help her out with what?" Travis asked, a sneer in his tone.

"The ranch," Matt said smoothly without missing a beat. "It sounded like she could use some help around here with things."

"Did she tell you why she needed help?" Walt asked, the question clearly leading somewhere.

"Her husband recently died and the men he'd had working for him moved on."

"Did she tell you her husband was murdered?" Travis demanded. "Shot to death in that very house? Or did you already know that?"

"As a matter of fact, she did tell me that," Matt said.

"And that doesn't make you nervous about working for her? It sure scared off the rest of the hands."

"I guess I'm made of stronger stuff than they are."

"What's your name again?" the sheriff asked, even though they all knew full well Matt hadn't offered it.

"Alvarez," Matt said. "Matt Alvarez."

Deciding she'd had enough of this, Elena spoke up. "Is there something I can help you with, Sheriff? Something must have brought you out here, since you didn't come about my truck."

Walt smiled thinly. "We just thought we'd stop by

and see if you remembered anything else about the night Bobby was murdered."

"No, I haven't," she said simply.

"In that case, I guess we'll be going."

He shot one final glance at Matt, then turned and headed back to his car. It took a moment for Travis to do the same, glaring at Matt, then Elena before following the sheriff.

She and Matt didn't speak as the two men climbed back in their vehicle. They watched in silence as the sheriff backed up, then headed down the driveway.

When the car was nearly out of sight, Elena finally spoke. "Why did you tell them that?"

"As soon as I saw who it was, I figured we were going to have to explain what I was doing here. That seemed like the best explanation."

"But now it'll look bad if you don't stay."

"I'm not going anywhere, not until I have some answers."

The determination in his voice sent a shudder down her spine. "I'm not sure your staying here is a good idea."

"Why not?"

"If anyone finds out about our…prior relationship," she said delicately, "it will look really bad that you suddenly showed up so soon after Bobby's murder and are staying here."

"It's been eight years. I doubt anybody will remember. I was nothing more than a ranch hand passing through, and we were careful about not being too public because you didn't want your father finding out, remember? Only a few people knew in the end anyway. Are the Nolans still around?" he asked, referring to the people who'd owned the ranch where he'd worked that summer.

"No, they sold out a few years ago," she admitted.

"What about Weston? Would he have told anybody about me?"

She glanced away. "I don't think he knew. I never told him and he never mentioned it."

"So it's unlikely anyone remembered."

"Small towns have long memories, especially this one. And at least one person in town clearly knows."

"Somebody who probably wanted to help you. Why else would they send me that article?"

"To cause trouble for me? Like I said, it could look bad having you here. Not to mention, how could they know you would come here to help me if they sent you a newspaper article?"

"Guess the only way to find out what that person's motives are is to find out who it is. Another reason for me to stick around."

She eyed him doubtfully, unable to shake the notion that this was a bad idea. The idea of having him here, so close at hand. Yes, she could use the help, if that was what he was truly here for. If the incident with her tires was any indication, it might be a good thing to have someone nearby.

But having this particular man, with his inexplicable motives and dark, compelling eyes, so close suddenly seemed infinitely more dangerous.

He met her gaze seriously. "Look, if you don't want me staying here, that's your call. This is your place. I can't force myself on you or your property. I can try to find somewhere in town to stay. But I'm not going anywhere until I have some answers. I want to know who sent me that article—and yes, why."

Elena felt her resistance—and most likely, her common sense—weakening. Yes, it could be a bad idea to have him here. No, she didn't understand what he was doing here, or why he would want to help her. But she believed he wanted answers, and with the rest of the town seemingly having already made up their minds, that gave them a common goal. Perhaps that was reason enough to keep him close, despite all the reasons she wasn't sure she should.

"All right," she said softly. "You can stay."

If he wondered why she'd caved, he didn't show it, simply nodding once. "Good. I was thinking we should go back into town and get your truck."

Elena automatically frowned at the suggestion. She was in no hurry to go back into Western Bluff after her last visit, especially so soon. But as she considered the idea, she realized he was right. They shouldn't leave her truck sitting on Main Street. God only knew what someone might do to it in the middle of the night, or if it would even be there the next day. Even if it were, she wouldn't put it past Walt or Travis to give her a parking ticket or trump up some other infraction just to cause her trouble.

"We'll need to change the tires," she noted.

"Do you have any spares?"

"There's one in the truck bed, and a few others in the barn."

He nodded. "Great. I'll load a couple in my truck and we can go."

"I'll show you where they are in the barn."

He automatically turned and headed in that direction. Elena waited a few seconds before following, watching him walk away with that same strange sense of unreality washing over her again. Her whole world seemed to have been upended again in a mere hour. It didn't seem possible that this was happening, yet evidently it was.

Matt Alvarez was back in her life, as suddenly as he'd once left it.

And it seemed, for the moment at least, this time he intended to stay.

Chapter Four

"Tell me about the sheriff," Matt said as they headed back into town.

Elena glanced over at him from the passenger's seat, grateful he'd raised the subject—any subject. Anything to distract her from her still unsteady emotions, and his closeness in the truck's cab. "All right. What do you want to know?"

He kept his eyes on the road, his profile hard as stone. "Is he good at his job?"

Elena considered the question. "I've always figured he was. Walt's been the sheriff for, I'd say, at least six years now, and he was a deputy for years before that."

"So there's a chance he might remember me from back then."

Elena frowned at the memory. "There's a chance," she agreed.

"We can worry about that when we need to. Ever had any trouble with him before?"

"None. I didn't have that much direct interaction with him, and when I did, he was always nice enough to me. When I was a teenager, there were a few times when he brought my father home, and he was always nice about it." Too nice, she thought with a trace of irritation. The kind of niceness that was really just pity. Far too many people had looked at her like that back then, if they'd acknowledged her existence at all.

Poor girl. Mother took off. Father's a drunk.

Of course, that was a lot better than the way people were looking at her now, she thought, as a grim smile touched her lips. She'd never imagined a day when being Ed Reyes's outcast daughter would seem like a step up to her. Or maybe that was the natural progression of things in some way. She'd turned out to be the bad seed her disreputable beginning had always made them think she'd be.

"So there's no reason to believe this is personal for him and he's not just trying to do his job."

"Not for him, no."

"But for someone else?" he concluded. "The deputy?"

"Travis is—*was*," she corrected with a wince, "Bobby's best friend. Was ever since they were little kids."

"No wonder he's gunning for you, if he thinks you killed him."

"It probably doesn't help that he never liked me to begin with."

"Why not?"

"He didn't think I was good enough for Bobby. But then, most people didn't. After all, he was a Weston. His great-great-grandfather was one of the founders of this town and Bobby's family was practically royalty around here. People used to say the town should have been called 'Weston's Bluff.' He was golden in this town. He could have had any girl he wanted."

"And he wanted you."

She didn't say anything for a moment. "Yes," she

said, her tone distant. "He did. In the beginning, at least."

As soon as she'd said the last words, she wished she could take them back. There was too much she didn't want to get into, things she didn't want to explain.

But if he wondered what had changed, he didn't ask. Maybe he didn't want to know any more than she wanted to get into it. A tiny bit of relief pierced her uneasiness.

"Did you ever think there might be another reason one of them is so determined to pin the murder on you?" he asked.

"What do you mean?"

"What if one of them is the killer?"

The idea was so absurd she nearly laughed. "Neither of them have motives."

"That you know of. You said nobody had a motive to kill your husband, but clearly somebody must have. After all, if you didn't kill him, somebody did, and there had to have been a reason. You just don't know what it is."

He was right, of course. She'd spent more than one sleepless night wondering who had killed Bobby—and why. The first answer depended on the second, but she hadn't had any luck answering either one, hadn't even come up with any remote possibilities. Rather than find a solution to her situation, her efforts had merely confirmed how dire it was.

She tried to wrap her mind around the idea of Walt or Travis killing Bobby in cold blood. It just didn't make sense, and not just for the lack of motive.

"If it were Walt or Travis, then why wouldn't they have left the gun, or planted it somewhere they could claim to have found it? Somewhere that would have made me look bad? The fact that the gun is missing is one of the only things keeping them from making an arrest. If one of them is the killer, then that person has the gun."

He fell silent for a moment, and she sensed him considering her words. "I don't know," he finally said. "That's a good point. I'm just trying to keep an open mind. We can't dismiss any possibility out of hand, no matter how far-fetched. We can't afford to overlook anything or anyone, not if we want to get to the bottom of this."

He was right, she acknowledged. This was the way it had to be. Sure, it didn't seem like anyone had a motive to kill Bobby, but someone clearly had. Until they figured out who it was, everyone had to be looked at as though they could be the killer.

It was only fair. After all, that was how everybody in town was looking at her.

"Okay," Matt said, pushing himself to his feet. "You're good to go."

Elena glanced at the two fully inflated tires, the truck now perfectly balanced on all four. "Thank you. Let's get out of here."

Matt had no trouble understanding her relief. He'd had his attention on the tires most of the time since they'd arrived back at her truck, but he'd been able to feel people watching them. No one had approached or said a word. It hadn't mattered. He'd known they were there. It wasn't a comfortable feeling.

Still, he wasn't ready to retreat just yet. Getting her truck fixed had been just the first item on his agenda when they got to town. He had other business to take care of.

"You go on ahead," he told her. "I want to poke around here a bit."

Her attention already drifting to the street and their unseen watchers, she turned back to him in surprise. Not that there was any reason for her to be surprised. It was, after all, what he was here for.

As if realizing it, she slowly nodded. "All right."

"I'll see you back at the house."

He waited, expecting her to turn and get into the truck. She didn't. She simply stood there, her eyes searching his face, her expression suddenly uncertain. It seemed as though she wanted to say something else.

And in an instant, he understood.

They were already saying goodbye, so soon after meeting again after so long. The strangeness of it hit him. It had always felt strange saying goodbye to her. He'd never been quite ready to do it. It didn't matter that they would see each other again in a little while. Or was she wondering if that was true, if she should say something, a more definitive goodbye than the last time, just in case?

This was actually a lot like the last time they'd said goodbye. They'd been on the street, not too far from here in fact. The difference was it had been night.

And they'd both had no reason to think he was ever coming back.

He *was* coming back, he almost felt like reassuring her. But he knew it wouldn't matter. Some part of her still wasn't ready to say goodbye to him, any more than it ever had been. And he realized maybe he wasn't ready, either, as the same innate sense of connection he'd had with this woman from the first moment he'd seen her clicked deep within him.

Eight years. It should have been long enough to wash away whatever feelings he'd once had for this woman. But as he peered down into the eyes staring back at him, took in her upturned face, he felt it just the same.

Whatever she might have wanted to say, she didn't. With another tight nod, she finally turned and rounded the front of the truck to the driver's side.

Stepping away from the vehicle, Matt watched her climb in and start the engine. He remained where he was as she backed out of the space. There was no reason for him to stay there. He needed to get going, needed to get started poking around.

But something held him in place, and he watched her drive away, the truck slowly heading down the street and fading into the distance.

"She's not somebody you really want to get mixed up with."

Matt recognized the voice without seeing the speaker behind him. It was the deputy who'd come by Elena's ranch earlier—Travis, she'd said his name was. He had the same sneer in his voice.

The man's tone rankled. The fact that Matt wasn't sure he disagreed with the statement did, too.

Not letting his expression show the slightest reaction, Matt slowly turned to face the man.

The sneer was on the deputy's face, as well. He peered at Matt, eyes narrowed as they studied him, like the guy was trying to figure him out. The scrutiny lasted long enough Matt was sure the man hadn't managed it.

"Is that so?" Matt said mildly.

"She's a murderer. Killed her husband in cold blood. Is that really somebody you want to be working for?"

"I figure if you had any proof against her she'd be locked up already."

"It's only a matter of time," Travis practically spat. "Everybody in this town knows she did it, and nobody's going to let her get away with it."

"Well, until that happens, she's still somebody with a job that needs to be done."

"As soon as she's locked up, you might find it hard getting paid for whatever work you've done."

"Guess I'll worry about that when the time comes."

The man grimaced, his mouth tightening with barely controlled anger. "Even if you don't believe she's a killer, take my word, she's no good. Probably no surprise there—her family wasn't, either."

The man let the comment hang in the air, probably expecting Matt to be curious enough to ask for more details. Heck, most people probably would be after a comment like that. But Matt already knew all about Elena's family. He'd met Ed Reyes himself, knew full well what kind of man he was. And Elena herself had told him more than this man could begin to, just as he'd told her things…

Not that he could admit that to this man. But even if he could, he wasn't about to. He didn't like bullies, never had. And Travis Gerard had *bully* written all over him. It made Matt wonder what kind of man Elena's husband had been, if this was the type of person he'd considered his best friend in the world. Matt's reflexive dislike for Bobby Weston grew deeper.

"Her old man was a drunk," the deputy finally said when the silence went on too long. "Her mother took off when she was just a kid. With a background like that, probably makes sense that she wouldn't consider her own marriage worth much."

"What's your point?"

"I'd think you'd want to know the kind of person you're working for."

"Why would her family make a difference when it comes to working for her? That's her family, not her."

Travis Gerard's eyes narrowed, fresh contempt shining from them. "So you're that kind of guy, huh? Doesn't matter what kind of person you work for?"

"I'm just wondering why you're wasting your time trying to scare me off. What does it matter to you if I get paid or not?"

"Her husband was a good friend of mine. I don't like the idea of her out there, going about her life like nothing happened, like she didn't kill a good man in cold blood."

"Then prove she did it," Matt said. "Trying to scare me off isn't going to get that done."

The deputy's face went dark red, his whole body tensing, and for a second, Matt was positive the man wanted nothing more than to deck him, was just about ready to throw that punch.

Matt held his ground, not about to back down, ready to take the blow if he had to. He was ready and willing to go toe to toe with this arrogant ass, but raising a hand against a Texas deputy was a surefire way to get in trouble, and there wasn't much he could do for Elena if he landed in jail his first day in town.

Finally, Gerard took a step back, giving his chin a belligerent tilt. "Don't say I didn't warn you."

"Don't worry, Deputy," Matt returned coolly. "I consider myself warned."

With a curl of his lip, Gerard turned on his heel and stomped away.

Matt watched him go, the knot of tension in the pit of his stomach only tightening. He didn't feel the slightest bit of relief that the deputy had backed down, his awareness of just how bad the situation was weighing down on him too heavily.

Whether or not Travis Gerard was right about the rest of the town—and the slashed tires indicated he just might be—the fact that the local law was gunning for Elena was confirmation enough that she needed help. Damned if he was going to stand by and watch her be railroaded. Unfortunately, she probably needed more help than he alone could offer, he had to admit. Luckily he might know someone who could provide some assistance.

Climbing into his truck, he pulled the envelope out of his pocket, found a pen in the glove compartment, then reached for his phone, hitting the speed dial.

A familiar voice answered after a few rings. "Triple C."

"Piper, it's Matt."

"Matt, where are you? Is everything okay?"

"Everything's fine," he said, dodging the first question. "I just need you to give me Pam's phone number."

She didn't say anything for a long moment, and he braced himself for her answer. "Everything can't be fine if you want to talk to an FBI agent."

"I just have a little bit of a situation here and I'm hoping she'd be willing to do something for me."

"Is there anything Cade and I can do to help?"

He had no doubt that if he said the word, she and Cade would hightail it to Western Bluff as fast as they could, no questions asked. That was the kind of people they were, not just the people he worked for but his closest friends in the world. "You can give me Pam's phone number," he said simply.

She fell quiet again, then slowly began to recite the digits. He immediately jotted them down on the back of the envelope. "Do you need me to repeat it?" she asked when she was done.

"No, I got it."

"We're here if you need us, Matt."

"I know," he said gently. "I appreciate that, Piper."

"Take care of yourself," she said, then disconnected the phone.

Swallowing a sigh, he dialed the number she'd just given him and waited for someone to answer.

The call was picked up on the third ring. "This is Pam," a voice almost exactly like the one he'd just spoken to said in a no-nonsense tone.

"Pam, it's Matt Alvarez."

She fell silent for a few moments much like her sister had. "Matt," she said flatly, her voice devoid of Piper's natural warmth. "This is a surprise." She gave no indication whether it was pleasant or otherwise.

"I'm sorry to bother you, but I'm in a situation and could use your help."

"What is it?" He quickly outlined Elena's circumstances. "This case doesn't fall within federal jurisdiction," she said when he was finished. "There's nothing I can do officially."

"I know that. I was just hoping for some information."

"What kind of information?"

"For now, anything you can give me on the town, on Elena and her husband, the sheriff and whether he can be trusted. Obviously, you have resources that I don't. I'm not asking for anything illegal or that would get you into trouble. Just anything you can give me that you think I need to know, though I might need to come back to you later the more I learn here."

She didn't say anything for a long moment again. "This woman must mean a lot to you."

His mind instantly wanted to deny the idea. Elena didn't mean anything to him. Not anymore.

He couldn't exactly say that. It would raise far more questions, ones he wasn't sure he was ready for and didn't like the answers to.

Instead, he simply said, "She's a friend."

Another silence. When she spoke again, all she said was "Give me a number where I can reach you." Matt quickly gave it to her. "I'll see what I can find."

"Thank you," he said, only to realize she'd already hung up. With most people the action would probably be considered rude, but he didn't take any offense at it. That was Pam—brisk, blunt, to the point. She was willing to help. That was all he cared about.

Lowering his phone, he glanced up, his eyes suddenly meeting those of a woman standing down the street a short distance away.

He could tell she'd been watching him for a while, her face reflecting surprise at having been caught. If he hadn't been so focused on the call with Pam he might have sensed it. Still, she didn't immediately glance away, continuing to look at him. He looked right back. Given the way he'd felt people watching him since he and Elena had arrived back here to change her tires, he figured he should get used to people staring at him. That didn't mean he was going to let them think they could intimidate him or make him in any way nervous.

But as he absorbed the woman's attention, he realized it was different somehow. She was an attractive woman in her fifties with dark hair and eyes and a nice face. There was a warmth to it, and her attention wasn't cold or judgmental. It was like she was studying him closely, looking for something. He half wondered what it was, not caring all that much. Maybe she was just curious about a stranger. It didn't seem like she meant him any harm, and as long as that remained the case, she could look as long as she wanted.

As though finally realizing just how long she had been staring, she abruptly looked away and started down the sidewalk in the other direction.

He watched her go for a few seconds before shaking his head and dismissing her strange behavior. He had bigger things to worry about.

Pam could likely get information that he couldn't, but he'd meant what he'd said. He intended to learn as much here as he could. It might still be early enough that word hadn't gotten out about who he was and why he was supposedly in town, so there might still be time to find someone willing to talk to him. And there was one place around here he figured was his best bet to find someone who would.

Chapter Five

Her hands were shaking.

The realization came with a strange sense of detachment, as though she was noticing something that was happening to someone else. Elena glanced down at the hands that were gripping the steering wheel tightly. Yes, they were shaking, she registered, barely feeling it. The steering wheel was shuddering beneath them.

No, she corrected faintly. Her hands weren't shaking. Her whole body was.

She looked back up at the road, only to discover that she was already outside of town. Blinking in shock, she tried to draw in a breath. It was impossible. Her lungs were too tight.

She quickly swung over to the side of the road and sat there, still clutching the steering wheel in a death grip, trying to catch that elusive breath. Thankfully, there were no other vehicles in view, no one in front of or behind her, no one to witness her meltdown. She was alone, truly alone for the first time since Matt's sudden reappearance in her life.

She wasn't surprised that she'd managed to get all the way outside of town without noticing where she was. From the moment she'd driven away from him, there'd been only one thing on her mind.

Matt.

Matt was back.

The image of the way he'd looked on the street came back to her.

She hadn't wanted to say goodbye. Not again. Not yet.

Suddenly, the flood of memories she'd barely managed to keep at bay when he was near finally broke free, filling her head with a million different thoughts, pictures, impressions. Things she hadn't thought about in years. Things she hadn't let herself.

Eight years. She could feel every one of the years that had passed since he'd left, and yet it seemed as vivid as if it were yesterday.

She'd been working at the diner that summer. She hadn't wanted to come back to Western Bluff, but she'd needed to save as much money as possible for school and it hadn't made sense to pay rent for an apartment when that money could be saved. Even with the scholarship she'd managed to get, she was barely making her way through college as it was. So she'd come home and waited tables. She'd worked at the diner all through high school, having been forced early on to get a job. Not only had she known she was going to have to pay her own way through college if she wanted to get out of this town, but her father hadn't been the most reliable of providers. She'd spent too many years experiencing the fear of not knowing if the bills would be paid and their needs would be met. College was her number-one priority, but if push came to shove, she would have something to dip into to cover any shortfall.

Lavonne had been nice enough to keep a job open for her and hire her on over the summers. The diner's owner had been the closest thing Elena had had to a mother figure after her own mother abandoned them. If there was one person Elena could imagine sending Matt the newspaper article to bring him back to help her, it was Lavonne, but she'd died five years ago, shortly after Ed.

It had been a fairly typical night. She'd been doing her best to stave off the boredom and her unhappiness about being in this town she'd hated so much, just trying to make it to the end of her shift, dreaming about being back at school.

He'd come in with a few other hands from the Nolan ranch. It wasn't uncommon for hands from the area ranches to make their way into town on their nights off. Lord knew there wasn't much else around here. Usually, they'd hit the bar on the edge of town, then make their way to the diner for dessert if they needed to sober up a bit before making their way home. Most of them would flirt with her. She'd always be friendly, keeping her tips in mind, but not *too* friendly. She had no interest in cowboys, in any guys from the area for that matter. Her future lay far from here, and she was too aware of that fact to get overly attached to anything she found here.

She hadn't seen him or his group when he'd come in, only registered that some people had. After finishing with the table she'd been taking care of, she'd picked up a few menus from the counter and turned to head over to the newcomers.

And then she'd seen him.

He'd been sitting at the corner booth with three other

cowboys, but he was the only one she saw. He was beautiful. Not in a way that she ever would have associated with that word before. He wasn't pretty. There certainly wasn't anything feminine about him. He was young, in his early twenties, not much older than she was, but there was no denying he was a man. He had thick black hair and deep bronze skin, his features strong and masculine. It wasn't a flawless face, not in the conventional sense. He was no model. No, he was too real, his face had too much character. And yes, to her eyes, he was, quite simply, beautiful.

Whether he'd sensed her attention or simply chosen to raise his head at that moment, he'd suddenly looked up, his eyes automatically and unerringly meeting hers.

In an instant, everything around them seemed to disappear, leaving only the two of them, looking at each other. Even across the restaurant she'd seen his eyes widen slightly. To an outsider, it might have looked like the reaction was surprise, and maybe that was part of it. But only a small part. Because staring into his eyes, she felt it, the same thing he must have, a click deep inside, an instantaneous connection, a cord formed between them and pulled taut.

Yes.

She didn't hear the word in her head so much as she felt it deep in her body, every cell sighing with rightness as she looked into this man's eyes.

Yes.

She knew immediately that he wasn't the kind of guy she was looking for. She didn't want a cowboy. She didn't want anyone even remotely connected to this town.

She also knew immediately that it didn't matter. Because the moment she saw him, the moment their eyes met, she knew. Whatever this was, it was right.

Yes.

She'd done her best to do her job and not let the rest of his table see her response to him, even as she felt his eyes on her every time she was in the main room of the diner, even as she couldn't stop sneaking glances at him every possible moment. And every time, he'd be looking back at her.

He'd lingered after they'd paid the check and the rest of his friends stepped outside, waiting at the end of the counter for her. She'd known why, too, as she walked over to him.

He'd leaned close. "Can I see you later?" he asked, low under his breath, directly into her ear, and she'd nearly shuddered. "Maybe give you a ride home?"

"Sure." She hardly lived far enough away to need a ride, but she wasn't about to turn down the offer.

"What time do you get off work?"

"Midnight." She'd told him about a spot at the end of the block, instinctively knowing she didn't want word getting out—getting back to her father—that she'd met some cowboy after work and driven off with him. That spot was close enough to be convenient, yet far enough away no one should pay much attention.

"I'll be there," he'd promised.

She should have been nervous. He was a complete stranger, and undeniably a man. She knew nothing about him. The prospect of being alone with him should have made her wary. But it hadn't.

She'd almost been afraid he wouldn't be there, that he'd change his mind. She'd hurried there after work, trying not to run, not wanting to look too eager.

He'd been waiting for her, in the shadows at the end of the block, a corner the nearest streetlamp didn't quite reach. He'd stepped out into the light when he'd seen her, his strong, sensual lips curving into a smile that took her breath away. And by the time she reached him she'd been smiling, too.

"I'm glad you came," he said, his voice low and deep, incredibly sexy.

"Me, too," she said. His truck was parked behind him. She waited for him to offer to help her in, maybe even make some pointless small talk about how the rest of her shift had gone.

Instead, there in the shadowed darkness at the end of the block, he'd kissed her.

It wasn't what she'd expected. She hadn't been ready for it. But as soon as his lips met hers she knew it was exactly right.

He'd kissed her, long and slow and sweetly, like she'd never been kissed before. She might as well not have been. Nothing she'd experienced before could begin to compare.

Things didn't get any less heady as the summer went on. They'd had to sneak around. She hadn't wanted her father to find out about them. He had never liked the idea of her dating. To call him overprotective would have been the understatement of the century. It wasn't just the usual protectiveness of a father toward his daughter, his only child. He'd watched her like a hawk ever since her mother had left them without a word. Elena had known he'd been afraid of losing her, too, had considered anyone who might take her away from him a threat. His drinking hadn't exactly made him any more rational about the matter, either. It had been a miracle he'd let her go away to school, but even that had required a great deal of arguing, until he'd realized she was going, and the only way to hold on to her at all would be to let her. And even then he'd made it seem like a betrayal.

So they'd seen each other in secret, whenever Matt could get away from the ranch, which wasn't nearly enough for either of them. Nights when she worked at the diner he would wait for her at their corner. At first he would drive her home, then they began to stay out later together. Her father was usually too out of it to notice. They would talk, and kiss, and when the time came that she was ready and couldn't wait anymore, they finally made love on a blanket stretched out on a field under the stars.

She'd never dated much in high school—never had the time—and had seen only a few guys casually in college. This was so much more than any of those fleeting experiences. They'd shared everything about their lives, her more than him at first. She'd told him about life with her father, about her mother leaving, the most ridiculously insignificant little details about her life. And he'd listened to every word, patiently.

"I just like hearing your voice," he'd told her once, the words warming her as none ever had.

He'd told her he'd never been close to his parents, either, and didn't have a relationship with them, though he wouldn't tell her why, simply saying it was complicated. It was only after a couple months, almost at the end of their time together, that he'd finally told her the details late one night. How he'd been raised by his mother, who'd moved them around various small towns in the Southwest. His father had been a rodeo cowboy she'd fallen hard for. He hadn't stuck around, not wanting a kid, and his mother had blamed Matt for ruining her life. It hadn't helped that he'd looked like his father, and every time she saw him she saw the face of someone she hated. He'd been the target of all her rages, until he'd done everything he could to get away from home. In one of the towns where they'd lived, there'd been a ranch nearby, and he'd spent hours by himself standing outside the fence watching the horses. When he was twelve he'd gotten a job mucking out stalls at another ranch, and gradually he'd learned more about horses and the cattle business, though he never got to stay anywhere for long. Eventually, his mother would be ready to move on.

He'd come home one night when he was fifteen to find his mother packing to leave with her latest boyfriend. She wasn't coming back, he wasn't invited. He hadn't been sorry to see her go. He'd been on his own ever since, managing to get hired on at ranches by lying about his age.

He'd met his father once, managing to track him down. It was like his mother had said, Matt looked a lot like him. There was no denying they were father and son. Except that was exactly what the man had done. He'd cussed Matt out, told him to take a hike, threatened to kick his ass if he didn't get the hell away from him. Not figuring the man was worth the trouble, he'd done just that.

His voice had been flat and controlled as he'd told it, but she'd been able to detect the emotion in his voice, the deep pain beneath the stoic exterior. She'd known, even before he admitted it, that he'd never told anyone else about any of that before. Only her. Because he trusted her. Because he loved her.

He'd told her that, too—finally—after several months. She knew the admission hadn't come easy, the vulnerability it required everything he'd learned to protect himself against. When she'd said it back, she'd seen the joy in his face, but also the relief, and it had broken her heart a little. She wondered if anyone had ever said that to him before. Everything inside her told her they hadn't.

They'd both been alone and basically on their own for most of their lives. But they weren't alone anymore. Now they had each other.

After a few brief, uneasy exchanges about the subject, they'd avoided talking about the future, about what would happen at the end of the summer when she went back to school. It didn't matter. She knew they'd work it out somehow. They'd found each other. They loved each other. There was no way they ever wouldn't be together.

Remembering it now, Elena shook her head. God, she'd been young. And so foolish.

Then her father had found out about them. She'd never discovered how, but she supposed by the end they'd been less careful than they'd once been. Nothing had mattered but being with him; every minute they'd been apart from each other had been unbearable.

Her father had erupted. He'd actually gone to the police to complain about the man messing around with his daughter, though she'd been an adult and obviously there was nothing they could have charged Matt with, even if they'd been inclined to bother.

But then her father had gone out to the Nolan ranch where Matt was working that summer. From what she'd heard in the whispers people hadn't managed to hide entirely behind her back, he'd made a fool of himself, screaming and flailing and demanding that Matt be fired, threatening to come back as much as he needed to until it happened. Unfortunately, he'd gotten what he'd wanted. Tom Nolan had a spread to run, and neither the time nor the interest to put up with Ed Reyes's nonsense. Even if he called the police to have him hauled away, Ed would have been back as promised once he drank enough. The summer was almost over, the season was winding down, and Matt was just another hand. It really wasn't worth the hassle of dealing with Ed to keep him around.

So he'd been let go. And there'd been nothing for him to do but leave town.

He'd asked her to come with him.

She'd said no.

A decision that had seemed like the right one—the only one possible at the time.

A decision she'd reconsidered more often than she could count.

The sunlight suddenly hit her eyes, blinding her. Raising a hand to shade them, she glanced up, gradually realizing where she was. She was still in her truck, parked on the side of the road. She must have been sitting there for a while. The sun had moved, sinking lower in the sky until it finally hit her face. A glance at the clock confirmed it. More than a half hour had passed.

With a sigh, she tried to shake off the remnants of the memories. She couldn't sit here all day. The longer she remained on the side of the road, the more likely someone would notice. She was lucky no one had passed by already. The last thing she needed was for word to get out that she'd been parked on the highway, having some kind of breakdown. Not to mention there was more than enough work waiting for her back at the ranch. She was only just managing to do the bare minimum to keep things going around there on her own.

Starting the engine, she shifted the truck into gear and pulled out onto the road. So much to do, beginning with learning how to put the past behind her and get her emotions under control. As long as Matt was here, it was something she was going to have to do. She had enough to worry about. She didn't have the time or energy to waste wallowing in the past.

He was just a friend. Here to help her.

She couldn't afford to think of him as anything else.

EIGHT YEARS AGO THERE'D ONLY been one bar in town. Matt had no trouble finding it on the edge of town just off the main street. There were no vehicles in the parking lot when he pulled in. It wasn't even five o'clock, he realized. Maybe too early to expect anyone to be here.

Sure enough, the place was almost empty except for one man seated—more like slumped over—at the bar, and one standing behind it. The seated man didn't react to Matt's entrance, though the bartender looked up. He appeared to be in his forties. Matt didn't recognize him, which might not mean much. If he was hoping people wouldn't remember him, there was a good chance he wouldn't remember everyone he'd met in Western Bluff eight years ago. Still, something told him he didn't know this man.

With a nod, Matt walked up to the bar and slid onto a stool. "Afternoon."

"Afternoon," the bartender said simply. "What can I get you?"

"A beer'd be good. Whatever you have on tap."

With a nod, the bartender moved away. The man certainly wasn't overly friendly, something that wasn't going to help Matt with his mission. He was going to have to hope tipping well would open the man up. Reaching for his wallet, he pulled out a twenty.

"You new around here?"

It wasn't the bartender who'd spoken, but the man seated a couple stools down from Matt. Matt glanced over at him, taking in the way he was hunched over the bar, the unsteadiness of his gaze. It may be early, but the man had clearly already had a few. Just as clearly he was in the mood to talk. Matt wasn't about to rebuff the friendliest greeting he'd gotten yet in this town.

"Yes, I am," Matt said easily. "Just got in today."

"And leavin' today, too, I reckon," the man cackled, laughing at his own apparent joke.

"What makes you say that?" Matt asked.

"Not much to see around here. Why would anybody stick around?"

"Looks like I'll be here for a while, actually. Just took a job. The Weston Ranch."

Out of the corner of his eye, Matt saw the bartender, who'd started back with his beer, suddenly stop. The drunk's eyebrows shot upward. He stared blearily at Matt for a few long seconds before reaching for his own drink.

"Might not be around as long as you think," the man said into his glass.

"Why's that?"

The bartender dropped Matt's beer down on the

counter in front of him so hard some of it sloshed over the sides of the glass. He made no move to wipe it up. "Woman you're working for's probably going to be in jail soon."

Matt met the man's steady gaze and returned it. He had no intention of being intimidated by the bartender any more than he had been by the deputy. The sooner word got out that he wasn't going to be a pushover, the better.

But the longer he held the man's eyes, the more Matt registered that what he saw in them wasn't anger or hostility. Just a cold matter-of-factness that somehow was even more disturbing.

If that was the man's attitude toward Elena, Matt really didn't feel like throwing a big tip his way. Not to mention he had the feeling now that not even a tip could get the bartender to open up. His new friend a couple stools down, on the other hand, seemed like someone he'd like to keep talking.

Matt set the twenty down on the bar. "Bring my friend here another," he said, nodding to the other man.

His lips thinning, the bartender took the bill and moved away again.

"Why, thank you," the drunk said, tipping his almost empty glass in Matt's direction. "Name's Roy Fuller."

"Matt Alvarez."

"See, Ben," Fuller said to the bartender. "He's not a bad sort. Besides, he's new. Might not even know about Bobby."

"If you mean the murder, I know," Matt said. "I met a local deputy. He tried to scare me off."

The drunk nodded so hard Matt almost expected his head to pop off his neck. "That'd be Travis. He and

Bobby were tight. Always were since they were kids. He's got to be taking this real personal."

That was putting it mildly. "That makes sense the way he was acting," Matt agreed.

"Yeah, Travis always did have a temper, and Bobby was like a brother to him. Not to mention he never did like Elena. He's got to be coming for her hard. Hell, most folks are. Bobby was the last of the Westons. That means something around here."

The bartender set the new beer in front of Fuller, who reached for it greedily.

"A family that important must have had some enemies," Matt suggested.

"You'd think so, wouldn't you? But no, not Bobby. He was a good one."

"*Everybody* has enemies," Matt pressed. "There wasn't anybody who had a problem with him?"

"Only that wife of his," Fuller snickered. "Why do you think she killed him?"

His words drew Matt up short. "You think she did it?"

"Of course. Folks liked Bobby. Nobody had a reason to want him dead. Nobody but her."

Matt felt his heart sink. Staring into the man's bleary gaze, Matt knew he wasn't lying or putting on an act. Fuller really did believe Elena killed her husband.

He glanced at the bartender to find him staring at him. The man nodded, the gesture seeming to say "I told you so."

"I heard he was having money problems," Matt said.

"Times are rough for everybody. Only person who cared about his money problems was his wife, who didn't want him spending any. He was always wanting to make changes and improvements on the ranch and she was always fighting him. Can't blame her, I suppose. Elena grew up poor, never had much. Makes sense she'd be tight with money." Fuller shot him a look. "I hope she's paying you well enough, especially since people might be giving you trouble for working for her."

"So he wasn't in debt to anybody?" Money could be a strong motive for murder.

"Not that I heard."

Which didn't necessarily mean anything. A lot of people kept money matters private. If Weston had been in trouble with someone, it was possible no one knew but him and the other person.

Matt wanted to believe he wasn't just clutching at straws. He couldn't quite manage it.

He tried to think of something else he could ask, another possibility he could pursue, but came up empty. Which wasn't good. Despite what Elena had told him, he'd figured there had to be someone out there who had a known beef with Bobby, maybe one she didn't know about if they were as estranged as she said. He'd meant what he'd said. Everybody had enemies. Heck, Elena seemed to have nothing but in this town.

Elena...

He frowned as a fresh thought occurred to him. Maybe he was just looking at this all wrong. Bobby Weston may not have had any enemies—though he still doubted that—but maybe this wasn't about him. Maybe it was about someone who did have plenty of people against her.

Elena.

Bobby Weston might be dead, but she was the one in a lot of trouble. Could all of this somehow be about *her?*

"Tell me more about this woman who hired me," he said to Fuller. "What's so bad about her?"

A laugh burst out of Fuller's mouth. "Killing her husband isn't enough for you?"

"She hasn't been convicted yet," Matt pointed out. "She hasn't even been arrested and it's been a couple weeks, so there must not be much real evidence against her. But it seems like the whole town's ready to believe she's guilty." He sent a pointed look the bartender's way, only to get the same stony stare in return. "And you said the deputy never liked her to begin with. She's got to be a pretty terrible person for everybody to turn on her like that."

Fuller waved a hand dismissively. "Eh, I never had a problem with her. Her mother took off and her father was a bum, but she was an okay kid. Not popular or anything. Quiet, kept to herself. One of those kids you could tell was dreaming of getting out of here."

"So why don't people like her?"

"I think it was mostly marrying Weston that did it. That's when people started looking at her different, and not in a good way. Before, they ignored her. After, they couldn't. Weston was too big around here, too much a part of the town. That made her part of the town, and people didn't like that. She wasn't in her place. Really it all comes back to the money again. Everybody knew that was why she'd married him. She was dirt poor with a bum for a father, and she ended up hitched to the biggest name in this town. People judged her for that, especially after they saw her and Bobby weren't really happy. They blamed her for that, for not making him happy. So when he turned up dead, nobody was surprised she killed him. She was in it for the money, and she finally killed him for it."

Matt let the man's words sink in. He had to admit it made sense—not her killing Weston, of course, but the reasons for the marriage and why the town had turned on her. He knew more than anybody how much security had meant to her back then. She'd married a guy who could give her that, so if it wasn't for the money itself, it was for what the money could provide. Why else would she marry him so fast, after only three months? She'd known Matt that long, and sure as hell hadn't chosen him.

The only other explanation he could think of was that she really had loved Weston—far more than she'd loved Matt, than he'd loved her.

He wasn't sure which answer he'd like less.

He was crazy about me, and I...was crazy about him.

A sharp pain shafted through him at the idea. Which was just stupid, he thought angrily, trying to shake off the feeling. It was the past. It had been eight years. He was over it, over her. There was no reason it should hurt to know she hadn't loved him as much as he'd thought he loved her.

But even as he thought it, the burn of that pain he'd felt in response lingered, too sharp to be shaken off that easily. He didn't even want to think about why that was.

"Hey, don't take it so hard," Fuller said, likely misreading whatever was on Matt's face. "I say go on and work for her. How many people like who they have to work for, you know? Unlike Ben here—" he raised his glass to the bartender "—I don't begrudge you the work. Times like these, a man's gotta do what he has to.

But don't get too comfortable, I'll tell you that. And you might want to get her to pay you up front. Fact is, your new boss is headed to jail. It's only a matter of time."

Chapter Six

For the first time in more than a week, when Elena heard the sound of someone pulling into the driveway, her heart didn't sink with dread. Instead, she felt a rush of anticipation, the feeling racing through her.

Then she realized the cause, the knowledge turning the small smile that had formed on her lips into a frown.

Matt. She was excited because Matt was back.

She shook herself. Good God, what was she doing?

Her husband had been dead for little more than a week. It hardly mattered that the feelings she'd once had for him had long since died. She had no business feeling this way about anyone right now, certainly not a man who'd suddenly reappeared in her life after eight years.

Nostalgia, she told herself. What she was experiencing was just the effect of old memories. Which made even less sense considering how everything had ended between them.

The reminder should have been enough to kill the ridiculous emotional response. Still, she had to squelch another little tremor of anticipation as she made her way out of the barn where she'd been giving the horses their feed.

But when she reached the barn door, she saw it

wasn't Matt's truck sitting in the driveway. Glen Marshall stood on the front porch.

Disappointment welled in her chest, the feeling just as absurd as the excitement she'd felt moments earlier. She tried to shake it off and forced a smile as she made her way up to the house. "Evening, Glen," she called when she was close enough.

He matched her smile. "Evening, Elena. Is this a good time to stop by?"

His smile was as warm as it had always been, and she felt another twinge of guilt for the disappointment she'd felt when she'd seen it was him. A hearty man in his fifties, Glen was a successful rancher and had been a close friend of the Westons for years. More important, he was just about the only person in the area who didn't treat her like an outcast. If anything, she should be glad to see his friendly face.

"Of course," she said, crossing the porch and pushing the door open. "Come on in."

Pulling his hat from his head, he stepped over the threshold and past her into the house. Elena closed the door behind him and nodded toward the living room. "Have a seat."

"Thank you." He took the chair on the far side of the coffee table, Elena taking the one opposite. "I heard you had some trouble in town today," he said with an almost convincing casualness.

"I'm sure you did. And I bet whoever shared that news with you sounded pretty pleased, didn't they?"

He had the grace to look away, but she could tell from the way he hesitated before answering that she was right.

"I wanted to make sure you were all right, and also talk to you about something."

"I'm fine," she said. "Already got my truck fixed and safely home, good as new. What did you want to talk to me about?"

"I'm sure Bobby probably mentioned that I'd offered to buy the ranch from him recently."

Elena nodded. "He did." And had been none too pleased about it. Glen and Big Jim Weston had been good friends ever since they were boys. After Big Jim's death, Glen had sort of offered himself as a surrogate father to Bobby and his brother Junior, especially when it came to ranching matters. He'd been there to guide Junior, and then Bobby, giving advice when it was asked for and a willing ear when needed. Bobby had taken Glen's offer as a sign the man didn't have faith in him and didn't think he could handle the ranch. Elena wasn't so sure that wasn't exactly the case. If anyone besides her had known how much Bobby had been struggling to keep things going around here, it was Glen. The fact that he'd thrown Bobby a lifeline when he needed one so badly probably wasn't a coincidence.

"I want to make the same offer to you, with the same terms, though I'm certainly open to negotiation."

The offer was a good one. More than good, really. Certainly more than the ranch would fetch on the open market in this economy. She'd wanted Bobby to take it. Of course, he hadn't. "I appreciate that. I'll definitely give it some thought."

She could tell it wasn't the answer he'd been looking for and suspected he'd thought she'd say yes right away. "Can I be completely honest with you, Elena?"

"I hope you will be."

"Look, I don't think there's any question a lot of people think you killed Bobby. Not me," he said quickly, "but a lot of people. And certainly Walt."

"True enough."

"Have you thought about hiring a lawyer?"

"Unfortunately, I have," she admitted. "If Walt and Travis have their way, I'm going to need one sometime soon. I just don't know how I'm going to pay for one."

"I figured as much. Which is another reason I thought I should reiterate my offer. If you sell now, you can use the funds from the sale to buy the best lawyer money can buy, not have to worry about that."

She couldn't argue with him. The longer the threat of an arrest loomed over her head, she'd wondered how she was going to pay for an attorney should the time come. And even without lawyer fees to pay, she could use the money. Even so…

"Thank you for your concern, but I think it's too early to consider making any kind of deal. I haven't even had a chance to deal with Bobby's will."

"I understand that. So I thought I'd let you know I would be willing to make an advance payment once the papers are signed. You could use the money right away."

The new twist drew her up short and actually made her consider it for a moment. He was certainly being more than generous. But even if she was ready to make a deal, she couldn't even afford a lawyer to handle that for her.

"I really do appreciate the offer, Glen, but I have to admit I feel a little like I'd be taking advantage of you. We both know the land's not worth as much as you're proposing."

"It is to me," he said. "The Westons have always

meant a great deal to me, and I'd hate to see the land they worked for generations sold to just anybody."

It was the same thing he'd told Bobby, and she knew it was true. "I understand, but with everything that's going on right now, I'm really not ready to face selling the ranch at the moment. But if and when the time comes I can sell, you can be sure I'll think of you first."

Again, she got the sense he was disappointed. She was almost afraid he would try to pressure her further, but instead he simply nodded. "I appreciate that."

She did her best not to let her relief show that he was letting the subject go for now. She knew his intentions were good, and she would certainly be hard-pressed to find a better offer, but this was the last thing she wanted to think about today.

The sound of a vehicle approaching outside met her ears. This time there was no rush of anticipation. There was no telling who it might be.

Glen glanced at her. "Expecting company?"

"It might be the new hand I hired to help out around here. He should be getting back from town."

She saw Glen's eyebrows rise in surprise. Before he could say anything, she quickly rose to her feet. He followed suit a moment later.

Together they walked to the front door, reaching the porch in time to see Matt climbing out of his truck.

"I didn't know you were looking for new hands, Elena," Glen said, in a tone she couldn't quite read.

"I wasn't," she said. "I needed to, but obviously I've had other things on my mind."

Before he closed the truck door, Matt's attention zeroed in on her and Glen. As he made his way to the porch, his gaze shifted from her to Glen and back. She read the question in his eyes, as though seeking a signal from her whether the man was friend or foe.

"Glen, this is Matt Alvarez," she said easily. "Matt, Glen Marshall, a good friend of my husband's family."

Glen shot her a quick look. "*Your* family, Elena."

She forced a small smile. "Of course." Glen might consider her a Weston, but if so, he was likely the only one around here who ever had.

"Well, I should be going," Glen said. "But again, think about my offer. I don't think you'll get a better one."

"I will," she promised again.

With a nod to Matt, Glen headed back to his truck. Matt and Elena watched him go in silence.

"Everything go okay in town?" she asked when Glen began to back out of the driveway.

"No problems. What offer?"

"To buy the ranch," she explained. "It was a standing offer he had with Bobby. He wanted me to know it's still on the table." She shook her head. "Not that it matters at the moment. I'm in no position to sell anyway. I haven't even been able to talk to Bobby's lawyer about his will."

"Why not?"

"Mostly because his lawyer seems to be avoiding me," she acknowledged with more than a little irritation. "Not that I'm surprised."

"What do you mean?"

"Jack Landry is the executor of Bobby's estate, not to mention the only lawyer in town. He also happens to be Bobby's cousin."

"I thought Bobby was the last of the Westons."

"He is. Jack's not a Weston. His mother and Bobby's were sisters."

"So he's probably not happy about the idea of you inheriting."

"Nope. I made a couple calls to his office, and was told he wasn't available. I left messages both times, and he hasn't returned them. With everything else that's been going on, I haven't had time to follow up further yet. And to be honest, I started to worry how bad it would look if it seemed like I was too eager to see what I'd inherited from Bobby. Everybody already thinks I killed him. I didn't want to give them any more reason to think so at the moment."

"You think this Jack Landry believes you're guilty, too, and that's why he's putting you off?"

"Probably. Most people figure my arrest is only a matter of time." Elena shot him a wry look. "Glen pointed out I could probably use the money for my up-coming defense, should I need it. He even offered to advance me the money from the sale."

"Nice of him," Matt noted drily. "Sounds like he wants the ranch pretty bad. He wanted to buy it when Bobby was alive?"

"Yeah. He made a very generous offer, too."

"Hmm. You ever wonder just how badly he wants it?"

"What do you mean?"

He looked at her with the utmost seriousness. "Badly enough to kill for it?"

Elena simply shook her head. "Hardly. Glen has his own spread. The Weston ranch is smaller than Glen's and isn't even adjacent so it's not as though he could combine them. Bobby's brother, Junior, was Glen's god-

son, and he and Bobby were about as close. He's just a
family friend trying to do a good deed for a family he
was close to for years and cared about deeply. The offer
really is just a gesture of pity, something Bobby knew
full well, which is another reason he refused to sell."

"Are you sure about that? There couldn't be some
other reason he wants the ranch?"

"Like what?"

"I don't know. That doesn't mean there isn't one,
something you don't know about. Something that could
be a motive. Are you really considering his offer?"

"I'd be a fool not to. It's a much better one than I'm
likely to get from anyone else, certainly more than I'd
get on the open market."

"And that doesn't make you suspicious?"

"I suppose it should." Elena exhaled sharply. He was
right. As she'd told him, her first instinct was to believe
no one had a motive to kill Bobby, yet clearly someone
had, so she must be missing something. Could Glen
really want the ranch so badly that he was willing to
kill Bobby to get it for some reason she wasn't aware
of yet? "And here I thought no one had any motives."

"Maybe you just needed a fresh set of eyes, somebody who doesn't know these people to look at them
with a different perspective."

Someone who was inclined not to trust easily?
Knowing what she did about his life history, she supposed this came naturally to him, not trusting people.
The idea made her sad, but at the moment maybe that
quality was exactly what she needed in her life.

"I guess it's a good thing you're here, then," she
said softly. Even to her own ears the words sounded

far more weighted with meaning and full of feeling than she'd intended.

His eyes went dark with some unreadable emotion, his expression enigmatic.

"Maybe it is," he agreed.

Chapter Seven

She ran as hard and fast as her body could manage, her lungs heaving, her legs pumping wildly, the pavement hard beneath her feet. And still it wasn't fast enough. She pushed her body harder, fear and adrenaline and pure desperation pounding through her veins. She had to get there sooner.

She had to get to him.

And then there he was, leaning against the truck he'd parked in the shadows at the edge of Main Street, barely out of reach of the nearest streetlight. It was their spot, the one where he'd met her that first night and all those nights after. It was as private a spot as the town had to offer, the rest of the street quiet and deserted at this time of night. She didn't have time to feel relief or take a breath. At the sight of him, she picked up a fresh burst of speed she wouldn't have thought herself capable of and ran even faster, hurtling toward him in the dark.

She saw the moment he spotted her, pushing himself away from the truck and moving forward to meet her, clearly as unable to wait for her as she was for him. The moonlight lit his face. It almost didn't seem necessary with the happiness radiating from his expression, the smile beaming on his lips. She immediately smiled, too, joy bursting within her. And when she launched herself at him, he was there to catch her, his arms wide and strong and open, closing around her and holding her tight.

"Elena," he breathed against her hair, the sound of his voice sending warmth rolling through her like a soft caress.

"Matt." There was so much more she wanted to say, but that single word—his name—was all she could manage to get out past the lump in her throat. And suddenly she realized she was crying, hot tears burning her eyes.

"What's wrong?" he whispered gently.

"I was just so scared I'd never see you again." Never look at his beautiful face. Never hear his voice. Never touch him. Never feel his arms around her.

He said nothing, only tightened his hold and held her even closer. It was answer enough that he'd felt the same way.

Finally, needing to see him, needing to say all those words she had inside, she pulled back to peer up into his face. "I'm so sorry. It's not right. It's not fair."

One corner of his mouth curved wryly. "Hey, can't say you didn't warn me. Your dad did go crazy."

Yes, he had, she thought, fresh anger surging inside her. There'd been times over the past several months when Matt had questioned whether it was really necessary for them to be so secretive. She herself had sometimes felt foolish about it. She was an adult, should probably be past the age when she should care about her father's reaction to her love life. Except Ed's re-

sponse when he'd learned about them had proven just how right she'd been to be worried.

He'd acted like a complete lunatic, ranting and raving to anyone who'd listen—whether they wanted to or not. He'd made a fool of himself, but he'd also accomplished exactly what he'd wanted—gotten Matt fired, ensured there was no longer a place for him in Western Bluff, so he'd have no choice but to move on.

She shuddered, fear striking directly at her heart.

"At least I know you weren't trying to hide me because you were ashamed of me or something," Matt said. The words were dry, laconic, but she knew him well enough to know the genuine fear he must have felt deep down, even if he'd never admit it consciously, even to himself. He'd been hurt too deeply, rejected too much by those who should have loved him the most, not to guard himself against the possibility of it happening again.

"Never," she said firmly, fiercely, meaning it as much as anything she'd ever said in her life. How could she ever be ashamed of him? He was the best man she'd ever known. It seemed impossible that they'd only known each other for three months. She couldn't imagine living without him.

Which brought them to this.

A sudden chill rolled through her. "So what happens now?" she made herself ask.

"I have to go," he said quietly.

She lowered her head and nodded faintly. Of course. She knew it was true. She just hadn't wanted to think about what it meant for them. She would be leaving soon enough herself, but she would be going back to school. And he... "Where will you go?"

"I don't know. Wherever I can get a job. It might take some time, but I saved up enough this summer to get by for a while until I find something. Hopefully it won't take too long."

A hesitant note entered his final words, betraying his uncertainty. Of course, he had to do whatever he could to find work. And the longer it took, the greater the likelihood the search would take him farther and farther away.

Far from here. Far from her.

His hands suddenly tightened on her arms.

"Come with me."

She raised her head, her heart racing, pounding, threatening to burst through her chest.

"Where?"

"Wherever I go," he said immediately. *"I don't know where I'm heading. But I need you with me."* He swallowed, and the flash of vulnerability on his masculine face made her heart twist painfully.

"I love you."

It wasn't the first time he'd told her that but it might as well have been from the rush of giddiness that soared through her, filling her with so much sheer happiness it didn't seem possible her body, her heart, her soul could contain it. And in that moment, she would have agreed to anything he said. Of course she would go with him. She would follow him to the ends of the earth and they would be together. Because he loved her. And she loved him. And that was all that mattered. Nothing else possibly could.

Nothing.

Except it did.

Like an insidious whisper, the thought slid through

her, a chill washing over her and extinguishing her joy as the full implications of his words settled in.

The image of him on the open road, traveling, looking for work, rose again in her mind. But this time she saw herself there with him. The uncertainty. The fear of not knowing what would happen or how they'd pay the bills, where the next paycheck would come from.

It was a life she knew too well. That was what it was like growing up with her father, the uncertainty, the precariousness. She couldn't live like that anymore. That was why she'd always been determined to get out of this town, to go to college.

College, where she was supposed to return in just a few weeks.

College, which she'd been working toward her whole life, which offered the promise of stability and certainty she'd craved and desperately wanted—needed—for so long.

How could she give up that bright future, all her hopes and dreams, to follow him into the dark unknown?

As fear gripped her insides, clenching her stomach, closing off her breath, she knew the answer without a doubt.

She couldn't.

But he loves me.

Yes, she thought, peering up into his dark eyes. She didn't doubt that. But she felt none of that love. She only felt fear.

He was still looking down at her, his face aglow, as though certain what she would say, as certain as she'd been only moments ago.

And she realized it had only been a few moments

since he'd made the offer. She felt so cold inside it was hard to believe she'd ever been happy and warm, let alone mere moments ago.

Still he waited for her answer, not yet realizing anything was wrong.

There was only one answer she could give.

"I can't."

He blinked, no other reaction on his face, as though the words hadn't had any impact.

"What do you mean?"

"I can't go with you."

He finally frowned, eyebrows furrowing in confusion. "Why not?"

"I have to go back to school. It's my future. It's everything I've been working toward for years." She almost winced. The words were all true, but they sounded so hollow spoken aloud compared to how they had in her head.

"You can have a future with me."

Again the words inspired a rush of emotion, of pure longing, at the possibilities they offered.

But then she remembered the costs. "Doing what? Going from town to town? Getting work on a ranch, too?"

"You've been waiting tables," he pointed out.

"For the summer! I don't want to do it forever. I want something more than that. I need to go to school." Suddenly inspiration struck, fresh hope flaring inside her. "You can come back to Austin with me when I go back to school." The idea was so perfect she could barely contain her excitement at hearing it voiced aloud.

His frown merely deepened. "And do what? Hang around while you go to school?"

"You can get a job."

"Doing what? Ranch work is all I've ever done. It's all I know. And I don't want to live in the city. I could never be happy in a place like that."

"Even if I'm there?"

His voice softened the slightest bit, but his expression was unyielding. "Even then."

"How do you know if you haven't tried?"

"I know," he said firmly. "How do you know you won't be happy on a ranch with me?"

"It's just not the life I want."

His expression hardened. "Or maybe I'm not what you want."

"You are!" she said without hesitation.

"Well, if you loved me, you would come with me."

"If *you* loved *me*, you would come with me."

"I can't," he said dully.

"Well, I can't, either."

He stared at her, and though he hadn't moved a muscle and his expression didn't change she could feel him slipping away from her. She almost reached out to grab on to him and hold him to her.

Before she could, he took another, inexorable step back. "Then I guess there's nothing left to say."

She wanted to argue. There was obviously so much to say. But as she stared into his eyes, panic gripping her throat, she knew there was nothing she could do. Nothing but to take it back and say she'd go with him. It was the only thing that could possibly dim the raw fury in his eyes.

But it wasn't the anger that made her heart squeeze and her lungs feel like they were being pummeled. It was what she saw beneath it. The hurt, the sheer agony.

And she knew she'd wounded him, just as she knew why. At least why it had to seem that way from his point of view.

But he was wrong. He had to see this was different. This wasn't like his mother, or his father or any of the other people in his life who'd rejected him and hadn't wanted him. That wasn't what she was doing.

Before she could begin to summon the words to deny it, he turned and walked away.

She watched him storm to his truck, his boots kicking up dirt with each angry step. The whole time she waited for him to stop and turn back, expecting it, knowing it would happen. It couldn't end like this. He couldn't just leave her. It wasn't possible.

The engine started with a roar. Seemingly a split second later, the truck began to back up, quickly turning and shooting out onto the road.

She stood there, her throat frozen in shock.

He'll come back. He'll come back. He has to.

She watched as the truck peeled away in the night, growing smaller, the taillights fading, until the tears finally blurred her sight and she could see nothing at all, the thought still echoing in her mind.

He'll come back.

He has to.

He'll come back…

ELENA BOLTED UPRIGHT IN BED, her heart pounding, her lungs squeezing so painfully she couldn't breathe. She leaned forward, desperately trying to pull in air. It felt as if she was being suffocated, as though she were dying.

Until she realized she *was* breathing, her chest falling up and down, the breath flowing into and out of her lungs. But it didn't ease the agony she felt in her chest, the sense that she was dying. And she realized it had nothing to do with not being able to breathe.

No, she remembered the feeling well, even without having dreamed it again. It was the feeling of having her heart broken, the worst experience of her life, the most painful thing she'd ever been through.

She sat there, trying to shake the awful feeling that continued to grip her. She began to push her hair back, only to realize the wetness she felt on her cheeks wasn't the remembered sensation of the dream. She brushed her fingers across her face to find it damp with tears. Damn. She hadn't had the dream in years, but it was as real to her as ever.

Those words continued to echo in her ears as loudly as though they'd actually been spoken an instant before.

He'll come back.

Except he hadn't. As long as she'd waited that warm summer night and the days and months that followed, Matt never had come back.

No, she realized with a start. It was different this time. Because after all these years, the dream had a different ending in reality.

He *had* come back.

And then her heart was beating faster again. It was eight years later, so much had happened—*was* happening—and it was nothing like she'd once imagined, but he was here.

He'd come back.

She sat there, trying to adjust to that basic fact that changed so much. It had been years since she'd had the dream, and it had returned only when the reality had changed.

He was here, in the bunkhouse just a short distance from where she lay.

Then she heard it.

A sound. A thump. Coming from somewhere outside.

Somewhere downstairs.

And for the first time it struck her that she hadn't simply woken from the dream.

No, something had woken her.

She quickly jumped from the bed, reaching for the gun she'd placed on the bedside table for safety's sake. From the moment she'd found Bobby dead downstairs, she hadn't felt completely safe in this house. The gun didn't do a lot to reassure her, but at least it was something. At the moment, she couldn't have been happier to have it there.

Matt was nearby, in the bunkhouse. He might as well have been a million miles away for all the good he could do her there. If there was trouble, it was here.

Or did he already know? He'd said he would try to keep an eye out overnight. At the time she'd appreciated the gesture, but thought he was being overly cautious. True, she was uneasy in the house, but deep down she didn't believe the killer was coming back. And while people in town were giving her a cold shoulder, she didn't see them coming after her out here. Of course, no one had slashed her tires before, either. She probably shouldn't count anything out at this point.

Moving to the window, she peered out.

She didn't see anything, but that didn't mean nothing was there.

A shadow suddenly shifted at the edge of the yard. Her heart jumping, she whipped her head toward it.

Just in time to see Matt step into the light.

Relief shuddered from her lungs and she relaxed slightly. Then she noticed he was armed, too, a gun lowered but held in his right hand. He stepped forward gradually, cautiously, slowly looking from side to side as he moved toward the house.

Elena automatically shoved away from the window and headed for the door.

She raced downstairs. Seconds later, she was at the front door. Quickly checking outside before opening it, she spotted Matt just reaching the front steps. He was frowning. He still didn't have his gun raised and didn't seem particularly concerned. No, he seemed angry.

Something had definitely happened.

Figuring it was safe enough and needing to know what it was, she pulled the door open and stepped out on the porch.

He drew to a halt at the sight of her, surprise flashing across his face.

"What is it?" she asked. "What happened?"

Matt stood there, staring at her with a distinct sense of unease, his mouth slightly open.

"What?" she demanded, unable to take the suspense.

"Elena—" Shoving his gun into the back of his waistband, he stepped onto the porch, then stopped again and swallowed, his eyes flicking over her shoulder for an instant. Just a tiny gesture, little more than a reflex.

And a telling one. It was enough. Curious, she turned around.

Then she finally saw them, the letters spray painted

in bright red on the front of the house to the left of the door.

She stepped back, partly from surprise, partly from revulsion, unable to escape the word the huge letters spelled out on the wall in such a garish tone.

MURDERER.

She flinched, the ugliness of it striking her like a punch to the face. It was all so ugly. There was no other word for it. The word itself. The garish red paint. The sentiment behind it. The fact that someone had come here, to her home, the one place in this world she should be safe, in the middle of the night and defaced it out of their hatred for her.

She dropped her head, unable to stand looking at it anymore, but unable to force her body into motion to turn away.

She sensed him come up behind her, approaching slowly, coming close enough that she could feel him there behind her.

"Hey," he said. "It's going to be okay."

"Is it?" she responded automatically, hating the quiver she heard in her own voice.

"Yes," he said firmly, his voice pulsing with anger. "They're not going to get away with this. I'm not going to let them."

Every word rang with certainty and determination, leaving her no doubt he fully intended to do what he promised. She just wasn't sure if even he was capable of it.

Them. It didn't matter if it was only one person who had done this. Because it wasn't just one person against her. It was the whole town.

This damn town. She should have gotten out when

she'd had the chance, should have left it behind her and never looked back.

Should have left with him...

Matt gently turned her around to face him, his hands laying lightly on her upper arms. "Hey," he said again. "Don't let them do this to you. You're going to make it through this."

It was the tenderness in his voice more than the words alone that called to her, making her raise her head to meet his eyes.

The kindness she saw there, the concern, nearly broke her. She couldn't even remember the last time anyone had looked at her like that, when anyone had so simply and genuinely cared about her feelings. To have it come from this man, a man she'd once believed she loved, a man she hadn't thought she'd ever see again just twenty-four hours ago, was almost more than she could bear.

She stared up into his eyes, this man who'd been out of her life for eight long years, who'd reappeared in her life so suddenly for reasons she still wasn't sure she understood, or maybe wasn't sure she believed. Once again she found herself studying him, trying to understand what he was thinking, what he was doing here. At least at first. Because, as it always had before, the longer she looked the more it struck her how beautiful he was. His face was more mature, even more masculine than before, and somehow even more beautiful.

Then she saw that look in his eyes change, becoming more heated, more intense, stroking over her face.

And out of nowhere, she felt her body respond. The emotions that had been churning within her ebbed away, replaced by an incredible sense of warmth that built from her core, pooling in her belly and flowing outward to fill every part of her.

She'd tried to tell herself that what she was feeling was the residual emotions from her memories. She wasn't really this attracted to him now.

But this wasn't nostalgia. This wasn't a remembered emotion. It was real, and it was more powerful than anything she remembered.

It was also madness. He'd been back in her life less than a day.

It didn't matter that her marriage had died long before her husband did. Bobby had been dead for less than two weeks. To feel something for someone else so soon, especially *this* someone else…

Would be a mistake, she reminded herself firmly. And she'd already made far too many of those in her life.

She deliberately took a step back, breaking the eye contact to glance down the empty driveway. "Did you see them?" she made herself ask. "Did you see who did this?"

"No," he said, turning to follow her gaze. "I'm sorry."

"It's okay. They must have come on foot. If they'd driven up we would have heard them." She frowned. "Though I did think I heard something…"

"An engine?"

"No, some kind of noise. That's why I got up. I thought I heard something outside the house."

Their eyes met, and she saw him coming to the same conclusion she was. If the noise had been made by the vandal responsible for this, then that person had been around not too long ago.

Could still be somewhere nearby now.

"Stay here," he ordered. Without waiting for a response, he bounded back down the stairs, grabbing his
gun from the back of his waistband. Checking in both
directions, he tore off around the back of the house to
the left.

Suddenly realizing she still had her own weapon in
hand, Elena raised it and held it poised in front of her.
She scanned the yard and driveway for any signs of
anyone. Logic said whoever had done this had probably taken off as soon as they'd completed what they'd
come here for, not wanting to get caught. But part of
her wondered if they might not have lingered, wanting to see her reaction, the result of their handiwork.

And she'd given them exactly what they most likely
wanted, she realized, remembering her reaction, the
way her first glimpse of the vandalism had hit her. She
was instantly angry, as much with herself as with the
person who'd defaced her home. She could just imagine that person standing out there in the dark, waiting
to see how she reacted, relishing in having been able
to torment her.

No more.

She didn't know if they were still out there—she
doubted it—but she still straightened her spine and
stared out into the darkness. She hoped they were
watching.

Because she'd had enough. She wasn't going to put
up with any more, and she'd be damned if she let anyone in this town see a hint of weakness from her again.

Chapter Eight

It was almost noon when Matt got up the next day. As soon as he saw the time, he felt guilty for having slept in, rising to his feet with a muffled curse. He'd intended to get up early and check on the horses and maybe the cattle, familiarize himself with the way things were around here. Elena had shown him around a bit last night after dinner, but he wanted to get a feel for the place on his own. If the two of them were going to keep this place running by themselves, they were going to have to figure out how to make it work.

Then again, there were more important things to focus on, and it wasn't like he'd gotten much sleep last night. He'd run around in the dark for what seemed like hours. There'd been no trace of the scumbag who'd vandalized Elena's house. As far as Matt could tell, the guy had most likely parked on the main road and walked up, approaching from the side. It wasn't that long of a walk, there weren't any lights along that way to reveal an intruder, and someone could likely get in and out pretty easily.

The guy might not know it, but he should really consider himself lucky for having gotten away. He probably wouldn't have liked what would have happened if

Matt had gotten his hands on him, not after he'd seen the look the bastard's actions had put in Elena's eyes.

He still might not, Matt amended. Somebody who'd pulled something like that once might be willing to try it again, and Matt had no intention of letting him get away twice.

In the meantime, there was ranch business to be taken care of, not to mention a murder investigation to deal with. Far too much for him to spend any more time in bed.

He showered and dressed quickly, intending to check on Elena first thing. She'd looked calmer, stronger, *angrier* when they'd met back up after his unsuccessful search for the intruder. He'd been glad to see her resilience in action, but he still remembered how shattered she'd looked when he'd been unable to keep her from seeing what the intruder had painted on the house, how lost.

And how beautiful, staring up at him in the moonlight.

Yes, he remembered that, too. It was just something else he didn't have time to deal with right now.

He was pulling his boots on when his cell phone rang.

Recognizing the number, he quickly answered. "This is Matt."

"It's Pam," she said shortly.

"Glad to hear from you," he said, meaning it. They really could use any help she had to give. "What do you have for me?"

"Not much on the town. It seems like a pretty typical small town without much to distinguish it. A fairly insular, static community. Not many people move there or leave. It generally hasn't made the news, barely makes the map."

Yeah, sounded like Western Bluff all right. "What about Elena and her husband?"

"Elena Reyes, born twenty-eight years ago. Robert Weston, born thirty years ago, died thirteen days ago. Both natives of Western Bluff. She graduated from UT, he went to Rice. They married at the county courthouse there seven years ago. Still married at the time of his death."

"What was their financial situation like?"

"Not great. The Weston ranch is heavily mortgaged and they're carrying a lot of debt."

So it was as Elena had said. "And the sheriff?"

"Walter 'Walt' Bremer was elected sheriff six years ago. He seems competent enough at his job. He's received the usual commendations from local and state law enforcement. Then again, his job usually doesn't involve investigating murders. There has been exactly one in his jurisdiction since he became sheriff."

Even if the sheriff had years investigating homicides under his belt, Matt wasn't sure he'd trust him to investigate this one.

It was all important information to have, but he wasn't sure what good it did him. Problem was he wasn't sure what else he needed to know. "Anything else?"

"Well, there is one thing I found interesting, though I can't say if you'll agree. Western Bluff did pop up on the Bureau's radar once a while back. A number of women were reported missing in the area over a seven-year span between twenty to twenty-seven years ago. Western Bluff was pretty much in the center of the reported disappearances, and there wasn't much else out there, so the investigation kind of focused on the town for a while. What really got someone's attention is that all the women matched the same general profile, Hispanic women in their twenties or early thirties. They were considering that the disappearances were connected, maybe a serial killer was operating in the area. Nothing much came of it, though. They were never able to prove that anything happened to any of the women. Some of them were Mexican nationals who might have just gone home."

Matt frowned. Twenty-five years ago one particular Latino woman had disappeared from the area, a woman who must have been in her twenties or early thirties when she apparently left town.

It was probably a coincidence, but at the same time, he couldn't help but wonder where Teresa Reyes had ended up. If anything, Elena might like to know, although there was no guarantee a happy reunion would be at the end, he thought, remembering his meeting with his father.

Still, he had to ask. "Can you see if you can find anything on Elena's mother? I believe her name is Teresa, Teresa Reyes. She left Elena's father twenty-five years ago. At least that's what everyone thinks."

"You think something else might have happened to her?"

"I don't know. But I'd be interested to know where she is now."

"I'll see what I can find."

"One more thing. Can you get me a list of possible criminal defense attorneys in the area, or maybe in all of Texas, who are damn good at their jobs?"

"You think an arrest is coming?"

"I don't know, but I want to be ready if it does."

"Sure thing."

"Thanks, Pam. I really appreciate it."

"You got it."

Matt was just about to shove the phone in his pocket when he spotted movement out of the corner of his eye. He whirled around to find a man standing inside the door, eyeing Matt warily.

"Who are you?" the man demanded.

He had some nerve, Matt had to give him that. "Somebody who's supposed to be here, unlike you. So I'm the one who's going to be asking the questions. Who are *you?*"

The man's lips thinned with anger, and Matt wasn't sure at first he was going to answer. "Carter Baines," he finally said. "I used to work here."

"*Used* to. You don't now, so you have no business being here."

"I lived here for years. Think I left something behind and came back for it."

"What is it?"

"My business, not yours."

"It is as long as *I'm* the one living here now. Either way, this isn't your property."

"I just wanted what was mine."

"You could have called Mrs. Weston and asked her to look for it."

The man's mouth curled in a sneer. "Had no interest in talking to *her*. If she was in jail where she belonged I could have been in and out of here without any of this hassle."

"You believe she killed her husband," Matt said, leaving it as a statement.

"Of course she did. Who else?"

"You tell me."

"Nobody," Baines spat. "She's the only one with any reason to kill him."

Matt figured that wasn't worth arguing. "If you worked here for years, you have to know Mrs. Weston pretty well. She really strike you as the murdering type?"

"She struck me as the greedy type, and there's no telling what somebody'll do for money."

"What made you think she was greedy?"

"Everybody knows she's the reason Bobby never had any money to spend around here. She was always on him about money, never wanting him to spend a dime. He should have had more men working this place, should have been making improvements around here, but he couldn't. Because she wanted all the money for herself."

Anyone could see Elena wasn't exactly living an extravagant lifestyle. "You really believe that?"

"Everybody knows it!"

"And where was she spending all this money?" Matt asked. "As far as I can tell she doesn't have any expensive clothes or jewelry. She doesn't have a fancy car, doesn't look like she travels much—"

"I don't know what she's doing with it," the man said. "All I know is it's all she cares about."

It didn't make much sense, but Matt was starting to figure Carter Baines wasn't the smartest guy around. There really wasn't any point trying to make him see logic. Matt didn't know why he was wasting his breath on the guy anyway.

He was about to throw Baines out when a woman's voice rang out. "What's going on here?"

Elena stood in the doorway. Her gaze slid between him and Baines, finally settling on the other man as her lips turned down in a frown. "Carter? What are you doing here?"

The man didn't answer immediately, his scowl deepening as he glared at her.

"Mr. Baines says he left something here," Matt answered for him. "He came to get it."

"You should have called," she told Baines. "I could have had whatever you left sent to you."

"Just wanted to get my stuff," he grumbled under his breath. "Easier to come and get it."

"Maybe," she said patiently. "But you don't work or live here anymore. That was your decision, which means you're no longer welcome on this property without my permission."

It didn't seem possible, but the man's eyes narrowed further, tight slits glittering malice. "Damn greedy bitch."

The bastard had barely gotten that last hateful word out before fury exploded in Matt's veins, instantly propelling him forward. "That's it. You're done here—"

Baines continued as though he wasn't even there, his focus solely on Elena. "Forget it, I don't need my stuff. Marshall hired me on, and he pays a hell of a lot better than Bobby ever could because of you."

Matt frowned, the comment drawing him up short. Glen Marshall, the rancher who'd made the offer on this place, had hired Baines? It didn't say much about his judgment, as far as Matt was concerned. Unless there was more to it....

"You finally got what you wanted," Baines continued. "Enjoy it while you can, because you're not gonna be able to when you're in jail where you belong."

Nearly on top of him, Matt reached for Baines's arm, ready to throw the man out on his ass. He opened his mouth to tell him off—

Elena spoke first, her tone steady, cold and unwaveringly calm. "I think it's time for you to leave."

For the first time, the man seemed to notice Matt's closeness, glancing up, his eyes flaring in surprise. He straightened his spine in an apparent attempt at dignity he didn't deserve. "I'm out of here," he said, as if he had a choice.

Baines headed toward the open doorway. He was nearly there when Elena spoke again.

"Carter."

The man's step faltered for the slightest of moments.

"You never did say what it was you left here."

"It doesn't matter," Baines shot back over his shoulder.

"It must've if you came all the way out here to get it."

"It doesn't matter anymore."

"Well, if I find anything I'll be sure to pass it on," Elena said with sugary sweetness.

Baines didn't acknowledge the comment. Stomping over the threshold, he disappeared into the midday sun.

Matt and Elena both remained where they were in the wake of the man's departure. Finally, the sound of a vehicle door slamming, followed by an engine starting, reached them.

Matt watched Elena relax slightly. "You okay?"

Elena waved a hand. "I'm fine."

Matt couldn't help but be impressed she'd remembered that detail in the heat of the man's comments. He had forgotten about it himself.

"Do you really think he left anything here?"

"I'm not sure. I haven't had time to go through the place and clean up since everyone cleared out, something I should have mentioned earlier," she said with a trace of apology.

"It was fine," he told her. "I've certainly slept in worse places."

"So there could be something here. But if he didn't leave anything, then that just means he came out here to cause trouble."

"Did you have problems with him before?"

"I was never his favorite person. He was tight with Bobby, so I'm sure he was treated to plenty of complaining about me."

"He said as much," Matt confirmed. "Nice guy you married. It seems he made you the fall guy for all the money problems the ranch was having."

Her mouth tightened into a thin line. "Things were tense between us the past several years."

He nearly snorted. "I guess so."

"He wasn't always like that," Elena said quickly, lowering her eyes, her expression softening.

Matt couldn't believe she was defending the guy. Anger churned in his gut. "I hope not," he said sharply. "He had to have treated you a lot better at the beginning if you were willing to marry the guy after three months. I know for a fact you wouldn't do that with just anybody."

As soon as the words came out he would have given

anything to take them back. He hated how petty they were, how childish. He hated how jealous he sounded, and that even he could hear the thread of pain in his voice. And most of all, he hated that wounded look that entered her eyes, and knowing that he'd managed to hurt her.

"You were never 'just anybody'," she whispered.

"Just not good enough," he said before he could stop himself.

"That's not true."

Her denial only stoked the fire he was trying to tamp down, the need to know. "Really? I must have been lacking something Weston had. Was it just the money?"

"No. I didn't marry Bobby because of money."

"Then why did you do it?"

"It's…complicated—"

"How complicated can it be? What was so damn great about him that you were willing to marry him after three months—"

"He was the first man who made me feel anything after—"

She slammed her lips together, her eyes flying to his face.

He stared back, a sick feeling in his gut.

She didn't have to finish. He knew what she'd been about to say.

The implications of it hit him hard, throwing everything he'd assumed about her into a new light. Even more than before, he wished he hadn't asked, wished he'd just let it be. Felt like hell for having forced her to admit something she clearly hadn't wanted to as she stood there, the blood drained from her face.

Oh, hell. He didn't know what to say. He didn't know

if he should try to apologize, if there was some way he could make it better, even while he was still trying to process what it all meant.

From the looks of her, it looked like he'd said more than enough already.

He needed to get out of here. He needed to think.

She lowered her head again, turning her face away. It didn't look like she wanted to deal with him, either.

Matt cleared his throat. "I should make a run into town. I figured I'd pick up some paint and take care that mess on the front of your house."

"Sounds like a good idea," she murmured.

Grabbing his keys, he nodded tersely, moved for the door and escaped into the sunlight beyond.

As she had when Carter left, Elena stayed where she was. But this time it wasn't caution that held her in place. It was sheer humiliation.

She couldn't have moved if she tried, every muscle in her body tightened hard with it. She stood motionlessly and listened as Matt got into his truck and drove away. She suspected there was some paint somewhere around the ranch they could use, but she didn't bother mentioning it. She knew it was just an excuse to get out of here—away from her—for a while. At the moment she could use the time apart from him as much as he could.

Even when the sounds of the truck receded and it was clear he was gone, she remained locked in place.

She couldn't believe she'd admitted that. She'd tried not to, but he'd kept pushing and pushing, until it had just come out. Almost subconsciously she'd managed to cut off the words at the last possible moment, instinct closing up her throat, though it was still too damnably late. She hadn't had to. From the expression on his face, he knew what she'd been about to say as well as she did.

He was the first man who made me feel anything after you.

It was utterly, painfully true, a truth she would give anything for him not to know. Because it spoke volumes about just how much he'd meant to her, just how hurt she'd been after he'd gone, and she wanted to hold on to what little pride she had left too much to admit it.

Because she *had* hurt. In the months after he left, after she went back to school and tried to resume her life, she'd hurt more than she could have possibly imagined. She'd felt gutted, as though all of her insides had been torn out, and most days she barely felt capable of standing. She'd cried, racking sobs that seemed to be ripping out what was left of her, more than she had when her mother had left. Time had passed, and there were days when she'd thought she was finally getting over it—over him. Then the shooting pain in her chest, the gaping emptiness, and the tears would return. For almost a year, she'd gone through the motions of her life in a daze, and her best days were the ones when she was simply, blessedly numb.

And then she'd met Bobby.

He'd been undeniably good-looking, and if her reaction hadn't been anywhere near as strong as what she'd felt the first time she saw Matt, she'd definitely felt a spark. Frankly, it had been a relief, because, yes, it was the first time in nearly a year that a man had affected her in any way. She'd clung to that feeling, so glad to be feeling anything at all. Bobby had been the opposite of Matt in many ways, outgoing and happy, and it had been nice to be around someone who didn't remind her of him at all. It was only later that he'd changed. He'd been good to her, they'd had so much in common, and everything had seemed so easy between them. And when he'd asked her to marry him, she'd set aside her misgivings, telling herself she wasn't going to make the same mistake twice and let the man she loved get away.

Later, she'd come to the painful realization that it wasn't so much that she'd loved him, it was that she'd *wanted* to love him, wanted to love someone so she wouldn't hurt so much anymore because of Matt Alvarez.

God, she'd been so young. And stupid. Stupid most of all.

She'd made foolish decisions for all the wrong reasons, and caused them both so much unhappiness.

And all these years later, she was still here, still in this town, still paying for those mistakes the way she was afraid she would be the rest of her life.

Chapter Nine

Contrary to what he'd told Elena, Matt didn't head into town, deliberately turning in the opposite direction once he left the ranch. He wasn't ready to deal with the townspeople and their suspicions. More than anything he needed to get away from all of this mess for a while.

Especially Elena.

Elena.

The memory of the way she'd looked when he'd pushed her to confess, when she'd finally blurted it out, loomed in his mind, haunting him.

He was the first man who made me feel anything after...

After Matt. It was the only possible answer, the only thing that would have gotten that reaction from her, caused the look of horror at having spoken it. Letting him know that losing him had hurt her so much she hadn't felt anything for a year, that she'd married a man simply because he'd made her feel something, anything, again after Matt had walked away from her.

He'd hurt her that much. Just as he'd hurt her today.

The sad thing was, at one point he would have believed he wanted to hurt her, just as much as she'd hurt him. But knowing that he had, not even realizing he had or how much, he would give anything to take it back.

What's more, everything he'd assumed about her relationship with Weston had been wrong. He'd figured either she truly had loved Weston or it really had been for the money, seemingly the only possible explanations. Either way, he'd just wanted her to admit it, needed her to say in plain words the reason she'd chosen another man when she hadn't chosen him.

She finally had. But even with the possibilities he'd considered, he hadn't expected the answer.

He should have known better. He should have known her.

Matt kept driving aimlessly, trying to sort through his thoughts, trying to work out his mixed emotions. He passed by the Nolan spread where he'd worked the summer he'd met Elena. She'd said they weren't there anymore. He half wondered where they might have gone and who owned the place now. Not that he really cared or that it mattered.

It was the name of the next ranch he passed that truly caught his interest, providing a welcome distraction from what had happened with Elena.

Marshall Ranch.

The only Marshall he'd heard of in the area was Glen, the man he'd met at Elena's yesterday. The man whose eagerness to buy the ranch out from under her still struck him as suspicious.

Matt considered where he was, gauging his distance from her ranch. Yes, it was far enough from her property to be the one she'd described, and sure enough, it seemed unlikely Marshall could want a spread so far from his own for any reasons but the one she'd given.

But at the moment, Matt wasn't inclined to believe any-one would be willing to pay a sizeable amount for a ranch simply out of the goodness of his heart.

He'd figured he'd like to talk to Marshall at some point, try to suss out the man's actual motives. As long as he was out here, this seemed as good a time as any. And now that he knew Carter Baines was working out here, he couldn't help wonder if Marshall had some-thing to do with the man's unexpected appearance that morning.

Making the turn, he thought about how he was going to approach this. By the time he pulled up in front of the house, he had a workable plan.

He was in luck. Marshall came striding out of the barn just as Matt put the truck in Park. Whether it was because his arrival had already been noticed or the man just happened to be coming out at that particular mo-ment, Matt didn't know. Either way, Marshall looked up and spotted him as Matt stepped out of the truck. Marshall headed toward him, his movements unhur-ried and relaxed.

"Mr. Alvarez," Marshall called out. Somehow, Matt wasn't surprised the man had remembered his name. "What brings you here?"

"We had some trouble out at Elena's place last night and I was hoping to get your help."

Matt didn't miss the way the man's mouth tight-ened slightly when he referred to the ranch as "Elena's place." Apparently, Elena should consider herself part of the Weston family, but the ranch was in no way hers as far as Marshall was concerned. Matt had to wonder whether he truly thought of her as a Weston, or if it had been a line he'd been feeding her to butter her up.

"Why don't you come in?" the man said. He nodded toward the house, then turned and led the way, leaving Matt to follow.

Once inside, Marshall led Matt down a hallway to the rear of the house, opening a door on what was obviously his study. It was a comfortable, masculine space, with a fireplace, dark wood paneling and brown leather chairs. A big desk sat along the far edge of the room.

Marshall motioned for Matt to enter first, then followed him in, closing the door behind them. "Now then," Marshall said, turning to face him. "What is it you think I can help you with?"

"Like I said, we had some trouble last night. Vandalism. Somebody painted the word *Murderer* on the front of her house."

Marshall swore lightly under his breath. "This town just won't give her a break, will it?"

"But you will?"

"I beg your pardon?"

"Elena said you made an offer on the ranch, said you'd advance some of the money from the sale for her so she could use it for her defense if she needs it. That's a very generous offer."

"It's the right thing to do," he said modestly.

"So you don't believe Elena killed her husband?"

The man hesitated for a split second—long enough for Matt to notice—before shaking his head with a sound of exasperation. "No, not at all. She wouldn't have it in her."

"Sounds like you're the only person around here who believes that."

"Yes, well, the Westons are—" he cringed "—*were* highly regarded around here, and Elena's folks weren't.

Unfortunately, most people are inclined to expect the worst of her. Plus most of them just want somebody to be held responsible for Bobby's murder, and she's the most obvious person to have done it."

"But not you?"

"I'd rather have the right person charged than just anybody."

Marshall was saying all the right things and sounded genuine enough, but Matt couldn't decide if he believed him. He wondered if his inclination to be suspicious was getting the best of him, leading him to read things into nothing.

But then there was Carter Baines's presence at Elena's place. Why had he really been there, and had Marshall known about it?

"Elena said you were close with the Westons."

"I knew Bobby all his life, and his brother, Jim Junior, too. Their daddy, Big Jim, was like a brother to me."

"And that's why you want the land?"

Marshall nodded. "I'd hate to see it sold off and broken up, which is what might happen if the bank takes it. That was a real possibility for Bobby, though he'd never admit it, and it won't be any easier for Elena."

"I'm sure Big Jim would have appreciated the gesture."

Marshall smiled faintly. "I doubt it. Jim always intended the land to stay in the family. Talked about how it'd always been owned by Westons and always would be." He shook his head sadly. "Of course he had no way of knowing how things would turn out for him and his boys. The past twenty years it's been one bad thing after another. It's almost like they're cursed or something."

"What do you mean?"

With a sigh, Marshall turned and moved over to a wall covered with framed photographs. He stopped in front of one of them, staring at it hard. "I don't know how much you know about the family. First Jim died so young. Heart attack at forty-two. Then his older boy, Junior, got sick. Now Bobby getting killed. Twenty years ago there was every reason to believe the Westons would be around for generations. Now they're all gone."

Marshall's voice was heavy with pain. Wanting to see what he was looking at, Matt came and stood beside him. The photo showed a group of people, a few parents and several children, at what looked like a picnic, posing for the camera. The two men were younger versions of Marshall and Big Jim, whom he recognized from pictures he'd seen on the walls of the Weston house. Based on the pose, the women were their wives, with their respective children all around them, as if they were all part of one family. Elena had said Marshall was close to the Westons and cared deeply about the family. That seemed apparent enough from the fact that he'd kept this photo, hung it on his wall.

Matt raised his eyes to scan the other pictures. Most featured children he assumed were Marshall's at various ages. One photo in particular caught his eye. Three men with their arms slung around each other, grinning at the camera. To the left was Marshall, with Big Jim in the middle. And on the right—

"Is that the sheriff?" Matt asked, pointing toward the third man in the photograph.

Marshall looked where he indicated. "Yep, that's

Walt. Of course, he wasn't the sheriff back then. He was fresh with the department. But that's him."

"So Big Jim was friends with Walt, too."

"Oh, yeah. Jim and Walt went way back. Used to go on hunting trips, fishing trips together every few months."

"You didn't go with them?"

Marshall grinned. "My wife didn't look too kindly on the idea of me taking off and leaving her with five kids to handle so I could go out and shoot things. Jim's wife passed when Bobby was still young, but he had a housekeeper who could watch over the boys for a few days, and Walt never married. It was easier for them."

Matt nodded, staring hard at the image of Walt with his arm around Big Jim's shoulder, a big grin on his face. This was the man in charge of Elena's fate, Big Jim's old hunting buddy. So Travis wasn't the only one who might have a personal stake in the case. He wondered why she hadn't mentioned it. Then again, given how long Big Jim had been dead, it was possible she didn't know. She would have been just a girl back then. Or maybe she just didn't consider it a strong enough motive for the sheriff to be taking the case personally.

Which he probably was. Great. Something else standing in the way of Elena getting a fair shake around here. No wonder they were gunning for her so hard. They were all letting their personal feelings get in the way of conducting an honest investigation.

The picture was a potent reminder of just how badly he needed to get to the bottom of this before Walt could railroad her into jail.

"By the way," he said, changing the subject. "Did you hire a man named Carter Baines?"

Marshall nodded. "Sure. I knew he'd worked for Bobby for years, and after Elena couldn't afford to keep him on anymore, he came looking for a job so I hired him. What about it?"

Another good deed for the Westons and their friends? Matt couldn't help thinking. "He showed up unexpectedly at Elena's place this morning, popped up in the bunkhouse claiming he left something there and wanted to go through the place. And when Elena noticed he was there and turned up, he insulted her."

Marshall grimaced. "I'll talk to him, make it clear I don't want anyone working for me to go bothering people like that."

"I appreciate it. Actually, he seemed to really dislike her. I was wondering if he was the type to go running around vandalizing somebody's house?"

"Carter? Nah," Marshall scoffed. "He's not the kind to go sneaking around pulling stuff like that. If he doesn't like somebody, he'll tell them to their face, as you unfortunately saw today."

Having seen the man's behavior toward Elena today, Matt could see Marshall had a point. Still, he wasn't quite willing to dismiss the possibility that a man with a nasty streak like Baines had shown would be above some dirty tricks.

"Well, you know this town better than I do. Any ideas who might be angry enough to have done that to her?"

Marshall sent him a wry look. "Pick up a telephone book."

"It's that bad?" Matt said, saying it as a question even though the man was only confirming what he already suspected.

"People are upset. Upset that nobody's been arrested, upset that she's still running around free. And they're only getting madder. I've never seen things this bad around here. I'm afraid until an arrest is made, things are only going to get a lot worse before they get better."

"You mean until *Elena* is arrested?"

Marshall gave a light shrug, his expression slightly regretful. "Somebody. I don't know if it has to be her, but somebody has to pay."

THIS TIME WHEN ELENA HEARD THE sound of an engine approaching the house, she felt no anticipation, only the familiar dread. Matt had been gone only an hour, and she wasn't expecting him back so soon. If it was him, she wasn't quite ready to face him, not sure what she was going to say.

As soon as she saw who it was, every thought of her conversation with Matt faded away, overshadowed by what faced her in the immediate future.

It was the sheriff's car. As it came closer she could make out two figures in the front seat.

Walt and Travis. Here for their daily visit.

Heck, this really should be routine to her by now, she acknowledged fatalistically. But every time she saw them coming, she knew the visit would be no more pleasant than their last and wondered what fresh surprises they might have to spring on her. Or if this would be it, the time they came to make an arrest.

She studied them carefully as they disembarked from the car, trying to prepare herself for what was to come. What she saw did nothing to ease her mind. Walt wasn't quite smiling, but he seemed happy somehow in a way that made her distinctly uneasy.

Travis, on the other hand, didn't seem happy at all. She hadn't thought it possible for him to look at her with any more hatred than he'd been treating her to the past few weeks, but somehow he was managing it, his face red, his eyes burning with rage.

"Afternoon, Elena," Walt said with false politeness.

"Sheriff. Travis," she acknowledged, nodding to them each in turn.

Travis didn't say a word in response, simply glaring at her with such undisguised fury her stomach sank even further.

Unlike his deputy's unwavering focus, Walt made a show of glancing around the area. "Your new hand around? What's his name again? Alvarez?"

Elena didn't doubt for a second that he knew exactly what Matt's name was. Not about to admit they had her on edge, she tried to keep her voice as even as possible and replied, "Yes, Alvarez. And no, he's not here. He went into town for some paint. As you can see, we have some damage to repair around here." She gestured toward the wall beside her.

Both men's eyes flicked briefly to the wall, though they must have seen what was there when they pulled up. If they hadn't already known. Travis's mouth curved in a cruel smile, so much that she almost expected him to release a bark of laughter. Walt betrayed no reaction, his eyes revealing nothing as they glanced at it then returned to her.

"Looks like you had some trouble," Walt said mildly.

"That's right. Any chance you'd feel like investigating that?"

The sheriff simply shrugged. "If you didn't see who

did it, probably not much chance of figuring out who it was. Most likely just teenagers playing a prank."

"Between this and what happened to my tires in town, the teenagers around here sure are busy," she said drily. "I wonder what they're going to have to pull before you do something about it."

"If you don't feel safe around here anymore, I'm sure you'll feel a lot safer in jail," Travis said. "All you have to do is tell us the truth about Bobby."

Elena stared back at him. "I have told you the truth about Bobby."

Travis's face reddened further, his hands fisting at his sides. He took a step toward her. "You lying b—"

"Travis," Walt cut him off without raising his voice. Travis seemed to regain control with visible effort, clamping his mouth shut and falling back into line at Walt's side. His eyes, narrowed to slits, never moved from Elena's face, his own remaining red.

"It's a shame your hand isn't here," Walt continued calmly, his tone instantly making her wary. She almost would have preferred Travis's open aggression to Walt's lightly insinuating caginess. "You never did say how you met him."

"He showed up when I needed him," Elena said easily.

"Right after your husband was murdered."

"Not quite," she returned. "It was almost two weeks later."

"And how did he just happen to show up right now, when you *needed* him?"

And just like that, she knew. He knew who Matt was, about their prior relationship. The trap Walt was laying for her was too obvious, Travis's eagerness—the way he was practically salivating at the idea of catching her in a lie—too clear. She suddenly understood his fresh anger all too well, as a chill rolled through her, her belly tightening with fear. It was exactly as she'd worried about. They knew about her and Matt—and it looked just as bad as she'd known it would.

It would look even worse if she lied about it, as they plainly expected her to. Her only hope was to go on the offensive. "Someone sent him a newspaper story about Bobby's death."

"And why would he care about Bobby's *murder?*" Walt asked, clearly making the distinction.

"Because we knew each other eight years ago. He was here in Western Bluff back then, working a summer for the Nolans. We dated that summer."

Neither Walt nor Travis had an immediate response to that, and she saw that she'd caught them off-guard. A small sense of satisfaction pushed away some of the fear.

Travis soon regained himself, his expression hardening back into a sneer. "So your old boyfriend just happens to show up right after your husband's murdered? You expect us to believe that's a coincidence?"

"No, I don't. I don't believe it's a coincidence at all. Someone sent him a newspaper story about Bobby's death to get him to come here."

Travis all but laughed. "Yeah, you!"

"It wasn't me. I hadn't had any contact with him in eight years. I had no idea where he even was."

"But somebody else just happened to and decided he should know?"

"Evidently."

"The man hasn't been in contact with you for eight years, and one newspaper article is all it takes to get him to run back to town?"

There was only one answer she could give to that. "Yes," she said simply.

This time he did laugh, the sound full of rage and no humor whatsoever. "You have to think we're idiots!"

Yes, she thought, though she wasn't about to say it out loud. "It's what happened."

"So an old boyfriend gets a story telling him your husband is dead and he hightails it to your side? Now why would he do that if you haven't seen each other or been in touch for years?"

"Because he knew I was no killer. He knew me for only three months and he knew that much. You both have known me a lot longer, so you should know it, too, even better than he does!"

"Yeah, well, we don't *know* you the same way he does," Travis sneered, the word filled with every drop of innuendo possible. "But rest assured, I do know you. I've known exactly what you were since the moment you hooked up with Bobby. I knew you were nothing but a no-good, worthless—"

"That's enough, Travis," Walt said, though there was no censure in his tone. "Now, Elena, you have to admit this story is hard to believe."

"It's the truth."

"Uh-huh," he drawled slowly. "And I suppose Alvarez can produce this mysterious newspaper article he received."

"Yes," she said. "I saw the envelope myself, complete with Western Bluff postmark."

"I look forward to seeing that," Walt said. "Why didn't you tell us any of this yesterday? You had to know it wouldn't look good when I figured it out."

"That's exactly why I didn't say anything. I didn't want you to jump to the wrong conclusions. How *did* you figure it out?"

"I'll admit it took me a while. Then I remembered that fella you were seeing that your daddy got riled up about and it all came back to me."

Exactly as Matt had suggested, she thought.

Walt eyed her shrewdly. "Pretty amazing that this guy would come back eight years later after all that trouble if he hadn't been in touch with you, just because somebody sent him a newspaper article."

Elena couldn't argue with that. "So it is."

"Indeed. When do you expect Alvarez back?"

"He didn't say."

"I guess we'll come back later then."

"Maybe we'll run into him in town," Travis said, the words sounding every bit like a threat.

"Maybe," Elena said mildly.

"Oh, and Elena?" Walt turned back with a casualness she didn't buy for a moment. "In case you or your new hand start to get any ideas about leaving town, don't."

"I'm not going anywhere." It seemed strange to say it, as long as she'd wanted out of this town. But even if she had the ability to leave, even if all her meager resources weren't connected to the ranch, she wasn't leaving now. Because she wasn't guilty, and damned if she'd convince anyone in this town that she was by running.

The look he shot her said he didn't believe her. She

wasn't surprised, nor did she bother to waste her breath arguing. She'd let her actions speak for themselves.

She wasn't her mother. She wasn't running. Not from this.

Not from anything.

Chapter Ten

When Matt finally made it into town, he took his time at the hardware store, ignoring the stares of the cashier and some of the other customers. Finding the right color of paint to match the front of Elena's house wasn't an easy task since he was operating from memory and so many of the shades were only slightly different from one another, but he wanted to get it right. He figured he could do that much for her.

He was finally loading up his truck, putting the cans of paint he'd bought in the truckbed, when he heard voices, the sounds of two men in conversation approaching on the sidewalk behind him. He didn't pay much attention to them and was about to close the tailgate when he heard one of them mention the sheriff.

"I'm telling you, Henry, you need to put more pressure on Walt and get him to make a damn arrest already. That woman should be locked up."

Matt froze, instantly tuning in to what they were saying. There wasn't a doubt in Matt's mind what woman the man was referring to.

Figuring it would look suspicious if he was just standing there not doing anything, he started acting like he was moving things around in the back of the truck without making any noise, keeping his ears peeled the whole time.

"Come on, Jack," the second man said. "Walt is doing his best. He wants her behind bars as much as we all do. He just has to get all the evidence together. You should understand that. You're a lawyer."

A lawyer named Jack. That sounded familiar. Matt quickly made the connection in his head. Elena had mentioned the lawyer in charge of Weston's will, the only lawyer in town. His name was Jack. Jack Landry. Weston's cousin.

"I understand it shouldn't be taking this long," Landry insisted. "It's been two weeks! Damn it, Henry. There has to be something you can do."

The man he called Henry sighed. "I'm just the mayor of this town, Jack. I can't force Walt to make an arrest before he's good and ready."

"Still, you—"

The other man cut him off, suddenly raising his voice, calling out. "There you are, hon. I was just on my way to meet you."

Curious, Matt gave a casual glance over to see who he was speaking to.

A woman was slowly making her way down the sidewalk toward them. It was the woman he'd spotted yesterday, the one who'd been looking at him.

Which was exactly what she was doing now.

Their eyes locked for a few seconds before she looked away, working up a smile as she turned her attention to the men as they met each other.

"Hi there," she said, kissing one of the men on the cheek—Henry, Matt figured—then nodding to the other. "Hello, Jack."

"Lynda," he acknowledged, barely concealing his annoyance that his conversation with the other man had been interrupted.

Matt studied the lawyer closely. He was roughly in his forties, with dark brown hair thinning on top. His desire to see Elena arrested for his cousin's murder made sense, but Matt couldn't help but look askance at anyone who was working against her, wondering if there wasn't more to his actions than it seemed.

Lynda turned back to Henry, who Matt assumed was her husband based on their interactions. "Ready for lunch?"

"I sure am." He gave a perfunctory glance at the other man. "I'll see you, Jack."

"Henry," Jack acknowledged.

The mayor and his wife started to turn away. Just before they headed down the sidewalk, she glanced at Matt one more time, this time quickly looking away.

He watched her go for a few seconds. Lynda, the mayor's wife. He'd have to ask Elena about her. She had to know who the woman was, might know if there was any particular reason for her attention.

Elena. He swallowed a sigh, reminded again how they'd left things, the mess he had to clean up. If they were going to talk about anything, that was probably going to be it. And he still didn't know what to say.

Even so, it was high time he got back. He finally closed the tailgate and turned away from the back of the truck.

When he arrived back at the ranch, Elena was walking across the yard heading toward the house, a bucket filled with what looked like cleaning supplies in one hand. She looked up at his approach, stopping in front of the steps to the house and waiting for him to get out of the truck.

Matt tried to gauge her expression, but couldn't read a thing from it. She was too contained, her face blank. Steeling himself, he climbed out of the truck.

"I cleaned out the bunkhouse," she said as he walked up, lifting her pail. "It should be a little more suited for occupation now."

"Thanks."

"Found this lodged between one of the dressers and a wall." She held up an item in her left hand. It was a belt buckle. "I think I've seen Carter wearing it before. I'm guessing this is what he came to get."

"So he really was looking for something he left behind," Matt said. It clearly wasn't just a belt buckle, but one he'd won at some point. Matt could understand why he'd come looking for it, even if he wasn't quite ready to assume there was no other reason the man had come poking around.

"Evidently. I'll send it on to Glen's so he gets it and won't have any other reasons to drop by." She didn't say anything for a few seconds, dropping her head and taking a deep breath. For a moment, Matt was sure he knew what she was about to say. She was going to bring up what had happened before.

She looked up and met his eyes. "Walt and Travis were here."

It wasn't what he'd expected her to say, and he couldn't hide his surprise, both at what she hadn't said and what she had. Then the implications of her words sank in, anger that he hadn't been here replacing his surprise. He knew whatever happened, it couldn't have been pleasant for her. Her expression confirmed that much. "What happened?"

"They know about you…about our history together. Just as I thought, it made things look even worse. Now they're even more convinced I killed Bobby."

"How'd they find out?"

"Walt said he remembered the fuss my father caused over our relationship back then. When he started looking into your background, it all came back to him."

"Or it never left," Matt said slowly.

Her frown deepened. "What do you mean?"

"Who better to track me down than a sheriff with police resources?"

"You think Walt's the one who sent you that article and brought you here?"

"Could be. It would explain how the person who sent the article knew where to find me. If he had something to do with Bobby's death and wanted to make you look bad, getting me to come here probably was a good way to do it."

"But Walt still doesn't have any kind of motive as far as I can tell. And why would he even bother to go to all that trouble when he'd already have plenty to try to frame me with here, especially since he had no reason to believe you would come?"

"I don't know," Matt admitted. "It's just a thought."

"I'm sure you're right about one thing, though. I knew whoever brought you here wasn't doing it to help me."

"Are you sorry I'm here?" he asked gently. He wouldn't blame her if she was. Not with the trouble his presence meant for her. Not after what had happened that morning.

Her eyes flickered to his face, then held, stroking over his skin intensely. He went still inside, not sure he wanted to know the answer.

No, that was a lie, he acknowledged. He knew what he wanted the answer to be. He just couldn't bring himself to admit it.

"No," she said finally. "No, I'm not."

The tightness that had gathered in his chest eased. "Good," he said. "Because somebody might not have intended for my presence to help you, but that's exactly what I'm going to do."

"What do you want to do?"

"Same thing as before. Get to the bottom of this. If the sheriff is even more determined to pin this on you, then we just have a little more motivation to solve this thing quicker."

Her lips twitched humorlessly. "I didn't really need any more motivation, but all right."

Matt suddenly recalled the conversation he'd overheard in town, the reminder that it wasn't just the sheriff who was out to put this on her. It was seemingly everybody in town, which she already knew. They might not need any more motivation, but they certainly had plenty of it.

Unfortunately, they were out of leads at the moment. He wasn't sure where they could go from here.

Then he looked up and saw the now-familiar word still screaming from the front of the house in bloodred paint.

MURDERER.

No, they didn't need more motivation. The crude vandalism was evidence of that. But at least that was something they could do.

He nodded at the wall. "I should take care of that. I got the paint. I'll get started now."

She followed his gaze. "Good idea. I'll help you. It'll be faster that way, and I want it gone as soon as possible. Just let me just put this inside," she said, indicating the bucket. "I'll be right back."

He watched her go, unable to help admiring her walk, glad to see the confidence, the purpose, back in her stride as she quickly climbed the front steps and moved into the house.

The fact that she looked damn good in a pair of jeans didn't hurt, either.

He shook his head, quickly turning away to start unloading the paint from the truck. Those were exactly the kind of thoughts he couldn't be having, for both their sakes. Things were messy enough between them.

He hadn't apologized for earlier, he realized, hadn't made it up to her. They seemed to have moved past it, and he doubted she'd be interested in bringing up what had happened any more than he really did. It didn't matter. That look on her face remained with him, reminding him just how carefully he had to tread from now on. He had no interest in seeing that look on her face again.

He'd hurt her enough. He wasn't going to do it again.

Chapter Eleven

A little after one-thirty in the morning, Matt made another slow circle around the house. He'd started his watch early that night, earlier than what he suspected was necessary, but he wasn't taking any chances. The night before, the vandal had shown up after two. If he made a return appearance tonight, it would likely be around the same time or later, deeper into the night, but it could be earlier, too. Either way, Matt wanted to be ready.

He doubted he'd be getting much sleep tonight anyway. After everything that had happened that day, there was too much going on in his head, too much on his mind. Weston. Marshall.

Elena.

Stopping in front of the house, Matt breathed deeply, pulling the air into his lungs to clear his thoughts, and stared out over the yard. As he stood there, a vague sense of unease washed over him, making his skin crawl in response.

He didn't have to wonder about its cause, as he took in the shadows surrounding him, the dark spaces nearby untouched by lights or the moon where anyone could be lurking, hiding. He didn't sense anyone watching, but his skin still tingled with awareness, the feeling of danger heavy in the air, the knowledge that trouble could be moments away.

Turning slightly, he glanced back at the house. They'd managed to get the front repainted. It seemed the fastest and easiest way to cover the graffiti, which was what mattered most. The paint he'd found almost matched the wall's original color. He doubted Elena would forget the message had been there, but she had seemed relieved not to have to look at it anymore.

They'd worked well together, he thought, his mouth curving at the memory. First painting the wall, then taking care of things around the ranch. They'd fallen into a natural rhythm that had come easily, picking up each other's cues, working in sync. It had been nice. He probably shouldn't think about it, give it more meaning than it deserved, but he couldn't deny it was true.

The lights were on in the house. He was sure she was still up, probably keeping a watch of her own. Maybe even looking back at him…

With a sigh, he turned away. He needed to keep moving. Not only was there plenty of ground he needed to cover, but it was the only hope he'd have of occupying his mind and thinking of anything else.

Distracted, he heard the muffled footsteps a split second too late.

It was the flash of motion that caught his eye, the sense that something was coming at him—fast.

He started to turn, spotting something arcing toward his head—

He automatically lifted his right arm to block the blow. Instead of his head, the object—hard, metal—slammed into his forearm. Pain exploded in the bone and shot up to the shoulder, his whole body seeming to be jarred by the hit. He reeled back on his heels, a reflexive roar of agony rising into his throat.

There was no time to release it or reach for the gun in his waistband. The attacker was already coming at him again, raising his arm to land another blow.

Seeing it coming, Matt erupted into motion. He threw out his left arm, aiming for the arm wielding the object, blocking it before the attacker could bring it down. Almost at the same time, he pivoted, sending his right elbow straight into the intruder's gut. The bastard folded over with a grunt. Before he could straighten, Matt brought his left arm down, the force of the hit making the guy lose his grip on the object in his hand.

With a growl of rage, the intruder lunged forward, his head still bent, driving his fist in Matt's ribs. Stomach tensing against the pain, Matt quickly returned the blow, then another, and another as the man came back throwing punches. They circled round each other, arms thrashing, hands landing punches and grabbing at clothes.

He caught only flashes of his opponent as they grappled. Tall. Broad shoulders. Black clothes. Ski mask covering the face. No way to identify him. More than anything he wanted to rip off the mask, see the bastard's face. The drive fueled him with every punch he threw, each one he dodged. He didn't care about getting hurt. Fending off blows was all about being able to get to the guy. Matt had to get to him, had to take him down. He had to be stopped.

"Hey!"

The woman's voice came as if from a great distance. He barely heard it over the thumping of his heartbeat as he battled with the intruder, unable to slow for an instant, not willing to give an inch.

In the far recesses of his mind, the identification was made.

Elena. She was out here.

The thought only pushed him to fight harder. She shouldn't be here. It was dangerous. This bastard was dangerous. He wanted to hurt her—

A gunshot sliced through the air, the noise nearly deafening.

Matt and his opponent froze simultaneously, both shocked into stillness by the loudness, the nearness of the gunshot.

What had happened? Had someone been shot—

The intruder recovered first, landing a blow to Matt's gut, which he never saw coming. Pain ripped through his abdomen, his body automatically folding over in response. The bastard gave him a hard shove, sending him crashing to the dirt.

Matt had barely landed before he was putting his hands out to ground himself, shoving the pain aside, ready to push back to his feet. Raw fury pulsing through him, he jerked his head up, already searching for his opponent, prepared to launch himself back into the fray—

Only to see the intruder making a break for it, sprinting toward the barn.

"Stop!" the female voice shouted.

The intruder didn't obey, vanishing into the shadows on the side of the barn.

Matt swallowed the curse he really wanted to yell at the top of his lungs. Not only had the bastard gotten the better of him—and that was reason enough for his fury—but he'd gotten away, free to come back and try something again.

Seconds later, he heard Elena hurry over, sensed her crouching at his side.

"Matt? Are you okay?"

He turned to look at her. She sat on her haunches, her gun still clutched in her right hand. With the moon shining down over her shoulders, she looked like some kind of avenging angel.

He sat up, grimacing as his body groaned in protest. "You shouldn't have come out here. You could have been hurt."

"Me? You were the one in a knock-down, drag-out fight." Rising to her feet, she extended her hand to him to help him up. "Come into the house. I have some pain relievers. I have a feeling you could use some."

"I'm fine," he said.

"I don't believe you."

He looked up at her. She stood there, hand extended, waiting.

Finally, with a groan, he took it. For a moment the feel of her soft hand in his threw him, and he nearly groaned again.

Soft. God, she was soft.

Then he felt her start to tug to help him to his feet. He nearly shook himself. Maybe the intruder had landed a blow to the head, knocking the sense out of him, without him noticing. He was starting to feel a little woozy.

He let her help without giving her his full weight. If he did, he'd only pull her down on top of him, and then…

No, that wouldn't be good at all.

Once he was on his feet, she released his hand all too soon and started for the house, leaving him to follow.

As he started to, Matt glanced behind him into the darkness. He wondered if the intruder was gone or lingering in the shadows, watching.

Just in case it was the latter, Matt did his best to hide how sore he felt, walking to the front steps as smoothly as possible. After he'd climbed them, he turned back, planted his legs on the porch's wooden planks, and slowly scanned the night, sending a message to the bastard.

He'd gotten away twice now.

He wasn't getting away a third.

"Have a seat," Elena said, waving toward the chairs at the kitchen table. Her heart still pounding in the aftermath of what had happened, she made her way to the counter and reached in the cabinet for the bottle of pain relievers she knew was there.

Pouring a glass of water from the sink, she turned around to find Matt had done as ordered. Seeing him in the light, he didn't look as bad as she'd feared he would. His hair was a mess, his clothes rumpled, but there weren't any visible bruises or scratches on his face or neck. But then, from what she'd seen, he and his attacker had been aiming most of their blows at their torsos. As she watched him shift in his seat, wincing as he twisted his upper body, she could only imagine how bad the damage was there.

She was tempted to ask to take a look, see whether he wanted her to check his injuries. Then a shiver rolled through her at the very idea of his bare torso, and she had to admit it would be a very bad idea.

Instead, she moved to the table, placing the glass of water in front of him. She uncapped the bottle and shook out two pills, holding them out to him. From the way his lips thinned, she was convinced he was going to refuse them. Finally, with visible reluctance, he took them. She almost rolled her eyes. *Men*. Always trying to act so tough.

"Are you sure you're okay? I have a first-aid kit."

"The thing that hurts worst is my pride." He shook his head. "Can't believe he got the drop on me."

"Not really," she pointed out. "You caught him just in time to block that hit."

He raised his head. "You saw?"

She nodded, the terror of those moments coming back to her so strongly it was like she was seeing it again. She'd been at her window, unable to sleep, when she'd seen Matt walking in front of the house, then the attacker had come rushing at him from out of nowhere, the tire iron clutched in his fist, aimed at Matt's head. She'd been helpless to do anything to warn him as it had come swinging down. She didn't know how, but he'd managed to sense the attacker's ambush just in time to dodge the blow. "I wanted to say something, warn you. When I saw him coming at you with that tire iron—"

"So that's what it was," he muttered. "Hurt like hell." He automatically moved his left hand to his right arm, no doubt over the spot where the blow had landed.

"Do you want me to take a look at it?" she asked.

He shook his head. "It'll just be a bruise. I'll live."

It wasn't as though she could insist. Pulling out one of the chairs, she sank into it, facing him. "Do you figure it was the same person who spray painted that word on the house last night?"

"Most likely."

"But why? Is he just getting some kind of sick pleasure out of tormenting me?"

"It could be, especially if he really believes you killed Weston. Or maybe he doesn't intend to let you get any rest until you confess."

She exhaled sharply. "Well, that's not going to happen, so I guess I won't be getting much rest. Not that I have been anyway…" She compressed her lips together, wishing she hadn't admitted that, though she was sure he would have guessed as much. Her current circumstances didn't exactly lend themselves to a good night's sleep, even beyond the impact he was having on her dreams.

"If he comes back, I'll catch him," Matt vowed. "He's not going to get away with this."

She believed he meant it, but after witnessing that brutal fight between the two men tonight, she was more concerned about the attacker catching *Matt*. It was a miracle he wasn't hurt worse. She wasn't sure they could count on that miracle to happen again.

"He came after you, you know. If he comes back, you could be hurt further."

"I can take care of myself," he said, and again it was all she could do not to roll her eyes.

Men.

She watched him shift in his chair, wincing again, and she nearly did the same.

"Sorry," she murmured.

"Not your fault," he gritted through his teeth.

"Isn't it?" she said. "I'm sorry you got sucked into all of this—"

"I'm not," he said firmly. The vehemence in his tone made her go still. She met his eyes.

"I'm not here because somebody sent me a newspaper article or you somehow made me. I'm here because I want to be."

Her heart lodged in her throat at the intensity, the purpose, in both his response and the way he was looking at her. Staring into his eyes, the question she'd been unable to answer, the one she hadn't dared ask, popped into her mouth, and this time she couldn't stop it from coming out.

"Why?"

The single word hung there between them, heavy in the air.

He didn't answer at first, his jaw tensing, simply looking at her, his dark eyes veiled.

"I mean, after all this time, after everything that happened…"

"Because I couldn't let them do that to you," he said roughly. "I couldn't let them railroad you and send you to jail. You don't deserve that."

It was a reasonable answer. An honest answer, she was sure. But there was so much more unspoken about it, so much she could infer that she didn't know if she should, no matter how much she suddenly wanted to.

"After the way things ended, I thought you hated me," she said softly.

"I did," he admitted. "For a while. Or at least I thought I did. But that was a long time ago."

"Yes, it was." Practically a whole other life. They'd changed so much since then. Yet sometimes when she looked at him, like now, she remembered as clearly as though it had happened moments ago, and nothing had changed at all.

Or maybe that wasn't a memory, she admitted as she held his gaze, warmth flooding through her. Sometimes it seemed so vivid because it wasn't being remembered, but experienced in the present.

Matt slowly lowered his eyes, looking hard at the tabletop. "Did you ever think what would have happened if you'd come with me?"

She paused again and hesitated, uncertain how much she wanted to admit. But she couldn't lie, not to him, not at this moment. "I used to. A lot."

"And what'd you think?"

She winced. "I thought…there was no point thinking about it. I couldn't change it and do things differently, so thinking about what it would have been like wasn't going to get me anywhere."

He nodded. "That was probably smart."

"What about you?" she asked. "Did you think about what might have been?"

He didn't say anything for a long moment. "No," he said.

She certainly understood. Sometimes it was just so much easier if they didn't think about things. But she knew just as well that some things simply couldn't be forgotten.

They sat in silence for a few moments until Matt finally said, "Can I ask you something?"

"Sure."

"If things were really that bad here, why didn't you leave?"

"You mean like my mother did?" She gave her head a firm shake. "I always knew that when I got married, it was going to be forever. I wasn't going to bail if things got tough or were less than perfect. When I said those vows I meant them."

"Even if it meant being unhappy?" he asked gently.

"Even then." And there'd been the guilt, she acknowledged to herself. For having married him when she hadn't loved him as much as she should have. For making a mistake that had caused them both such unhappiness. If he'd asked for a divorce, she would have given it to him without question, without asking for anything in return. But even if she had been willing to leave, it hadn't seemed right that she be the one who made that call.

"What about him? It doesn't sound like he was any happier. Did he ever say anything about ending the marriage?"

"No. He always had enough to worry about with the ranch. I'm sure our marriage was the least of his concerns."

"Or maybe deep down he still loved you," he said quietly.

"I don't know. By the end, he sure didn't act like it." She shook her head again, not really wanting to think about Bobby for the time being. "What about you? Eight years is a long time. You must have had somebody serious in your life."

His whole body seemed to tense, then he shook his head once. "Nope."

She knew she should probably leave it alone. Of all people in the world, it was likely her business least of all. But she couldn't manage to keep from pressing, wanting to know, needing the answer. "You didn't want that?"

"Nope," he repeated.

She didn't like thinking of him alone. She wasn't naive enough to think he'd been completely without female company in those years, but there was a big difference between sex and having a meaningful relationship with someone. And he was as alone as he'd ever been.

She couldn't help but feel a pang of guilt, knowing that she must have played a part in that. Of course his childhood had left scars that had never quite healed. The difference was, despite what he'd been through, there'd still been hope for him. He'd opened up to her, opened his heart and soul to someone for the first time, trusted her.

Loved her.

And she'd thrown it back in his face.

She winced at the idea. It wasn't what she'd intended, but she'd known even back then it was how he would take it.

Maybe it was something most people would have gotten over, recovered from, over the years. But not him. Even in those early days, when they were happy from the start, he hadn't revealed his deepest self to her. It had taken months, until right before the end, before he'd let the walls down completely. It didn't surprise her he hadn't let down those walls again, had protected himself this strongly against getting hurt again. But knowing it was true didn't make her happy.

"What's your life like in New Mexico?" she asked, hoping to hear something happier.

"Good."

She almost smiled. He was still as forthcoming as ever. "So you're working on a ranch?"

He nodded. "I'm the foreman on a cattle operation

out there. A guy I worked with a few years ago hired me on when he bought his own place."

"And you're happy there?"

"Pretty much," he conceded after a while.

"But not entirely?" she asked carefully.

Again he fell quiet for a minute, this silence lasting longer than the last. "The Triple C's a good place, and Cade and Piper are good people. I know I have a place there as long as I want it. I've just been thinking lately about how long I want that to be. They just got married, and they're settling down and making all these plans. It's got me considering what I want to do. I think every man thinks about wanting something of his own someday. Maybe my own place. Maybe something else. I don't know."

It seemed some things hadn't changed, she acknowledged. His life wasn't completely settled and his future was unknown, just as it had been before. The difference was that this time his words inspired no unease in her. Maybe it was because she was different, old enough to know by now there was no certainty in this life. Maybe it was he who was different. He wasn't that young man finding his way in the world. There was something so solid about him, so strong. Everything about him spoke of a man capable of making his own way and getting things done. She had no doubt he'd decide what he wanted and get it.

Suddenly she wished she hadn't asked. Talking about the future just reminded her how uncertain her own was, and how whatever future he had wouldn't have her in it.

"I'm sure you'll figure it out," she said, pushing to

her feet. "It's getting late. We should probably try to get some sleep."

"Good idea."

Together they made their way to the front door. She was about to open it when she froze. "Do you think he'll come back? Or that he's still out there?"

"I doubt he'd come back," Matt said. "I think I got in enough solid shots that he should be nursing his wounds somewhere if he left. And he should be long gone by now."

Pulling the door open, she scanned the scene beyond, unconvinced.

An idea suddenly hit her. He should move into the house. He would be safe here. They both would be safe here, in this place where she hadn't felt truly safe from the moment she'd come home to find her husband shot dead in his study.

More important than her safety, she needed him nearby.

Needed to know he was safe.

The idea was so foolish she instantly rejected it. It would be a huge mistake. She could barely sit at the same table with him without feeling…something, something unsettling and confusing.

And exciting.

She kept her mouth shut. He moved past her and stepped outside. "Good night," he said.

"Good night," she echoed. She watched him go, tracking his progress the whole way, unable to take her eyes from the broad shoulders, the wide back and slim hips. In the yard he bent to pick up something from the ground. The tire iron, she thought with a shudder, the memory of just how close it had come to his head returning to her. So close. Too close. He turned back slightly and waved it at her, and she smiled. At least he was the one with the tire iron now. If the intruder was still around and tried coming at him, Matt would have the advantage.

She continued to watch him go until he was long out of sight, a solitary figure walking off into the moonlight, her stomach doing a little flip. And knew that everything she was feeling was new, not a memory. A response to the man he was, not the man he'd been.

The man she still ached for after all these years.

Chapter Twelve

As expected, Matt woke up sore the next morning. When he pushed himself up from the bed, his body seemed to scream in protest, every bone aching.

He swore under his breath, vowing once again that he was going to take down the intruder the next time he showed up around here.

Dressing quickly, he was just stepping out of the bunkhouse when a ringing erupted from his pocket. He fished out his phone and checked the screen.

Pam.

"Hey there."

A beat of silence echoed over the line. "You don't sound so good," she noted.

"Rough night," he muttered, starting toward the house.

"Hmm. Should I even ask how it's going, then? Any progress?"

"Not really," he said, unable to keep the frustration from his voice. "We've been asking questions, but mostly running into dead ends."

"Has your friend been arrested?"

"No." *Not yet.*

"Well, that's something at least. Things could be worse."

Matt knew she was right. He didn't even want to think about how much worse they could get. "You find anything on your end?"

"First, I got a list of highly regarded defense attorneys I can send you so you'll have them if the time comes you need them."

"Thanks," he said, inspiration striking. "I hate to ask this, but can you find the names of a few attorneys who handle estates and inheritance issues, too? We're having some issues with the lawyer in charge of Weston's estate. He's Weston's cousin and is making things difficult for Elena. I'd like to find out what her options are."

Pam was quiet for a moment. "His cousin, huh? Jack Landry? About that…"

Matt could practically hear her mind working. "What is it?"

"When his name came up as Weston's only other possible heir I thought I'd do some research into Texas state inheritance law. In Texas, being convicted of killing someone doesn't necessarily stop the killer from inheriting. But if there are other possible heirs, they can file suit and make a claim on the estate to prevent the killer from inheriting. In that case it would go to them."

Matt had no trouble following where she was going. "Which means if Elena is found guilty of killing Bobby, Landry can claim the ranch."

That certainly could explain why he was so determined to see her locked up. And if he was pushing this hard to make it possible for him to inherit, who knew what else he might have done to get the ranch.

He should have thought of it sooner. "Thanks, Pam, that's a big help."

"There's one more thing." She paused for a beat. "I also did the search you asked for on Teresa Reyes."

His pulse kicked up in anticipation. "Did you find her?"

"Nope. Not a trace in the past twenty-five years."

He didn't know which answer he'd been hoping for, but as soon as he heard Pam's answer his heart dropped. "Does that mean what I think it does?"

"Most likely," Pam said bluntly. "She's either done a perfect job covering her tracks—something I have a hard time believing she could have done without a lot of help—or she's not alive and hasn't been for the past twenty-five years."

"Do you think there could be a connection between those women who went missing back then and the disappearance of Elena's mother?"

"There could be. If there was a killer at work at the time, it's too much of a coincidence not to be considered. But then again, it was never proven that those missing women were connected or that there was a killer operating. We have to keep that in mind."

"True," he agreed. "I don't suppose there's anything more you can find out?"

"I'm already on it. I've scheduled a meeting with the agent who headed the investigation. He's retired but still in the area."

He wasn't surprised. Pam was nothing if not thorough. "Thanks, Pam. Let me know if you find anything else out?"

"Will do." As always, she ended the call without another word, their business having been concluded.

Matt took his time lowering the phone from his ear, trying to absorb this new information. If what he suspected was true, then everything Elena believed about her mother was wrong. It could change so much about how she viewed her family, her life.

"Who was that?"

He jerked his head up to find he'd reached the house without realizing it. Elena stood on the porch, arms folded over her chest. Damn. He could have used some time to process this, to think about what he would say, or if he would say anything before he knew more.

Hoping she couldn't read much in his expression, he climbed the steps to join her. "Pam Lowry. She's my boss's sister-in-law and an FBI agent who works in Dallas."

She blinked in surprise. "You know an FBI agent? Why didn't you tell me?"

"Guess it just didn't come up. I asked her to do some research for me on the town, the people…"

"And me?" she asked. There was no discernable trace of anger in her voice, only curiosity.

He nodded his confirmation. "I needed to know as much as I could about all of this as quickly as possible."

"What did she have to tell you?"

"Not much I didn't already know, unfortunately." He hesitated, not sure how to handle this, not sure whether he should tell her, not sure what it meant. "There was one thing, though…."

"What is it?" she prodded when he didn't continue.

"I asked her to look up your mother."

She simply blinked at him, her expression utterly blank. "My mother?" she repeated flatly. "Why?"

"Travis brought her up back in town on my first day

here, how she took off, so when I had somebody on the phone with the resources to track her down, I asked."

"Oh," Elena said, unable to come up with a single alternate response. She supposed she'd once wondered where her mother had gone and what she was doing, but Teresa Reyes had been gone so long now Elena seldom thought of her at all anymore. "All right then. What did your friend have to say?"

"She didn't find her," he said gently.

Elena felt no disappointment, only the same numbness that seemed to have blanketed her from the first moment he'd brought up the subject. "I guess she did a good job covering her tracks then. She really must not want to be found."

"That's just it," Matt said carefully. "She didn't just do a good job. Pam couldn't find anything at all, something that shouldn't be possible if your mother's still out there. Which means she most likely—"

"Is dead," Elena finished when he didn't. She saw the open concern in his eyes. She understood it, was even touched by it a little, even if it was unnecessary. How could she begin to mourn someone who'd been dead to her for years?

"There's more," Matt said. "Earlier I asked Pam if she could find any background information on the town, anything interesting I should know. She said there wasn't much, but Western Bluff was mentioned in connection with a number of Latino women in their late twenties to early thirties who were reported missing in the area twenty-five years ago. That's about when your mother supposedly left, isn't it?" he said when she didn't respond.

"Yes," she admitted weakly, not sure where he was going with this.

No, it was obvious where he was going with this. She just didn't like it. "What are you suggesting? That my mother didn't leave? That she was…taken?"

"I don't know. The cases were being investigated as possibly being the work of a serial killer, but no evidence was ever found of that."

"So there's a chance it might not be true."

"A chance, yes."

But not a likely one, she acknowledged. The FBI wouldn't have been looking into it if it hadn't seemed suspicious. And it would have been. This wasn't the city, there weren't all that many people in the area to begin with. For several women with at least a similar ethnic background and age to go missing in the same general area, it would seem more likely than not there was a connection.

But her mother? Was it possible she hadn't left? Had something happened…?

Elena couldn't even begin to process the significance of that. She had far too much on her mind at the moment that mattered so much more.

She did her best to push the thought aside for another time, sometime when she could try to come to terms with it. Sometime far in the future. "That's not important right now," she said. "Bobby's murder is the only thing that is."

Matt looked at her for a long moment, as though he wasn't sure about that. She steeled herself, silently willing him to let it go. She really couldn't deal with this right now. She was barely handling everything else on her plate—the ranch, Bobby's death, *him*. She couldn't cope with one more thing, especially one whose implications threatened to be this unsettling.

He finally nodded. "All right. Let's focus on the murder."

Elena exhaled, only then realizing she'd been holding her breath. "Good. Any ideas what we should do now?"

He appeared to consider the question. "About his cousin. How was Jack Landry's relationship with Bobby?"

"Decent, I suppose. They weren't close. I can't remember Jack coming out here even once since I'd been married to Bobby, but that might have had more to do with me. Jack is one of those who figured I married Bobby for his money. They got along well enough. Why you do ask?"

He quickly explained what Pam had told him about the inheritance law. She was frowning when he finished. "You think Jack might have killed Bobby to inherit the ranch?"

"It's a motive, a pretty good one. We have to consider it, especially since we don't have a lot of other leads."

"True, but the ranch isn't really worth inheriting. It's in so much debt it's not much of a prize. It's definitely not worth killing somebody over."

"From what you said and what I heard in town, I got the feeling Bobby's debts weren't exactly common knowledge. It could be Landry doesn't even know about them."

"True."

"And is it possible he knows about the offer Marshall made on the place? In that case, even if he knows about the debts, he would also know he could make money from selling it."

"It's possible. I doubt Bobby would have mentioned it, but I don't know who Glen's told."

"I want to try to talk to Landry, see if I can get anything out of him."

"Do you really think he'll talk to you?"

"I'll just have to do my best not to give him a choice. Do you want to come?"

The idea of confronting Jack the way she was feeling right now seemed like far more than she could handle at the moment. "I don't think so. Jack isn't going to talk to me. If you really think you'll get anything out of him, you're better off going on your own."

The look he gave her said he recognized it for the excuse it was. "If you're sure…"

Elena nodded. "I have enough I need to get done around here. The horses need to be fed. I need to check the stock. You know how it goes."

"Do you want me to stay…"

"No. Go. See what you can find out."

"I'll be back in a little while then."

"Okay."

He hesitated, as if there was something else he wanted to say, as if there was something he *should* say. Finally, with one final nod, he headed to his truck.

Elena watched him go. After he stepped into the vehicle, she finally released a breath she'd been holding. It didn't help. Her chest still felt tight. So very tight.

She lurched into motion, moving toward the barn. She'd meant what she'd said. She had so many things to do. And more than anything else in this world at the moment, she needed to do them.

MAYBE HE SHOULDN'T HAVE TOLD her, Matt thought as he drove away from the ranch. At least until he'd thought about what it meant and all the ramifications. He'd told himself he didn't want to hurt her, but it was obvious she'd been thrown off by the revelation at the very least. But he hadn't felt right keeping it from her.

Maybe he shouldn't have left her, but he'd had the distinct sense she wanted to be alone.

By the time he'd made it to Western Bluff, he still didn't have an answer. He finally had to set the question aside to focus on what he was going to say to Jack Landry.

Landry's law office was located on Main Street, not far from the police station. Matt remembered spotting it on his way into town. Giving the police station a wide berth, he parked at the other end of the block and made his way back to Landry's office.

Stepping inside, he found himself looking at Landry himself, recognizing him from the street the day before. The man stood at a desk in what was a small reception area, speaking to the woman seated behind it. Both of them looked up at his entrance, Landry's eyes narrowing, lips compressing into a thin, angry line. Matt supposed that meant the man knew who he was, too.

Still, he figured it would be best to go with an introduction, to try to get things off to an easy start. They were probably going to get heated soon enough.

"My name is Matt Alvarez. I'm working for Elena Weston."

"Oh, is that what people are calling it these days?" Landry snorted. "You can cut the crap, Alvarez. I know who you are."

"I'd like a word with you."

"Not interested."

"Well, I'm going to be talking. I can do it right here in front of your assistant, but I'm not sure you're going to want her to hear what I have to say, or we can do this in private."

Landry eyed him, and Matt could tell the man was gauging his seriousness, and how much he cared about whatever Matt might reveal. From the desk, the woman's head swung back and forth as she slowly looked between them.

"All right," Landry said. "I'll bite. Let's hear what you've got to say." He turned and walked through a door behind him.

Figuring that was as much of a cue to follow as he was going to get, Matt did. The second room was clearly Landry's private office. Once Matt was through the door, the lawyer closed it behind him and moved to the desk. "If you've come to declare her innocence to me, you're wasting your time—and mine."

"No, I'm here to talk about inheritances."

Stopping behind the desk, Landry glared at him. "I'm not discussing my cousin's will with you. It's privileged, not to mention none of your damn business."

"No, I want to talk about the law. See, I recently learned a little something about inheritance law here in Texas. It turns out that if a murder victim's primary heir is convicted of his murder, then another heir can petition to inherit his estate instead. Besides Elena, you're Bobby's only other living relative, aren't you?"

The man's jaw visibly tightened. "What are you suggesting?"

"Only that it gives you a motive for murder—and to see Elena put in jail for it."

The man's eyes flared in outrage. "This conversation is over."

Matt held his ground. "You were pushing pretty hard for that to happen the other day when I overheard you talking to the mayor, trying to get him to pressure the sheriff into making an arrest."

"Because she murdered my cousin. Everybody in this town knows it."

"Everybody in this town is wrong. She didn't do it."

"And we're all just supposed to take your word for it?"

"No, you can take the evidence's word. There is none."

"Yet."

"It's been two weeks and the police haven't exactly been sitting on their heels. Don't you think if there was anything to find, they would have come up with something by now?"

Landry held up a hand. "I told you you're wasting your time if you're going to argue her innocence with me. Just like you're wasting your time with the rest of that garbage you mentioned. This also is none of your business, but if it'll get you out of here, I'll go ahead and say it. What you didn't mention about that law is that the other heir has to petition to inherit, it doesn't happen automatically. I have no intention of doing that. So even when Elena is convicted—and she will be—I won't inherit, because I don't want to."

"Really?" Matt scoffed. "You expect me to believe you wouldn't take the ranch?"

"I don't care what you believe. And no, I wouldn't take the place if you paid me to."

Landry was so vehement Matt actually believed him,

the realization as surprising as the man's statement. "Why not?"

"I don't want anything from the Westons. There's too many bad vibes surrounding them. And I can't stand the ranch," Landry said frankly.

"Why?"

"I just can't. Even when I was a kid I hated going out there to visit my aunt and my cousins. There's just something about it. As long as I've been alive, nobody's been happy out there. First my aunt, Bobby's mother, was thrown from her horse and killed. She was young when she died. So were Big Jim, Junior and now Bobby. I don't know what it is. Maybe I'm just being superstitious, but the place didn't feel right to me even before my aunt died. And nothing about it has changed my mind since."

Seeing the intensity burning in the man's eyes, Matt felt a shiver roll along his skin. He didn't doubt Landry meant every word, his unease with the place communicated so loud and clear Matt could feel it himself.

He suddenly remembered the feeling he himself had had last night. He'd thought it was simply the feeling of danger, the knowledge that someone could be—and likely was—lurking in the darkness. Was it possible it was something more?

As soon as the thought occurred, he recognized how ridiculous it was. He didn't believe in curses or anything like that. Although, considering it brought back Marshall's comment yesterday. He'd said the Westons seemed like they were cursed or something. He'd been talking about the family themselves, not the ranch. Either way, Matt didn't buy it. The Westons had just had bad luck. It happened.

But looking at Landry, his face pale, his expression tense, he believed everything he was saying.

Even so, Matt hadn't come all the way here not to play all his cards. "You wouldn't have to keep the ranch. I'm sure you've heard about Glen Marshall's offer to buy it."

Landry showed no surprise. Matt took that as confirmation that Landry had already known.

"I don't want the money. Bobby was my cousin and I loved him, and he was my only living relative, too. No amount of money could make up for that. Now will that be all, or do you have any more accusations to throw at me?"

"That's it."

"The door's right there. Use it." With that, Landry finally pulled the chair out from behind his desk and sat in it, rolling forward to the desk and focusing on the papers on top of it as though Matt wasn't there.

Turning the conversation over in his mind, Matt opened the door and left. Moments later he was outside on the sidewalk.

It was possible Landry was lying, of course. He was a lawyer; chances were he was good at it. But Matt's gut told him the man had been telling the truth. Which made this just another dead end.

As he made his way back to his truck, he couldn't help but think about Landry's words. So many bad things happening to one family. Including Elena, he thought. She may not have died like the other Westons, but she'd had a rough time of it. A rough time that was still ongoing. Damn. All this, and they were still no closer to the identity of Bobby Weston's killer. And like the man had said, everybody was left still thinking Elena had done it.

He was almost at his truck when he looked up and spotted her, just as he had the last couple of days.

Lynda, the mayor's wife, the woman from the street, the woman who'd been watching him.

Just as she was now. Their eyes met once again. This time she quickly glanced away and didn't look at him again, though the deliberate way she wasn't was just as telling.

He'd asked Elena about her. She'd said the mayor's wife was a woman named Lynda Clayton and her husband's name was Henry. The two of them had never been particularly warm toward her, so Elena figured the woman's attention was no different from anyone else's, believing he was working for a murderer. Still, he couldn't escape the feeling there was more to it. Who was this woman? Why did she seem so interested in him?

With Landry's talk of curses and bad vibes ringing in his mind, he half wondered if the woman even existed, or if she was just a ghost haunting him for some reason.

No, she was definitely real, as she unlocked the Mercedes in front of her and climbed in. As he watched her start her engine, he realized that while he hadn't gotten the answer to the biggest question on his mind, he could get an answer to this one. He didn't have to ask Elena. He could go straight to the source and ask the woman herself.

She was already backing out of the space, getting ready to leave. There was only one thing he could do.

He got in his truck and followed her.

She drove to the east side of town, what he guessed was the good side judging from the look and size of the houses on the street she finally arrived on. She pulled into the driveway of one of them, and he figured that meant she was home.

He parked against the curb and quickly got out of the truck, making his way up the driveway.

She was just opening the front door when he called out, not wanting her to get inside before he could speak to her. "Excuse me, ma'am?"

She glanced up and looked back at him. He saw immediately that she recognized him, a trace of nervousness entering her eyes.

Matt smiled, trying to look reassuring. "Mrs. Clayton, is it?"

She looked at first like she wasn't sure she wanted to answer before slowly nodding. "That's right."

Something in her eyes held him. It wasn't the wariness of a woman who'd found a stranger on her doorstep. Instead, there was something speculative in her steady gaze, as though she were studying him, trying to gauge him in some way. He recognized the feeling. It was the same way she'd looked at him in town, though he was only now close enough to read it.

"Ma'am, my name is Matt Alvarez. I'm working for Elena Weston out at the Weston Ranch."

After a moment, she nodded. "Yes."

He tried to figure out what to say. "Hello, I've noticed you staring at me," wasn't really going to cut it.

Trying to find the words, he surveyed her, this attractive, well-dressed woman in her early fifties...

Which was about how old Elena's mother would be if she were still alive.

He wondered if he just had Teresa Reyes on his mind, given his conversation with Elena. But he had to admit, in a town this size, chances were the two women had known each other, maybe grown up together. He couldn't help but ask.

"By any chance did you know Elena's mother? Teresa, I believe her name was?"

The flash of emotion that passed over her face before she could hide it was all the answer he needed. Lynda Clayton not only had known Elena's mother, but the name meant enough to her to stir an emotional reaction. And suddenly he was sure he had the answer to a question he'd been asking for days.

He leaned closer, watching as her eyes widened slightly though she didn't back away, and said quietly, "You're the one who sent me the article, aren't you?"

There was no missing the flare of alarm in her gaze, but she waited too long to deny it to claim she didn't know what he was talking about. Even as she opened her mouth to respond, he spoke again.

"Do you really want to have this conversation out here? Because I'm not going anywhere. I've been wanting to talk to you from the minute I opened that envelope, and I'm not leaving until I have answers."

She didn't move, staring at him, doubt etched across her features, until he figured a softer tack might be called for. He gentled his tone.

"I believe you sent me that article because you wanted to help her. Has that changed?"

He saw immediately he'd been right. She stepped back out of the doorway, pushing the door open farther. "Come in then. Quickly."

Matt did as ordered, stepping over the threshold and

past her into the house. As soon as he had, she shut the door behind him.

"So you did send me the article," he said, still wanting the confirmation.

She nodded tersely without looking at him. "Yes. You might as well come in." She moved past him into a room on the left. It was the living room. With a heavy sense of weariness, she lowered herself into the nearest seat.

Matt remained in the entryway to the room, giving it a quick glance and checking the other entrances. There was no one in sight and a heavy silence hung over the house. Both seemed to indicate no one else was around. He doubted she would have invited him in if there was.

He refocused his attention solely on her. "Why?" he asked.

"Like you said, I wanted to help Elena."

"But why contact me?"

"Because there was no one else."

"There was you. You could have helped her."

Lynda opened her hands in a helpless gesture. "What could I do? Everyone in this town believes she killed Bobby, and no one was going to believe me just because I said otherwise. And if I started opposing Henry they'd all think I was crazy. So I did the only thing I could. I reached out to someone who might be able to do something."

"Again, why did you pick me out of all the people in the world? You could have hired her a lawyer, a private investigator…"

"I don't have the money to do either of those things. If I took the money out of our joint account, Henry would have stopped the payment, and at the very least I'd have to explain why I did it."

"Why *did* you do it? What difference was it to you?"

Lynda swallowed, her gaze becoming distant. "Teresa Reyes was my best friend growing up. I don't even know how many people remember that now, it was so long ago. When we were little girls and all through high school, she was like a sister to me. You may not know it looking at me now, but my folks were poor, and so were hers. We were two of a kind, us against all those rich, snobby mean girls. Then I started dating Henry, and things started to change. I had Henry's approval, so the rich girls started to notice me. Accept me. Teresa and I started drifting apart." She gave her head a hard shake. "No, that lets me off the hook more than I deserve. We didn't drift apart. I cut her loose. She was my best friend, and I pretty much just stopped talking to her. Our lives weren't the same anymore. We were living in different worlds, especially after she started seeing Ed, and Henry and I got married. Henry didn't want me around Teresa and especially Ed. They weren't his kind of people. The 'right' kind of people. And I went along with him. I didn't really feel like I belonged with his friends, and Teresa was kind of a reminder of why I didn't. It was easier to not be friends with her anymore. At least for me.

"Henry and I started having kids, and of course Teresa had Elena. When Teresa left Ed, ran away from her own daughter, I felt so awful. I'd seen her in town sometimes. I knew she couldn't be happy, but I had no idea things were so bad that she would decide to run away like that. She needed a friend. I should have been that friend. I should have been there for her. It was too late for that. But I could at least try to be there for Elena.

"I kept an eye on her over the years. I knew Henry wouldn't want me getting involved. That wouldn't have stopped me if I'd been able, but the one time I tried talking to Ed about her, offering to help in any way I could, he just screamed at me and threw me out of his house. He knew Teresa and I had been close, of course, and he didn't want anybody around who reminded him of her. Not to mention he remembered how I treated Teresa. He had no use for me, said I was probably one of the things in this town she'd been trying to get away from. I suppose I couldn't blame him for that at least.

"So I did what I could. Not as much as I should have, but something. Elena needed money for school, so I pulled some strings with a ladies' organization I belong to out of Dallas that offers a scholarship. It wasn't much, nowhere near as much as I would have liked. I should have tried harder. I'd hoped she'd be able to get out of Western Bluff, make a fresh start somewhere. But then she married Bobby and stayed."

"And then he was murdered," Matt concluded.

Lynda nodded grimly.

"That still doesn't explain why me."

"I saw you that summer, the two of you," she said, surprising him. "Long before Ed found out and made a ruckus about the whole thing. I knew there was something between the two of you. I'd see you at the diner, the way you couldn't take your eyes off her, the little private smiles you shared, like you were all alone in a room full of people. And when I tried to think of somebody, anybody in this world who might care enough to help her, I remembered you."

"How did you find me?"

"I have a friend whose son does background checks for the state. It was easy enough. There are a lot of Matt Alvarezes out there, but I knew about what age you were. It was just a matter of tracking down the right one."

"Weren't you worried it would look bad, a guy she dated a long time ago showing up right after her husband was murdered?"

"I didn't believe it could get any worse. How could it? She already had the whole town against her, the police determined to prove she was guilty. What she needed was someone on her side."

"And you thought somebody she knew for a few months who'd been gone for eight years was the best person out of everybody in the world to be on her side?"

"No, I thought somebody who once loved her might still care enough not to want to see her in prison."

Loved her? Matt tried not to let his surprise show at the woman's words. And it was a surprise. Not that he'd loved Elena—he knew that, of course—but that anyone had known, especially someone he hadn't been aware of and hadn't spoken to before in his life. The way he and Elena had felt about each other had been private. He'd never told another soul, and other than perhaps her father when he'd tried tearing them apart, he didn't believe she had, either. It had been between them, theirs and theirs alone. But there wasn't the slightest doubt in this woman's voice. To hear her put it so simply, to find out that someone else had known came as a pure shock. "How did you—"

She eyed him knowingly. "I saw the way you looked

at her back then, the way she looked at you. You loved each other."

He couldn't deny it.

"What about Bobby Weston?" he asked before he could stop himself. "How'd she look at him?"

"Not the same way. I think she wanted to. It was like she was trying her best, but it wasn't the same."

The answer gave him no pleasure, imagining Elena unhappy like that. "And Weston?" he asked quietly. "Did he love her?"

A hint of sadness entered her eyes before she lowered them. "Yes," she said. "I believe he did. Certainly in the beginning. He looked at her the way she never looked at him."

It was the last thing Matt ever would have expected, but damned if he didn't feel a twinge of sympathy for the man. But then, he knew what it was like to love Elena more than anything, and to believe she didn't love him the same way. He wouldn't have wished that feeling on anybody, not even the man who'd gotten to marry her. And while he couldn't condone the way Bobby had treated her, he could understand it. Because he also knew what it was like to think he hated her. He couldn't imagine what it would have been like to be married to her, be around her every day, and feel that way. As much as he hated to admit it, he wasn't sure his behavior would have been any better.

Hell, he'd walked away from her, leaving her crying on the street. He really wasn't much better.

But he could still make it up to her.

No, he *would* make it up to her, he thought fiercely. Whatever he had to do, he'd make amends for ever having made her that unhappy.

"You love her."

Matt glanced up to find Lynda watching him, a small, sad smile on her lips.

His first impulse was to deny it. It was ridiculous. He really hadn't been carrying some kind of pathetic torch for Elena all these years.

But despite his intentions, the words never came.

Because it didn't matter what he'd thought, what he'd felt, when he'd first come back to town. It wasn't what he felt now.

He loved her. Just the thought of losing her again, in any way, sent a sharp, agonizing pain straight through his chest.

Lynda studied him, her smile deepening. "I was hoping you cared enough about her to not want to see her in jail, but I didn't know if there'd be any romantic feelings left." She leaned forward, her smile fading, a serious gleam in her eyes. "Whatever happens, don't let her go this time. Life's too short."

"You're right about that." He didn't tell her that he had no intention of letting Elena go again. The first person he intended to tell that was Elena herself.

He'd waited long enough.

Chapter Thirteen

After Matt left, Elena tried to focus on the work she had
to do around the ranch. But no matter how much she
tried to avoid it, her thoughts kept returning to the unexpected information he'd delivered about her mother.

Was it possible? Had her mother not left her after
all? On the one hand, she supposed she should find
that comforting in some way, that her mother hadn't
abandoned her, hadn't rejected her as she'd always believed. But to suspect that something had happened to
her instead, that she'd met with some terrible end,
wasn't comforting at all. Elena wasn't sure if she should
hope it was true, or if she shouldn't, or if she should do
anything at all.

She hadn't arrived at any answers or found the slightest peace when she heard the vehicle coming up the
driveway. Instantly going on alert, she immediately
moved to the front door. A sigh of relief worked its way
from her lungs once she saw who it was.

Matt. He was back.

Stepping out onto the porch, she watch him park out
front. Once he had, he didn't get out of the truck immediately. Elena could tell he was looking at her, could
feel the heat of his gaze on her. What was he doing?

Frowning, she waited for him to climb out and join her on the porch, her concern growing the longer he didn't.

She was considering walking down to the truck to check on him when he finally opened the door and slowly got out. He took his time gently closing the door behind himself, then made his way to her, his steps deliberate, his head lowered slightly as though he were deep in thought. She felt her unease build. He looked as though he was carrying the weight of the world on his shoulders.

Matt finally reached the steps, moving up them until he stood on the porch with her.

"Is everything all right?" she asked carefully.

"Yeah," he said simply.

The vague answer did nothing to put her mind at ease. "Did you talk to Jack?"

Matt nodded. "Didn't get anything out of him. He denied everything, of course."

"No surprise there."

"I also talked to Lynda Clayton. She was the one who sent me the article about you."

"Lynda Clayton?" she blurted out. She knew who the woman was, of course. That didn't mean the words made any sense. She couldn't remember the last time she'd even spoken to the woman, or frankly if she really had.

He nodded. "She was friends with your mother growing up," he explained. "Best friends, the way she tells it. Sounds like she married up and your mother married down, and she kind of cut your mother loose. After your mother...left..." He glanced away awkwardly, lingering on the word in a way that made it clear he wasn't entirely comfortable putting it like that and reminding her rather painfully of their earlier conversation. "Well, she felt bad for the way she treated her and tried to keep an eye on you. Sounds like she's been looking out for you in various ways over the years. After the murder she figured you might need more help than she could give and...well, here I am."

For the second time in one day he'd managed to completely throw her for a loop, delivering new information she didn't know how to process. First her mother may not have left them, may have had something happen to her. Now Lynda Clayton, a woman who she would have thought was only marginally aware of her existence, had been looking out for her?

Elena had had no idea Lynda and her mother had been friends. But then, her father had barely spoken of her, and never much in the way of personal details. No one else really had, either. There was so little she knew about Teresa Reyes, her friends, the life she'd led. She only knew that she'd left.

And now maybe she didn't even know that.

Shaking her head, she opened her mouth to question him further when she realized he was staring at her, his eyes haunted, his expression pained. The sight of his expression filled her with fresh apprehension. It seemed he was nervous to tell her something. She braced herself, wondering what more there could possibly be.

He finally spoke. "I'm sorry."

"For what?"

"For eight years ago. For...expecting you to give up all your plans to follow some cowboy without a job God knows where. That wasn't fair to you. I was wrong. You deserved better than that."

The words stunned her into silence. She'd never expected to hear them, had no idea what had brought them about, didn't know how to begin to respond.

"You were never just some cowboy," she whispered, the words coming automatically.

It was what she'd tried to tell him before, that he'd never been just anybody to her. This time he didn't blow the comment off, a pained look flashing across his face. "Still, it wasn't right. I knew it was no kind of life for you. I shouldn't have gotten so mad." He swallowed, his voice softening. "I shouldn't have walked away from you."

"It's okay. I understood why. I'm sorry. I wish I'd been able to come with you, strong enough to take the chance. If I'd known how things would turn out…"

He stepped forward, moving so achingly close to her. "Don't," he said. "You can't do that to yourself. We never know what's going to happen. The time just wasn't right for us."

Maybe it was as simple as that, she acknowledged as she peered up into his eyes. Maybe no one had been at fault. They'd wanted different things, different lives. And at that time there'd simply been no way for them to work.

"And now?" she whispered.

"I don't know if it's the right time. I just know I don't want to let you go again."

"Then don't." The words caught in her throat, practically coming out on a sob, filled with every ounce of feeling she was experiencing, every soul-deep need.

Don't let me go.

She didn't have to say anything more. He reached out and took her in his arms.

A lump rose in her throat, and she pressed her lips

together against the sob she was certain would come out if she opened her mouth. She'd missed this, hadn't realized just how much she'd needed it until now. To feel his arms around her. To feel him holding her, simply holding her, so very close. It was just as she remembered. His arms felt different, his body harder, more muscular, after all these years. It didn't matter. She recognized the feel of his embrace as well as if he'd never let her go.

It felt like coming home.

They simply clung to each other, and at first it was enough. This was all she needed. But gradually she began to soak in the heat of his body, his warmth seeping through the layers of clothing and into her skin. Like a slow-acting drug, it spread through her from head to toe, filling her to the core with his heat. The first flickers of awareness sparked to life deep in her belly, the stirrings of arousal building in strength and power. Each moment brought awareness of something new, each fresh discovery adding fuel to the fire. The broad muscularity of his chest beneath her cheek. The strength of his back beneath her fingers and palms. His intoxicating male scent filling her lungs. And she knew she had to have more.

She wanted him, as much as she ever had before, if not more.

As if realizing it exactly at the same time, he eased his hold on her and leaned back slightly. Elena raised her head from his chest and tilted it back to meet his eyes. The dark heat she saw burning in those black depths made it clear she wasn't alone in feeling what she was. Even the sight of it there pushed her awareness, her need, higher.

Then he slowly lowered his mouth to hers.

He kissed her softly, sweetly, with a gentleness that drove a sigh from deep in her throat. His warm, sensual lips stroked against hers, tasting, inviting them to open for him. She responded in kind, deepening the kiss with each subsequent caress. His tongue pushed forward, finding hers, teasing lightly, retreating, then finding it again. A chuckle rumbled deep in her chest at the joy of it, giddy delight bubbling up inside her. She'd forgotten how much fun kissing him could be. It was heady and arousing, but also playful and joyous. He continually surprised her, made it interesting, kept her on her toes, which only made it more exciting.

He broke away to work a trail of kisses along her jaw and down her neck. She automatically leaned her head away to allow him easier access, savoring each lap of his tongue, each brush of his lips against her soft skin.

Her eyes drifted open for just a moment, allowing her to see where they were. Out in the open where anyone could see. More important, on the porch of the house that had never really been hers, where generations of Westons had lived before. The realization immediately diminished her fire slightly. Instinctively knowing where this was heading, where she wanted it to go, she knew she couldn't do this here. They needed to go someplace that was hers and hers alone as much as anyplace in the world was.

She moved her mouth to his ear. "Let's go upstairs," she whispered.

He lifted his head to look into her face. "You sure?"

"Yes." She couldn't recall ever being as sure of anything in her life.

One corner of his mouth moving upward in a slow,

sensual smile, Matt released his hold on her. Reaching down, she took his hand and pulled him inside.

They made it to her bedroom, Elena stepping in first, when he suddenly stopped, his resistance bringing her to a halt, too. She glanced back to find him standing just outside the doorway, eyeing the room with a distinct sense of unease.

"Did you and…"

Elena understood immediately. She shook her head. "This is my room. I moved in here once things got too broken between us. We stopped sharing a bed—in any way."

Matt nodded, both relief and a trace of apology in his eyes. It wasn't what she wanted to see there. She wanted the dark heat back in them, wanted him to look at her with that raw fire that said he wanted to devour her.

She wanted him. Wanted him with far fewer clothes for starters.

Moving toward him, she reached for the buttons on his shirt. Popping the first one, she murmured, "Any more questions?"

She sensed his smile. "Nope."

"Good," she said, continuing to release the buttons, pulling him farther into the room by his shirt. She didn't want this to go too fast, needing to take in every moment, every part of the experience. So long. It had been so long since she'd seen his body, since she'd touched his skin, since she'd felt every part of him. She'd never thought she would again. She wanted to relish it, bask in every sensation. She finally finished with the buttons and opened his shirt, revealing his long, lean torso to her. A breath caught in her throat as she simply looked at first, at his firm musculature, his flat belly, his smooth bronze skin. He'd gotten bigger, stronger. He was still the most beautiful man she'd ever seen.

When she started to push the shirt from his shoulders, Matt pulled the gun from the waistband of his jeans and placed it on the bedside table, then turned back to her.

They undressed each other together, taking their time, moving slowly, working together. Boots were tugged off, buttons were released, fabric slid from shoulders and arms. All the while, they touched and explored, as if amazed by every next bit of flesh that was revealed. Which she was. She knew his body so well, the line of his shoulders, the length of his torso. It was all so familiar, yet so different at the same time, leaner in some places, more muscular in others. She could only imagine he felt the same, as his fingers stroked her breasts, her belly, her hips. She knew her body was different than it had been. She'd gotten older, rounder in places. A trace of anxiety flickered through her. She hoped he liked what he saw.

One glance at his face, his eyes unerringly focused on her, said he did.

Finally, there was nothing else covering them and they stood bare before each other. His hands trailed along her sides as he stepped forward and kissed her once more. They almost immediately deepened it together. His arms went around her, his hands finding her hips and lifting her off her feet. Her breasts pressed against the hard wall of his chest, the heat of his skin burning against her own. She wound her arms around his neck as he stepped forward, carrying her to the bed. There was a sound when his legs hit the edge of it. Then he was lowering her onto it, easing her on the mattress, stretching out beside her.

As his hands moved over her body, his mouth over hers, it struck her that they'd never done this before, never made love in an actual bed. Back then, they'd had to find a place together wherever they could, and a bed had never entered the equation. Instead, they'd made love in the bed of his truck, parked in an isolated, out-of-the-way spot, or on a blanket spread out under the stars. They'd certainly never lacked for not having been in a bed. Wherever they'd been, it had been lovely. All they'd needed was each other.

But still, it was nice to be in a bed this time. It was like a new experience for them, as if it were their first time. And it was, their first time since they'd found each other again. It seemed right somehow.

They took their time exploring each other's bodies, until it wasn't enough. He rolled away and reached for his wallet, pulling a packet from it and covering himself. Then he came back to her.

Elena parted her legs, letting him move between them, wanting him there. Matt positioned himself above her and leaned forward to kiss her again. She breathed in the experience of it, basking in the weight of him above her and between her legs. The tip of his erection nudged insistently against her folds, as though asking for admission. She was more than ready. And when Matt finally thrust into her, she raised her hips to meet him.

The breath caught in her throat as they remained there for an instant, locked together. It was so right. She smiled, unable to believe she'd existed without this, without him for so long, that giddy joy spiraling through her. He smiled back at her, that gorgeous smile he offered far too rarely, that the world seldom got to see. Her heart felt on the verge of bursting, from this moment, from this man, from the beauty of his smile.

They began moving together in perfect rhythm, hips moving apart, finding each other again. Elena wrapped her arms around his neck again, unable to get enough of touching him, needing to feel as much of him as possible. Bracing himself above her on his arms, he drove into her, harder, faster, pushing her to greater, seemingly impossible heights. She stared up into his eyes, watching his face, the emotions flashing across it, the pleasure. As she came closer and closer to the edge, she saw him approach it with her, the tension building in his face, his neck and shoulders. And when she reached it, he was right there with her, looking deep in her eyes at the moment of their release.

And as the waves of her release ebbed away, they left amazement in their wake. Amazement at the rightness of this moment, of having found each other again, of a new beginning she'd never dreamed possible.

Yet here it was.

Here *he* was, back where he belonged.

With her.

Chapter Fourteen

Matt woke to darkness.

Drifting awake, he slowly peeled his eyelids open to peer into the shadows above him. It was night, he registered. The ceiling above him was unfamiliar. So was the bed.

Still, he didn't have to look to see where he was. He knew. He recognized the feel of the woman at his side, the sweet smell that was uniquely hers, as a deep, warm contentment spread through him at the knowledge.

He was with Elena. Where he belonged. There was nowhere else he ever wanted to be.

His mouth curving in a smile, he lay there and simply basked in the feeling, better than anything he'd ever known. He couldn't remember the last time he'd ever been this happy. Maybe not since they'd parted ways before, maybe never at all. He breathed in the scent of her, absorbed the thump of her heartbeat from where her body was pressed against him, listened to the soft sound of her breathing.

He didn't know how he'd survived without this, without her, all this time. He only knew that he couldn't again. God willing, he would never have to.

He would have loved nothing more than to remain

where he was, closing his eyes and drifting back to sleep with this amazing woman curled up beside him. But even as he started to do so, he remembered what had happened last night, and the night before.

He opened his eyes fully once more. It had still been early evening then. Judging from the darkness, it was now much later, well into the night. The time their nasty visitor liked to come out and play.

Hard determination replaced the contentment that had filled him just moments before.

He was going to catch the bastard. He wasn't getting away with anything tonight.

He should do a check of the grounds. At the very least, he should make sure the house was secure. He couldn't remember if they'd locked any of the doors, and it was worth checking out. Their troublemaker had been getting bolder. He'd feel a lot better if he knew more definitively that they were safe.

Swallowing a sigh of regret, he eased himself from the bed and quickly dressed. Sitting down to tug his boots on, he glanced back at Elena. The sight of her there, curled up on her side facing him, nearly cracked his resolve and made him crawl back in beside her.

Soon. He'd be back soon enough. In the meantime, he had work to do.

He retrieved the gun he'd placed on the bedside table, keeping it in hand. With one last, lingering look, he headed downstairs.

The house was still and quiet. His footsteps as silent as possible on the hardwood floor, he kept his ears peeled for the slightest noise, the faintest disturbance. He detected nothing as he made his way down the stairs to the front.

He stopped at the front door, checking the lock, giving a perfunctory glance outside through the window. So perfunctory he almost missed seeing it, the shadow at the edge of the barn moving toward the house.

He'd been about to turn away from the door. Instead, he froze, eyes returning to the figure as it crept forward, trying to remain in darkness as much as possible. The figure was dressed in black, a ski mask covering his face.

Triumph surged from deep in Matt's gut. This was it. He was going to get the guy.

Not about to wait and see what the bastard had in mind, to miss the chance to catch him, Matt quickly considered his options. If he went out the kitchen door and circled around the back, he should be able to get the drop on the person.

But only if he moved quickly.

As soon as he thought it, he sprang into motion, bursting away from the door and racing through the house on the balls of his feet to the back.

Reaching the kitchen door, he slowly pulled it open, careful not to make a sound. When he had it open just wide enough for him to pass through, he slipped through the gap and hurried outside.

It took him less than thirty seconds to make his way around the side of the house to the front. He paused at the corner, carefully looking around the edge to scan for the trespasser.

He instantly spotted him, standing almost in front of the house. The man was looking down, something clutched in his right hand. A glass bottle. In his left he held a lighter, which he started to ignite. Once he had a flame he started lifting it to something dangling out of the mouth of the bottle—

Recognition slammed into Matt.

It was a fire bomb. Which could only mean one thing.

He was planning on throwing it into the house.

No.

Without a second thought, Matt burst from the shadows and charged the bastard, automatically shoving the gun into the back of his waistband with one hand, fighting to outrace the rag's ignition. At the last second the trespasser must have spotted the motion out of the corner of his eye, jerking his head up in Matt's direction.

Too late to do anything about it.

Matt crashed into him, locking his arms around the trespasser and knocking him clear off his feet. In the back of his mind, he heard the bottle the man had been holding crash to the ground and break into pieces. The smell of gasoline filled the air.

They landed hard on the ground, rolling away from the odor, tumbling against the packed dirt. The man started to fight him, throwing his arms and knees and his body weight against Matt as best he could. The bastard was strong as hell, Matt had to give him that. Matt fought to keep a hold on him. He finally managed to get on top of the intruder, straddling him with his legs. He pulled back long enough to draw a fist, driving it hard into the man's masked face. The punch was enough to get the bastard to stop struggling for an instant. Matt drew his fist back again and landed another blow, making the man weaken further. Matt wasted no more time, reaching for the gun he'd shoved at the small of his back and aiming it directly between the intruder's eyes.

"Stop it," Matt ordered when the man would have started fighting back again. He cocked the weapon, drawing the intruder's attention. The bastard froze, eyes slowly focusing on the barrel of the gun less than six inches from his face.

Matt read the calculation in those narrowed eyes. "Go ahead," he said, satisfaction pulsing through his veins. "You don't know how badly I want to pull the trigger."

They stared at each other for a long moment, locked in a silent battle of wills. There was no way Matt was going to blink first.

Finally, the other man relaxed slightly, his eyes reflecting his acknowledgment that he'd been bested—and fury that he had been.

Matt barely restrained a triumphant grin. This wasn't the time to get cocky. Remembering their battle the night before, he knew how quickly the balance could change. "Now let's see who the hell you are."

Reaching down with his free hand, he ripped the mask off, baring the man's face. He wasn't at all surprised at what he saw.

As expected, Deputy Travis Gerard glared back at him, his expression mutinous, unrepentant.

It was all Matt could do not to drive his fist into the deputy's arrogant face one more time. "I should have known you were behind this, you bastard," he forced out, his jaw tight. Keeping the gun steady, Matt slowly rose, never shifting his aim. Travis never took his eyes from the gun, either.

When Matt was on his feet, he took a couple steps back and away from the man. "Get up," he ordered.

From the look Travis shot him he was tempted to defy the order just for the hell of it. But he gradually climbed to his feet, taking his time, making a big show of it. When he finally straightened, he brushed some of the dirt off his clothes and stood facing Matt, meeting his eyes.

Matt stared back, his sense of victory quickly dimming as he considered the reality of the situation at hand. Because he hadn't just caught someone committing a crime on private property. He'd caught a sheriff's deputy doing it. A sheriff's deputy in a department that wasn't going to be inclined to believe anything Matt had to say, that would probably have no problem with his actions or with covering them up.

"So what the hell are you going to do now?" Travis snapped, regaining some of his bravado.

That was the problem. "I haven't decided," he said coldly. "If I call the sheriff, he's not going to believe me, is he? He'll somehow turn this around on me, probably charge me with assaulting an officer and let you off scot-free, won't he?" And if he got arrested, Elena would be alone out here, openly vulnerable to whatever attack Travis decided to launch next. Which he would, of course. If he got away with this there'd be nothing holding him back from trying again.

Travis's smirk said he shared Matt's analysis—and fully expected everything to unfold as described.

At the sight of the man's smugness, Matt saw red, nearly hitting his breaking point with this dirtbag and this whole situation. In an instant, all he wanted was to see the bastard squirm.

"Hell, I might as well shoot you then," Matt said, gratified to see the smirk slowly fade from Travis's mouth. "If I do, then there's no way he can turn this around on me. We have you dressed all in black, trespassing here in the middle of the night. I could always claim I didn't know who you were. Nobody could blame me for shooting some guy who was getting ready to throw a firebomb into the house."

"You wouldn't," Travis challenged, not looking entirely sure about that. "You'd never get away with it."

"I should," Matt said. "It's what you deserve. A firebomb? What the hell were you thinking? She could have been killed!" Travis simply stared back at him, as if Matt wasn't telling him anything he didn't already know, or something he couldn't care less about. "Did you slash her tires in town, too?"

He said nothing, his mouth a tight line, but the glint in his eye looked too much like pride.

"You bastard. Do you have any idea what you've put her through?"

"Good. It's what she deserves."

"What the hell do you want from her?"

"I want her to confess! I want her to admit what she did. Until she does she doesn't deserve a moment's peace. She doesn't deserve to have a good night's rest in this house that she damn well doesn't deserve to own."

In the wake of his outburst, Travis stood there, chest heaving, face mottled with emotion. But there was more than anger in the man's words. There was pain, in his face, in his voice, almost like he was on the verge of tears. The man truly believed Elena killed his best friend, practically his brother, Matt acknowledged. He could understand the man's motives, even if he damn well couldn't condone his actions.

The best he could do was try to come to some kind of understanding, some way to get him to back off.

"All right. I'm going to tell you this once, Gerard. The sooner you realize this, the sooner you can start figuring out who's really responsible. Elena did not kill Bobby."

"Then who the hell did?"

"Maybe if you opened your damn mind and even considered the possibility that someone else is responsible you'd figure it out."

"You think I haven't? You think I haven't considered every single person in this town, thought of every possible reason any one of them would have killed Bobby? I haven't come up with a damn thing. The only person with a reason, the only person who could have done it is *her*."

"Just because you haven't found the answer yet doesn't mean it's not there."

"Or else I've already found it."

"Damn it, Gerard. I can promise you, Elena didn't kill him."

"And how do you know that, huh?"

"Because I know her. And you should, too. You should know she's no killer."

"Yeah, I know her," he scoffed. "I know she's a gold digger who trapped a good man into marrying her when she didn't even love him. It took him a while to realize it, but Bobby knew it. It used to eat him up. She didn't love him. He just didn't know that she was hung up on somebody else. It was you, wasn't it? All this time. And now you come back here the minute he's dead, sleeping in his house, with his wife—"

"It's not like that—" Matt began.

"The hell it's not!" Travis said. "So don't tell me she didn't do it. You don't tell me a damn thing, because I sure as hell don't believe a word you say."

They stood there glaring at each other in the moonlight. It hardly mattered that Travis didn't want to hear what he had to say, because Matt didn't know what he even could say. If he were in Travis's shoes he'd probably feel the same way about things. Short of finding the real killer, there wasn't going to be any convincing him Elena was innocent. And as for the rest… No, Travis wasn't likely to believe them about any of that, either.

That didn't mean Matt was going to put up with any more of the man's garbage. He probably couldn't count on the sheriff to do anything to stop him, which meant he was going to have to find some way—

His only warning came a split second before it happened. Travis's gaze abruptly moved behind him, his eyes widening slightly in response to what he saw.

Matt didn't have time to react.

Then he couldn't.

A split second later, something heavy crashed into the back of his head. His vision blurred and he stumbled forward. He tried to regain his balance as the world seemed to swim around him and his feet seemed to have disappeared. Then he was falling, falling endlessly. Until…

Nothing.

SOMETHING WOKE HER.

Something loud, a noise of some kind. It prodded her

to wakefulness, pushing her from the best sleep she'd had in a long time.

Still half-asleep, Elena registered that she was cold. A source of warmth she'd gotten used to wasn't there anymore. Matt.

Without opening her eyes, she reached out to find him.

And found only cold sheets.

She opened her eyes to glance at where Matt had been lying at her side.

His half of the bed was empty. He was gone.

Frowning, she slowly sat up, more confused than concerned. "Matt?"

The sound of her voice echoing through the open doorway and down the hall emphasized the emptiness of the house and the sense that she truly was alone.

No answer.

She glanced toward the window, noting the darkness outside. It was the dead of night.

The trouble they'd had the past couple nights suddenly came rushing back to her. Had something happened? Had he heard a noise? Their troublemaker again? Why wouldn't he have woken her?

No, if he'd heard something he would have woken her, wouldn't he? He wouldn't have simply left her alone and helpless in bed.

Everything was probably fine.

Still, she couldn't quite shake the feeling of unease crawling along her nerve endings. The house was so quiet. Too quiet. And there'd been that noise, she remembered, trying to place it, trying to recall what it could have been.

Climbing from the bed, she reached for her clothes

and quickly tugged them on, then moved to the window. Standing to the side of it, she gently pulled the curtain back an inch, then leaned over and peered out.

Everything appeared to be still. It was a cloudy night, the moon and most of the stars hidden from view behind the dense coverage. It made the darkness more opaque that usual. Some light from the house spilled out into the yard and driveway, and the light fixed on the post next to the barn did its job illuminating most of the area directly in front of it. But there seemed to be far more shadows than usual, stretching across the ground, keeping much of it in darkness. She couldn't see much out there, except—

It took her a moment to understand what it was she was seeing. And then—

A gasp lodged in her throat.

A man lay on the ground in front of the house.

Everything inside her tensed in shock, in horror.

No.

He wasn't visible enough for her to make him out much, just out of range of the big light out front, hidden in the shadows on the edge of the driveway. She couldn't see his face, couldn't really make out his clothes. She only saw a silhouette, the figure large enough it looked like a man to her.

Had the intruder come back? Had he done something to Matt?

She tried to peer closer, desperate for any indication it was Matt. But if it wasn't, where was he?

Whether or not it was Matt, something must be wrong. There was no reason for someone to simply be lying there on the ground unless he was hurt...or dead.

She shoved the thought aside. She couldn't afford to think like that. She had to figure out what to do.

She could call the police, but somehow she doubted Walt or Travis would rush out here, even if they did believe her. And in the meantime, Matt could be dying.

The hell if she was going to cower in her house while the man she loved was out there, possibly on the verge of drawing his last breath.

Moving back to her bedside table, Elena retrieved her gun, not about to go out there unarmed. And this time, if there were someone who meant her harm, who'd done something to Matt, she wouldn't be firing into the air.

When she reached the bedroom door, she was about to step out into the hall when she paused, thinking quickly. If someone had gotten to Matt, there was a chance they'd already managed to get inside the house.

They could be here now, coming for her.

Holding her pistol up in front of her, she slowly eased her head through the door frame, looking down the hall to the stairs.

Nothing. The hall was clear.

Not about to take it for granted that would continue to be the case, Elena quickly and silently moved into the hall, her gun poised and ready to be aimed at the slightest sign of motion. She headed for the stairs, checking open doorways along the way, then made her way down to the first level. Nothing stirred. Keeping her breathing as silent as possible, she didn't hear a single sound in the house or from outside. The quiet only made her more nervous. It was almost *too* quiet, unnervingly so.

At the bottom of the stairs, the front door beckoned to her. She ignored it. She couldn't go out the front. It was too open; she'd be entirely exposed. Not to mention this could be a trap. Someone could be trying to lure her out of the house, and if so, they'd likely be waiting out there, maybe even by one of the sides of the door, waiting for her to open it, ready to ambush her. She had no choice but to go out there—as long as there was a chance that Matt was vulnerable, hurt, she had to do something—but if this were a trap, she was going to do her best to avoid it. She'd go out the back, stick to the darkness along the side of the house. While there might be someone out there, it would give her the best chance to remain as unseen as possible.

Once she had a plan, she executed it quickly, hurrying to the kitchen. The door was already slightly ajar, drawing her to a halt. What did that mean? *Was* there someone in the house?

If so, that was more reason than ever to get out.

Moving to the open doorway, she pressed herself against the wall and looked out. There was no one lying in wait, at least not on that side. They could still be on the other.

Only one way to find out.

Taking a breath, she raised the gun next to her head, then reached for the doorknob.

One…two…

Three.

She whipped the door open, jumping out and aiming her weapon at the side she'd been unable to check.

Nothing. There was no one there.

She didn't waste time letting relief sink in, instantly moving forward and around the house.

When she made it to the front, she stopped at the corner, her eyes immediately going to the spot where she'd seen the man. It took her a few seconds to make him out, but he was there, exactly where he'd been before. She quashed every instinct that wanted to rush to his side. That was exactly what she couldn't do, of course.

Instead, she moved forward slowly, carefully making her way to the figure, keeping her head moving and her eyes shifting in every direction at all times, not about to let anyone sneak up on her.

All the while, she kept glancing back at the man, constantly checking if she could make out his face, her heart climbing higher and higher in her throat the closer and closer she came.

And then she was there. Close enough. She saw his face.

She lurched to a stop, the shock of it too great to let her feel any relief.

The man on the ground wasn't Matt.

No. It was Travis.

Travis, dressed entirely in black, lay on the ground. Travis, unblinking, stared sightlessly up at the sky.

Travis, mouth agape with horror, had a hole in the middle of his forehead.

A gunshot, she realized, staring in disbelief at the horrible sight. That must have been what woke her. She'd heard the gunshot. But who could have done this? And where was Matt—

"Drop it," a voice ordered behind her, snapping her out of her daze. The command was punctuated by the sound of a weapon being cocked.

The voice sent relief rushing through her, because she recognized it too well.

Oh, thank God.

"I said drop it," the man repeated, the voice unmistakably that of Sheriff Walt Bremer.

She opened her fingers and let the pistol tumble from it.

He slowly shifted in front of her, allowing her to see she hadn't been mistaken.

"Don't move," he ordered. With one quick motion, he kicked the gun away. Keeping both his eyes and his weapon on her at all times, Walt slowly moved to where he'd kicked the gun, then bent to retrieve it, shoving it into the back of his waistband.

His eyes glittered with coldness and…something else.

He reached down to his belt with his free hand, grabbed a pair of handcuffs, then threw them at her feet. "Put those on."

Her relief instantly died, replaced with fresh fear. His deputy was dead. Walt already thought she'd killed Bobby. He probably thought she'd killed Travis, too.

"I didn't do this," she said quickly but firmly.

Walt simply gestured toward the cuffs with a jut of his chin. "Put 'em on."

There didn't seem to be any point in arguing, not with that look in his eyes, not with the gun he kept on her with unwavering focus. Heck, he might just be looking for a reason to pull the trigger. She definitely wouldn't be able to defend herself if she was dead.

She bent down to retrieve the cuffs, moving slowly to demonstrate she wasn't going to try anything and wasn't a threat. The metal was cold in her hands. She carefully locked one cuff around her left wrist, then moved to fasten the other.

"Tighter," he barked out.

Biting her tongue, she complied, squeezing the cuffs until they were taut against her wrists, yet not tight enough to dig into her skin. That didn't make them feel any less unbearable. She'd imagined the moment Walt would take her away in cuffs, of course, the image haunting her. But never had she pictured it like this. And, of course, she'd imagined Travis would be there in an entirely different context, grinning smugly the whole way.

"I didn't shoot Travis," Elena tried again.

One corner of his mouth tilted upward in a humorless smile. "Sure you did, Elena. You and your boyfriend. It's the only explanation. Travis here had the two of you under surveillance. He saw you were about to run and tried to stop you. The two of you got away. It's clear as day. Nobody will have any trouble believing it."

The straightforward way he laid it out made it seem eminently reasonable. Listening to him tell it, she almost might have believed it, too. Except for one thing.

"But I didn't get away," she pointed out, even as a warning bell was clanging in the back of her mind, even as the puzzle pieces were clicking into place and she understood that she was in even more trouble than she'd imagined. "I'm still here."

"Are you?" Walt simply smiled, as though they were sharing a private joke, or maybe he was telling one and waiting for her to get the punchline. Which she already had, she acknowledged, as she realized what she'd deduced had to be true.

This was bad. So very bad.

Because the only thing worse than Walt believing she was guilty of a second murder...

Was if he was the killer himself.

Chapter Fifteen

"*You* killed Travis."

There was no need to say it. She already knew it was true. It was the only possible explanation, the only thing that made any sense. Except it didn't make sense, not at all. Part of her really did need him to confirm it, that this was really happening.

Walt smirked. "Why would I do something like that?"

"You tell me," she shot back, desperately needing him to, desperately needing to understand any of this.

The smirk didn't fade, but there was still a perceptible change in his demeanor, his expression hardening, his eyes growing colder. "It's time to end this. I've waited long enough."

"For what?"

His expression barely changed, but something in the way he looked at her made her skin crawl. "You'll find out soon enough."

He was clearly insane. She couldn't believe he'd simply murdered Travis like that in cold blood.

No, not just Travis, she suddenly knew, the knowledge hitting her hard. He must have also—

"You killed Bobby."

He raised one shoulder and tipped his head slightly, as if it were nothing. The gesture was so infuriatingly casual her anger spiked.

"Why?" she demanded.

He shook his head. "Bobby had that damn fool idea about digging up the back of the spread. I couldn't let him do that. I couldn't let him dig up what's out there."

That was what this was all about? "What's out there?"

"Souvenirs. Big Jim was a fool, too, liked to keep his women close. Buried them on his own damn property. Of course, he never thought anyone would be digging out there. He certainly didn't count on dying as young as he did."

Souvenirs? Women? Buried on the property? It felt as if he was talking in riddles. She wished he would just cut to the chase and spill it already.

Only one thing was clear enough. Walt had killed Bobby. He was behind all of this.

Which still didn't make any sense. She thought of the reason she'd dismissed him as a possible suspect. "I don't understand. If you killed Bobby, you must have had the murder weapon the whole time. Why not just plant it and arrest me?"

"Because I didn't want to arrest you. I just wanted you to look guilty enough that everybody would believe you ran to escape justice when you disappeared."

"Disappeared?" she echoed faintly.

Still smiling, his eyes stroked over her, trailing down her body with a thoroughness and such open interest she went cold from head to toe. "I've been waiting for this for a long time."

Oh, God. "Waiting for what?" she said warily, fearing she already knew.

"You're a beautiful woman, Elena. Grew up real nice. Your mother was beautiful, too. You look a lot like her."

It didn't occur to her to question why he was bringing up her mother. She automatically knew. He was talking about making her disappear. Her mother had disappeared, no one questioning that she'd run away. And Elena knew, the realization hitting her like a blow straight to the gut.

"My mother didn't run away. You killed her." And not just her, Elena knew, her horror growing. The other women who'd gone missing, possibly victims of a serial killer.

Big Jim's women. His souvenirs. Buried out in the back of the spread.

So that was it. What Walt had been worried Bobby would dig up. The reason he'd had to die.

His smile deepened, the sight piercing her numbness and filling her with sudden rage. "She was so beautiful," he said wistfully, his gaze growing dreamy and distant. "Normally we wouldn't have taken someone so close to home, someone we knew, someone we knew had people who would miss her. But she was just so beautiful. Jim wanted her bad. So did I. Finally, we just had to have her."

He lapsed into silence, not elaborating on what had happened then. He didn't have to, as Elena saw his smile, the gleam in his eye, the sheer grotesque happiness he displayed as he remembered. Elena felt bile rise in her throat and nearly gagged, from horror, from revulsion, at the idea of what must have been done to her mother at those men's hands.

For just a moment, guilt surged from the pit of her stomach, washing over her, nearly overwhelming her. She'd spent practically her whole life hating her mother, believing she'd left them, left *her*. And she'd been dead the whole time, taken away by this monster.

This monster who now wanted her.

The reminder brought her crashing back to reality. She was the one now facing those same dire straits her mother once had. She had no trouble believing Walt was capable of making it look like she'd run away. He'd done it before.

But not before he did God only knew to her.

The hell he will.

Everything within her rejected the idea, a fierce determination gripping her. Teresa Reyes couldn't have known what would happen to her beforehand. Most of the other women probably didn't, either. But Elena did, and she damn well wasn't going down without a fight.

If there was any outward change in her demeanor, Walt didn't react to it. His gaze remained far away, that despicable smile on his face. Elena wondered if it would be possible to make a move while his attention was elsewhere, distracted by his own disgusting thoughts. Maybe she could go for the gun—

Whether she tensed or he simply realized he'd let his mind wander too long, Walt suddenly sharpened his focus, his eyes narrowing on her face, the gun centering on her chest.

"And now it's time for you to go," he said.

"Do you really expect me to just go with you willingly, knowing what you intend to do to me?"

"I think you will. Because if you don't cooperate, I'll kill your boyfriend."

Matt. Fresh shock rolled through her. It seemed impossible, but somehow, in the midst of processing the truth about Walt, about her mother, she'd forgotten about him.

"Where's Matt?"

Walt waved with his free hand. "Right over there."

Elena whipped her head in the direction he indicated.

It took her a moment to spot him in the dark. Once she finally saw him, she nearly shuddered with relief. He was lying on his side, facing her, his arms bound behind his back. She tried to see if he was injured, still breathing—

His eyelids suddenly popped open, his gaze meeting hers.

His eyes weren't easily visible in the dark, but she could make them out, his stare direct and purposeful. He glanced toward Walt, then back at her. She quickly interpreted the silent message he was sending her.

Keep him talking.

Of course. He was trying to come up with a plan. Maybe he could manage to sneak up on him as long as Walt didn't know he was still awake, or provide some kind of distraction allowing her to act.

She quickly turned back to Walt. "Is that supposed to be an incentive? Obviously you're planning on killing him anyway."

"Yes, but you want me to delay as long as possible, don't you? The longer I put it off, there's still a chance he can escape, make some big move and save you both, isn't there?" His tone was plainly mocking, making it clear how likely he thought that would be. "That's what he's doing over there, isn't he? Trying to come up with a plan?" He turned slightly as though to include Matt in the conversation. "I know you're conscious, Alvarez. Good. Let's get this over with."

"What over with?" Elena asked.

"We're getting out of here."

"And going where?"

"You'll find out soon enough." His voice hardened. "Alvarez, I said get up."

After a moment, Matt slowly rose to his feet, no easy task with the use of his arms restricted. He still managed it, keeping his head high and proud, staring down Walt the entire way.

If Walt was at all intimidated, he didn't show it. But then, he was the one with the gun. He jerked his head toward the side. "Come on, the both of you. I had to park far enough away from the house that no one would hear me approach, and I have no intention of carrying you both. Walk."

"And if we refuse?" Matt asked.

"If one of you refuses I'll shoot the other. Nowhere that'll prevent you from walking, but enough that it'll hurt like hell. Shoulder wounds aren't much fun. If you both refuse, you both get shot. Easy as that."

"You won't get away with this," Matt pressed. "I have a contact with the FBI I've been in touch with throughout this. She knows Elena is innocent and she'll know we haven't run. If anything happens to us, she'll be down here in no time, investigating our disappearances."

His eyes narrowed with suspicion, Walt surveyed Matt carefully. "Even if I believe you really do know someone with the FBI, it won't make any difference.

Let her look all she wants. She won't find a trace of you. This isn't my first time. I know how to set up a disappearance and get rid of a body so it won't be found. The FBI's come looking around before and they didn't find a thing. She won't, either."

"Technology's a lot more advanced than it was twenty-five years ago," Elena pointed out. "They have new ways of finding people, bodies. You don't think there's a chance they won't poke around the ranch, maybe find those bodies Big Jim has buried out there?"

"They're not going to dig up the whole ranch on some damn scavenger hunt. I'll take my chances."

"Then what?" she asked. "With Bobby dead and nobody left to carry out his irrigation plan, are you just going to leave those bodies out there?"

"I'll move the bodies soon enough. Should have done it years ago. As soon as enough time has passed and nobody's poking around, I'll take care of it. After you're gone, it'll take some time before the ranch's ownership is settled. It should be vacant for a while. I'll be able to take care of what's out there without anyone noticing."

"Even if you can make it look like we ran, my friend at the FBI isn't going to believe we shot a deputy before running," Matt said.

"Really? Even when Travis was clearly out of control and threatening Elena here? It seems pretty obvious things just got out of hand. Enough people knew what Travis was doing. Now here he is, dressed all in black, the remains of a homemade Molotov cocktail with his fingerprints on it nearby. Anyone can see what he came here to do. You stopped him, there was a struggle, and he got shot. Killing a sheriff's deputy in Texas? That's not something anybody's going to take lightly, no matter the reason. You had to know you were looking at a heap of trouble, and Elena already had enough of her own. It only makes sense you'd run."

The scary thing was, it did make sense hearing him explain it, as he was no doubt prepared to do after they "disappeared" and he had to present this version of events as fact.

"I don't understand," Elena said. "Why did you kill Travis?"

"He was always going to have to die. He was too hell-bent on seeing you pay. Once you disappeared, he would never have stopped trying to track you down, and when the trail got too cold, he might just realize how suspicious that was, might start asking questions. No, he served his purpose, setting up the events that everybody would believe made you run. There wasn't much further damage he could do, not after this. It was time to end this."

She wasn't surprised that he could be so cold-blooded about everything, not with all she now knew him capable of, but it still came as an unpleasant shock to hear anyone discuss killing another person with such an utter lack of feeling. The man truly was insane.

"Now," he said. "Enough talk. Let's go. I haven't got all night."

She and Matt exchanged a glance, clearly having reached the same conclusion. They'd exhausted all their arguments for the time being, and Walt had swatted them away one by one as though they were nothing. There didn't seem to be anything they could do at the moment but comply.

Walt had them walk straight out behind the house and into the pasture beyond. They moved in silence.

Elena spotted the truck long before they arrived at it, the vehicle slowly growing larger as they approached. Her dread grew with every step, her desperation for a plan—any plan—that could get them out of this rising with each second. What would happen when they got there? Would he no longer need Matt to be alive and capable of walking?

No, she realized. She shouldn't have underestimated Walt's laziness. If he killed Matt here, he still would have to get him back out of the truck and carry him to wherever he intended to dispose of his body. His plan required Matt to disappear, seemingly with her. No trace of his body could be found. They had some time.

Just not very much.

They finally made it to the truck. Matt and Elena stopped behind the vehicle and glanced back at him.

Walt was frowning. He eyed the truckbed, then the two of them. She could see his mind working, watched him try to figure out what to do. Elena considered their own options, her thoughts likely leading her to the same place his were. He couldn't have a very steady grip on his weapon while he was driving. If one of them was in the front with him, they could try to make a move, go for the gun or the wheel. If it was her, he'd be more hesitant to shoot, not wanting to kill her, not before he could do what he wanted with her. If it was Matt, he would be even stronger, have more of a chance to fight back. And if one of them was in the back, they could try to jump out and make a run for it. Or better yet, they could hop out the side and try to get into the driver's side to him and the gun.

They were all good possibilities—for them, offering at least a chance. So she wasn't surprised when he didn't go with any of them.

Walt reached into his pocket with his free hand and pulled out his keys. He tossed them at Elena's feet. "You're driving. Alvarez, you're in the middle, and I'm riding shotgun." His lips curled back, revealing a lot of teeth. "Literally. I'm going to have my gun in your side the whole time. Elena, you try anything funny behind the wheel, and I pull the trigger. Alvarez, you try making a move, same result. Got it?"

Elena swallowed hard, her heart plummeting. Walt might be lazy and deranged, but he wasn't completely stupid. It was the best scenario—for him at least, keeping them both firmly under control.

Walt was still waiting for an answer. There was just one problem with his plan. She raised her bound wrists. "How am I supposed to drive with these on?"

He eyed her for a long moment, as though wondering if she was trying to pull something. Or maybe he just wasn't happy about having a big flaw in his plan pointed out.

In one swift motion he reached down to his belt, unhooked one key from a loop and tossed it onto the ground in front of her with the keys to the truck. "There," he said. "Unlock the cuffs, but don't even think of trying anything."

Elena made herself nod, unable to squelch a tiny sense of triumph. It would be much more possible to do something with her hands free. What that would be, she didn't know. It wasn't much, but it was a start.

"Okay," he said. "Let's get going."

He motioned to the keys, and Elena slowly bent to retrieve them. When she had the handcuffs off, she tossed them back to him on the ground in front of him, then reached for the keys to the truck. Once she had them in hand, Walt gestured for her to go to the driver's side, Matt to head to the passenger's. Once they'd done as ordered, Walt fell into step behind Matt, keeping his gun aimed at his back.

With numb fingers Elena opened the door. She was about to climb inside when the passenger door opened, Matt standing on the other side. Their eyes met across the length of the cab. He gave a barely perceptible nod, his gaze narrowed and hard, his expression resolute. It was a signal to her, an indication he had a plan and everything was going to be all right.

And she knew, her heart stopping dead in her chest. He was going to try something. He was going to make a move or go for the gun or…something. Something reckless and stupid that would put him in danger, all with the intention of trying to save her.

Staring at him in shock, she almost shook her head. She didn't want him risking his life for her, damn well didn't want him *sacrificing* it.

Even if she'd been foolish enough to try to communicate a message to him, she didn't get a chance. He ducked his head and climbed into the cab, sliding across the seat to the middle. Walt followed quickly behind.

Elena had no choice but to get in, too. She landed right beside Matt, their thighs and arms squeezed tightly together. The feel of him there offered no comfort, only reminding her of how much danger he was in.

Closing the door, she slowly stuck the key in the ignition and started the engine. "Where are we going?" Elena asked, trying to keep her voice steady.

"I'll let you know. Just head straight."

She did as he said, shifting the vehicle into Drive and pressing down on the gas, sending the truck straight on into the night.

They drove across the back pasture, out into the heart of the spread. Elena might not know exactly where he was taking them, but she could imagine too well. The back acreage offered access to a vast number of isolated spots—both on the property and beyond—where no one would notice them heading, and where Matt could disappear with little hope of being discovered for a very long time, if ever. And then Walt would have her all to himself.

She continued to go through every available option. There had to be something, anything, she could do.

If she slammed on the brakes, Walt could be startled into pulling the trigger. All that would result in was Matt being shot. She wouldn't be able to do anything, not for him, not to Walt with an injured Matt between them.

If she suddenly swerved in either direction, same result. Walt startled into firing, Matt shot, her helpless. No good.

What if—

Matt bumped his knee into hers twice, the action deliberate enough to let her know it was no accident.

She tried not to betray a single reaction, giving no indication she'd noticed the gesture.

Out of the corner of her eye, she saw him tilt his head slightly to the left. A few seconds later he repeated the motion, again leaving her no doubt it was no accident.

She glanced down. He made a tiny, downward motion with his hand.

Nothing else immediately followed, leaving her pondering the meaning behind his cues.

Something…left and down. What could that mean? Obviously he wanted her to do something.

He bumped her with his elbow, nudging her toward the door.

Left. Down. Door.

No.

She couldn't be reading him correctly. He couldn't possibly want her to do what she thought he did.

Because if she was correct, he wanted her to jump out of the truck.

Under different circumstances, she might have gawked at him. If that was what he wanted her to do, then he was out of his mind. What good could that do? She wasn't concerned about her own safety. Falling out of a moving vehicle would hurt, but at this speed, she would be fine. And if it would save him, she would do it. But if she threw the door open and suddenly fell out, he would immediately shoot Matt.

Or would he?

Jumping out of the truck wouldn't jostle him the way hitting the brakes or swerving would. It would surprise him, but not in the same way. It would take him a second to understand what was happening, to react to it. Which meant he likely wouldn't pull the trigger right away. No, there would be that split-second delay, which Matt might be able to use to his advantage to do…something.

Maybe. He still had his hands fastened behind his back after all.

It was a big hurdle, possibly an insurmountable one. Frankly, she couldn't see how he'd overcome it—

Matt nudged her again with his elbow. Harder this time. Insistent.

She wanted to nudge him back—hard—but was afraid Walt would notice. They were lucky he hadn't called them on any of these signals yet.

She had to trust he was right on this. And she did, to a degree. She trusted he believed this would save her. She just didn't trust he intended for it to do the same for him.

It couldn't happen. She couldn't lose him. They hadn't come this far, found each other again after so long, only for her to lose him now.

Still, she couldn't delay forever. They had every reason to believe that Matt was already living on borrowed time. Walt could very well intend their destination, wherever it was, to serve as Matt's final resting place. She saw the way Walt kept leaning forward slightly and glancing over at her. He couldn't keep his eyes off her. How had she never noticed how creepy the way he looked at her was? Whether he'd managed to hide it better before, he wasn't now. He wanted her alone, to have her all to himself. Which meant Matt's time was running out.

No, wherever they were going, she had to act before they got there.

She had to do this.

She quickly went through everything she had to do. It was simple really. Grab the doorknob. Open the door. Fall out. Whatever Matt had planned, that would be the tricky part.

She could do this. She *had* to do this.

She braced herself against the door.

It happened in seconds, faster than she'd imagined.

She grabbed the handle.

The door popped open.

She tumbled out, her leg slamming against the door as she went.

She barely noticed it, because it seemed that almost instantly she hit the ground, the landing jarring every bone in her body. Weeds and shrubs hit her, scratched her, as she rolled over and over, dirt filling her nose and eyes.

She finally managed to slow her momentum, until she flopped over onto her back and landed. Coughing, blinking to clear her vision, she immediately pushed herself up, ignoring the aches and pains in her bones and hand, seeking out the truck.

Then she saw it, still rumbling along, but gradually slowing, the driver's-side door hanging open. It was too far away for her to make out what was happening in the cab.

Elena pushed herself all the way to her feet, preparing to break into a run. She had to try to help Matt. She couldn't let Walt hurt him.

A gunshot rang out.

She'd just begun moving. Instead, she stumbled to a stop, her whole body tensing in horror.

No.

It couldn't be. Matt had somehow managed to get the gun away. Nothing else was possible. He couldn't have been shot. He couldn't be hurt or bleeding or gone....

Her legs nearly gave way and she almost fell to her knees.

Her vision began to burn again, harder this time, no longer from the dust, but from the sheer agony gripping her body, squeezing her heart, compressing her lungs.

She remembered this feeling. It felt as if she was dying.

The way she'd felt the first time she'd lost him.

The seconds ticked by. She needed to move. She needed to go and see.

But somehow, no matter how hard she tried, she couldn't compel her body to move. Because if something had happened to him, she couldn't face it, not losing him, not forever.

Once again she wouldn't have gotten to say goodbye.

The truck continued to roll forward, still slowing gradually, its progress across the flat earth eerie in the moonlight.

Suddenly, as though hitting an invisible wall, it slammed to a halt.

She waited. If Walt stepped out of the truck, she would need to run. Even if she hardly felt the need to fight anymore.

Then she heard it.

"Elena!"

She recognized the voice immediately.

Matt. It was Matt.

The air wheezed from her lungs.

He didn't sound hurt. He sounded fine. He sounded safe.

She lunged into motion, running the rest of the way to the truck as fast and as hard as her legs could carry her, stumbling and lurching the whole way.

Then she was there, at the still-open driver's-side door.

And found herself staring at Matt's back and cuffed wrists.

She gaped in disbelief, not understanding what she was seeing.

He sat in the driver's seat, his back to the open doorway. She peered over his shoulder. Walt was slumped in his seat, his chin to his chest, clearly unconscious.

"How did you—"

Matt glanced back at her, meeting her eyes. "Go around the other side and get the keys to the cuffs," he said. "I need you to unfasten mine and get a pair on this bastard before he wakes up."

She wasted no time doing exactly that, hurrying around the front of the truck to the passenger side. Walt's arm and shoulder were against the door, so she opened it slowly, careful not to jar him or let him fall out. When she had the door open, she leaned in and over him. She spotted the keys looped to Walt's belt, along with another pair of cuffs, maybe the ones she'd taken off. Grabbing the cuffs, she fastened them on Walt's wrists—extra tight, just the way he liked them. Without bothering to close the door, she took the keys and raced back to the other side.

As soon as she was there, Matt shifted to allow her easy access to the cuffs. She had them open in ten seconds flat.

Then he was shifting in the seat, sliding out of the cab, stepping onto the ground and forward to catch her in his arms.

Elena threw her arms around him, sagging against him.

"I don't understand. How did you do it?"

"My hands were bound, so I had to use my feet. As soon as you opened the door and I saw his head turn, I twisted and slid over onto the driver's side and started kicking, going for the gun first, then his head."

She gaped at him in horror. "He could have shot you."

"But he didn't."

"You're out of your mind."

"It worked, didn't it?"

"You're lucky it did."

"I was thinking earlier we were due a little luck, weren't we?"

As she looked into the humor laughing in his eyes, she couldn't help it. A laugh escaped her lips, too. "I guess you're right."

Yes, she thought, after everything they'd been through in the past few days, it had been time for something to go their way. And it had. It hardly seemed possible, but they'd made it. They'd won. They were still standing.

Together.

Chapter Sixteen

Elena stood on the back porch and stared out into the night. It was a clear, warm evening. A multitude of stars glittered in the inky-black sky, and the moon cast its glow upon the land that stretched before her as far as the eye could see. Weston land. Her land now, though not for long. She'd wanted to leave here for so long. The ranch had been connected with so much unhappiness for her—more than she'd even known—but she couldn't deny the beauty of the land.

It was a lovely night. Peaceful. So peaceful that it was almost impossible to believe the ranch had been the scene of so much activity and turmoil in the past few days.

In the wake of Walt's attack, Matt had wasted no time contacting his friend Pam with the FBI, wanting someone on their side as they dealt with the aftermath. With a deputy dead and the sheriff responsible, they knew they were going to need all the help they could find to get anyone to believe their story and take their word over his. Pam had made the initial contact with the state authorities, who had quickly descended on the scene. Pam had arrived soon afterward with several of her own colleagues, the Bureau's standing investigation into the missing women and possible serial killer giving them some claim for jurisdiction in the case.

As expected, the state authorities had initially been hesitant to believe Matt and Elena over Walt, with his long history in law enforcement. But there was too much about the circumstances of that night that didn't line up with his version of events, like why Matt and Elena would have driven off with him instead of killing him like Travis if they were the killers. A search of his home turned up additional evidence that Walt had been involved in Big Jim's murderous activities—and had continued on his own in the years since. It seemed Big Jim wasn't the only one who liked to keep souvenirs close at hand.

It hadn't taken the crime scene investigators long to find where Big Jim had buried the bodies of his and Walt's victims on the ranch property. Elena had been there when the remaining bones had started to be uncovered. It would be some time before the bodies were accurately identified, if they ever could be, and there was no way of knowing yet whether Teresa Reyes was among them. Elena was aware of that. She hadn't cared. After all the times she'd hated her mother for leaving them, blamed her for what her father had become, wondered how she could have abandoned her child, she'd needed to be there. So when the first bones began to emerge, she'd been there to witness it, tears in her eyes, trying to hold back the sobs, until they'd finally broken free and Matt had taken her in his arms and held her while she wept.

He'd been by her side that day, and every day since that night, her only constant in a world that seemed to have turned upside down on her. She didn't know what she would have done without him. She hoped to never have to experience that again.

Even as she thought it, she heard the screen door behind her squeal softly as it was opened. She didn't have to look to see who it was. Even if there was anyone else it could have been, she had no trouble recognizing him, her body instantly responding to his nearness, attuned to his presence on a molecular level that was undeniable.

He didn't say anything as he came up behind her and wrapped his arms around her waist. She leaned back against him, resting her head on his shoulder, sinking into the sensations of his body and his touch as her eyes drifted shut.

"Hey," he murmured against her hair. "You okay?"

"Yeah," she whispered back. "Just thinking."

"Having second thoughts?"

"No." The land might be beautiful, but more than ever she knew she couldn't stay here. Selling was the right thing to do.

In the midst of everything that had happened, she hadn't had a chance to contact Glen until tonight to see if his offer still stood. He'd admitted that he hadn't been certain he still wanted to buy the ranch, now that he knew the truth about Big Jim. Elena had guessed as much when he hadn't tried to contact her himself sooner. She wouldn't have blamed him for taking back his offer, though she would have been disappointed. It was only natural that the property would be tainted in a lot of people's minds due to what had happened here. If Glen no longer wanted it, it could take her a long time to find another buyer.

Fortunately, Glen had decided to continue with the

sale. Big Jim may not have been the man he'd believed him to be, but that didn't change the work generations of Westons had put into the land. Junior and Bobby had still been his friends, practically his sons, and for their sake, he would go forth with his original plan to try to maintain the property, the way they would have wanted.

And she had a feeling he would have a much better time of it. Matt had told her about Jack's belief that the place had bad vibes. Elena wasn't sure she believed in that, but she had to admit that in the days since the bodies had been removed from the property, the ranch felt different. Happier.

"And you're really sure about letting this place go?"

She nodded. "I'm sure." Even if the ranch wasn't connected with so much unhappiness for her, Bobby had given his heart and soul to running it and he hadn't been able to make it work. There was little chance she could succeed where he'd failed, especially when she wasn't nearly as invested. Glen would have a much better chance of doing something worthwhile with the ranch than she ever could. "It's the right thing to do. And the amount of money Glen's offering should be enough to pay off the remaining debts here, with enough left over for me to start over somewhere else."

"Where do you want to go?" he asked softly.

It was a very good question. "I'm not sure," she admitted. "I haven't really had a chance to think about it."

She just knew she needed to get away from Western Bluff. The past few days had made that clear enough. No one had apologized for their suspicions or the way they'd acted toward her. If anything, things were just as tense and uncomfortable as they'd been immediately after Bobby's murder. A lot of people were still avoiding her or looked away when they saw her in town, but now it was more out of embarrassment than distrust.

The only exception had been Lynda Clayton. After the news had gotten out about the true fate of Elena's mother, Lynda had arrived on her doorstep, tears in her eyes.

"Does Henry know you're here?" Elena had been unable to keep from asking.

"I don't know, and I don't care," she'd said without hesitation.

Her tone was honest enough Elena hadn't doubted she meant it. Still, she hadn't known quite what to do as Lynda had stared at her, her eyes poring over Elena's face with unnerving scrutiny, the tears coming harder.

"You look like her," Lynda had finally whispered.

The wrenching pain in her voice had cracked something open in Elena and suddenly she'd been crying, too. She'd barely known how to begin grieving for her mother, a woman who'd been gone most of her life and whom she hardly remembered. But seeing Lynda's profound anguish had somehow released Elena's own sorrow. This woman she barely knew, who'd brought Matt back into her life, was the only person grieving her mother, too, who cared about her as a person. Even more, she was the only one who could tell her about Teresa. Her tears flowing freely, Elena had automatically opened her arms, and Lynda had fallen into them. They'd clung together for a while before going inside for a long talk. Lynda had shared just a fraction of her memories, and for the first time Elena had been able to learn about who Teresa had been. Not just the abstract idea of a mother who hadn't been there, but the real flesh-and-blood woman she was. They'd talked for hours, and Elena knew that wherever she went, her newfound relationship with Lynda was one connection to the town she would keep.

It was likely to be the only one. Once the ranch was sold there would be nothing keeping her here. She could go practically anywhere. She had a college degree she'd never used. She could start a career like she'd always dreamed of, doing almost anything she wanted. The vast number of possibilities that lay before her were overwhelming.

This was what she'd wanted practically her entire life, to get away from this town. And now that the moment was finally here and the whole world was available to her, she didn't know where she wanted to go.

There was only one thing she did know: wherever she went, she wanted it to be with Matt.

She opened her mouth to say just that when he reached over and turned her to face him.

She peered up into his eyes, her heart leaping into her throat at the sight of him and the intensity in his gaze.

"Come with me."

Past and present merged in front of her. She'd lived this moment before. Yet here it was again, a second chance she'd never dreamed possible.

"Where?" she asked, suddenly breathless.

"Wherever I go."

"Back to New Mexico?"

He hesitated, then lifted one shoulder in a helpless little shrug. "To start. I want you to meet everybody there. But maybe not forever. Like I told you, I don't know if I want to work on the Triple C the rest of my life, not to mention I can't imagine there being enough for you to do there. Maybe I want my own place. Maybe I should try something new. I don't know where I'm going any more than you do. But I know I want you with me. If you'll have me."

It was exactly what he'd offered her before, exactly what she'd feared the most. A life of uncertainty. It wasn't what she'd dreamed of, it wasn't what she'd ever wanted for her life.

But this time she wasn't afraid. How could she be? After everything they'd been through, everything they'd overcome, she couldn't imagine anything that they couldn't deal with together. And second chances were so rare in this life. She wasn't about to let this one get away.

"Yes," she said, happiness soaring through her. The feeling only grew, surging higher and fiercer as she watched the smile dawn on his face, the sheer joy in his eyes.

He lunged forward and caught her in his arms, lifting her straight off her feet and pulling her tight against him.

Laughing, Elena held on to him just as tightly, never wanting to let go, knowing she never would. The future lay before them, vast and unknown, not scary, but thrilling.

Because they didn't need certainty. They didn't need a plan.

They needed only love. And each other.

They had that.

And she couldn't wait to discover the beautiful future they'd find together.

* * * * *

"That shouldn't have happened," she said, her voice not much louder than a whisper.

"No. It shouldn't have." He didn't try to kiss her again.

She leaned her head against his chest. "It won't happen again."

"Count on it." He held her into the night as she fell into a troubled sleep. She clung to him, her body shaking, her head twisting back and forth as nightmares disturbed her slumber.

In the small hours of the morning, Pierce spooned her body against his, his gaze on the dying embers of the fire, his thoughts swirling around the shooting, the dirt bike, Roxanne and the bullet and wrapper they'd found in the cave.

Sleep escaped him with her body close to his and the wad of evidence in his pocket. The more he mulled over everything, the more dread filled his chest, crushing him with worry.

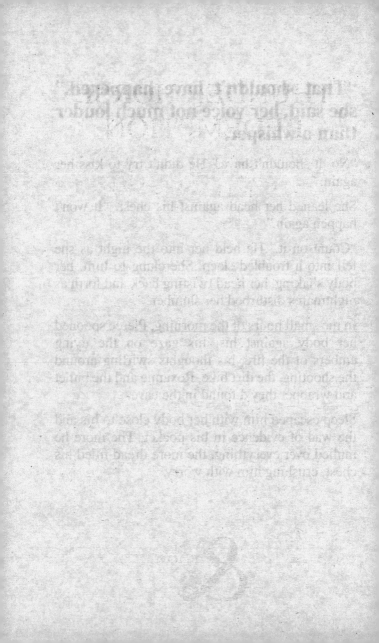

THUNDER HORSE REDEMPTION

BY

ELLE JAMES

MILLS & BOON

First published in Great Britain 2013
by Mills & Boon, an imprint of Harlequin (UK) Limited,
Eton House, 18-24 Paradise Road, Richmond, Surrey TW9 1SR

© Mary Jernigan 2012

ISBN: 978 0 263 90634 9
ebook ISBN: 978 1 472 01200 5

46-0613

Harlequin (UK) policy is to use papers that are natural, renewable and recyclable products and made from wood grown in sustainable forests. The logging and manufacturing processes conform to the legal environmental regulations of the country of origin.

Printed and bound in Spain
by Blackprint CPI, Barcelona

A Golden Heart Award winner for Best Paranormal Romance in 2004, **Elle James** started writing when her sister issued a Y2K challenge to write a romance novel. She has managed a full-time job and raised three wonderful children, and she and her husband even tried their hands at ranching exotic birds (ostriches, emus and rheas) in the Texas Hill Country. Ask her, and she'll tell you what it's like to go toe-to-toe with an angry 350-pound bird! After leaving her successful career in information technology management, Elle is now pursuing her writing full-time. She loves building exciting stories about heroes, heroines, romance and passion. Elle loves to hear from fans. You can contact her at ellejames@earthlink.net or visit her website at www.ellejames.com.

This book is dedicated to the brave men and women who serve our country in the military, in law enforcement and as first responders. Their dedication to making our country and world a better place is selfless and commendable. Thank you.

Chapter One

His tailbone bruised, his thighs protesting the prolonged position, Pierce Thunder Horse shifted in the saddle. He hadn't been on a horse in over two months. There wasn't much call for FBI special agents to saddle up.

His typical visits to the family ranch were short. He loved his mother and brothers and would do anything for them, but the ranch held too many memories. Pierce didn't come home often—it hurt too much.

With Tuck's upcoming wedding, he couldn't avoid returning. The frenetic wedding planning served as a stark reminder of Pierce's own wedding that wasn't. When his mother had mentioned that someone should really check on the local herd of wild horses, Pierce had jumped at the chance to get away from the hubbub. But he'd ridden half of the day and had yet to find the herd. Soon he'd run out of Thunder Horse Ranch property and cross over onto the Carmichael Ranch.

Roxanne Carmichael.

The redheaded hellion, his former fiancée, had been the love of his life. She was also the one who'd called off their wedding when her brother Mason had died on the job, thanks to Pierce's mistake.

His chest tightened, his hands gripping the reins so tightly his knuckles whitened. Why couldn't he locate the blasted herd? He was out here to find the horses, not mull over what had happened.

Every member of the Thunder Horse family had a deep connection to the wild horses of the badlands. They always felt they needed to make sure the herd was healthy and thriving, even though official responsibility for the area's wild horses rested with the representative of the Bureau of Land Management—Roxanne. Damn! Had he really thought riding out to check on the herd would *stop* him from thinking about her? If so, he was a fool. Their love of the wild horses had brought them together.

Pierce remembered as if it had been yesterday the night he and Roxanne had saved a lost horse from a snowstorm. Roxanne had asked Pierce to help her bring the filly to her barn, where they'd nursed her to health and kept her warm and fed until the mare could be located and the two reunited. He'd known Roxanne for years, but that was the first time he'd realized what an amazing woman she'd become. It had been the beginning of their courtship. Eight months later, he'd asked her to marry him. And two months ago, she'd ended it.

Since then, he'd buried himself in his work to avoid the pain, the blame and the loss. He'd made it his objective to dodge memories and force to the back of his mind the date of his own wedding that hadn't happened and never would. But now that he was back at the Thunder Horse Ranch, Pierce had way too much time on his hands. Plus, the ranch carried too many memories—not just of Roxanne, but of Mason, who had been Pierce's friend since they were kids. The familiar settings only managed to dredge the painful memories back to the surface, a constant reminder of his failure professionally and personally.

A cold chill slithered down Pierce's back, chasing away the warmth of an early summer day in the North Dakota badlands.

He glanced up at the position of the sun as it dropped toward the horizon, his gaze lowering to the landscape. Nothing moved and only the sound of his horse's hooves clomping against the ground and the creak of leather interrupted his tumultuous thoughts.

With the sun so close to setting, Pierce wasn't going to find the herd and still have time to return to the ranch house before dark. Pierce had tugged his reins to the left, aiming the horse toward the barn, when a loud bang ripped through the silence.

Was that gunfire?

Bear, his stallion, danced beneath him, whinnying his fright.

Pierce spun back around and squinted against the setting sun, his gaze panning the prairie. Firing a weapon on the plains was rare but not unheard of, although it wasn't hunting season. Should he check it out? The sound had come from somewhere on the Carmichael Ranch. He hesitated, not at all anxious to cross over onto Carmichael property. He couldn't see anything, but his gut told him someone could be in trouble.

Another shot rang out.

Pierce nudged his horse.

Already nervous, Bear leaped forward, his legs stretching into a gallop, eating up the distance on the sparsely vegetated ground between him and whoever was shooting.

A smudge rose above the landscape, capturing Pierce's attention. From this distance, he couldn't tell if it was smoke or dust.

If the cloud was smoke, it meant a wildfire on the prairie.

The puff grew as Pierce approached. In the middle of the cloud of dirt rising from the dry prairie grass, a horse and rider emerged, riding hell-for-leather.

The rider leaned far forward, almost one with the horse, urging it faster.

As they neared, Pierce made out a small vehicle in pursuit. A dirt bike, the man steering it bent low over the handlebar.

As the horse and rider approached, the cowboy's hat flew from her head and a mass of deep auburn hair spilled out, flowing behind her.

Pierce couldn't mistake that red hair. It had to be Roxanne Carmichael, riding like her life depended on it.

His heart thumped, pressing hard against his ribs, making it difficult for him to breathe. Every instinct to protect what had once been his reared up in Pierce's consciousness. He spurred his mount to move faster.

Before he could reach her, another shot rang out and nicked the hindquarters of Roxanne's mare.

Already in a state of agitation, the horse bucked, then reared so suddenly that Roxanne toppled from the saddle, landing hard, flat on her back.

The mare took off, racing away from the dirt bike, leaving Roxanne at the mercy of the shooter.

The dirt bike, which had stopped while the driver fired his gun, now roared toward her again, speed increasing instead of decreasing, aiming directly for the woman lying on the ground.

At the last moment Roxanne rolled to the side, avoiding being hit.

Still too far away to intervene, Pierce pulled his rifle from the scabbard on his saddle and fired a round into the air. At the same time he dug his heels into Bear's flanks, pushing him to close the distance.

The shooter slowed and spun the bike to face Pierce, his dark helmet hiding his face. He lifted his hand, pointing it toward Pierce.

Sun glinted off the metal of the pistol he carried.

Pierce yanked Bear's reins to the side, forcing the animal to zigzag toward his target.

Another shot rang out.

Pierce answered, firing his rifle, careful to aim high to avoid hitting Roxanne. With the horse's movements the shot could go just about anywhere. All he might hope for was to scare the bastard away.

When Pierce didn't back down, the man on the bike spun his vehicle, the rear tire skidding sideways, kicking up dust in a dense cloud. The rider sped off across the prairie in the opposite direction. Within seconds, he disappeared over a rise, leaving a faint haze of dust in his wake.

Pierce raced to where Roxanne lay on the ground, ignoring the instinct pressing him to pursue the rider. His own need to find and capture the man who'd shot at Roxanne mattered far less than making sure Roxanne herself wasn't badly injured. He jerked back hard on the reins, forcing his horse to rear and spin all in one motion. As soon as Bear's hooves touched ground, Pierce flung himself out of the saddle and ran toward Roxanne.

She lay flat on her back, cursing beneath her breath.

Pierce let out the gulp of air he'd been holding and chuckled. She couldn't be hurt badly if she had the energy and wherewithal to form coherent curses.

Roxanne pressed her fingers to the bridge of her nose, her eyes squeezed shut. "Did you get the license plate of the truck that hit me?" she asked.

Dropping to his knees beside her, Pierce ran his hands over her arms and legs, searching for fractured bones.

"I'm pretty sure there's nothing broken," she said, pushing his hands away as her eyes fluttered open. "Hello, Pierce." Her wide blue gaze was cool and wary. It hit Pierce like a gut punch to see her look at him with none of the warmth or love he'd cherished. He reminded himself that he was lucky she was even talking to him. After what he'd done, he wouldn't blame her if she never spoke to him again.

His chest tightened as his fingers slid up her arms. "Hello, Roxy. Are you okay?" He touched her gently, his hands moving around to the backs of her shoulders to help her sit up.

She leaned away from his touch then swayed and would have fallen back if Pierce hadn't reached behind her and steadied her with his arm. "Just had the wind knocked out of me in that fall. I'll be all right," she replied.

He leaned her against his chest to keep her from toppling over and further injuring herself, his heart clenching at the familiar aroma of her hair—honeysuckle and hay and the incongruous scent of copper, indicating fresh blood. When his right hand pulled away from her shoulder, it was red with her blood. "You've been injured, and not from the fall. Care to tell me how?"

"What?" She stared at the blood on his hand. "I'm bleeding?"

"Yes." He ripped off his denim shirt and the clean white T-shirt beneath, tearing a piece from the hem. He folded the soft fabric into a tight square wad and pressed it to the wound on her left shoulder, frowning of my brothers back to check on her. But right now, you've got a bullet hole in your shoulder, and every sign of a concussion. You need to go where people can take care of you."

"And you think *you* can take care of me?" As soon as the words came out, they both flinched. She knew it was a low blow to throw Mason in Pierce's face, even if he *had* fallen short on his promise to keep her brother safe. They both knew what Pierce had done—he'd never offered any excuses for what had happened to Mason, not even when she'd begged him to explain.

"It's my responsibility to personally verify the status of the wild horses," she said, choosing to change the subject. She glanced behind them as if she could see to where she'd left Sweet Jessie. "I can't just let someone else take care of it." *I've got responsibilities, too,* she wanted to say—but didn't.

"The sooner you stop arguing, the sooner you can get fixed up enough to leave. Until then, you're on *my* horse and we're going to *my* house."

She stared up into his face and recognized that Thunder Horse stubborn streak in the tightness of his jaw. He wasn't going to budge on the matter.

The ache in her head intensified and her shoulder burned where she'd been nicked. She willed herself to be stronger, squeezing closed her eyes as a wave of nausea washed over her. When she opened her eyes, her vision was no less blurry, maybe having something to do with the tears of frustration threatening to fall.

Dear God, she refused to cry in front of Pierce. She'd already spent the past two months crying when no one was looking.

With her horse gone, the shooter still at large and herself just about too tired and bruised to muster up

as he evaluated the injury. It appeared to be just a nick, but it could have been so much worse.

"The shoulder doesn't hurt as bad as the back of my head." She pressed her fingers to the back of her skull.

Pierce brushed her hand aside and parted her hair, finding a soft knot. "More than likely, you'll live. The shot to your shoulder was just a flesh wound. Are you up-to-date on your tetanus shot?"

"Had one a couple weeks ago." She snorted. "Stepped on a nail."

Pierce shook his head. "Sounds like you. You seem to follow trouble."

Roxanne sighed. "Yeah, that's me."

"What just happened here? Why was that man shooting at you?"

She started to shake her head, until the movement made her wince and clutch at the back of her head. "Remember the filly we rescued from the snowstorm two years ago?"

Pierce swallowed hard on the lump clogging his throat, remembering the night he'd fallen in love with Roxanne. "Sweet Jessie?"

"Yeah, that one." Roxanne opened her eyes wide and blinked several times. "I was following Sweet Jessie toward the canyon, hoping she'd lead me to the herd of wild horses, when I heard a shot from behind. I felt a sting and when I turned around, that dirt bike was behind me. I took off, he followed after me… You know the rest."

"Do you have any idea who the biker was?" Pierce hadn't been able to make an identification, but it had been years since he'd lived full-time on the ranch. Roxanne would be more familiar with the locals—and their bikes—than him.

"No." She pinched the bridge of her nose again. "It's a bit blurry. I must have hit the ground pretty hard, just now. I was good until then."

Pierce stared into her eyes. "You could have a concussion. Can you get up on your own?"

"Absolutely." She pushed away from him and staggered to her feet. Then she swayed and her knees buckled, tipping her over into Pierce.

Pierce straightened, then hooked his arm beneath her knees and scooped her up, settling her against his chest. He glanced around, searching for Bear. He gave a short, sharp whistle.

The stallion trotted toward him, snorting and tossing his mane, still hyped up from the mad dash to save Roxanne.

"Easy, *Mato Cikala*." Little Bear. Pierce spoke low and slow in his native Lakota language as he approached the spooked horse, maintaining eye contact with the animal the entire time.

Ultimately, the stallion calmed, his dancing hooves settling to a stop in the dry prairie grass.

Pierce lifted Roxanne up onto the saddle, seating her sideways. He placed her hands on the saddle horn and said, "Hold on."

Roxanne's lips tightened. "I know how to ride a horse."

"I know," he said, before he placed his boot in the stirrup and mounted behind her. Then he slid into the saddle, lifting her to sit across his lap.

"This is silly. I can handle a horse by myself."

"You may be fully capable, but I don't intend to walk all the way to the ranch."

"My mare—"

"Is halfway back to the barn by now." He bit hard

on his tongue to keep from saying more. He knew she didn't want to be anywhere near him, so the least he could do was make the trip as unobtrusive as possible. Besides, when they weren't talking—arguing—he could almost pretend that things were the way they used to be. Pretend she didn't hate him…and that he didn't hate himself.

The stubborn look on her face didn't match the glazed look in her eyes and the way she swayed as she sat there alone.

His heart clinched. "Try not to argue, for once."

"I DON'T ARGUE," SHE muttered, her body naturally leaning against his, despite her better judgment.

With her brain somewhat fuzzy, she had to work to remind herself that Pierce Thunder Horse wasn't someone she could trust.

When she realized he was headed away from her ranch, Roxanne frowned. "You're going the wrong way."

"I'm taking you home with me."

"I can't go home with you! Some maniac is out there on a dirt bike shooting up every rider he sees—I need to get home so I can call the sheriff and tell him what happened. Then I need to check on my horse and make sure she got back safe and isn't badly hurt. And when that's done, I'll need to saddle back up to go check on Sweet Jessie—I think the bullet that winged me migh have hit her, too, but I didn't have a chance to check

"You can call the sheriff from our house—for the good that will do—and you can call your fore to check on your horse. Jim knows your stables a as you do, and he'll be able to take care of the r anything's wrong. As for Sweet Jessie, I'll s

the energy to do anything at all, she decided not to argue with the man. Instead, she clamped shut her lips and tried to keep as far away from Pierce as possible. A difficult task, considering she was sitting in his lap.

After a few minutes, the sway of the horse lulled her into a daze. Giving up the fight, she leaned into his body and stayed there the rest of the ride back to the Thunder Horse Ranch.

The scent of leather and denim and the familiar earthy, musky male aroma set her heart beating faster and heat radiating throughout her body, reminding her of better times and of all they'd lost.

If she hadn't called off the engagement then she and Pierce would have married by now. They might even have had a baby on the way. She'd loved Pierce so much, had been so sure that she'd finally found someone she could count on, someone who could be a real partner in her life as well as a lover. Losing that hope had hurt. It *still* hurt.

A sob rose in her throat, choking off the air to her lungs. Her head aching with each passing mile, Roxanne stiffened and tried to move away from Pierce.

The arm around her tightened, pinning her. Short of making a big fuss and possibly falling off the horse, Roxanne had no choice but to stay put.

Rather than relive their final days as an engaged couple, Roxanne forced herself to think through what had just happened. "What do you think that man was after?" she wondered out loud.

"I don't know, but he seemed pretty determined to shoot you." Pierce's grip tightened on the reins.

The stallion danced sideways, seemingly confused by his rider's instruction to slow.

A slight movement of Pierce's legs, and loosening the reins, set the horse in a forward motion again.

"If someone wanted to shoot me, why would he wait until I was out in the canyon? There are easier ways to find me, in places where he could have gotten close enough to get a much better shot."

Pierce liked that thought even less if the way he tensed was any indication, but before he could reply, the stallion beneath them stumbled, jolting Roxanne. She winced, pressing a hand to the back of her skull. "Ouch. Must have hit my head harder than I thought."

"I'll get the doctor to come out as soon as I've got you settled."

"I'm fine. Just a flesh wound and a bump on the noggin. I'll be back in the saddle by morning."

"Not if you have a concussion." His voice was firm, unyielding. "The doctor will have to clear you to my satisfaction before I let you leave the ranch."

"Hey, get this straight, mister." She poked him in the chest. "The decisions about what I can and cannot do are between me and the doctor. You've got no part in them, or in anything else that has to do with me."

She recognized the mulish expression on his face and knew what he'd say before he even opened his mouth. "When you don't know what's good for you then somebody has to step in."

"*You're* not good for me—we're not good for each other. We can't even ride a couple of miles of trail together without fighting." She took a deep breath, forcing her voice to sound calm, collected. "Just let me go home, Pierce. I'm not your problem anymore, and I can take care of myself. I've been running a ranch by myself for years. I think I can make my own decisions."

Another jolt and the pain reverberating around the

inside of her skull made her cringe. Well, darn it all. Why did she have to be so weak in front of the one man she'd sworn to never show an ounce of vulnerability again?

"Look," Pierce said. "I don't want you at the ranch any more than you want to be there. But I won't let you go home until the doc says you can."

Her chest tightened at his harsh words. Once they could barely stand to be apart. Now they could barely stand to be together. Too much had happened. Irreversible actions and words with permanent consequences. "Okay, I'll stay until the doctor can convince you that I'm all right. Which I am."

Roxanne didn't relish the idea of being at the Thunder Horse Ranch with Pierce there. She'd been over a couple times to meet Tuck's fiancée and get measured for her bridesmaid dress, but she'd left as soon as possible to avoid any chance of running into Pierce.

Why did he have to be the one to find her out in the canyon? Why couldn't it have been Tuck, or one of Pierce's other brothers? Why did her already horrible day have to sink to the new low of having to depend on the man who'd encouraged her brother to join the FBI and then let him die in that explosion?

What had happened had been inexcusable and irreversible. She knew that for sure. Not because of the FBI—the official word they had given her was that Mason's death had been ruled unavoidable.

No. Roxanne knew Pierce was responsible for her brother's death because that was what he had told her himself.

Chapter Two

Pierce insisted on carrying Roxanne into the cavernous great room of the Thunder Horse Ranch house, despite her objections. The feel of her body against his brought back so many memories he could barely breathe.

"I can walk, really." She kicked her legs and pushed against his chest. "Let me down." Twin flags of color rose in her cheeks as he entered the room where two of his brothers and his mother stood gaping at them.

Stopping just inside the entry, Pierce braced himself for the onslaught of questions his family was sure to ask.

His mother was the first to remember her manners. "Roxy, good to see you, sweetie," she said as though it was an everyday occurrence for her son to stroll in carrying his ex-fiancée. "Oh, dear, is that blood?" She lifted a hand to her own cheek, her eyes widening. "For goodness' sake, Pierce, let her have the lounge chair," she commanded. "I'll get some coffee. Maddox, you call Doc Taylor. Pierce, give Dante the details of what happened in case you need his help with anything else."

Pierce smiled despite the gravity of the situation. Though thin and petite, his mother had a will of iron, with a bossy streak to match. She didn't hesitate to tell her boys what to do, no matter that they were all grown men who now towered over her small frame.

"Yeah, what happened?" Dante planted himself in front of Pierce, his gaze taking in the torn shirt and bloodstains. "Are you hurt, too?" His arms crossed over his chest, his eyebrows knitting in a fierce frown, clearly ready to take on anyone who might be a danger to their family.

"I'm fine, Roxanne's the only one hurt," Pierce said. "Found her out on the northernmost corner of the ranch." Pierce's jaw tightened. "Someone was using her for target practice."

"The chair?" Roxanne tipped her head toward the chair Pierce's mother had indicated. "At least put me down. It's not like I can't walk."

"Yeah, why are you carrying her?" Dante asked. "Are her legs injured, too?"

"She's not all that steady on her feet. Her horse threw her and she hit her head. I think she might have a concussion." Pierce relented and eased Roxanne into the chair.

"What were you doing out by the canyons?" Dante asked, turning his focus to Roxanne.

"I was checking on the wild horses." Roxanne sat in the chair, her chin tipped upward, one hand feeling the back of her head. She winced. "I was following Sweet Jessie. I found her by the watering hole near North Canyon. When I went down to check on her, I heard a loud bang. Something stung my arm and almost knocked me out of the saddle. Whatever nicked me, hit Jessie—most likely in the shoulder, but I couldn't say for sure. She might have tripped or been hit because I think I saw her drop to the ground before my mount took off. The shooter came after me. That's when Pierce found us."

Dante swore. "Did you see who it was?"

Roxanne sighed. "No. I didn't. He was on a dirt bike in full-coverage gear, including a helmet."

Tuck entered the room, carrying his baby girl, Lily. "What's going on?"

His beautiful blonde fiancée, Julia Anderson, followed him. When she noticed Roxanne on the chair, she hurried around to stand in front of her. "Good Lord, Roxanne, are you all right?"

Pierce frowned. Apparently the two women had already met while Pierce had been wrapping up his previous assignment in Bismarck. What else had he missed?

Roxanne smiled. "Don't worry, Julia, I'll be fine for the wedding." She pushed against the seat cushions, preparing to stand.

Julia laid a hand on her uninjured shoulder. "I'm not worried about the wedding. I want to know what happened to you. Holy smokes, you're bleeding." Julia reached out to touch Roxanne's other arm where Pierce had wrapped his shirt around her injury.

"It's nothing. Just a flesh wound." Roxanne shot a glance toward Pierce. "Pierce patched me up and it's not bleeding so badly anymore."

The baby, clearly picking up on the distress in Julia's voice, leaned away from Tuck, reaching for her mother.

Julia turned automatically to play with Lily's hands, rather than take the baby, keeping most of her attention on Roxanne. The baby giggled and buried her face in Tuck's shirt.

A sharp pang tugged at Roxanne's gut. She knew things hadn't been easy for Tuck and Julia. A quickie Vegas-style marriage—followed by an even quicker divorce—had separated the couple only hours after they'd met. Tuck hadn't even known their brief union had resulted in a daughter until a few weeks earlier. But now that their differences had been worked out, the little family looked so natural and beautiful together, full of so much love and happiness.

"It doesn't make any sense," Pierce's oldest brother, Maddox, said as he paced the floor. "Who would want to shoot at you?"

"It doesn't make sense to *you*?" Roxanne snorted softly. "I was the one being shot at and it makes no more sense to me. Maybe he wasn't shooting at me at all. He could have been aiming for the horse for a little target practice." Her lips tightened. "There are idiots out there that get a kick out of killing defenseless animals."

Pierce's jaw clenched. "They're idiots, all right, but they're not stupid enough to shoot at the horses in front of a potentially hostile witness. And it's not like he didn't realize you were there. If you were in between the shooter and Sweet Jessie, he had to be shooting at you."

Maddox inhaled and let his breath out slowly. "I'm glad it was only a flesh wound." His shoulders pushed back and he looked around the room at his younger brothers. "We'd better get out there and see if we can find out who did this." He turned to Dante and Tuck. "You two take the truck. I'll take the four-wheeler."

"I'm going by horse." Pierce straightened, anger building with each breath he took. Someone had shot at Roxanne, tried to run over her and almost killed her. The bastard needed to be found. If he'd been faster, smarter…maybe he could have taken the guy into custody back in the canyon. It was his fault Roxanne was still in danger. Pierce should have gone after him while he'd had the chance.

Dante grabbed his cowboy hat from the coat tree in the hallway. "We have to find whoever did this. The prairie and canyons are dangerous enough without people shooting at one of us."

"Who would want to hurt Roxanne?" Tuck handed the baby to Julia, who nestled Lily into the crook of her arm, a frown marring her brow.

"I don't know, but we sure as hell are going to find out." Pierce clamped his hat on his head, grabbed a box of bullets from the gun cabinet and headed for his father's office. For what it was worth, he placed a call to the sheriff's department. When the dispatcher came on, Pierce explained the situation and the approximate location.

The dispatcher promised the sheriff's department would be out to investigate as soon as they had a deputy available. Pierce hung up, shrugging. He'd done the right thing by reporting the incident, but he didn't have a whole lot of faith or respect for the local sheriff. The man still stood by the theory that Pierce's father had fallen from his horse and died of head injuries. Pierce and his brothers disagreed. No way their father had fallen from his horse. The man could ride before he learned to walk. But the sheriff refused to put in the effort to find the truth. And Pierce refused to let Roxanne's safety depend on that kind of man. Whether she liked it or not, he still considered her *his* responsibility. He wouldn't let her down, not this time. Not again.

Pierce grabbed a couple of walkie-talkies from a shelf and emerged from his father's office.

At the same time Amelia Thunder Horse reentered the living room, carrying a large tray filled with thermoses of coffee, and plastic bags filled with sandwiches and trail mix. She eyed the box of bullets but didn't say anything about them. "No one's leaving without food. You never know what's going to happen out there on the plains or in the canyons. They didn't name it the badlands for nothing."

Pierce tossed a walkie-talkie to Maddox, grabbed a plastic bag of trail mix and one with a sandwich from the tray, snagged a thermos, kissed his mother's cheek and headed for the door. "Thanks, Mother."

She called out after him, *"Wakan Tanka kici un."* May the Great Spirit bless you.

He smiled, a tug of nostalgia tightening his chest. His mother didn't often use the Lakota language his father had taught her and all of his sons. Only when a greater need arose.

In the barn, Pierce removed the saddle from Bear, rubbed him down and settled him in a stall with feed. He led his own stallion, Cetan, out of his stall, threw a saddle over his back and cinched it. Pierce was guiding the horse out into the barnyard when a voice called out.

"I'm going with you."

Pierce turned toward the sound, his pulse quickening, his jaw growing rigid.

Roxanne stood with her feet planted wide, hands fisted on her jean-clad hips—more beautiful than he remembered and just as stubbornly determined.

"We don't need your help." Pierce turned his back on the woman and led the horse away from the barn door. "Besides, isn't the doctor on his way to check out your noggin?"

Roxanne strode for the barn. "I've been falling off horses since I was five years old—Doc's not going to tell me anything about concussions that I don't already know. But don't forget, I wasn't the only one injured. While you boys play detective, someone needs to check on Sweet Jessie, and her foal. I'm the local contact for the Bureau of Land Management when it comes to those horses. It's my—"

"Responsibility." Pierce turned back. "And it's *my* responsibility to catch that madman with a gun before he gets a chance to come after you again. You're staying."

"I'm *not* your responsibility, and you don't get to decide where I go. Maddox said I could ride Sassy." She marched into the barn and grabbed a bridle from a nail on the wall.

"Did the fact escape you that you were the target of a shooter?"

"No, it did not." She squared her shoulders, standing taller. "I wasn't prepared before. I'm aware now and will take precautions."

"And how will you do that?" His gaze panned her lithe form. "You aren't carrying any kind of protection, are you? Where's your rifle?"

"I don't carry one. Besides, you have one." She frowned. "Look, Pierce, I'm being sensible. I could have snuck off on my own once you were gone, but instead I'm going with you. I'm willing to be careful, I'm willing to take precautions, but I'm *not* willing to sit around and do nothing when there's so much that needs to be done. Accept that I'm going and stop wasting precious time by arguing. It'll be dark soon."

She held his gaze a moment longer, then disappeared into a stall and emerged leading Sassy, the sorrel mare.

Pierce didn't wait around to bicker with the confounded woman. He didn't want to see Roxanne; he wanted the hell away from her, especially when fire blazed in her beautiful eyes and she stood so defiantly.

Planting his foot in the stirrup, he swung up into his saddle and yanked the stallion around to the north. Named after the Lakota word for hawk, Cetan could outrun even the swiftest of the wild horses in the canyon. He could easily outdistance any of the other horses in the barn, if Pierce chose to let him have his head.

But it would be foolish to expend the horse's energy when they had a long ride ahead of them. Instead of galloping off into the distance, Pierce nudged the stallion into a canter. That way, Roxanne wouldn't have any trouble catching up with him. He still didn't like the idea of her riding out while the gunman was still at large, but the idea of her sticking close and letting him protect her was a hell of a lot better than having her ride out alone.

In the short time they'd been in the ranch house, dark clouds had rolled in. The weather in North Dakota could change at the drop of a hat. Thunder rumbled long and low in the west. *Wakan Tanka* grew angry. Perhaps the Great Spirit reached out to punish those who brought violence to the people and the creatures of the plains.

The approaching storm reflected Pierce's mood. He growled under his breath. Sure, he'd expected to see Roxanne as part of the wedding party. She and Tuck were the same age and had been friends throughout high school. They had been like brother and sister.

Despite the differences between Pierce and Roxanne, Pierce couldn't deny Tuck's request to have Roxanne as one of Julia's bridesmaids.

He'd told himself that he'd be fine seeing her again, but he'd been wrong. Time hadn't healed old wounds, as his mother always liked to say. Nothing could cure death. Roxanne had made it clear that when her brother had died, she wanted nothing more to do with Pierce. No wedding, no future…nothing. Even though he knew it was no more than he deserved, it still made his gut twist just to think about it.

All the old feelings he'd had for her hadn't waned one bit. No amount of dating or bedding other women would wipe Roxanne from his mind. He'd barely even tried, the wounds to his heart still too fresh. He told himself he preferred to be alone. No, he *deserved* to be alone.

Truth was, no woman measured up to Roxanne and he'd failed her so completely, the damage could never be healed.

At the approaching thunder of hooves, Cetan pranced to the side.

Pierce pulled back on the reins, but the stallion would have none of it. His competitive spirit wouldn't let another horse catch up or move ahead of him. He arched his back, kicked his hind legs into the air and would have thrown a less experienced rider.

Accustomed to surprising mood swings in the horses he'd tamed from the wild herds of the canyons, Pierce rode out the rough bucking and brought Cetan to a halt.

Roxanne approached with a hint of a smirk curling the corners of her lips.

Pierce's back teeth ground together. When she pulled in beside him, he eased control on Cetan's reins and let the stallion take the lead in a steady trot. Pierce didn't speak or acknowledge her presence. He was afraid of what he might say. Yet, he kept an eye on Roxanne, just in case. She was hurt, and she was in danger. Even though she hated him, he knew he couldn't live with himself unless he kept her safe.

ROXANNE'S GAZE BORED into Pierce's back. She should have ridden with Dante and Tuck in the truck. But she knew where she was most comfortable. When trouble struck the badlands of North Dakota, Roxanne preferred to be in the saddle. Besides, she was more likely to find

Sweet Jessie and her foal off the beaten path, and they were her priority right now.

The fact that *she* had been injured, along with Sweet Jessie, wasn't something Roxanne let herself think about. She didn't know why anyone would choose to target her—or if he would try to attack her again—but sitting around and thinking about it would drive her crazy. With all the problems she'd been having with the ranch and her finances, the thought of another disaster in her life threatened to crack her self-control. The only way she knew to deal with the strain was to focus on something else—a problem she could fix.

Checking on the horses fit the bill, even if it meant riding with her ex-fiancé.

She'd avoided Pierce since her brother's death. The only time she saw him was from a distance when they happened to be in Medora, the small town where she purchased supplies. She had noticed that Pierce hadn't been home much since the explosion, and why should he? His work with the FBI kept him busy. Just like it had kept Mason busy when Pierce had lured him into that danger-filled world.

A booming clap of thunder shook the earth and air around her. The mare beneath her skittered sideways, tossing her head in the air with a frightened whinny.

Roxanne glanced at the incoming storm, doubt tugging at her gut. Maybe they should have waited until the following day to be out on the prairie. With no trees within sight, that left the two horses and riders as the tallest spires within miles—lightning rods for what looked like a nasty storm about to break over the landscape. Easy targets for a determined shooter, should he choose to return. But no, she wasn't letting herself think about that now. She'd set a mission for herself, and she wasn't going home until it was completed.

A flash of lightning snaked across the sky, followed closely by an answering rumble. Sassy pulled against the reins and swung back toward the barn and shelter from the oncoming storm.

Roxanne struggled to turn the horse in the direction Pierce and his stallion rode. They had to get to the watering hole and find Sweet Jessie and her foal before wolves or two-legged snakes claimed their lives. The rain would wash away the horse tracks…and the tracks of the dirt bike the Thunder Horse brothers would use to try to track down her shooter.

Ahead, Pierce sat tall in the saddle, his shoulders broad, his dark Lakota hair hanging down just below his collar, straight, thick and jet-black. The cowboy hat on his head shielded his eyes from what little light shone around the approaching cloud bank. Every time Pierce glanced behind him, Roxanne's heart flipped, stuttered and burst into a frantic pattering.

Damn the man. He'd always had that effect on her. When would she ever get over him? No man had ever captured her heart or imagination like Pierce Thunder Horse.

The truck with two of the other Thunder Horse brothers passed them, followed soon by the four-wheeler. They honked and swung wide of Pierce and Roxanne, kicking up a cloud of dust from the dry prairie floor.

Roxanne settled into a bone-jarring canter, slow enough to conserve the horse's energy. If they had to go down into the canyon to find Sweet Jessie and her foal, the rain would make the trail even more dangerous than it already was.

Sassy would need all her strength for a coordinated and sure-footed descent.

As they neared the watering hole, Roxanne let out a sigh, half-relieved when she didn't find the wild mare's body in the dirt. The wound mustn't have been too bad, if she was able to get up and leave the area. Still, Roxanne wanted to gauge for herself.

Pierce paused briefly at the watering hole to check for hoofprints and tire tracks, and to compare notes with his brothers.

Roxanne urged her mare slowly toward the canyon's rim, her gaze darting right and left as well as scanning the ground. Having been shot at once made her paranoid. Every noise caused her to jump. She tried to force herself to focus. The brothers were taking care of the shooter—Roxanne's job was to take care of the wild horses. She couldn't let herself get distracted from that. If she did, she'd be reminded how vulnerable and frightened she felt at the thought of a gunman on her trail.

Sweet Jessie had been shot by the pond. The herd had to have been close by at the time of the shooting. Noise from the gunshot would have sent them into the canyon to hide.

In the dirt leading away from the watering hole, Roxanne discovered a trail of dark brown dots. Dried blood and hoofprints. At first they headed for the canyon, but the prints veered south before reaching the canyon's edge. Unfortunately, where Sweet Jessie's prints headed south, another, smaller set of hoofprints led directly to the canyon.

"The foal and mare are separated." Roxanne glanced across at Pierce as he came abreast. "The little one won't stand a chance if she doesn't find her mother soon."

At the edge of the gorge, Roxanne paused, searching

for the trailhead where the horses would have dropped down into the canyon below.

"Are you trying to get shot again?" Pierce angled his horse in front of hers. "You're exposed here on the edge of the canyon. If someone wanted to shoot you once, wouldn't you think they might be interested in shooting at you again?"

"And like I said to you before, if someone wanted to shoot me, there are better places for them to try than here where there's next to no cover to get a good position—especially now that I'm surrounded by angry-looking men with guns." She straightened her shoulders, her gaze darting toward the canyon below. "I refuse to run scared. There's a foal down there who will die without her mother. Lead, follow or get out of my way."

Pierce's brows dipped. "You're a stubborn woman. Anywhere along the trail is easy pickings if someone is down there in the canyon aiming up."

"Do you see any tire tracks leading down into the canyon?"

Pierce leaned over in the saddle, scanning the trailhead. "No. But this might not be the trail he used to get down there."

"You do see horse tracks, don't you?"

"Yes."

Roxanne raised her gaze to the sky again. "If we don't hurry, it won't matter. The rain will keep us from finding the foal. She could die and no one will care but me."

He shifted in his saddle, glancing out across the gorge, squinting. Finally he faced her. "Damn it, Roxanne, I care."

She waved her hand toward the trail, choosing to ignore his statement. "Then let's go."

"Wait here." Pierce took off at a trot toward his brothers. Over his shoulder he called out. "And I mean wait."

Roxanne's gaze followed him.

Pierce conferred with his brothers and returned, reining in beside her and her mare. "They want to stay up top and continue searching for clues as to who the shooter might be before the rain washes away any evidence, but Maddox will cover us while we go down."

"Good." She didn't wait for him. Pressing her heels into Sassy's flanks, she clucked her tongue and spoke softly to the horse as she picked her way down the steep and narrow trail.

Roxanne focused on the path ahead, refusing to look to her side where the ground dropped away in a slope too steep for man or beast. If a shooter popped off a round, he wouldn't even have to hit her. The noise alone could cause her horse to spook and toss her or, worse, tumble down the steep slope with her. And even without the shooter, if her mount took one faulty step, both horse and rider would plummet to the bottom of the canyon with nothing to slow their fall.

Her breath wedging in her throat, Roxanne clung to the saddle horn, her fingers light on the reins, giving the horse her head. Roxanne's feet dug into the stirrups as she leaned back in the saddle to keep from pitching forward. Sassy picked her way to the bottom at her own pace.

About halfway down, the sky opened, rain gushing from it like a fire hose spraying down full blast.

Blinded by the torrent, Roxanne could do nothing but hold on and pray Sassy remained sure-footed as the trail turned slippery and more treacherous by the minute.

Not until the path leveled out and the canyon floor rose up to meet them did Roxanne release the breath she'd been holding and push the hair out of her face to glance behind her.

Cetan descended, easing his way down the last few feet of the narrow trail. Rain dripped from the edges of Pierce's cowboy hat, his face set in stone beneath the brim.

"We'll be lucky to find the foal in this," Roxanne called out as Pierce reined in beside her.

"We're here, we might as well try." His heels pressed into his horse's sides and he headed north along the base of the cliffs rising up beside him.

Her head down, Roxanne wished she'd taken time to grab a cowboy hat at the Thunder Horse Ranch. Hers had been lost earlier in her wild ride to get away from the shooter. She could barely see through the rain running down her face. Sassy fell in step behind Cetan, seemingly content to let the larger horse lead as they pushed forward.

Roxanne followed the man she'd sworn to hate for the rest of her life. Weak and tired from the long ride and the injuries she'd sustained from being shot and thrown, she did something she swore she'd never do again. She let the tears she'd been holding back for two months, mingle with the rain coursing down her cheeks.

If Pierce looked behind him, all he'd see was a pathetically wet woman with water streaming down her face on the back of a bedraggled horse. He would never know she cried.

After riding in the torrential downpour for several hundred yards, Pierce's horse tossed his head into the air and took off.

Startled by the sudden movement, Sassy danced sideways.

Blinded by the rain in her eyes, Roxanne scrubbed a hand across her face and peered ahead.

Several yards in front of Pierce a blurry shadow darted toward the shallow river cutting through the center of the narrow canyon. The foal? She could only hope so. Because if it was the shooter, she didn't know what she could do to protect herself.

Roxanne dug her heels into Sassy's flanks. The horse leaped forward as the sequence of events unfolded before her.

With one hand, Peirce held the reins, while his other hand reached for the rope hanging from the side of his saddle. His arm rose high above his head, the rope swinging in a wide loop. When Pierce launched the lasso, the ring dropped over the head of the small horse that appeared too young to be weaned.

Pierce's horse dug his hooves into the slippery soil, sliding forward with the force of the foal's tug on the rope.

As soon as the two beasts came to an unsteady halt, Pierce dropped from his saddle and raced toward the filly.

Roxanne reached them at the same time, slipping from her horse's back to the ground. She stumbled, regained her footing and ran forward, flinging her arms around the filly's neck to add her weight to Pierce's hold until the frightened animal calmed.

Pierce spoke to her in a deep, monotone voice, whispering the words of his forefathers, the Lakota language rolling smoothly off his tongue.

Not only did it soothe the frightened animal, it helped steady Roxanne's racing heart.

The foal finally settled, eyes still wide, nostrils flaring, body quivering, her ribs expanding with each frantic breath she took. At least she didn't try to break free of Pierce and Roxanne. A fierce surge of triumph filled Roxanne. Despite everything that was wrong—and increasingly dangerous—in her life, at least they'd managed to do this. They'd found and caught the foal, which felt like the first thing that had gone right in her life in way too long.

With the lighting flashing above the canyons and the thunder booming against the rocky cliffs, Roxanne stared across the filly's neck at the man she'd once loved. Their gazes met and held.

Sometime during the struggle with the young horse, Pierce had lost his cowboy hat. Black hair lay plastered to his head, his high cheekbones standing out, glistening in the rain. His eyes glowed so darkly Roxanne couldn't fathom what thoughts hid behind their inky depths.

All she knew was that her traitorous heart was not her own and hadn't been since the day she'd fallen in love with Pierce Thunder Horse.

Chapter Three

Pierce's heartbeat thundered along with the storm-ravaged sky as he gazed into Roxanne's eyes. It took all his willpower and a little help from *Wakan Tanka,* the Great Spirit, to break eye contact and focus on the task ahead. "We need to get the filly back to the ranch."

Roxanne glanced back in the direction from which they'd come. "The trail will be too slippery to get out of the canyon."

Pierce knew that, but he couldn't bring himself to stay with Roxanne any longer than necessary. "We have to try."

She shook her head. "No. We can't risk it. Not when the filly is so scared to begin with. At least not until the rain stops. It wouldn't be safe for us or our horses, either."

He knew she was right. "Get the halter hanging on the side of my saddle."

"Are you sure you have her?"

The filly bucked beneath his hold. Pierce refused to let go, his hands clamped around her neck. "Yes," he said between gritted teeth. "Get it."

Roxanne raced for the saddle, snatched the halter and a lead rope and returned at a slower, more steady pace so as to not spook the foal. She slipped the straps over the pony's nose and buckled the clasp behind her ear. Once she had the lead snapped onto the ring at the side, she nodded. "I've got her."

Slowly, Pierce let go of his hold around the filly's neck.

Immediately, the young horse reared.

Roxanne dug her heels into the ground, but the little horse dragged her through the mud anyway.

Pierce grabbed Roxanne around the middle and held on. With his other hand he reached for the lead rope.

Together, they wrestled the filly to a standstill, Pierce's hand closing around Roxanne's on the rope.

Not until he had the foal under control did Pierce note how close he was to Roxanne. Her drenched body pressed against his, the cold rain doing nothing to cool the heat pooling in his loins.

His hand curled around her hip, dragging her closer. He sucked in a deep breath, inhaling the scent of honeysuckle, the knot in his gut tightening. "Why did you have to come back into my life?"

Her body stiffened, the hand beneath his convulsing around the rope. "Trust me, I had no intention of crossing paths with you." Despite her harsh words, her voice shook.

"Then get away, and stay away from me." He pushed her away from his body, both hands wrapping around the lead rope.

"I can't, until this storm clears." With her back to him, she walked several steps away, then swung around to face him. Hands perched on her hips, her blue eyes flashed through the rain running down her face. "Pending clear skies and dry trails, we're stuck with each other. Not my choice, but I'll deal with it. For now, we need to find shelter until this storm blows over."

"Got anything in mind?" The foal bucked and Pierce gritted his teeth, holding on.

"There are some caves somewhere around here. My brother…" Her voice caught and she looked away. "We used to camp close by when we fished in the river." She grabbed her horse's reins and Cetan's and left Pierce standing there holding on to the filly.

He could choose to follow or continue arguing with the rocks in the rain. For a moment he debated staying put, convinced the cold rain seemed a whole lot cozier than holing up in a cave with an angry ex-fiancée. One look at his charge and he knew the filly deserved better. Besides, until the shooter was caught, Pierce knew he wasn't going to be comfortable having his eyes off Roxanne for long, no matter how hard it was to look at her and know that she'd never be his again. Pierce fell in step behind Roxanne and the two horses, dragging the stubborn little beast with him.

Within fifteen minutes of trudging through rain and mud, Roxanne located the first of a series of caves she'd spent many summers camping in with her brother and father. The memories they evoked made a cold lump rise in her throat, reminding her why she could never forgive Pierce Thunder Horse.

A jagged crevice, wide enough for two horses to stand abreast, allowed them to enter without ducking, bending or otherwise forcing the animals through. The opening also allowed a moderate amount of light inside. The cave's interior, carved out of solid rock through years of erosion, was the size of a barn.

Getting the filly inside took a little more time and patience, but with Roxanne's help, Pierce maneuvered the frightened animal through the passageway, tying her to a boulder large enough to anchor her.

"I'll be right back. I need to radio my brothers and let them know we're okay and will stay here until the rain lets up." He went back through the crevice to stand at the opening of the cave, far enough away from the horses the static wouldn't bother them. The distance from Roxanne helped him to think as he made contact with his brothers. Too bad he couldn't come up with any solutions to keep Roxanne safe and also far, far away from him.

TIRED AND COLD TO THE bone, Roxanne dragged the saddle from Sassy and let it fall to the floor. What had happened to her strength? She felt as weak as a kitten. Determined to pull her own weight, she lugged the saddle up onto a large rock to dry. She used the saddle blanket to rub down the horse, then stretched the damp blanket over another rock.

Pierce reentered the cave.

"They didn't try to come down the trail after us, did they?" Roxanne asked.

"No. But they were about to when I called. They'd been searching the area and were fortunate enough to find some bullet casings before the rain hit. I told them where we were, and sent them back to the ranch. They're not going to find anything else out there in this weather. They'll contact the sheriff's department and let them know about the casings."

Once both horses were cared for, Roxanne trudged her way through the darkness, searching for anything they could use for firewood. When she and her brother had last been inside the cave years ago, they'd left enough fuel to burn for the next visit, knowing firewood was scarce on the plains.

In the shadows farther away from the entrance, she

located the ring of stones they'd arranged for the fire. That was expected. Less expected was what she found at the center of the circle—charred firewood, discarded cans and plastic wrappers that had definitely *not* come from her or Mason.

"Someone has used this cave. By the looks of this trash, fairly recently." Roxanne lifted a plastic wrapper and something shone brightly beneath, catching the little bit of light from the cave's access. "Interesting." She pushed the object out of the dirt. "It's a bullet." From the shooter? Well, who else could it be? This cave was on Carmichael property, and there certainly wasn't anyone who had permission to be using it.

Pierce caught her hand as she reached for the shiny metal. "Don't. We might be able to lift prints. And let me have that plastic wrapper." He tore the tail of his shirt off and picked up the unexploded round and the wrapper using the piece of fabric, tucking the wad into his jeans pocket.

Roxanne rearranged the ring of stones, searching for any other items of interest. "You think the man who camped here is the same man who shot at me?"

His lips thinned into a straight line. "We won't know until the state crime lab can perform the forensics on the casing and compare it to the ones my brothers found."

"Hopefully, the sheriff made it out to the ranch and has started the investigation."

Pierce's jaw clenched at the mention of the sheriff.

Cold slithered across Roxanne's skin, reminding her of what she'd been searching for in the first place. She inched her way to the darkest corner, hoping any critters who might have called this cave home had scurried out, preferring the warmth of the summer prairie to the cool darkness. She found the stash of tinder and dry wood they'd left well before her brother's death, still hidden behind a boulder.

As she emerged into the meager light carrying an armful of firewood, Pierce had pulled out the bag of sandwiches and trail mix his mother had insisted on him bringing. When he saw what Roxanne held, he dropped the bag next to the stone ring and relieved her of her burden. "You shouldn't be carrying that. You might get that gash bleeding again."

She thought about arguing but decided it wasn't worth it. Besides, her arm really did hurt. If he wanted to take care of the fire himself, that was fine with her.

Within minutes a cheerful fire burned brightly, lighting even the darkest corners of the cavern, chasing away the shadows and spiders.

Roxanne laid her saddle blanket on the ground beside the flames to dry, and then collapsed in the dirt close to the fire, grateful for the warmth as the chill of damp clothing set in. Her teeth clattered together, the ache in the back of her head intensifying as the painkiller she'd taken earlier wore off. She rubbed the knot at the base of her skull, kneading the soreness, hoping to ease the ache in the absence of medication.

"Here, let me," said a brusque voice from behind her, and her fingers were brushed aside.

Warm, callused hands curled around her neck. Thumbs avoided the lump, smoothing the hair and skin in gentle circles.

Tense muscles relaxed, the soreness fading as Roxanne pushed aside the fact that Pierce was the source of her relief. For a moment, she let the heat of his fingers chase away the chill inside, leaning back into his broad chest.

The thumbs stilled, and his hands froze against her skin.

A shiver, originating at the base of her spine, rocketed all the way up her back, shaking her violently. Once the trembling began, it didn't abate.

His hands jerked away from her and he stood, backing up several steps. "You have to get out of those wet clothes."

"And w-what am I s-supposed to wear in the m-mean time?" she quipped, the chattering of her teeth taking the barb out of her response.

"Wearing nothing is better than keeping the dampness against your skin. The moisture conducts heat away from your body."

"I know that." Still, she couldn't quite stomach the thought of undressing in front of him. With everything that had happened with the shooter and her injury, she felt too vulnerable. Common sense told her that she needed to get the clothes away from her skin, but every instinct protested. She couldn't let herself be weak where Pierce Thunder Horse was concerned, lest it create a leak in the dam of emotions she'd held in check since he'd returned.

Stubbornly, she wrapped her arms around her knees, pulling them up against her body for more warmth. Her body's trembles turned into bone-shaking shivers, so violent she thought she'd rattle apart.

"Good grief, woman. It's not as though I haven't seen you naked before." He grabbed her hand and urged her to her feet, standing her in front of him. His hands clamped down on her shoulders and he rubbed them through the damp cotton of the T-shirt she wore.

"You're freezing. I suspect shock is setting in from your fall and injury. If we don't get you warmed up, you could have some serious problems, and we both know that there's no way I could get you some help until the weather clears."

"Well, when you put it that way." She pressed her hands into his chest, pushing against him. "I can undress myself."

He let go of her, his lips twisting. "Go for it."

Her fingers fumbled with the hem of her shirt. They shook so hard, she couldn't manage to pull it up over her torso. "I don't know…what's…wrong…" Tears welled in her eyes, and before she could stop them, ran down her cheeks. Now she couldn't even see what she was doing.

"Give it up." Pierce's whispered words stirred the wisps of hair beside Roxanne's ear, his breath warming her cold skin.

"Never," she said, though her hands fell to her sides. Giving it up would have to mean trusting him, and she couldn't do that. She *couldn't!* But when he reached out to her again, she found that she couldn't quite bring herself to stop him, either. She'd been cold for so very long…and Pierce was always so warm.

Deft fingers made quick work of tugging her shirt up and over her head, easing it past the wound on her shoulder and the back of her scalp.

Roxanne's breath lodged in her throat and her gaze traveled upward to connect with the darkness of the Lakotan's eyes. Months of sorrow, of love lost and families betrayed couldn't begin to melt away in one look.

She wanted to say *no,* wanted to shake her head, push him away, stay strong all on her own, the way she had for months. But God help her, she also wanted to say *yes,* to relax and let someone else take control, maybe even take care of her for a little while.

In the end, she didn't say anything at all. Neither did

he. Instead, his lips lowered, so slowly she had plenty of time to resist, to turn away and run.

But she didn't.

EVERY THOUGHT, NERVE, beat of Pierce's heart centered on Roxanne. Her fiery red hair lay wet and curling against her face, her mouth opened, her tongue flicking out to slide across her lips.

He bent to capture her full bottom lip between his teeth, sucking it into his mouth.

The lace of Roxanne's bra rubbed against his shirt. The urge to rip aside the fabric swelled inside him. He had to touch the full, rounded softness of her breasts, to smooth his hands over the swells, rediscovering the curves and warmth of Roxanne's naked skin.

He buried his face in the curve of her neck, nipping and sucking at the pulse beating wildly there.

When Pierce realized she was just as affected by him as he was her, he continued his assault, tossing her shirt to the floor. He unclasped her bra, easing the straps over her shoulders and down her arms, his gaze following its progress as her breasts sprang free. He cupped one in his palm and touched the rigid nipple with the tip of his tongue, lost in the taste of her.

Her chest rose on a gasp, her head falling back. Roxanne's hand reached out to circle Pierce's neck, bringing him closer so that he could suck the nipple into his mouth, pulling hard.

Her other hand groped for the top button of his jeans, fumbling with the hard metal rivet. His head rose and he stared down into her smoky blue gaze, seeing the woman he'd fallen in love with, the woman who was his equal, his soul mate, the only one for him. He pulled her hard against his chest and held her, giving in to the way it felt to have her back in his arms. He wanted her so badly his entire body shook with his need.

He had difficulty forcing his thoughts beyond the moment. If he followed his base instincts, he'd throw caution to the wind and take her there, in the darkness of the cave, their naked bodies writhing in the firelight.

But if he did that, she'd never forgive him. When they both came to their senses, Roxanne would remember all the reasons she had to despise him, all the reasons they would never be a couple again, never have a future together.

Pierce dragged in a deep breath and let it out, loosening his hold on her.

This was Roxanne. The woman he still loved with all his heart. The sister of one of the men whose death was his fault.

Pierce couldn't change the past or undo what had happened to Roxanne's brother. He couldn't stop her hating him and hadn't been able to keep her from leaving; nor had he tried. Today was the first time they'd managed to even have a conversation since ending their engagement, and it had been more than enough to show him how angry she still was. Right now, she was cold, and scared, and hurting and she was willing to let his touch make the world go away for a while, but it wouldn't last. Making love to her wouldn't change anything. She still hated him and no matter how perfect she'd been for him, Special Agent Pierce Thunder Horse was the wrong man for her.

He tugged her bra straps up over her shoulders and eased them both down to sit near the campfire, holding her close to share his body warmth.

"That shouldn't have happened," she said, her voice not much louder than a whisper.

"No. It shouldn't have." He didn't try to kiss her again.

She leaned her head against his chest. "It won't happen again."

"Count on it." He held her into the night as she fell into a troubled sleep. She clung to him, her body shaking, her head twisting back and forth as nightmares disturbed her slumber. Because of her possible concussion, he had an excuse to wake her from her dreams every two hours.

In the small hours of the morning, Pierce spooned her body against his, his gaze on the dying embers of the fire, his thoughts swirling around the shooting, the dirt bike, Roxanne and the bullet and wrapper they'd found in the cave.

Sleep escaped him with her body close to his and the wad of evidence in his pocket. The more he mulled over everything, the more dread filled his chest, crushing him with worry.

Whatever Roxanne had stumbled on that had caused the shooter to attack, it was much bigger than some idiot taking potshots at wild horses.

If he wasn't mistaken, the piece of plastic and the claylike substance clinging to it wasn't a candy wrapper for gum, but the packaging used around plastic explosives.

Chapter Four

A horse nickered, stirring Roxanne awake. Her eyes blinked open to the muted light of predawn filtering through the window. Only it wasn't a window, and the cool air brushing across her skin wasn't coming from outside her house.

Her back was warm. An arm draped around her middle and the solid mass pressing against her generated enough heat to chase away the chills, keeping her from freezing in the cool morning air.

Then it all came back to her and she jerked to an upright position, her hands covering her breasts. She breathed a sigh of relief when her hands connected with her bra.

Pierce Thunder Horse pushed up on one elbow, a wary expression on his face. "Morning. Sleep well?"

"Fine." She leaped to her feet, snatching up her T-shirt and jeans. Turning her back to the Lakotan, she jammed her feet into the jeans and shivered as she shimmied the cold but dry fabric up her legs. Thank goodness her shirt and jeans had dried in the night, or moving about in the cool North Dakota morning air would be very uncomfortable. She finger-combed her hair to smooth the curls before she felt confident enough to face Pierce.

Good Lord, what had she done? She'd almost made love to this man.

Without looking him in the eye, she faced Pierce.

He'd pulled his denim shirt over broad shoulders, leaving it hanging open, exposing his smooth, dark chest.

Roxanne realized too late that staring at his chest was every bit as dangerous as looking into his eyes.

"I need to get back to my ranch." The sooner she got away from Pierce, the better.

Pierce frowned as he buttoned his shirt. "It's not safe to go there without an escort. And I'll need to go with you, anyway, in order to bring Sassy back with me." She started to protest, but his jaw tightened and he held up a hand. "Give it up, Roxanne, I'm not taking no for an answer. You're still in danger, and I'm not going to let you ride around this area by yourself."

Roxanne fought the urge to scream in frustration. She couldn't deny that he was right about the danger of riding alone, but she hated to think that she was dependent on him, that she needed his help or protection. She'd spent the past two months convincing herself that she was fine on her own, that she didn't need Pierce or anyone else. Then on the very day that he rode back into her life, she found herself forced to rely on him. And worse, in spite of all her strong, fervent resolutions, she'd even ended up falling back into his arms.

"Just because we…"

"Almost made love?"

"Just because we almost had sex," she corrected him firmly, "doesn't change anything between us. It was a mistake that will never happen again."

Pierce nodded slowly, his dark eyes black and intense. He looked as hurt and tormented as she felt, and in spite of all her anger and pain, part of her still longed to reach out to him, to comfort him and be comforted in return. But that wasn't possible.

"I know," he said, and walked away.

THEY EMERGED FROM THE cave cautiously, Pierce leading the strange little group of humans and horses. Roxanne blinked in the sunlight, her eyes adjusting from the shadows.

Cetan whinnied, shifting from side to side at the end of his lead.

The colt twisted and reared, tugging at the end of the rope Pierce used to lead her out.

A quick scan of the canyon floor revealed the presence of the herd of wild horses. Separating herself from the rest, Sweet Jessie trotted toward them.

Roxanne studied the way the mare moved. "She appears to be all right."

"I can see where she was hit. She has a streak of blood on her right shoulder. But it doesn't seem to bother her."

Roxanne chewed on her bottom lip. "I'd like to inspect her more closely, but I'm afraid capturing her might cause further injury."

The colt pulled hard against the lead, squealing in a high-pitched cry for her mother.

"We'll keep an eye on her."

"*I'll* keep an eye on her," Roxanne replied. "It's not like you'll be around once the wedding is over, anyway. You'll be back to your FBI work."

There was a pause as Pierce seemed to be wrestling over what to say. The foal took the decision out of his hands as she struggled against the rope until Pierce could barely maintain his grip. "In the meantime, this little one wants her mama. I can hold her, if you can loosen the buckle on the halter." He held the frightened animal steady.

Roxanne slipped the straps free of the buckle and slid the halter over the filly's head, her fingers brushing against Pierce's arm.

As soon as the filly was free, Pierce let go. Without pause, the colt bolted for her mother, tossing her head as if in defiance of her time held in captivity.

Sweet Jessie met her halfway, sniffing, nuzzling and herding her errant baby toward the herd.

On a rise a hundred yards from where Pierce and Roxanne stood, the herd stallion rose up on his hind legs, calling out to the mares.

Cetan snorted, his eyes rolling back. He tugged on the reins Roxanne held.

Pierce relieved her of her hold, his hand rising to stroke his stallion's neck, speaking to the animal in his native tongue.

"Come on," Pierce said, his voice low, insistent. "We could do without a fight between stallions."

Roxanne gathered Sassy's reins, placed her foot into the stirrup and swung up into the saddle, her shoulder stiff from her wound and a night sleeping on the hard floor of the cave. She headed for the trail leading out of the canyon, without looking back over her shoulder at Pierce.

The work they'd done to help the filly had been challenging and worthwhile, seeing the colt reunited with her mother. But now that it was done, all of Roxanne's other worries came crashing back in. The shooter who might still be after her. The financial problems she was facing at her ranch. And most troubling of all, the feelings she had for Pierce Thunder Horse that refused to die down.

That didn't make Pierce any less guilty of talking her brother into joining the FBI, or sending him into the situation that eventually got him killed.

Roxanne pushed the past to the back of her mind, the dangerous trail her more immediate concern. She let Sassy choose her footing on the way up.

She waited long enough to ensure Pierce made it out of the canyon. Thankfully, the shooter wasn't watching for them. Neither were the other Thunder Horse men. Based on the angle of the sun hovering over the horizon, it was very early in the morning.

If she was lucky, she could get in a good day's work, despite having lost the day before to the attack. The cattle auction was coming up soon and she had to have her animals loaded and shipped before that day or she'd be in even worse shape financially than she was physically. The thought of the shooter still disturbed her, but it wasn't as if she could go into hiding. She had a ranch to run.

As Pierce and Cetan cleared the rim, Roxanne nudged Sassy into a canter, headed toward the Carmichael Ranch. She could hear Pierce and Cetan behind her, but didn't rein in to wait for them. She was in too much of a hurry to get home. Having been out of contact for over half a day, she wondered if anything else had gone wrong while she'd been gone.

Thirty minutes later, she rode into the barnyard and dismounted.

Before Pierce could climb down off his horse, Roxanne handed over Sassy's reins. "Thank you for the use of your horse. You can go now."

Pierce's lips quirked at the corners for a moment,

but he quickly grew serious again. "You can't dismiss me that easily. What happened with the shooter could happen again."

"Yes, it could. But you sticking around won't change that. He didn't hesitate to shoot at me in front of you before."

Pierce hesitated, his eyes narrowing.

"I have four ranch hands and a foreman running around the place. If that man comes back, he'll definitely be outnumbered. I'll be okay. You can leave now."

Pierce didn't budge.

"Fine," Roxanne said. "I'll make sure I don't ride alone and I'll carry my own rifle." She planted her fists on her hips. "Satisfied?" She shook her head. "You'd think I didn't have a mind of my own."

"The man who attacked you didn't give up easily. He might come back to finish the job."

"Let me worry about that." She dropped her hands to her sides. "Now, if you'll excuse me, I have a ton of work to do, and I want to get it done before I head back out to check on Sweet Jessie." Roxanne strode toward the barn.

Nothing moved behind her, leaving her in no doubt that Pierce wasn't heading home yet.

"My brothers and I will ride out this afternoon and check on Sweet Jessie and the herd," Pierce called out. "No need for you to do it."

Roxanne halted just outside the barn door and faced him, squinting up at him in the morning sunlight. "It's my responsibility. I'll do the checking."

"And we'll be there to help. Three o'clock this afternoon. Don't go out there until then." He waited for her response, glaring down at her.

"Three o'clock." She turned to enter the barn, her gaze avoiding his. She'd go earlier, just to avoid the man.

Pierce's voice carried to her in one last attempt, "Maybe I should stay."

Her head poked out the door, her brows furrowing. "No." With that final response, she entered the barn, refusing to go back out.

She waited for her eyes to adjust to the dim lighting inside the barn and for the sound of retreating hoofbeats to indicate the barnyard was clear of Pierce Thunder Horse.

As the interior of the barn came into focus, she gasped, her heart fluttering against her ribs.

Across the walls and doors, slashes of red spray paint marred the otherwise clean surfaces.

"STAY OUT OF THE CANYON!"

WITH SASSY'S LEAD ROPE tied to his saddle horn, Pierce headed toward home, reminding himself he was no longer a part of Roxanne's life. The fact that they'd come very close to making love had changed nothing—at least, it didn't seem to have changed anything for Roxanne. It was a different story for him. Having her in his arms again had only lengthened the time it would take to get over her. But he *would* get over her. There wasn't any other option.

Pierce knew now that they weren't meant to be together. Not just because they would both always blame Pierce for her brother's death, but also because, with Mason's death, Roxanne was the only Carmichael left. The woman needed a man who'd be around to help her manage the huge Carmichael Ranch. Not some adrenaline-junkie special agent who'd only drop in long enough to get her pregnant before he left on his next mission.

And she didn't need the worry of waiting by the phone for the call that would inform her that yet another member of her family had given his life for his country. No. Roxanne deserved a better man than Pierce Thunder Horse. Even if she did forgive him for her brother's death, he couldn't add to her heartache by being an absentee husband and father.

The image of her lying near-naked in his arms on the floor of the cave flashed through his mind, weakening his conviction. He wanted to hold her again.

His jaw tightened, along with his resolve. Pierce Thunder Horse would have to get over Roxanne Carmichael. For her own good, if not his own.

As he rode into the Thunder Horse barnyard, his brothers streamed out of the barn, carrying bridles and horse blankets, in the middle of saddling their horses.

Maddox met him first, taking Sassy's reins. "Did you run across the shooter?"

Dante held Cetan's head as Pierce dismounted. "Where's the filly?" he asked.

"More important, where's Roxanne?" Tuck asked, bringing up the rear.

"No more encounters with the shooter, the filly was reunited with Sweet Jessie, Sweet Jessie is wounded but holding her own, and Roxanne insisted on returning to her ranch."

"How was it, spending the night in a cave with your ex?" Dante chuckled. "Prickly?"

Yes, and also very much no. Pierce tipped his head down, hoping the shadow of his cowboy hat would hide any expression on his face. "We made do." He dropped to the ground and led Cetan into the barn. "What did you hear from the sheriff on the bullet casings?"

"Nothing."

Pierce dug in his pocket for the bullet and plastic wrapper, unfolding the wad of cloth surrounding the items. "I take it you kept one of the casings?"

"I did." Tuck's lip curled upward on one side. "Whatcha got there?"

Pierce handed him the wadding. "Get the casing and this bullet and plastic wrapper to the state crime lab, personally. Have them check for a match between the two and see if they can lift prints or even partial prints on any of it."

"Got it." Tuck unfolded the cloth and stared down at the bullet. "Looks close if not exact on the casing. Is this what I suspect it is?"

Pierce's gut clenched. "The wrapper usually found around plastic explosives? Yeah."

Maddox whistled. "Where did you find it?"

"In the cave. Seems our shooter has been camping out on Carmichael property." His fists tightened at the thought that Roxanne wasn't safe on her own spread.

He loosened the girth around Cetan's middle and slipped the saddle over his back. "What I don't understand is why someone would target Roxanne."

Dante replaced Cetan's bridle with a halter and tossed a brush to Tuck, who started running it across the animal's back. "I can't figure that one out at all," Dante said. "The Carmichaels have been a part of this community for a long time. As far as I know, they have no enemies."

"For some reason, Roxanne does now." Pierce hefted the saddle onto a saddletree in the tack room and hung the bridle on a hook. "And she doesn't seem to understand how serious the situation is."

Tuck grinned. "You, of all people, know she's not going to let a little thing like being shot at slow her down. When she sets her mind to getting something done, hell better get out of her way."

Pierce nodded. He remembered.

The woman was as hardheaded as any one of the Thunder Horse brothers. She had to be, in order to run a ranch on her own after her father's death. Even when her brother had been alive, she'd been the one to manage the daily upkeep and operations, while Mason followed his own dreams of being an FBI special agent.

Pierce remembered how excited Mason had been when he'd started his FBI training. Despite Roxanne's belief to the contrary, Pierce had tried to talk Mason out of joining the FBI, telling him that he needed to help his sister with ranch operations. But Mason had that Carmichael stubbornness, too, and in the end, Pierce hadn't been able to change his mind. At the time, he'd consoled himself with the thought that he would always be there, both to help Roxanne with the ranch and to keep an eye on Mason. Now, he couldn't do either.

Pierce shook his head, pushing the thoughts away. That was the past. The present held more pressing matters. With a currycomb, Pierce tackled Cetan's other side. "Did the sheriff ever go out to the site of the shooting?"

Tuck shook his head. "No."

Pierce snorted. "Didn't expect he would."

"Seemed satisfied with the bullet casing. Like it would catch the culprit."

"The man's a waste of the badge he wears," Dante said.

"Came out, flirted with Mom and left," Maddox added. "Seemed like he couldn't have cared less about the shooting, taking the opportunity to investigate as an open door to our mother."

Tuck stuffed the wad of fabric containing the bullet into his jeans pocket. "He did say he'd go to the Carmichael place and ask Roxanne a few questions today."

Pierce's teeth ground together. He'd like to be there when the sheriff stopped by Roxanne's. The lawman would be more hassle than help.

Again, he had to remind himself Roxanne Carmichael would no longer accept his help.

"Julia's worried about Roxanne." Tuck's words interrupted Pierce's thoughts. "Do you suppose one of us should camp out at the Carmichael ranch until they find this guy?"

"She wouldn't let us if we tried."

Tuck grinned. "I know. Just thought I'd suggest it. It would make Julia happier."

"You two have your own worries, what with the wedding coming up fast. How many days now?"

"Five." Finished on his side, Tuck rounded the horse's backside and collected the currycomb from Pierce. "But if things get worse with that shooter, we might have to postpone."

"No way. You two deserve each other."

Tuck laughed. "I'll take that as a compliment." His smile straightened and he clapped a hand on Pierce's shoulder, leaning in to speak so that only Pierce could hear. "Look, Pierce, I know this was supposed to be your time. You should have been married by now, not me. I just wanted you to know, I'm here for you if you need to talk."

"About what?" Pierce stepped away from his brother, letting Tuck's hand fall to his side. The last thing he needed was his brother's pity.

"You could talk about Roxanne, the wedding…" He shrugged. "You know…things."

Pierce took the brush and currycomb back from Tuck's hand. "I've got nothing to say. Our breakup is old history. I'm over her."

Tuck hesitated for a moment, as if he wanted to say more. Then he nodded. "The offer is open. Whenever you need me, I'm here to listen." He didn't wait for a response, instead leaving the barn. Maddox and Dante followed him shortly after.

Pierce stood with the brush in his hand, his chest squeezing so tight he couldn't breathe. If he was so over Roxanne, why did he feel like he was having a heart attack?

He forced himself to go through the motions of brushing Cetan from front to rear, one more time. His hands moved slowly, one steadying stroke at a time until they quit shaking and he could breathe normally.

All the while, he pictured Roxanne lying next to him on the cave floor, her pale white skin almost glowing in the darkness, her soft curves nestled against him.

Yeah, he was over her.

Chapter Five

Roxanne called the sheriff's office as soon as she'd discovered the paint in the barn.

Deputy Shorty Duncan showed up in less than an hour to question her on the events of the day before and to take pictures of the damage done in the barn.

He spent time with each of her ranch hands, questioning them about their whereabouts during the night, but nothing came of it. According to their accounts, no one had seen anything and Roxanne hadn't been there to verify.

As he slipped the pad he'd been taking notes on into his pocket, the deputy faced Roxanne. "I've got what I need."

"Any idea who would do this or why they'd want me to stay out of the canyon?"

Duncan shook his head. "No, ma'am, but I'll be checking into it. You can be sure of that." He tucked his pen in with the pad. "In the meantime, I suggest you stay out of the canyon. Sounds like trouble."

"Aren't you going to check out the canyon to see why someone would want me to stay out?"

"Soon as I get some backup to go with me, I sure will. Don't you worry."

"Not much help, was he?" Jim Rausch, her ranch

foreman, said as he stepped up beside her to watch the deputy drive away.

"Wonder when he plans to be back out to check the canyon?"

"No tellin'."

Roxanne sighed. "We can't wait for the law—we have cattle to round up. We'll save the canyon for last."

Jim nodded toward the hands gathered with their horses and called out, "We're burnin' daylight. Mount up."

Roxanne spent the rest of the morning and part of the afternoon with her ranch hands, mending the fences and loading chutes, preparing for the roundup. It made no sense to herd the cattle into the corrals until all the preparatory work had been taken care of. And maybe the routine mending would give the sheriff and his men time to check out the canyon.

Two of the hands worked a downed fence on the northern perimeter, while the other two worked the fences in the holding pens.

Roxanne and her foreman removed and replaced weathered boards on the loading chute.

She'd worked through lunch while her men had stopped for sandwiches, preferring the solitude to sustenance. She couldn't have eaten had she wanted to, her stomach remaining knotted since Pierce had left.

The work was slow and steady…and very tiring. As two o'clock rolled around, she strode over to her foreman. She hated to slow down the work by taking him away from his duties, but after being shot at the day before, she knew she couldn't risk riding out alone, especially to the canyon. Despite Pierce's promise to check on the horses along with his brothers, she knew she needed to see for herself that the herd hadn't been harmed. And for her own peace of mind, she wanted to see to that *without* Pierce beside her.

"I need you to ride over to the canyon with me to check on Sweet Jessie."

"Sure you want to do that, Miss Carmichael?"

"I need to make sure Sweet Jessie and the rest of the herd are okay."

Jim gathered his reins and turned his horse, glancing down at his watch. "Didn't Mr. Pierce say to meet them out there at three o'clock?"

"And we will. But I wanted to get a jump on finding Sweet Jessie to save them some time and the possibility of trouble in the canyon," she lied. She really wanted to get out there, find Sweet Jessie and get back to her ranch without spending any more time than she had to in the presence of the Thunder Horses, one in particular.

"I'd feel better with them there." He pushed his hat back on his head and stared to the north. "There's safety in numbers."

"We'll be fine, with you as my backup. There was only one shooter."

"Still not likin' it, but if it's what you want, let's get a move on. There's still lots to be done out here."

Jim and Roxanne saddled up and headed out across the prairie.

Roxanne clamped her cowboy hat down on her head, glad for the shade as the sun beat down on her shoulders. The heat of summer had settled into the badlands of North Dakota. Without a tree in sight, the land baked, waves of heat radiating from the dry earth, making the early-morning chill a dim memory.

A trickle of sweat slipped down between Roxanne's breasts and she shifted in her saddle, her jeans clinging to her damp legs.

Roxanne slowed her paint horse to a walk. The heat would tire the horses faster than the speed and she wanted to conserve energy for their return.

Jim rode up alongside her and settled into the slower, steadier pace. After a while, he glanced over at her. "You know, Pierce is a good man."

At the mention of Pierce's name, Roxanne's heartbeat kicked up a notch. "Can we talk about something else?"

Jim shrugged. "Just saying." He rode in silence for a few more minutes.

Roxanne breathed easier after a while, certain Jim wasn't going to continue selling Pierce.

Then he cleared his throat and said, "You two had somethin' special. You don't find that often, you know."

She glared at her foreman. "I don't want to discuss the man. Besides, you're one to talk. Since when are you an expert on relationships?"

Again, the older man shrugged. "I was in love once."

Roxanne's brows rose. "I didn't know that. I've never even seen you with a woman."

He frowned. "I go to town on my days off. Not that it's any of yer business, little girl."

She smiled, glad they weren't talking about her and Pierce anymore. "I'm not so little anymore."

"My point exactly. You're getting older and need to settle down while you're still breedin' age."

"Jim Rausch, you make me sound like a broodmare." She shook her head. "I don't want to settle with or for anyone. Not now or anytime soon. I'm doing just fine on my own." It was mostly true. She'd *make* it true. Just as soon as she convinced her silly heart not to pine for Pierce.

"You ought to reconsider your opinion of that Thunder Horse boy. He's still pretty stuck on you."

"Don't go there. You know he's the reason Mason joined the FBI, and that it's his fault Mason got himself killed."

"Not the way I see it." Jim rode in silence for a long second or two, before adding, "Mason had his own reasons for joining the FBI. You can't blame it on Pierce."

"Pierce sent him into that building that blew up."

"Now how was he supposed to know the building would explode?"

The image of a fiery explosion had haunted her dreams and memories for months. Roxanne didn't need a reminder. "I'm the wrong one to ask. I don't know the details, and Pierce refused to tell me." *Even when I begged him to explain, to tell me what had happened.* "All he'd say was that Mason's death was his fault. I'm not marrying Pierce Thunder Horse and nothing you can say will change my mind."

"A woman's got a way of changing her own mind."

"Don't hold your breath." She nudged her horse to go a little faster, trying to put distance between her and Jim.

Unfortunately, he remained abreast. Jim glanced at her, his lips curled ever so slightly. "Just saying."

Roxanne clamped her lips shut, refusing to further the conversation by replying to him.

As they neared the canyon's rim, she slowed her horse, her gaze darting right and left. As far as she could see, nothing moved across the edge. That didn't mean a shooter wasn't lurking, but for now, Roxanne felt confident they were alone on the plains. She patted the rifle protruding from the scabbard on her saddle. Between her and Jim, it was two against one, and they were both armed. That ought to keep the attacker from making a move.

"I'll go down first. When I'm close to the bottom of the trail, you can start down. In the meantime, keep your rifle ready."

"I got yer back, Miss Carmichael." Jim pulled his weapon out and checked the chamber.

She smiled at the man she'd known for as long as she could remember. "Thanks, Jim. When I get to the bottom, I'll cover for you."

Domino, her black-and-white paint gelding, wasn't too keen on the narrow trail. After a little gentle persuasion, Roxanne got him headed in the right direction.

He picked his way down the steep trail, his steps slow and nervous. At several particularly dangerous points, pebbles slipped over the side and tumbled to the bottom.

Domino tossed his black mane and nickered, his eyes rolling back.

Roxanne smoothed her hand across his long, sleek neck. "Easy, boy. Just a little farther."

Ten feet from the bottom, she pulled the rifle from her scabbard and waved it up at Jim.

The foreman began his descent more easily. His horse was older, more docile and sure-footed.

Roxanne twisted in her saddle, careful to check all directions for a possible threat.

When Jim and his bay mare hit the halfway point, the hair on Roxanne's arm stood on end and she glanced over her shoulder. Nothing. She turned in her saddle to get a better look behind her.

A movement along the canyon rim caught her attention, and Roxanne's heart stopped. Someone was up there.

A jumble of rocks and boulders tumbled down the hill toward Jim and his horse, kicking up dust and more rocks in its path.

"Get out of the way!" Jim shouted, urging his horse to hurry in an attempt to beat the landslide.

Domino reared and backed away from the base of the trail, whinnying wildly.

With one hand holding the rifle, Roxanne struggled to keep her seat and maintain control of her gelding.

The rattle of rocks grew to a roar as a large boulder bumped down the steep slope.

Roxanne's breath caught in her lungs and she froze.

Jim and his horse were directly in the boulder's path.

"Move!" she shouted, waving the hand holding the rifle. "Move!"

Jim glanced behind him, his eyes rounding. He dug his heels into the horse's flank, startling the horse.

The mare leaped forward and reared as the boulder passed by, narrowly missing them both. The mare recovered her footing, but Jim lost his seat and tumbled out of the saddle.

As if in slow motion, he landed on the downhill side of the trail, bouncing off the rocky slope and cartwheeling downward, picking up speed with the landslide of rocks and gravel.

The foreman somersaulted, slid and bounced the rest of the way down the five-hundred-foot drop, landing in a rush of stones and gravel with a sickening thud.

Roxanne dug her heels into Domino's sides and raced to the base of the slope, her heart hammering against her ribs so hard it hurt.

"Jim. Oh, dear God, Jim," she cried as she dropped to the ground and crouched over the older man's still form.

Pebbles and small rocks continued to slide down, pelting her face and arms, some of them sharp, drawing blood.

Roxanne didn't care. Jim was her only family, the man who'd been a father to her when her own had died.

"Jim." She reached for the base of his throat and pressed two fingers to his skin, praying with all her heart for a pulse.

"Please be alive. Please."

She held her breath, willing her shaking hands to steady. Finally a faint pulse bumped against her fingertips and she let out a long shaky sigh. "Thank God."

But when she took stock of his form, her vision blurred and she sat back hard on her heels.

Jim lay at an awkward angle, his ankle twisted beneath a rock, his face pale, scratches bleeding across every exposed surface. And never once did he open his eyes.

Roxanne raised her face to the sky and cried, "Help! Please, oh please, help!"

"Sittin' light in the saddle today, brother?" Dante settled his cowboy hat on his head, pushing it down tight as he swung up on his black gelding.

Pierce eased himself into his own saddle on Cetan. "I got saddle sores from riding the past two days."

"Need to rebuild the calluses on your butt, brother. Becoming a softy in the agent business," Maddox teased. "I'll take the truck with the medical supplies."

"Says the man who rides horses for a living," Pierce quipped.

"I'll let you two do all the fun stuff in the canyon while I provide cover from above. Besides, someone's got to haul the medical supplies in case Sweet Jessie needs them, and they ain't gonna fit on the back of your horse."

"Yeah, yeah. You'll be napping, old man." Dante

clicked his tongue and his horse trotted out of the barnyard.

Maddox caught Pierce's gaze, all kidding wiped from his face. "Nothing from Tuck, yet?"

"Nothing more than what you already know. The bullet and casings are a match. He couldn't lift any prints. He's trying to get a trace on the plastic explosives, but there wasn't much to go on."

Maddox nodded. "You two will catch this guy. I know I can count on my FBI brothers to always get their man."

"I just hope we get him before he gets Roxanne."

"Yeah." Maddox's head dipped and he fiddled with the leather gloves he carried. "Speaking of Roxanne…"

Pierce held up a hand. "Don't go there. We're history."

"Spending the night in a cave alone with her didn't stir up any lingering anything?" Maddox gave him a pointed stare.

"We weren't alone. We had three horses in the cave with us."

Maddox snorted. "You're avoiding the question."

"No, I'm not answering it. Come on, we'll be late for our three o'clock with the woman at this rate."

Before he could leave the barnyard, Pierce spied Maddox's fiancée running from the house toward them, carrying a pair of walkie-talkies.

"Maddox, you got company."

The pretty, dark-haired princess of a breakaway Russian nation skidded to a halt, breathing hard. "You almost forgot your radio." After she handed him one, she stood for a moment, staring up at him, the love shining from her eyes. "Be careful, please." Then she flung her arms around his neck and pressed her lips to his.

Maddox's arms circled her tiny waist, pulling her close, deepening the kiss.

Pierce's gut knotted.

Maddox and Katya were so in love it made Pierce want to gag.

He dug his heels into Cetan's flanks, startling the animal into a jerky lope. Pierce didn't slow the horse until he was well out of eyesight of the barn, his brother and his brother's fiancée.

He told himself he was better off single. He'd be no kind of husband to any woman, and especially not to Roxanne.

Tuck was crazy to think a relationship between him and Julia would work out while he stayed an agent, even though Julia had already told Tuck she wouldn't stand in the way of his career, that she wanted him to follow his dream of being an FBI special agent.

He'd end up quitting the FBI in order to stay home with his wife and baby daughter. From what Pierce had seen, Tuck would give up breathing for Lily and Julia, and Pierce had seen the worry in Julia's eyes every time Tuck headed back to the office in Bismarck. She'd worry about him until he returned, even though Tuck was a good agent who'd given her no reason to doubt his ability to come home to her at the end of the day. Not like Pierce, who had already let Roxanne down when his mistake ended in her brother's death.

Even if Roxanne forgave Pierce for Mason's death, he would never forgive himself. Pierce couldn't ask her again to be his wife. Being the cause of her brother's death would always stand between them, not to mention the loneliness, heartache and uncertainty of being the spouse of an agent.

Pierce caught up with Dante and they rode side by

side in silence the rest of the way out to the canyon on the border of the Thunder Horse and Carmichael ranches. Dante didn't mention Roxanne and Pierce didn't bring her up, preferring to push on, keeping his thoughts completely to himself.

As they neared the trailhead Pierce and Roxanne had ascended earlier that morning, a slew of emotions rippled across his consciousness, the foremost being regret.

Regret that things hadn't worked out differently, that it had been inevitable they turned out the way they did.

What if Mason had lived? What if he and Roxanne had continued with their wedding plans? They'd be married now.

And their marriage would have been a huge mistake. Roxanne deserved a man she could count on, and that could never be him.

A distant cry echoed off the canyon walls, pushing thoughts of what might have been to the back of Pierce's mind.

"Did you hear that?" Dante asked.

Both men pulled on their reins and listened.

"Help!" The desperate sound rose from somewhere down in the canyon.

Pierce's pulse leaped. "Roxanne?" He slapped his reins on his horse's flanks. Cetan burst into a gallop, heading straight for the trail.

"Pierce, wait!" Dante called out behind him.

At the last moment, Cetan skidded to a halt, sending a shower of pebbles and gravel over the edge.

"Help! Please, help us!" Roxanne's voice called out.

Pierce dropped down off Cetan's back and peered over the rim of the canyon.

Roxanne knelt beside a distorted figure lying among

the rocks. When she glanced up, she pointed her rifle up at him and shouted, "Who's there?"

"Roxanne, it's me, Pierce." His voice echoed several times off the walls of the canyon.

"Thank God," Roxanne said, and laid the rifle on the ground, kneeling in the dirt beside the man.

"I'm going down." Pierce handed his reins to his brother.

Dante caught his arm. "Be careful, Pierce. Looks like there's been an avalanche." He nodded toward the edge where a large chunk of the rim had recently fallen away.

Pierce's throat constricted. Roxanne could have been the one lying hurt at the bottom of the canyon. He left Cetan at the top and walked down the steep trail, his boots slipping on newly loosened stone. At one point the trail all but disappeared, ripped away by a rush of stone and debris.

When he reached the bottom, he hurried across to where Roxanne sat on the ground, holding Jim Rausch's hand, the tears trickling down her face forming long trails through the dust caked to her skin. She glanced up at Pierce. "Don't let him die."

Pierce dropped to his haunches next to Jim's body and felt for a pulse. "He's still with us. How long has he been out?"

"Fifteen, twenty minutes, maybe." She shook her head as she stared at the man. "He fell most of the way down and I couldn't do a thing."

"Moving him could cause more damage. We'll have to get an airlift to get him out of here."

Pierce glanced up to the rim of the canyon. Maddox had arrived and waited beside Dante. Pierce stood and waved at his brothers.

Dante started the long trek down the damaged trail.

"I'll be back." As Pierce turned to go, Roxanne's hand grabbed his leg.

"Hurry." Her voice broke, and another tear slipped down her cheek.

Pierce forced himself to move away, climbing the trail as fast as he could to meet Dante halfway up.

"Is it Jim?" Dante asked, his gaze moving past Pierce to the man lying so still. "Is he dead?"

"It's Jim and he's still alive. Tell Maddox to radio back to the house and have someone call nine-one-one. We need an emergency medical helicopter here ASAP."

"Got it." Dante turned and scrambled back up the trail.

Pierce returned to the base and Roxanne.

He sat on the ground beside her and gathered her in his arms. "He'll be okay."

She turned her face into his chest, her fingers bunching his shirt. "Promise?"

"I can't promise, but we'll do the best we can."

She didn't reply…but she didn't let go, either.

For the longest time they sat there, waiting for the reassuring thumping of rotor blades beating the air.

When it finally came, Pierce stood, gathered the horses' reins and held them steady as a helicopter hovered over the canyon and then landed on a flat patch of ground on the canyon floor. At the same time, a handful of emergency medical personnel descended from the rim of the canyon, carrying medical supplies and a backboard.

Pierce pulled Roxanne away from Jim, leaving him in the care of the professionals. He stood with her hand clasped in his, his heart aching for her. Pierce knew what Jim meant to Roxanne.

Jim Rausch was more family to Roxanne than employee. Having survived her brother's death, she'd be devastated by the loss of her foreman.

He prayed to the Great Spirit to spare the man's life for Roxanne's sake. She didn't need to go through all that again.

Roxanne broke away from him and followed the medical team as they carried Jim on the backboard to the waiting helicopter.

After they loaded the foreman into the helicopter and it lifted off the ground, the technicians returned to clear their equipment.

Roxanne trudged back, her head down until she reached Pierce. "He has to make it."

"Jim's a tough guy. He'll pull through."

Roxanne's face turned up to his, her normally bright blue eyes nearly gray, shadowed. "I watched him fall all that way down."

Pierce pulled her into his arms. "You couldn't have done a thing to help. It was an accident."

"No it wasn't."

"She's right—it wasn't."

Pierce turned at Maddox's voice.

His brother was stepping off the trail onto the floor of the canyon.

Roxanne straightened. "I know I saw someone, standing at the ledge right before the avalanche started. Was it him? Did he do this?"

Maddox nodded, his mouth set in a grim line. "You'll want to take a look at this, Pierce. From the tracks he left behind, there's no denying it. Someone forced that boulder free, setting off that avalanche."

Chapter Six

Roxanne paced the corridor of the St. Alexius Medical Center in Bismarck, the acrid scent of rubbing alcohol and disinfectant burning the insides of her nostrils, bringing back nothing but bad memories.

She hated hospitals. Every time she'd gone to one, someone she'd loved had died. Her father, her mother and, more recently, her brother. Now Jim lay in a hospital room—and it was her fault. She should have heeded the warning not to go into the canyon.

Pierce leaned against the wall, his arms crossed. "Getting yourself all worked up won't help Jim."

"I don't need advice, I need answers." She stopped in midstride and glared at Pierce. "Who did this? And why?"

He shook his head. "We don't know. We didn't see any dirt bike tracks this time."

"I didn't hear a motorcycle, but then I was at the bottom looking up…." She scuffed her boot across the polished tiles. "I should have seen more, enough to identify the bastard."

Pierce grabbed her shoulders and forced her to look at him. "Once you realized what was happening, you kept your eyes on Jim. And from what you said earlier, if you hadn't been watching him, he could have been hit by a boulder traveling at top speed."

Roxanne's body shook with her anger. "This psycho has to be stopped before someone is killed."

"My brothers are searching the canyon rim for more tracks. He couldn't have gone far without a horse or an ATV. If there are tracks, Maddox and Dante will find them."

"Why Jim?" Roxanne asked, her brows drawing together.

"Do you mean, why not you?" Pierce shot back at her. "You can't blame yourself, Roxy."

"I was stupid, I should have heeded the warning."

Pierce frowned. "What warning?"

Roxanne tipped her head back, running her hand through her hair. "When you dropped me off this morning, I went inside the barn and found a message spray painted across the walls."

Pierce shook her slightly. "What did it say?"

"'Stay out of the canyon.'" She broke free of his grip and walked away. "And I didn't."

"Why didn't you call me?"

She spun to face him, anger at herself digging a hole in her gut. "I didn't want you to come back around. It wasn't your problem. I called the sheriff and Deputy Duncan came out, asked questions and said he'd check into it."

Pierce snorted. "You should have called me back before I'd even left."

She flung her hand in the air. "Hindsight isn't doing Jim any good now."

A nurse emerged from Jim's room, pushing a cart of bloody gauze and surgical equipment. She gave

Roxanne a reassuring smile. "Dr. Rhoads will be out shortly."

Her stomach knotting, Roxanne quickly settled herself in a chair as she felt her knees start to give way. Her breath caught and held in her throat as she waited for the doctor to appear. A crash cart hadn't been wheeled in. That had to be a good sign. The nurse had smiled. Another good sign.

Jim had to be all right.

She gulped back the sob that threatened to rise in her throat, calling on all the anger that had been simmering to force herself to stay strong and in control.

When the doctor emerged, Roxanne practically pounced on him. "How's Jim? Will he be all right?"

The doctor's brows dipped. "Are you his next of kin?"

"I'm his boss and the only family Jim has. That makes me next of kin." Roxanne stared up at the doctor. "I have power of attorney, but the paperwork is back at the ranch."

"Good enough." Dr. Rhoads nodded and laid a hand on Roxanne's shoulder. "He's pretty banged up, but for a man his age, he's in good physical condition and should pull through just fine."

Roxanne let go of the breath she'd been holding. "Thank God."

"He's got a broken arm, sprained ankle and two broken ribs. Had a helluva time getting his boot off. Ended up cutting it away. Since he took such hard knocks to the head, we'll keep him overnight to make sure he doesn't have any swelling on the brain."

Roxanne's chest tightened at the recurring image of Jim tumbling down the steep walls of the canyon. "He fell a long way."

Dr. Rhoads laid a hand on Roxanne's arm. "We'll keep him in the intensive care unit overnight and check on him every half hour. The good news is that he did recover consciousness while we were patching him up and asked for Miss Roxy. I assume that's you?"

Roxanne's eyes clouded with tears. Jim hadn't called her Roxy since her father had died. "That's me. Can I see him?"

"He's hooked up to monitors and oxygen, but yes, though only for a few minutes. He won't be awake for long, I have the nurse administering a sedative in his IV. It should kick in pretty quickly."

Pierce flipped out his credentials. "I'm with the FBI. If he's awake, I'd like to ask Jim some questions about what happened."

Dr. Rhoads's lips tightened. "Don't take too long. He's been through a lot."

Roxanne shook the doctor's hand. "Thank you so much for taking care of him." Then she scooted around him and into the room, Pierce close behind.

Another nurse was inside, adjusting an IV bag. When she saw them, she smiled and left them alone with the foreman.

Jim lay in the hospital bed, his rugged, sunbaked skin a sharp contrast to the crisp white sheets.

Her chest squeezing tight, Roxanne tiptoed to his bedside and took his work-worn uninjured hand in hers, carefully, afraid she'd hurt him.

Her old friend's eyes blinked open and stared up at her for a long moment. "Watch that first step," he said, his voice like gravel, rough and broken. "It's a doozy." He chuckled and winced.

A tear slipped from the corner of Roxanne's eye. Jim always had a way of making her laugh when times were at their worst. "You never did like following the leader," she said. "You had to go and make a path of your own, didn't you?"

He closed his eyes and whispered, "Faster."

She squeezed his hand, reminded of just how quickly it had happened, even in the slow motion of her traumatized view. "Show-off." Her voice caught on a sob.

Jim's brow furrowed. "Hey, what's this? Cowgirls don't cry."

She brushed a tear away, but more followed. "This one does."

"Go home, Miss Roxy." He squeezed her hand.

"Not without you."

"Gonna be there soon enough."

She smiled, feeling better at the reminder that he wouldn't have to be in the hospital for long. "You better."

"Now go, cowgirl." His voice faded.

For a moment Roxanne thought he'd drifted to sleep. She held on to his hand, afraid that if she let go something bad would happen.

Jim's lids twitched open. "Got my eye on one of the nurses. You're cramping my style."

Pierce touched her shoulder. "Come on, the old man needs his rest."

"And a good-lookin' nurse." Jim glanced up at Roxanne. "I'll be fine. Just need a little nap." He closed his eyes again and his breathing grew slow and steady.

Roxanne laid his hand on the bed and backed away, reluctant to leave.

Pierce hooked her arm and led her through the door.

"I should stay," she said, staring at the closed door.

"And do what? The nurses are going to keep an eye

on him all night. It's getting late and we need to get back."

Roxanne knew he was right, but leaving Jim…

"Look, Dante went by your place earlier to let them know what was going on and get a look at that spray paint. I'm sure your ranch hands would appreciate an update."

Roxanne's shoulders sagged as her world rushed back in, reminding her of her responsibilities as a ranch owner. With her foreman out and herself here in Bismarck, there was no telling how the cattle roundup was progressing. She couldn't afford to lose another day or she'd miss the sale and her only opportunity to make enough money to keep the ranch afloat through the winter. At that rate, she'd have to lay off all the hands and she wouldn't have anything to pay the mortgage, the men, Jim or his medical bills. "You're right. I need to get back to the ranch." She spun on her boot heels and headed for the exit.

Since Maddox had brought the truck to the canyon, Pierce and Roxanne had taken it all the way to Bismarck to check on Jim while Dante and Maddox had taken care of getting the horses home. Pierce would have to take her back to her ranch.

Roxanne left the hospital and climbed into the truck cab, sinking back against the seat, letting the worry for Jim's safety roll off her.

She breathed in the earthy scent of hay and leather gloves, remembering the many times she'd ridden in this old truck, worked alongside Pierce as they loaded hay onto trailers, hauling it back to be stored in the barn. The memories reminded her of hot summer days and cool, lazy nights, sitting on the porch of her ranch house, just the two of them in the swing her grandfather had built for her grandmother. The old couple had been married over seventy years when they'd passed on within months of each other.

Roxanne had assumed she and Pierce would be like them, sitting on the porch swing, growing old, celebrating their seventieth year together with their grandchildren gathered around.

She shook her head, sitting up straighter in her seat, her eyes focusing on the road ahead. She had been mistaken. Their union wasn't meant to be.

After Pierce pulled onto Interstate 94, he glanced across at her.

"You should stay at the Thunder Horse Ranch tonight."

His words ripped through the silence, startling a response out of her. "What?"

"You heard me. Someone has made a point of going after you and your people. It's not safe for you to go back. My brothers and I can protect you better at our place."

"And leave my ranch and the hands at the mercy of some lunatic?" She crossed her arms over her chest. "Thanks, but no thanks."

In her peripheral vision Roxanne could see him staring at her, but she refused to look his way. She'd leaned on him entirely too much that day already. It wasn't as if he'd be there always. He'd told her she couldn't rely on him, and she'd taken him at his word.

In this, as in everything else in her life, she was on her own.

SILENCE SETTLED AROUND them in the cab of the pickup as Pierce accepted that this was one battle he wasn't going to win. He knew that Roxanne couldn't leave her ranch hands to fend for themselves. Much as he'd like to spirit her away from it all to keep her safe, her sense of responsibility wouldn't let her go.

The warning message led him to believe the canyon was the only place the shooter had issues with, so perhaps she was safe as long as she stayed on the ranch. But the message had appeared inside her barn, close to her home. Pierce didn't trust that the attacker wouldn't make it more personal. How could he keep her safe?

The rumble of tires on the road vibrated through his chest. The thought of Roxanne staying on her ranch without the foreman ate a hole in Pierce's gut.

Jim was the oldest and most trusted employee she had and he'd stayed in the ranch house since the deaths of Roxanne's parents. With Jim out of the way, someone might take advantage of the opportunity and make a move on Roxanne, a lone woman in an empty house.

By the time he pulled onto the long gravel driveway leading up to the Carmichael ranch house, he'd made up his mind.

Now all he had to do was convince Roxanne.

He shifted into Park in front of her house.

She glanced sideways at him. "Thanks for taking me to Bismarck."

"I'd have gone anyway." Pierce switched off the engine. "I wanted to see that Jim was okay. He's a good man."

When Roxanne opened her door and climbed down, Pierce did the same.

She stared across the cab of the truck at him, without closing the door. "I can take it from here. You don't have to stick around."

"I'm staying." He closed the driver's door.

"Oh, no, you're not." She slammed her door and

rounded the front of his truck, grabbed his door handle and opened it again. "Tuck needs you to help him with wedding planning."

Pierce shut the door again. "I'm staying."

"I don't need you to. I have four ranch hands as backup."

"And they stay in the bunkhouse while you are alone in the main house." He crossed his arms over his chest and stared down at her, feet braced, ready for the fight. "I'm staying."

She frowned. "You're not welcome, so go home."

"You need protection. I'm it."

"I have a gun. I'll provide my own protection." She jerked her hand toward the truck. "Go."

He shook his head, his lip lifting on one side. "Sorry. No can do. You're stuck with me."

"You're not staying in the ranch house." She heaved a sigh, her shoulders sagging, the shadows beneath her eyes deepening. "Please leave."

"Not going to happen. Look, if you don't want me in the house then I'll sleep outside." He raised his hands above his head and stretched. "Been a few years since I slept under the stars. Reckon it will be good for me."

She dragged in a breath and blew it out through her nose like an angry bull. "You're a stubborn man, Pierce Thunder Horse."

"I can be."

"Fine. If you're staying, it has to be in the bunkhouse with the hands."

"Kind of missing the point, aren't you? I won't be close enough to help you if someone tries to come after you."

"That's as good as it gets, cowboy."

Pierce's eyes narrowed. At least she wasn't booting

him off her property or calling the sheriff to have him removed. "Done."

He opened the rear door to the cab and unearthed a sleeping bag he kept rolled up behind the seat in case of a breakdown. Being prepared meant the difference between life and death during the North Dakota winters. Granted it was summer, but the bag remained in the truck year-round, just in case.

Roxanne turned toward the house, her voice carrying over her shoulder. "I'll fix a sandwich for you. I'm sure the hands have already rustled up their grub. Give me twenty minutes."

He nodded and took off toward the bunkhouse. He still didn't plan to sleep there—the distance to the house was too much for his comfort. However, it was his chance to check out Roxanne's employees. One of them could be the troublemaker.

As he entered the long barracks-style building, four heads turned his way. "Evenin'." He touched the brim of his hat and strode in. "Looks like I'll be helpin' with the roundup. Miss Carmichael said to bunk here."

Pierce nodded at Abe Hunting Bear and Fred Jorgensen, men he'd known as long as he'd known Roxanne.

"We could use the help, Pierce." Abe offered his hand. "Seems the herd is scattered farther than normal this year. The early drought has them ranging wide to get enough to eat."

Pierce braced himself as the Lakotan gripped his hand hard enough to crush bones. When Abe let go, Pierce shook his hand, letting blood rush back in. "Good to see ya, Abe."

Fred proffered a hand, his gaze direct. He didn't utter a single word, just shook Pierce's hand and let go. The man turned to his bunk, dropped down on the thin mattress and tipped his hat over his eyes. Typical of the shy cowboy. The man had a painful stutter that worsened under stress. He'd rather fake sleep than carry on a conversation.

Pierce stepped past the first two bunks and nodded at the kid. "You're new here."

The blond-haired, blue-eyed gangly boy shook Pierce's hand with a surprisingly strong grip. "Name's Toby Gentry. You might know my oldest brother, Jake. I think you two went to high school together in Medora."

A smile spread across Pierce's face. "He played football, didn't he?"

Toby grinned. "Starting quarterback for three years straight."

"You'll have to tell him hello for me next time you see him."

"I will. We Skype once a week. Jake's in the army now, deployed to Afghanistan." Instead of a sad look, Toby's shoulders straightened, his thin chest pushing out, pride for his brother apparent.

The fourth ranch hand sat on his bunk, an unlit cigarette dangling from his lips. He didn't get up to greet Pierce. Instead his eyes narrowed.

Pierce refused to back down. "Hi, I'm Pierce Thunder Horse."

The younger man's nostrils flared, but he gave a nod of acknowledgment. "Ethan."

"I'll be helping Ms. Carmichael through the roundup."

"Whatever."

Toby motioned Pierce toward the bunk beside his. "You can bunk here."

"Thanks." Pierce unfolded the thin mattress and

dropped his bedroll on it, eying the sullen ranch hand as he settled his sleeping bag. "I'd better get back up to the ranch house. The boss said she'd have a sandwich for me."

"I'll go with you. I'm kinda hungry, too." Toby led the way.

Pierce followed the boy out of the bunkhouse.

When the door shut behind them, Toby glanced at Pierce. "Don't worry about Ethan. He's not the friendly type. Likes to work alone."

Pierce fell in step with the young man. "What's his problem?"

Toby shrugged. "He's always been kinda a loner, but he ain't been right since his girlfriend died a couple months back."

"What happened to her?"

"From the little he's told us, she was in a fire or somethin'." Toby scuffed his boot in the dirt. "He doesn't like to talk about it and we don't ask. No sense in poking a man where he's hurting already."

Pierce could definitely understand that, and in spite of himself, he felt a little pity for the morose young man. "Thanks for the warning. Does he always have such a bad attitude?"

Toby's brows wrinkled. "Well, he ain't all that friendly, but he wasn't hired to chat. He does his job and he don't talk back. Don't know if he's planning on sticking around, though. Miss Carmichael hired the two of us on as temporary until she gets some fences mended and all the cattle in. If the sale goes well, we might stay on for good. If not…" his shoulders raised and lowered "…guess I'll be looking for work again."

"Does Ethan have a last name?"

"Mitchell. He answered Miss Carmichael's advertisement. Came from Bismarck. I think he has some local friends, though. Saw him talkin' to Shorty Duncan on his day off."

Pierce slowed. "Deputy Shorty Duncan?"

Toby turned to face him. "Somethin' wrong with that?"

"No, no. Just seemed odd. When was this?"

"Last Sunday." Toby's head tipped to the side. "Why?"

"No reason. Just curious."

Toby stepped up on the porch and strode toward the back door. He knocked.

"Come in," Roxanne called from inside.

The door opened into the large kitchen.

Roxanne stood at a butcher-block cutting board, wearing the same dusty jeans she'd worn all day, her feet bare and her auburn hair hanging down around her shoulders in wild, loose curls.

She'd taken time to scrub clean her face and arms and she looked young, sexy and so beautiful it hurt Pierce to look at her.

When she glanced up, her frown swept upward in a smile for Toby.

Pierce's fists clenched, the stab of jealousy completely unexpected and unwarranted. He had no claim to Roxanne anymore.

"Hey, Toby," she said. "I'm glad you came up to the house. I have some extra chicken here—could you use a sandwich?"

Toby grinned. "Thanks, Miss Carmichael. I sure could. Abe cooked tonight and it wasn't nearly as good as what you make. Not that I'm complainin'. Just saying."

She handed one of the two sandwiches she had prepared to him and the other to Pierce.

"Won't you have a seat?" She motioned for Toby to sit at the long solid pine kitchen table.

"Nah, but thanks. I think I'll eat this on the way back to the bunkhouse. It's gettin' late, and I wanna catch some shut-eye. Got a long day ahead."

Roxanne smiled and held the door for the young man. "See ya in the morning, then." She stood staring out at the night for a few minutes before she turned back into the kitchen.

Pierce laid the sandwich on the cutting board and sliced it down the center, handing her one side. "Eat."

"I'm not hungry."

"Do it for the ranch then. Your hands won't want to play nursemaid to you if you pass out from malnutrition."

She glared at him, but she took the sandwich and bit into the end of it.

"What do you know about Ethan Mitchell?"

"Only that he works hard, and came from Bismarck." She bit off another piece and chewed. After she swallowed, she asked, "Why?"

"He's got a chip on his shoulder. I just wondered if you knew why?"

"Started a couple months ago. Apparently his girlfriend was killed in an accident back in Bismarck. Happened around the same time as Mason..." Roxanne set the sandwich on the cutting board. "Why do you want to know?"

"Have you ever said or done anything to make him angry?"

"No." She shook her head. "He's been a little bad

tempered, but it never really seemed aimed at me. I assumed he was going through a grieving process."

"Angry for two months? You'd think he'd have moved on by now."

Roxanne's mouth quirked up on the corners then straightened. "It's not that easy, and you know it."

Pierce stared down at the sandwich in his hand. "Guess you're right. I'm still angry over my father's death, and at the sheriff for not doing any more than he did to investigate." Pierce's fingers tightened around the sandwich, as images of his father's body being laid out in the Thunder Horse ranch house crowded into his memory. The mix of anger, frustration and crushing sadness had meant that he'd wanted to lash out at everyone in the immediate vicinity.

Yeah, he could understand Ethan's anger. Pierce glanced at Roxanne. She'd been angry when they'd told her about Mason's death. Pierce had been angry as well—at himself—and he'd lost none of that anger or self-blame since.

He'd understood when Roxanne called off their wedding. But his heart had still broken, and not just from her rejection. Mason had been his friend, too. He'd grieved for the loss, as well, and mourned even more that he couldn't hold Roxanne through her sorrow.

Roxanne wrapped her arms around her middle and turned to stare out the window at the night. "Maybe you'd better go get some rest like Toby. We'll be up early tomorrow."

Pierce took his sandwich and left the kitchen, feeling no closer to bridging the chasm that had opened between him and Roxanne the day her brother died. Nor was he sure he wanted to bridge the gap.

She deserved better. Someone to be there for her, not someone who'd let her down.

As he headed back toward the bunkhouse, he tossed the sandwich into the bushes. After the eventful day, hunger for food was the farthest thing from his mind. Hunger for Roxanne? Well, he'd just have to get over it.

Chapter Seven

Roxanne headed toward her bedroom determined to follow her own advice and get to bed early. When she passed by her office, she remembered the stack of correspondence she'd put off as long as she could. Had all gone well today, she'd have tackled it as soon as dinner was over.

Tired to death and heart weary, she wanted to pass the door and ignore the bills, but she couldn't. If she didn't pay a couple of them, she'd be turned over to a collection agency. Not only would they hound her for payments, her credit rating would suffer and she'd never get another loan to tide her over through the rough months when cash flow was an issue.

Dragging her feet into the office, she sat behind the desk and stared at the mound of envelopes and the ancient computer on which she kept the ranch's books.

She opened the first envelope. A bill with a thirty-days-past-due notice. Her gut clenched. Her father had prided himself on always paying his bills on time.

"Well, Daddy, a lot has changed and I'm not so sure you left the ranch to the right person."

Her father hadn't had much choice. Roxanne had been one of two children. Mason had had an equal interest in the ranch, but he hadn't wanted to stay and work it, preferring to join the FBI instead. That left Roxanne to take care of the ranch, the cattle and horses, not to mention her responsibilities as the Bureau of Land Management representative in charge of monitoring the wild horses of the badlands.

Roxanne loved the ranch and couldn't imagine herself doing anything other than what she was doing, but sometimes the struggle to keep things going was almost more than she could bear. Especially when the bill collectors came to call and she couldn't afford to pay.

The economy had tanked, cattle prices fallen and her mortgage had come due. The sale of the cattle would only stall the inevitable. Sooner or later, she'd lose the ranch and be homeless and jobless.

Then why the hell didn't she just get up from her desk and go to bed and sleep until next Wednesday?

Because Roxanne Carmichael didn't give up. It wasn't in her blood. She came from a long line of hardheaded Carmichaels who didn't know when to call it a day.

Determined to find the money to pay the bills, she tapped the keyboard.

Nothing happened.

She checked the plugs and the connections and tried rebooting.

The computer wouldn't reboot, the screen remaining dark.

Self-pity slammed into her like a mini-tsunami, crashing over her and sucking her down.

Tears filled her eyes. She rose from the chair, a rush of anger bubbling up and over. Roxanne shoved the stack of papers off the desktop and slammed her palm on the scarred wooden surface. "What next? Good Lord, haven't we suffered enough?"

With the walls closing in around her, Roxanne flung open the French doors leading out onto the deck and stepped through. She breathed deeply, hoping to calm the rising panic.

"How will we survive? How will I pay the men?" Roxanne dropped into the porch swing, burying her face in her hands. "I should just give up."

PIERCE DIDN'T MAKE IT back to the bunkhouse. Instead he performed a perimeter check of the ranch house and the outbuildings, circling each structure, checking inside, around the outside and anywhere danger might lurk.

He found nothing.

Before returning to the bunkhouse, he made one more pass around the ranch house. A light burned in the kitchen and one in the study. Roxanne was probably still awake.

Pierce wondered why. Was she worried about Jim? Suffering from insomnia after being shot at and almost getting caught in a landslide?

A soft sobbing sound reached him. He tilted his head to listen. Had it been the rustle of the leaves in the tree shading the house from the moonlight?

The breeze died down and the sobbing continued, accompanied by the repetitive creak of metal on metal from the direction of the porch.

Easing his way up the steps, Pierce tiptoed across the wooden planks until he stood in front of the old porch swing he and Roxanne had shared on many occasions.

The woman sat hunched over, her face buried in her hands, moonlight glinting off the moisture spilling through her fingers.

Seeing Roxanne, an incredibly strong woman, reduced to tears of despair tugged at Pierce's heart. All his self-made promises to keep a distance faded away as he reached out and pulled her into his arms.

Roxanne gasped, her eyes widening.

When she realized it was him, she stiffened. "What are you doing here?"

"I heard you crying."

She sniffed. "Cowgirls don't cry."

"Right." Pierce thumbed away a trail of tears on her cheek. "Must have been the wind I heard in the trees."

She sniffed again, her eyes pooling with a fresh wash of tears. "What am I doing wrong?" Roxanne buried her face against his shirt, her fingers clutching at the fabric. Her shoulders shook with each sob, the sounds muffled against his chest.

He stroked her hair and held her steady, comforting her, whispering words of his ancestors into her ear, soothing her.

When her tears slowed to a trickle, he tipped her face up and pressed a gentle kiss to her forehead. "Everything will be okay."

"How do you know?" She stared into his eyes, her own red rimmed and glazed with moisture.

"Because you're strong. You always come through."

Her head dipped, her gaze dropping to where her hands rested on his chest. "I'm not strong enough to protect my ranch and the people who work for me."

"You shouldn't have to worry about that. Let the sheriff find the shooter. It's his job."

She gave him a confused look, and for a moment, he wondered if she had other problems, troubles that she hadn't shared with him. But her expression closed off before he could analyze it further. "You of all people are one to talk. You never trusted the sheriff's investigation on your father's death. Why should I rely on him now?"

She had a point.

"These men can take care of themselves. You aren't their bodyguard."

She shoved her hair out of her face. "But they work for me. I'm responsible."

"Then give them the choice. Tell them what's going on, and then say that they can work for you and run the risk, or walk." Pierce cupped her chin. "You can't take care of everyone."

"But—"

"You can't," he said softly.

The fight seemed to go out of her, and she leaned into him. "I want to," she murmured. "I know it's wrong. But I can't help it. It's who I am."

"The person I fell in love with." Pierce laced his fingers through her hair and pulled her closer. She melted into him and he slid his finger under her chin, tilting her face up toward him before leaning in closer...closer...

A rustle in the bushes made him freeze, his head jerking up. He listened, trying to make out the noise.

Then a loud crash broke through the night.

"What the hell?" Pierce jumped to his feet and bolted off the porch, racing around the side of the house. He thought he saw a shadowy form running away, but before he could get a lock on where the person was going, there was a burst of light that dazzled his eyes and completely disoriented him. Turning his head toward the source, he let out a gasp of shock.

Someone had set the house on fire. And they'd started with Roxanne's bedroom.

RECOGNIZING THE SOUND as broken glass, Roxanne had rushed into the house as soon as Pierce had left the porch. Running into her room, she was shocked and horrified to see smoke and flames rising up the side of her bed, licking at the fabric of the quilt her mother had made especially for her.

"No!" Roxanne rushed forward, grabbing a throw rug from the floor, using it to beat at the flames, ignoring the way the acrid scent of gasoline filled her lungs along with the smoke.

"Roxanne!" Pierce called out through the shattered window. The next thing she knew, he'd barreled into the room, too.

Flames spread from liquid spilled on the wood flooring, and climbed up the curtains on either side of the broken window.

Roxanne yanked the quilt from the bed and tossed it to the floor, smothering the flames beneath her rug.

Pierce ripped an area rug up from the hallway and laid it over the flaming fluid, snuffing out the fire. Then he opened the broken window, yanked the burning curtains, rod and all, from the wall, and shoved them out onto the ground.

After the fire was out, Roxanne stood in the bedroom surveying the wreckage, her heartbeat finally slowing from the panic she'd felt only moments before. A fresh breeze helped clear the smoke from the room. Roxanne coughed, noticing for the first time the burning sensation in her lungs when she breathed. She stared at the damage. "Why is this happening?"

"I don't know," Pierce said. "But it has to stop."

Roxanne bent to lift her mother's quilt and inspected the damage. A giant scorch mark marred one corner, the rest was only blackened by smoke. A good washing would clean it up. But would it erase the stench of smoke? The lingering taint of fear?

She hugged the blanket to her body.

"I'm going to call the sheriff." Pierce headed down the hall.

"Miss Carmichael, you okay?" a voice called from outside the house.

"Yes, Toby," Roxanne answered. "I'm fine. I'm coming out."

While Pierce placed the call, Roxanne briefed the ranch hands on what had happened.

"Sorry, boys, but the sheriff will probably question everyone. I ask you all to cooperate."

Pierce stood on the porch, his gaze taking it all in.

Roxanne wondered what was going on behind his dark gaze. Did he have any lingering regrets that their moment together on the porch had been interrupted?

Outside, with the cool North Dakota night breeze chilling her skin, Roxanne had been having second thoughts. Perhaps the interruption had been destiny's way of saying *don't go there*.

The men returned to the bunkhouse and waited for the sheriff to arrive. Denying the urge to clean up the mess in her bedroom, Roxanne made a pot of coffee and sat on the porch, pretending to drink a cup, lost in her thoughts on where she and Pierce had been headed and the damage done both between them and to her house.

Twenty minutes later, Deputy Shorty Duncan showed up and took their statements. He gathered the bottle fragments, dropping them into an evidence bag.

"Someone used an accelerant and what looks like a beer bottle to make a Molotov cocktail." He brushed his hands off on his trousers and met Roxanne's gaze. "Easy enough for even a grade-school kid, and damaging."

"Tell us something we didn't know," Pierce said.

"I'll have the bottle fragments dusted for prints."

The deputy stepped back, his gaze panning the room. "No guarantees."

"I've heard that before. When are you going to actually do something about the man trying to kill Miss Carmichael?" Pierce asked. "After she's dead? No wait, you don't even investigate murders, do you?"

"You got a problem with me, Mr. Thunder Horse?" Shorty Duncan puffed out his barrel chest and moved toe-to-toe with Pierce. The deputy stood six inches shorter than the Lakotan, but he was no less self-assured.

Roxanne's pulse raced, sure she would witness a fight if she didn't do something. She eased between the two men. "Look, guys, I'm tired and I want to get some sleep in what's left of the night." She stared up at Pierce, holding his gaze.

"I'll do my job, just keep him on a leash, will ya?" Shorty snapped a few pictures, using a camera he'd brought from his SUV. "If you have any more troubles, just call nine-one-one."

Roxanne nodded. If they didn't find prints on the glass, the deputy's trip to her ranch would turn out to be nothing but a waste of time. At the rate the sheriff was investigating what had happened, someone was sure to die before they resolved the case.

It was time to take action.

After Deputy Duncan left, Pierce helped her clean up the glass and mop the remaining gasoline from the floor. When they'd finished, the clock had pushed past midnight.

With a full day of roundup ahead, Roxanne groaned. "I'm getting a shower. You don't have to stay. You can go back to the bunkhouse."

Pierce shook his head. "You take the first shower. I'll grab my gear and sleep on the couch."

Too tired to argue, Roxanne nodded. "Thanks."

"I'm just glad I was here."

"Me, too." She avoided his eyes and ducked into the laundry room where she gathered clean if wrinkled clothing that didn't smell of smoke. She hurried down the hallway to the guest bathroom.

She rushed through a shower, scrubbing the smoke and soot from her hair. Her chest felt tight, her throat raw, but thankfully the smoke in her room hadn't been too thick.

When she'd combed the tangles out of her hair and smoothed cream into her skin, she stepped out of the bathroom wearing a T-shirt and sweatpants. Nothing at all sexy.

Pierce had been to the bunkhouse and returned with his bedroll. He'd removed his shirt and had just set his boots beside him on the floor.

When he straightened, Roxanne's breath caught in her throat at how big and handsome the man was. He wore his Lakota heritage with pride. She cleared her throat. "The shower's yours," came out in a gravelly croak. "Towels are in the cabinet beneath the sink. If you need anything else, let me know."

Roxanne stood for a moment longer, unable to tear her gaze from him.

He inhaled, his naked chest expanding, then he let it out on a sigh. "It's been a long day. Go to bed, Roxanne."

As if all the wind had been sucked from her lungs, Roxanne hesitated only a moment longer. Then she performed an about-face and escaped into the guest bedroom, shutting the door firmly between them. She leaned against the wood panels, her heart racing, her body on fire with flames hotter than any Molotov cocktail could inspire.

Hell yeah, it had been a long night, and likely it would get even longer.

Chapter Eight

Pierce lay awake into the night, kicked back in the recliner in the Carmichael Ranch living room. His thoughts hadn't strayed far since he'd returned to the badlands. All centering on Roxanne, her bright auburn hair and incredibly blue eyes.

Two months had done nothing to shake her from his thoughts and dreams. Being with her again only reawakened the longing, making it stronger than before. If he'd thought he could just walk away from her, he'd been wrong.

He must have slipped into a troubled sleep, because the sun rising up over the horizon spilled into the living room of the ranch house, nudging him awake.

Shouts outside had him up and moving across the floor to peer through the window at the rear of the house.

The ranch hands had their horses gathered in the barnyard and were climbing into their saddles. Toby glanced toward the house, said something to Abe and nudged his horse, sending it forward.

Pierce shoved his feet into his boots and his arms into his shirtsleeves, buttoning as he strode through the house to the back door.

Toby arrived on horseback at the back porch as Pierce stepped out.

"Would ya let the boss know we'll be rounding up the cattle in the north pasture?" The horse danced sideways and Toby pulled the reins tight before continuing. "No need for Miss Carmichael to get out this mornin'. We can handle it."

Pierce nodded at the boy. "Good, because she'll be staying around the ranch house today, helping me with repairs."

"I will?" a voice said.

Pierce didn't have to turn to know Roxanne stood behind him. "She will."

Toby glanced from Pierce to Roxanne, his cheeks reddening. "Either way, we'll be back around sunset." He turned and rode away at a swift trot.

Pasting a smile on his lips, Pierce turned to face Roxanne.

Her curls lay around her shoulders, tousled as if she'd just risen from bed. She still wore the T-shirt and sweats from the night before. Twin flags of color rode high on her cheeks, and her blue eyes practically snapped at him. "Look, cowboy, this is my ranch and I'll call the shots."

He saluted and strode past her into the house. "Then call them. I have work to do in order to make your house temporarily livable."

She grabbed his arm as he moved past. "And I have cattle to round up. No cattle means no lights or payday."

"Like the cowboy said, they have it covered." Pierce held back a grin as he played his trump card. "Do you want Jim to come home to all this smoke damage? Might give him a coronary on top of his other injuries."

Roxanne let go of his arm, her eyes narrowing. "No, of course I don't want that."

"Right, then I'll need a hand getting it all cleaned up and ready. I'll bet the hospital will cut him loose this afternoon. He's bound to hear about what happened—can't expect the ranch hands to keep it to themselves—but if we clean up the worst of it, then we might be able to calm him down. But we'll need to have the place ready or he'll try to ride out after the bad guy himself."

Her gaze shifted to the window, her fingers twisting a long strand of hair. "I hate it when you're right." The stiffness leached out of Roxanne's body. "Since you're so smart, you can cook breakfast."

"I can handle that." He went one way, Roxanne the other.

In the kitchen, Pierce found the skillet and rummaged through the refrigerator for eggs and ham.

By the time Roxanne emerged in a clean pair of jeans and a faded and wrinkled chambray shirt that was two sizes too big for her, Pierce had omelets on the table.

"I loaded the washer with my smoky clothes. Remind me to switch the loads before I head out to the roundup. Mmm, that smells good." She pulled up a chair and lifted a fork, digging in.

Pierce loved that about Roxanne. She wasn't a girlie girl who picked at her food. She rode hard, worked harder and ate to keep up her strength. Add to that the pale face of an angel and auburn curls a man could lose himself in and...

Pierce swallowed hard and reined in his thoughts and desires. He wouldn't get much done at this rate.

They passed the meal in silence.

As soon as the dishes were cleared, Pierce headed

for the barn, collecting hammers, nails, plywood and a circular saw.

When he returned, Roxanne was busy scrubbing the soot off the walls with a vinegar-and-water solution. She'd stripped the bed and tossed the sheets and the damaged quilt into the laundry room.

"You don't waste time," he commented.

Without pausing, she quipped, "Got cattle to get to the market."

"The men will handle it."

"It takes more hands than their four pairs and I've only got two more days to get the job done."

"Or what?"

"I miss the sale."

She started to say more but clamped her lips shut and went back to work on the walls. Making her way around the room, she cleaned the walls and then started in on the ceiling.

Pierce knocked the remaining shards of glass out of the window frame, careful to collect all the pieces and put them in a box to be recycled later. He cut a square of plywood out of the scrap he'd found in the barn and fitted it into the window, nailing it to the window frame, finding it strangely sad when the board blocked his view of Roxanne. Up until that moment, they'd been working quietly together, neither speaking, but for Pierce's part, he didn't feel it was an uncomfortable silence. He liked being around her. The woman wasn't afraid of work, whether it was washing walls or roping steers.

After returning the tools and remaining supplies to the barn, he entered the house through the back door.

Roxanne's voice drifted through the hallway from the ranch office. Her tone was one of distress.

His need to protect this woman pushed Pierce forward. He stopped before the door, out of sight but within listening range. Guilt over eavesdropping gnawed at his gut, but the need to help won out.

ROXANNE HAD BEEN ELBOW deep scrubbing the walls and the ceiling when the phone in the office had pulled her away from her task.

She'd answered the call, thinking it would be the hospital with news of Jim.

"Ms. Carmichael?"

"Speaking."

"This is Mr. Palmer from the First Bank of Medora."

"Hello, Mr. Palmer." Her stomach twisted into a knot and she sat in the chair behind the desk, bracing herself for what came next. "Did you get my application for the line of credit loan?"

"We did, and we've reviewed it." He paused. "I understand you've had some problems out there at the ranch."

"Nothing major," she lied.

"We received word that your foreman is laid up in the hospital with multiple injuries and is unable to perform his duties." The man paused waiting for her to confirm or deny.

"And?" Roxanne asked, her voice terse.

"We also heard there was a fire and some damage to the ranch house last night."

Roxanne wasn't surprised. News traveled fast in small communities. She'd bet good ol' Deputy Duncan had passed on that little tidbit. If not, perhaps the dispatcher had shared the only incident on a boring night over coffee at the diner.

Her patience wearing thin, she cut to the chase. "I'm

sorry, Mr. Palmer, I have a busy day ahead. Is there a point you're trying to get to?"

"Ms. Carmichael, in light of the recent events, the bank executives and underwriters have reviewed your request for the line of credit and have determined you to be high risk."

Blood drained from Roxanne's head and a ball of lead settled in her belly. "High risk? What does that mean?"

"That you are too much of a risk to loan the money to."

"I've always made my mortgage payments on time. I've never declared bankruptcy. I'm good for it. I just need a temporary loan until I can get the cattle sold."

"We understand, but in your case…"

Roxanne rose from the desk chair, blood boiling, her fingers clenching the handset so firmly her knuckles turned white. "In my case I'm a woman running a ranch in a typically male environment. Well, Mr. Palmer, let me tell you—"

Keep your cool, her inner common sense implored.

Roxanne caught herself before she spewed all her frustrations out on the telephone. She clamped her tongue between her teeth so hard she could taste the coppery flavor of blood.

Clearing her scratchy throat, she started over. "I'll be in town soon to discuss the situation with the bank president. Have a nice day," she ended, forcing the words between clenched teeth.

"That won't be necessary—" Mr. Palmer started.

"Oh, yes it will. Thank you, Mr. Palmer." She hit the end button and threw the phone across the room. It hit a shelf full of books then crashed to the floor and broke in half, the plastic pieces falling to the floor with a loud clatter.

Roxanne turned toward the French doors, staring out into the bright sunshine, and wondered how the sun could keep shining so optimistically when her world was falling apart.

"Anything wrong?" Pierce's voice cut through her thoughts, reminding her that she had more than a couple of unresolved issues in her life, her ranch finances and the attacker being two, Pierce Thunder Horse making it three.

With her back to the infuriating man she planted her hands on her hips. Her heart thumped hard inside her chest, feeling like it might explode. "Have you stooped to eavesdropping now?"

"Couldn't help overhearing. Is the bank giving you troubles?"

"No. Everything is perfectly *fine*." She pushed through the French doors and out onto the porch, needing to get away from him, from the banker and from everyone who pulled at her.

The thickheaded man didn't get the hint. He followed. "If you need a loan, I'm sure the Thunder Horse Ranch can front you the money to tide you over to the sale."

She spun to face him, closing the distance to stand directly in front of him. "Get this straight, Mr. Thunder Horse, I. Don't. Need. Your. Money. Or *anything* else from you." She poked his chest with her index finger on every word. "Not now, or ever."

He captured her wrist and held it, his black eyes so intense she felt them burn a hole right through her. "Are you that proud you'd risk losing everything you've worked so hard for just to save face?"

"I don't want to rely on you or any man. I can do this on my own."

"Damn it, Roxy, you're making it hard for me to help you."

"I didn't ask for your help," she said through gritted teeth. "I didn't want you to come back into my life."

"Well, that's too damn bad. I'm here and there's not much you can do to make me go away until this mess is resolved."

She stared up into his eyes, all the heat of her anger making her breathe hard, her chest rising and falling, pressing against his arm with each time she inhaled. As angry and frustrated as she was with him, it was still hard to fight her body's natural instinct to lean in closer to him.

His dark gaze bored into hers, sucking her into that black abyss. He seemed to be struggling, too. "I didn't want to come back into your life, but you make it hard for me to resist."

They were so wrapped up in the electric connection between them that the sound of a horse's hooves didn't register until the beast whinnied and snorted.

Roxanne glanced up, her eyes glazed, barely able to focus on the man astride one of her horses.

Ethan sat in the saddle, his hands gripping the reins, his eyes narrowed and, if Roxanne wasn't mistaken, angry.

She pulled away from Pierce and ran a hand through her hair. "What is it, Ethan?"

He hesitated, his hands clenching and unclenching around the leather straps in his hands. "I came back for some more fencing supplies to repair the corral."

Roxanne frowned. "You know where they are."

"Right." He nudged his horse with his heels and the animal leaped forward, heading for the barn.

If not for Ethan's interruption, she might have thrown herself at Pierce. What was wrong with her?

"Roxanne—" Pierce's hands rested on her arms and he tried to turn her to face him.

She shook free of his grip and stepped out of reach. "I need to get out on the range and help with the roundup. We're done here."

THE NOTE OF FINALITY IN her voice made Pierce let go.

Roxanne reentered the house, picked up her cowboy hat and hurried toward the barn.

Torn between leaving and following her, Pierce made the only decision he could. He followed, jogging toward the barn, worried that she'd get so far ahead of him that he wouldn't be able to catch up or find her. She was still in danger, the target of an idiot bent on some evil revenge or something equally insane. He hadn't figured it out yet, but he needed to soon.

At first he'd thought maybe it was something to do with the horses or the canyon. But with the attack moving to the ranch house, it looked more and more like Roxanne was the target, not the wild horses of the Dakota badlands or anyone within the vicinity to the canyon. Narrowing down the targets should make it easier to find the attacker, but in spite of that, Pierce couldn't claim to be pleased with the latest piece of the puzzle.

At least out on the open range, he'd see a threat coming at them from a long distance away.

Pierce swung by his pickup and grabbed the rifle and scabbard he'd loaded in the rack behind the backseat. If there was trouble ahead, he wanted to be ready.

Roxanne led her mare from the barn, the saddle

hanging loose on the mare's back. She tied the animal to a hitching post and cinched the girth.

"What horse do you want me to ride?" Pierce asked.

"None," Roxanne answered through gritted teeth.

He shrugged and entered the barn, gathered a lead rope and came back out to the pen where the horses gathered, hoping for a snack or a bale of hay to munch on.

He selected a large black gelding, snapped the lead on his halter and opened the gate to bring him out.

By the time he'd captured his horse, Roxanne had the bit between her mare's teeth and was buckling the bridle behind the horse's ears.

Knowing he wouldn't get his gelding saddled in time to catch her, Pierce stopped in front of her. "Wait for me."

"I'm just going out to the north pasture. The others are out there now, moving the cattle. I'll be safe. You don't have to come."

"You're a stubborn woman."

"And you're an equally stubborn man." She swung up into her saddle and dug her heels into the mare's sides, sending her speeding off across the prairie.

"Damned woman." Pierce led the horse into the barn and threw a saddle on him.

He hoped he could find Roxanne quickly. On a spread the size of the Carmichael Ranch, that could take some doing. At least he knew what general direction she'd chosen.

Out in the barnyard, Ethan Mitchell was loading supplies onto a four-wheel-drive all-terrain vehicle, tying them down with bungee cords.

"I thought you'd be helping the others rounding up cattle," Pierce said.

Ethan ignored Pierce, climbing onto the ATV.

Pierce stood in front of the vehicle, determined to get to the bottom of Ethan's bad attitude toward him. "Did I do something to piss you off?"

Ethan glared at him and revved the engine. "No time to sit around jawing—I've got work to do." The ATV leaped forward, missing Pierce by inches.

Anger burst through Pierce's veins, but he had more important matters to attend to. Pierce mounted his horse and rode out in the same direction as Roxanne, hoping she hadn't altered course.

She had ridden off without anyone watching her back. If Pierce didn't find her soon, there was no telling what might happen.

Chapter Nine

Roxanne headed out across the prairie, just as she had a thousand times before. Alone, without a bodyguard. But for the first time ever, she felt nervous and downright paranoid. Every noise, every shadow made her jump. Not until she caught up to the rest of her crew did she settle down.

She found three of her ranch hands working the herd, guiding them toward the pens closer to the ranch house. Once they had the entire herd in the pastures closer to the road, the animals would be corralled and loaded up to be transported to market.

The herd wasn't as large as it had been earlier that summer.

She rode up to Abe, settling her horse into an easy walk beside his. "Where are the rest of them?"

"All we can guess is that they made their way down into the canyon. Won't be easy getting them out."

"Damn." She needed all of the cattle brought in so that she could cull those that would go to market and those that would stay back for breeding stock for next year's herd.

"We'll have to move what we have into the holding pens today. Tomorrow we can work the canyon. It'll take every one of us."

Abe nodded. "Won't be easy. Too many places they can hide."

"W-w-what a-a-about th-th-the message in th-th-the b-b-barn?" Fred asked.

Roxanne pinched the bridge of her nose, willing her headache to go away. "We have to try. We won't stick around long—just get the cattle and leave. And no one's to go out there alone, is that understood?"

She hated the thought of putting her ranch hands in harm's way, but the sale was too important to let any of the herd go unaccounted for. Especially with the bank denying her loan application. The money in the bank might reassure the powers to be that she could run a ranch, despite the troubles of late.

Troubles that were impossible to forget as long as Pierce Thunder Horse kept hanging around, she thought as she watched the Lakotan ride up. As least he seemed willing to work. Without Jim, they needed every set of hands they could get.

PIERCE FELL IN STEP WITH the others, locating strays and bringing them into the herd, moving the cattle to the pen.

Chasing after one particularly stubborn steer, Roxanne got separated from the others. After leading Roxanne on quite a chase, the animal was finally trotting off in the right direction to rejoin the herd when Roxanne realized just how far she was from the ranch hands and Pierce. If any danger popped up, she couldn't just shout for help. They'd never hear.

She wondered how long it would take for Pierce to notice she was missing and come looking for her. Hopefully she'd get back before then. She was just turning her horse to return to the pen when a sound that didn't belong to the badlands reached her ears.

A motor's whine reached to her across the prairie.

Her mare danced in a circle.

A plume of dust rose from the dry earth as a dirt bike raced straight for her.

The biker maintained a direct path to collide with Roxanne and her horse, his speed insane, his body hunched low.

Cut off from her men, Roxanne raced the opposite direction of the dirt bike, hoping to make a wide circle and head back toward the ranch hands and safety.

She hadn't loaded her rifle and scabbard onto her horse, thinking she'd be fine working among the men all day. Hell, she wasn't used to bringing her rifle every time she went out to work the cattle. It wasn't supposed to be this way.

The faster her horse ran, the faster the motorcycle came at her.

The mare wouldn't last long at full speed. Roxanne had to do something before the cyclist came within range to shoot at her.

She topped a knoll and rode straight down into a copse of stubby trees. Swinging out of her saddle, she slapped her horse's hindquarters, sending her off in another direction, while Roxanne dove into the underbrush.

Seconds later, the bike burst over the hilltop, going airborne for a moment, then slamming to the earth, roaring ahead after the disappearing horse.

Roxanne remained hidden until the sound of the motorcycle vanished into the distance. She hoped her horse would find its way back to where the others were, or back to the barn. Whichever, as long as the animal was safe from the man on the cycle.

After five minutes of silence passed, Roxanne rose from her hiding place and began the long trek back to where she'd left the men and the herd.

Halfway there, she spotted a lone horse and rider, galloping toward her. For a moment she considered ducking behind a tree or bush, but as she studied the way he sat straight and tall in the saddle, she knew it was Pierce.

When he reined his horse to a halt in front of her, his face was set in an angry scowl.

"You don't have to say it. I know." She stared up at him. "I shouldn't have left without telling you."

Without a word, he dropped down from his saddle and gathered her in his arms. She knew she should pull away, but after the near miss she'd had, she couldn't resist the allure of being close to him, feeling safe again even if it only lasted for a little while.

"You scared the crap out of me, you know that?" he whispered against her ear.

"I scare myself sometimes."

He leaned her away from him. "What happened?"

She tipped her head in the direction the attacker had gone. "The guy on the dirt bike came back."

Pierce held her at arm's length. "He didn't shoot at you?"

"Not this time. I didn't let him get close enough."

"Where's your horse?"

She chewed on her lip. "The barn, I hope. I ditched her and hid behind a bush. The guy on the bike chased her."

Pierce's lips curled into a smile. "I should be really angry with you." He tugged her close again, hugging her.

"You have every right. I should have paid more attention to how far I'd gotten from the group." She stared out across the rise, frowning. "I hope Sheba will be okay."

"Come on, your men will be worried." He mounted his horse and held out a hand for her.

She took it and, placing her toe on top of his, swung up behind the saddle.

They caught up with the hands as they neared the holding pen. No one questioned why she was riding double with Pierce and she didn't offer an explanation.

She slipped off the back of the horse, dropped to the ground and ran for the gate, throwing it open. The herd streamed through and raced across the pen to the other side where a gaping hole led out onto the gravel road beyond.

"Damn it! Abe, Fred, get over there and head them off before they get too far," Roxanne yelled above the sound of the cattle mooing.

Abe and Fred rode through the herd to the hole in the fence and dropped down out of their saddles, ducked beneath the top barbed wire and out onto the road.

Roxanne looked around. "Where the hell's Ethan? I thought he was working the repairs on the fence."

"Haven't seen him since he went back for supplies." Toby eased in behind the herd and worked his way across the pen to the hole in the fence, blocking other cattle from making their escape.

Pierce herded the stragglers into the pen and closed the gate. "Missing someone?"

"Ethan." Roxanne shook her head. "Something's gotta give."

About that time an engine's roar sounded behind them.

Pierce and Roxanne turned as Ethan zoomed across the prairie toward them.

When he pulled up beside Roxanne and Pierce, Roxanne bit down hard on her tongue to keep from yelling at the man. "Where have you been?"

"Had trouble with the ATV. It quit working out in the middle of nowhere and took me a while to fix it."

"Seemed to be working fine when you raced out of the barnyard," Pierce said, his eyes narrow.

"And it's working now," Roxanne added, crossed her arms over her chest.

"Well, it quit for a long time. Had to jimmy a few wires and fiddle with it to make it this far. You want these supplies or not?"

His antagonism triggered Roxanne's own anger. "You could have been here faster walking. Now, get over there and help the men gather the cattle who made it through the hole you were supposed to mend." She pointed to the broken fence.

Ethan swung his leg off the ATV and sauntered across to where the men were having a tough time getting the cattle back through the hole in the fence.

"I've a mind to fire him," Roxanne muttered.

Pierce nodded but didn't say a word.

While the men worked hard to retrieve all the cattle and mend the fence, Roxanne had Pierce take her back to the ranch house ahead of the others to prepare the evening meal. The men would be tired and hungry.

No words passed between them.

Roxanne cast a glance his way, noting the dark shadows beneath his eyes. He hadn't gotten any more sleep than she had. Tonight had to be better. She couldn't keep up this pace, especially with the grueling work of bringing in the strays from the canyon on the next day's agenda.

When they arrived at the barn, her mare stood waiting patiently for someone to remove the saddle from her back.

"I'll take care of the horses," Pierce said. "I know you have other work to attend."

She chewed on her bottom lip and sighed, too tired to argue. "Okay. But I don't like being beholden to you."

"You're not. Consider it a favor to the horses." His lips twisted into one of the crooked smiles that had always made her laugh.

Damn the man.

Roxanne hurried toward the house. Once inside, she slammed cabinet doors and pots and pans to relieve a little of the tension that spun up every time she was around Pierce.

She scrounged in the refrigerator, took stock of the contents of her freezer and almost cried. With barely enough staples to make a pot of stew for the men, her cupboards were frighteningly bare.

Doing the best she could, she threw the ingredients into a pot and had it ready by the time the men arrived, hungry and grumbling.

By the time they sat down to the table in the kitchen, it was dark outside. Roxanne had showered and was ready for a quick run into town, hoping to get there before the bank and the grocery store closed. A glance at the clock made her shoulders sag. Sadly, the bank would be closed. She wouldn't have a chance at talking to the bank president as she'd threatened Mr. Palmer. But she still needed to get to the store. Hopefully, she had enough room on her credit card to buy supplies for the pantry.

While the men consumed the stew, Roxanne gathered her keys and wallet. "I'm headed to Medora for supplies. I'll be back later."

"We're all out of sweet feed for the horses," Abe said. "And we're just about out of fuel for the ATVs, plus barbed wire and nails to shore up the pens and chute."

The more items Abe added to her list, the heavier the weight of her finances grew. She could only hope Mr. Batson at the feed and supply store would let her use her credit card or add those items to her account. She barely had cash to pay for the groceries she needed to feed her employees. She didn't even want to think about how she was going to pay their salaries.

Pierce blocked her at the door. "Wait until morning. The feed store will be closed."

"But I need to be out bringing in the stragglers from the canyon tomorrow."

"You're tired." He took the keys from her hands and turned her around. "Go to bed."

She wanted to, but there was so much riding on her. "I can't."

"Yes. You can."

He walked her back into the house and down the long hall to her bedroom. "Go to sleep. I'll clean up the kitchen."

For once, she didn't argue, too tired from all the hard work of the roundup, not to mention being chased by the bike and all the worry from her responsibilities closing in on her. Roxanne changed into a soft jersey T-shirt and crawled into her freshly laundered bed. The lingering stench of smoke was not enough to keep her from falling straight to sleep.

THE NEXT MORNING SHE WAS up early, ready to hit the road to town so that she could get back before most of the day was wasted. Pierce was nowhere to be seen. The couch didn't even look slept on.

Roxanne stepped out of the house and strode toward the barn to perform a flyby inventory of feed before heading to town.

As she emerged from the barn, Pierce joined her.

She stopped and faced him, guilt for taking up all of his time eating at her. "I don't need you to babysit me all the way to town."

"I don't consider myself a babysitter." He crossed his arms over his chest. "I like to think of myself as more of a bodyguard."

"Well, nothing's gonna happen today, and I'm only going to town. I seriously doubt anyone will try to harm me on my way in and back."

"I came out to tell you the hospital just rang. Jim is being released and needs a ride home."

Roxanne sighed, glad her foreman was well enough to come home but regretting the amount of time it would take to drive to Bismarck and back. "I'll have Abe get the supplies while I go pick up Jim." She started for the house, but Pierce's hand caught her arm.

"I have some things I want to check at the bureau in Bismarck. Let me get Jim."

Her brows narrowed. "You don't mind?"

"Jim's a good man. I don't mind in the least."

Roxanne stared harder at him. What was the catch? "You trust me to go all the way to Medora and back by myself?"

"Absolutely."

A truck pulled into the barnyard and stopped next to Pierce. Dante smiled and waved, then shifted into Park.

Pierce leaned close to Roxanne. "It's not you that I don't trust. It's the bastard who's trying to hurt you." He opened the driver's door for his brother. "My brother has graciously volunteered to take you to Medora for the supplies you need, haven't you, Dante?"

Dante's smile curved downward, his brows dipping. "I have? Mom sent me out to check on you two. She's been worried."

"And I have to make a run to Bismarck to pick up Jim from the hospital." Pierce clapped his brother on the back. "Perfect timing on Mom's part, wouldn't you say?"

"As I was saying…" Roxanne glared at Pierce. "I don't need a babysitter."

"She's got a point," Dante agreed. "She's all grown up."

"It's either go to Medora with Roxanne or stay here with her. Those are the choices." Pierce's mouth pressed into a thin line. "After the latest attack, I don't think she should be left alone."

"Yeah, heard about that." Dante's arms crossed over his chest and he gave his brother a tight look. "Mom heard from Sheriff Yost that Roxanne had another encounter with the dirt bike yesterday and that you had a little fire out here the night before. Nice to get that kind of news from the grapevine. Mom was not happy that you didn't call."

"The fire happened in the middle of the night. I didn't want to worry her."

"All it would have taken was a single phone call." Dante's arms dropped to his sides. "But I understand. Roxanne, are you ready to go?"

She stood with her feet braced, her arms crossed over her chest. "I don't need you to take me to town."

"The longer you argue, the longer it will take to get there and back. And I know you're dying to get back to the roundup." Dante hooked her elbow and tugged her toward the truck.

Roxanne glared over her shoulder at Pierce. The smirk on his face didn't make her any less mad. "Don't think you can order me around, Pierce Thunder Horse. I'm only going with Dante because it will take less time than me arguing with your sorry carcass."

"See you in a few hours. Don't go lookin' for trouble." Pierce tipped his hat and took off for his truck.

Roxanne climbed up into the cab of Dante's four-by-four pickup and sank into the leather seats. "I'm not happy about being babied." Not only did it put a hitch in her confidence, but it made her worry about how it would look to the bank president if he saw her being escorted by the Thunder Horse men, as if she couldn't take care of herself.

Still, she had to admit that it was nice not to have to be on alert for the whole drive. Even after a full night's sleep, she was still exhausted by the previous day's work and the thought of another tough day in the saddle ahead. She tipped her hat over her eyes and feigned sleep to avoid conversation with Pierce's brother.

Dante seemed as content to drive in silence as she was. By the time they drove into Medora twenty minutes later, Roxanne's muscles had relaxed and she'd almost fallen asleep.

Dante pulled into the feed store. A young clerk was sweeping the front sidewalk as Roxanne jumped down from the truck.

"You can wait here," she told Dante. "I'll only be a minute."

Typical Thunder Horse, Dante climbed out of the truck and followed her in.

The teen frowned, set his broom aside and moved to let her by. "You're early, Ms. Carmichael."

"I have a couple things to get. It will only take me a minute."

With Dante in tow, Roxanne raced around the store, gathering nails and a roll of barbed wire.

"I need four sacks of sweet feed, too," she called out to the boy.

Dante helped the teen stack the four fifty-pound bags onto a hand truck. By the time they met back at the register, Roxanne had the items she needed.

The teen rang up the purchases. Roxanne handed over her credit card and held her breath.

Dante wandered off toward the hunting equipment and rifle cabinet, giving Roxanne a little much-needed privacy on her transaction.

After swiping her card twice, the clerk glanced up. "It's not going through."

Heat rushed up into Roxanne's face. She'd pushed her credit to the limit the last time she'd come to town. She'd hoped her credit card company would increase her limit just enough to allow the charges to go through. Glancing around at the items she had to have to keep her animals healthy enough to do the work they had to do, she sucked up her pride and asked, "Can I put it on my account?"

The clerk looked up her account number, entered the amount in the computer and shook his head. "Sorry, ma'am, your account is maxed out."

Out of options, Roxanne glanced down at the supplies. "I'm sorry to have held you up."

To Dante, she said, "I'll be getting groceries." Then

she turned and left the feed store, her heart dragging around her feet.

She had to pass the diner on her way to the market. Mr. Palmer pushed through the door, almost hitting her in the face. When he saw it was her, he turned the other way.

"Mr. Palmer," she called out.

The man stopped and hesitated before he faced her. "Yes, Ms. Carmichael?"

"Do you know if the bank president will be in this morning? I'd like to set up a meeting about my line of credit application."

"As I said on the phone, it will be a waste of your time. The choice has been made. Nothing you can say or do will alter the decision."

"Without consulting me?" Her fists clenched and she stepped closer to the banker, standing eye-to-eye with the man. "What kind of bank are you running? Well, forget it. I'll find a bank that will loan me the money."

"Good luck with that, Ms. Carmichael. You're not a good risk—no one will loan you the money."

"You'll eat those words, Mr. Palmer. Just you wait and see."

Sheriff Yost emerged from the diner, his back to them as he spoke to someone inside. When he closed the door, his brows rose. "Is there a problem here?"

Anger still seething, Roxanne let Palmer escape as she turned her ire on the sheriff. "Yeah, what have you done to capture the man who shot at me and then tried to burn down my house with me in it?"

He raised his hands, a placating smile spreading across his face. "Now, now, Ms. Carmichael, we're doing the best we can. I have Deputy Duncan leading the investigation. I'm sure we'll get our man."

"Yeah. I'm reassured." She pushed past him. "In the meantime, I have to have a bodyguard because you can't do your job and keep the citizens of this county safe. Excuse me while I do something more productive than talk to a waste of taxpayer dollars."

Roxanne entered the supermarket, collected what little groceries she could afford, paid with the last bit of cash she had in her wallet and carried the bags outside to wait for Dante.

As she stepped out on the sidewalk, Dante's truck pulled up alongside her.

Good. At least she wouldn't have to stand around and risk running into more of the people who made her life hell. As she dumped the bags onto the backseat, she glanced into the back of the pickup at the four sacks of sweet feed and the roll of barbed wire she'd been forced to leave behind at the feed store.

Anger bubbled up yet again. She opened the passenger seat door and stared across at Dante. "Tell me you didn't pay for my feed and supplies."

"I didn't. I paid for your *animals'* feed and supplies." He grinned. "There is a difference."

She pointed toward the feed store. "Take them back."

"I can't."

"You sure as hell can."

"No, the store's closed until tomorrow morning."

"Liar."

His grin faded. "Roxanne, get in the truck, you're making a scene."

"I don't give a damn if I'm making a scene. I won't be the object of pity or charity."

"Then get into the truck." He shifted into Park and reached for his door handle. "Or I'll help you in myself. That'll make a nice, big scene if that's what you want."

"Damn you, Dante." Her voice shook as she climbed into the pickup and shut the door. "Damn you and all of the Thunder Horses."

"We've all been down at some point in our lives. I'm just trying to give you a hand up."

"I never wanted to be beholden to anyone."

"And you aren't now. Consider it a gift."

"It's charity."

"A *gift*." Dante shifted into Drive and headed out of Medora.

Roxanne sat in her corner, staring out the side window as the scenery raced by, fighting a wall of tears threatening to crumble around her.

Not far out of town, she leaned her face against the cool glass, wishing a hole in the ground would swallow her up. Her burdens had become so onerous she didn't think she could stay afloat long enough to swim to shore.

Perhaps it would be a blessing if someone finished her off. Then she wouldn't have to worry about the ranch being taken from her or where her next meal would come from.

Good grief, girl. Get a grip.

Roxanne sat up straight and swiped at the moisture in her eyes. Her daddy hadn't raised a quitter. Let her attacker bring it on. She'd be ready.

Chapter Ten

During the long drive to Bismarck, Pierce couldn't help but think about Roxanne and what had almost happened on the porch. If not for the fire…

He groaned. How was he supposed to stay focused on keeping her safe if he couldn't keep his hands off her? Maybe it was for the best for her to spend some time on Dante's watch instead of his. Without her distracting presence, Pierce might actually be able to make some progress on finding the man who was targeting her.

Pierce had called ahead to the hospital, letting them know that he'd be by to collect Jim after he stopped at the bureau. Tuck had been there working since he'd handed over the bullets, plastic and casings they'd found. While his absence—with a wedding to prepare for in less than a week—had to be driving his future bride nuts Pierce couldn't help but feel relieved that he could depend on his brother's help.

He pulled into the bureau parking lot in Bismarck and stared up at the building. It felt as if it had been months since he'd been there when, in fact, it had only been days. So much had happened at the ranch that he hadn't had time to stop and think. Some vacation.

Inside, he found Tuck at his desk, poring through computer files.

"Anything on the casings and bullets?" Pierce asked.

"Good to see you, too, Pierce." Tuck chuckled as he rose and hugged his brother. "They do match, but we couldn't lift any prints off them. Nor could we get a trace on the plastic explosives."

Pierce smacked his palm against the wall. "Damn."

Tuck resumed his seat in front of the computer. "I've been checking the databases on Roxanne's ranch hands. As expected, there's nothing on Abe and Fred. Clean as a whistle. But then you suspected that. They've been with Carmichael Ranch for a while. Toby had a speeding ticket a couple months back, but nothing alarming in his files."

"What about Ethan Mitchell?" Pierce leaned over his brother's shoulder and stared at the screen.

"Did you know he's a local boy from Bismarck?" Tuck clicked a few icons.

"Yeah, I gathered that much from Toby."

A mug shot of Ethan Mitchell appeared on the screen, his hair longer and dirtier, but with the same sullen face. "He had an arrest a while back for disturbing the peace. His neighbor called the cops when an argument took to the streets."

Pierce's chest tightened. "Convicted?"

"He paid a fine and that was the end of it. Apparently the woman he was arguing with was his girlfriend. He claimed it was a simple domestic dispute that got out of hand."

"What did the girlfriend say?"

"She refused to make a statement."

"Too afraid of him?"

Tuck shrugged. "Maybe. Probably. But I can't really say for sure."

"Nice to know the man respects women." His fingers

tightened around the back of Tuck's chair, the urge to return immediately to the Carmichael Ranch so strong he had to fight himself not to give in.

"Yeah," Tuck was saying. "You should warn Roxanne that he might be trouble."

"Think he could have been the one who shot at her?" Pierce asked.

"I don't know. I didn't find any weapons charges against him."

"Dig deeper. He's got a real attitude. The man is surly, argumentative and rude."

Tuck snorted and smiled up at Pierce. "Making friends, brother?"

"See if you can find out where his girlfriend was."

"Why are you interested in her?"

"One of the hands thinks Ethan's got a chip on his shoulder because his girl died in an accident."

Tuck's brows rose. "An accident our friend Ethan caused?"

Pierce frowned. "Just dig."

"Will do." Tuck turned back to his computer.

"Anything I can do from the ranch?"

Tuck shook his head. "Other than watching out for Roxanne, keeping an eye on Ethan and finding more evidence to go on…I can't think of a thing."

"I'm on it." Pierce straightened. "Let me know if you hear anything."

"Same with you. Some vacation you're on. You'll need to come back to work to rest up." Tuck rose from his seat and walked with Pierce to the door of his office. "Oh, one other thing. You need to stop by the tuxedo shop and check the fit on your tux for the wedding. Only a couple more days before *this* Thunder Horse ties the knot."

"I'll slip by on my way to pick up Jim at the hospital."

"Thanks, then I can tell Julia to mark you off her bad list."

Pierce chuckled. "Didn't know she had a bad list."

"She doesn't. Julia's an angel. I'm the bad guy, using my position as groom as an excuse to boss my brothers around." He smiled, his gaze on the photograph of Julia sitting on his desk. "She deserves to have it turn out great."

Pierce's chest tightened. "You love her, don't you?"

"Never thought I'd admit it, but I do. I think from the moment I met her over a year ago, I've loved her." He shrugged and grinned. "I was just too stubborn to see it."

Pierce had to force a smile. Seeing his brother so happy only made him realize how empty his life was. "Thunder Horse stubborn?"

Tuck clapped a hand to Pierce's back. "You got that right."

Pierce envied his brother's joy. "You're a lucky man."

"On that note, I'll agree. Now leave so I can get back to work. My fiancée would like to see me again before the wedding."

Pierce left the bureau building and drove straight to the tuxedo rental shop, whipping into the parking lot and shoving the shift into Park a little harder than was necessary. He was anxious to get back to the ranch as soon as possible.

Apparently Tuck had called ahead. The owner pushed the door open as Pierce stepped down from the truck.

Within minutes he'd tried on the suit, confirmed that it fit perfectly, changed back into his regular clothes and been sent on his way, arriving at the hospital a few minutes later, coming to a stop in the drive-through pickup area.

Jim waited in a wheelchair inside the lobby, surrounded by the scent of disinfectant. There was a sheaf of discharge papers in his hands, and a frown creased his forehead. "About time you got here. Been stewin' in my juices for nearly half an hour. I could use a breath of fresh air. Damned hospitals. Can't stand the smell."

"Couldn't wait to go home?" Peirce asked, wheeling the chair through the door and out onto the curb.

"No, they couldn't wait to get rid of me," Jim grumbled, pushing to his feet. "And here I was about to make a move on the good-looking nurse."

"Probably why they booted you out of your room." Pierce wheeled the chair back inside and returned to help Jim.

In a hospital-provided boot, Jim limped toward the truck on his sprained ankle.

Pierce opened the passenger seat door and reached out to the older man.

Jim shoved his hands away. "I'm not a damned cripple. Let me do it myself."

Pierce stepped back as the man tried to maneuver himself up into the truck without applying pressure to the cast covering his broken arm, or the boot encased around his foot.

He grabbed the handle above the door and leveraged himself into the seat, dropping down with a wince.

Before the foreman could protest, Pierce leaned in, dragged the seat belt over his shoulder and snapped it in place across his lap.

Jim grunted his thanks, holding his injured arm out of the way throughout the process.

As Pierce headed out of the parking lot, the SUV's

steering wheel pulled hard to the right. At first Pierce attributed it to the uneven pavement that took a beating during the winter's icy weather. But as Pierce maneuvered the truck onto the interstate heading west, the vehicle continued to pull to the right. He couldn't remember running into anything to knock the wheels out of alignment and the tires had all appeared inflated properly when he'd left the hospital.

He kept driving, determined to get to the ranch. He'd take the truck to his mechanic when he was sure Roxanne was safe.

"Miss Carmichael doin' all right?" Jim asked, taking Pierce's mind off the front wheel.

"She's holding her own. I sent Dante to Medora with her to keep her safe. She had some things to get and he promised to look out for her while I went to Bismarck."

Jim nodded. "I heard you had a fire in the house night before last."

Pierce shook his head in rueful resignation. He'd hoped they'd be able to keep the news from Jim, but really, he'd always suspected the man would find out. "How'd you hear about that?"

"I may be old, but I've got friends."

Jim had been a part of the western North Dakota community all his life. It didn't surprise Pierce that he had already heard about the fire, considering it was in the same house he lived in. "Someone tossed a Molotov cocktail into Roxanne's bedroom window."

Jim shot a concerned look his way. "Was she in there at the time?"

"No she was on the porch." *With me,* Pierce didn't add.

Jim's jaw tightened. "I don't know who the hell is

trying to sabotage her life, but he'd better stop before I put a bullet right between his eyes."

"Believe me, if I knew who it was, it would have stopped already. He's not leaving much for us to go on." His fingers tightened around the steering wheel, his frustration bubbling up. Reminding himself that Jim didn't need more worry to add to his injuries, he asked, "What's the doc say about you and riding?"

"Not to ride horses." Jim breathed hard out his nostrils. "Didn't say nothing about driving a truck or a four-wheeler."

"You'll have a challenge driving with a sprained right ankle, and limited to one-handed steering."

"I'll manage. The cattle have to make it to the sale come hell or high water."

"Are things that tight?" Pierce asked.

"They ain't loose if you know what I mean. That girl's been working her fanny off to make that ranch pay enough to survive on."

A smile quirked the corners of Pierce's lips just as the truck jerked hard toward the shoulder, the right front end dipping toward the pavement. A loud screech ripped through the air as metal ground into concrete.

Pierce fought to keep the truck from careening off the interstate into a ditch. As fast as he'd been going, he couldn't maintain a straight trajectory. The vehicle slid off the road, bounced over the gravel and shot into the ditch, coming to a hard stop when the front end hit the embankment.

The force of the impact threw Pierce forward, the seat belt catching and stopping him from slamming into the steering wheel or flying through the front windshield.

When the world came to a complete stop, the cab of

the truck tipped forward at a steep angle, buried in the embankment.

Pierce shot a glance at Jim.

The man's seat belt held him from falling forward into the dash. His eyes were squeezed shut and his face was creased in a grimace.

"You okay, Jim?"

"Been better," he said through gritted teeth. "This seat belt is pressing against some of those broken ribs."

"Hang on, I'll get you out."

"I'm not goin' anywhere."

Pierce released his belt, falling hard into the steering wheel. He shoved his door open and scrambled out, ducking back to search the floorboard for his cell phone.

He found it lodged between his seat and the console. The screen was cracked and no manner of shaking or rebooting the device would make it work.

Tossing it aside, he hurried around the other side of the truck and pulled the door open.

Careful not to hurt Jim further, Pierce helped the injured man down onto the ground. Once he had the foreman settled, he rounded to the front of the truck and stared down at where the tire had been.

Both the wheel and tire were missing and, from what Pierce could tell, the axle had broken. A spare tire wasn't going to fix this truck; nor was he going to be back to the Carmichael Ranch anytime soon.

His chest tightened. Was it simply bad luck that the truck's wheel had fallen off? Or had someone loosened the lug nuts in an attempt to sabotage Pierce's truck and keep him from returning to check on Roxanne?

As soon as she'd stowed the groceries in the refrigerator and pantry, Roxanne headed for the barn.

Dante stood beside the truck, poking at the keys on his cell phone.

"You won't get any reception out here."

"A man can always wish." He glanced up. "Mind if I use your landline? I wanted to check in with Pierce and Tuck."

"Help yourself."

"I'll be just a minute. You won't go anywhere while I'm inside, will you?"

Roxanne shook her head. She'd ditched her body-guard once too often lately, and what had it bought her? She'd nearly been run down by a motorcycle and buried in a landslide. "I'm not planning on going any farther than the barn for now. I'll stay put until you're done. But then I have to get out to the canyon. Today's the last chance I have to get those cattle into the sale."

As Dante jogged toward the house. Roxanne entered the barn.

While she'd unloaded the groceries, Dante had stacked the feed sacks inside the barn, but they still needed to be transferred into the right containers. Feed had to be stored in metal cans to keep the mice from getting into it. They could chew through a paper feed sack in less time than it took to pour the feed into one of the metal trash cans they kept for storage.

Hefting a fifty-pound bag onto her shoulder, she carried it across the barn to the row of cans lining the wall. Each contained a different kind of feed. She located the sweet feed can, tossed the lid onto the ground and tore open the sack.

As she emptied its contents into the can, the door to the barn swung closed, shutting out the daylight she'd relied on to see what she was doing. Assuming it had been the wind, she thought nothing of it beyond the inconvenience of pouring feed in the dark. Still, she knew the barn more than well enough to finish the task in the dark, so she didn't bother going over to reopen the door.

As she emptied the bag into the bin, the combination of oats, corn and barley along with the sweet scent of molasses filled Roxanne's senses. She'd always loved the smell of sweet feed. The horses loved it and needed the additional nutrition boost to keep up with the amount of work they performed during roundup.

As she laid the empty paper sack in the stack to be recycled, another aroma seeped into her consciousness.

The acrid, biting stench of smoke, coming from the back side of the barn where they kept the stack of hay bales they fed to the livestock on a daily basis.

Had something set off a fire in the hay?

A flash of concern sent her scurrying through the dark barn toward the door. She had to get outside and determine the source of the smoke and put it out before the barn went up in flame.

But when she pushed on the door it didn't open. She tried to lift the large wooden braces that locked the door in place—they wouldn't budge.

Smoke sifted through the walls. Sheba stamped her feet in her stall and whinnied.

"I know, girl." Roxanne spoke to the horse in a soothing voice, as much to calm her own nerves as the animal's. "I'm working on it. Something's jammed. It'll just be a minute."

No matter how hard she leaned on the latch, it wasn't going anywhere. Roxanne abandoned that exit and raced for the small side door. Again it wouldn't open, the lock jammed.

Smoke was filling the interior of the barn.

Sheba kicked the inside of her stall, her frightened cries echoing against the old oak timbers.

Roxanne ran her fingers along the wall beside the door and flipped the light switch. Nothing happened. Panic spiked as Roxanne realized this was no accident. Someone had started the fire on purpose—and beforehand, they'd deliberately locked her in. She raced back to the larger barn doors and pounded her hands against it. "Help! Someone help us!"

The men were out on the range, which left Dante as the only one who could free her from the barn. Surely he'd see the smoke rising and come out to help. But would he come soon enough?

Roxanne dragged in a deep breath to yell again. Instead smoke filled her lungs and she coughed uncontrollably. "Help!" she cried, coughing, falling to her knees to avoid the worst of it, praying for someone to come.

Roxanne crawled across the floor searching for something to pry the doors open. Then she remembered the pitchforks and shovels used to clean the stalls. Pulling her T-shirt up over her nose, she rose to a crouch and raced across the floor for the tools.

"We'll be okay, Sheba. Just hold on."

PIERCE AND JIM HITCHED a ride with a trucker on his way west. When they reached Medora, Pierce borrowed a car from a waitress he knew at the diner and drove the rest of the way out to the Carmichael Ranch, Jim beside him, his face pale but determined.

"I don't like it. Too many accidents to be considered accidental," Jim commented.

Pierce's thoughts exactly, and the reason he didn't wait to find a ride from Medora. Now as he turned onto the drive leading up to the Carmichael ranch house, his stomach clenched. A plume of smoke rose behind the house.

"You seein' what I'm seein'?" Jim sat forward.

"Damn." Pierce gunned the accelerator, shooting the little car forward. He skidded to a stop in the barnyard and leaped out.

Dante was running from the direction of the house, holding a hand to the back of his head, blood caked in his dark hair.

"What the hell happened?" Pierce asked.

"I don't know."

"Where's Roxanne?"

"Last she said, she was going to the barn."

Pierce ran for the barn door. A heavy metal lock held the latch in place. He grabbed it and yanked hard. "Roxanne!"

"Help. I'm in here." Her voice sounded thin, gravelly.

"Get a crowbar from my truck."

"You didn't drive your truck and I don't have a crowbar in mine," Dante said.

Pierce remembered his truck was somewhere between Medora and Bismarck, stuck in a ditch. With nothing around to break the lock, he had only one choice. He reached his hand out. "Give me your keys."

Dante dug into his pocket and handed Pierce the keys to his pickup.

"Get away from the doors!" Pierce shouted to Roxanne, then ran for the truck.

Chapter Eleven

Roxanne's first attempt to force the door by shoving the pitchfork between the two large doors and throwing all of her weight into it hadn't worked. The door hadn't budged an inch. She'd been on the verge of tears when she'd heard the voices murmuring outside, carrying through the thick wood doors of the barn.

Pierce's voice called her name. She forced herself to answer as loudly as she could, and was startled by his response. "Get away from the doors!"

She hesitated. Had she heard right? Her haze-muddled brain kicked in and Roxanne leaped to her feet. Smoke filled her lungs and stung her eyes as she threw herself to the side.

An engine raced, the sound moving toward her fast. Then the wooden doors exploded in a shower of broken boards and splinters as the hood of a pickup burst into the barn. Smoke spilled out through the opening.

The truck backed out through the hole.

Stumbling to her feet, Roxanne flung herself out of the barn and into a strong pair of arms. When she blinked the smoke from her eyes, she could have cried anew. Pierce held her, a fierce frown denting his beautiful brows. "Oh, thank God, you're here." She coughed and pointed back inside the smoldering interior. "Sheba. Please, help Sheba."

Pierce shoved Roxanne into Dante's arms and flung the damaged doors wide. Then he covered his nose and mouth with his arm and ran into the smoke.

He remained inside for what felt like a very long time.

Sheba's frightened whinny was followed by the smack of a stall door sliding sideways on its runners.

Sheba burst through the barn door, tossing her head and trotting as far from the flame-belching building as she could before she stopped and stamped her feet.

Roxanne held her breath until Pierce emerged, his eyes red rimmed and his face gray.

Jim hobbled toward her from a strange car parked in the barnyard. "Looks like it's comin' from behind the barn."

Pierce and Dante took off at a run, vaulting over corral panels and ducking through fences to reach the back.

Roxanne followed, not as fast, her lungs burning from all the smoke she'd breathed.

When she reached the other side, Pierce and Dante were tossing burning hay bales away from the back of the barn.

Roxanne ran forward to help.

"Stay back—you'll get burned," Pierce shouted.

"So will you!" Roxanne continued forward.

"Just do it, Roxy. You've already breathed too much smoke." Pierce ripped the shirt off his back and beat at the flames licking up the wooden slats on the back of the barn.

Roxanne ran to the front where Jim was wrestling with a water hose one-handed. "Take this." He handed the hose through the corral panels.

She raced to the back of the barn with the hose while Jim turned on the water.

When she arrived, Pierce and Dante were in an all-out battle against the rising flames.

Roxanne aimed the nozzle at the fire and hosed down the wood, praying with all her heart that the thin spray of water would be enough. She couldn't lose the barn.

Pierce and Dante wet their shirts and beat at the burning hay bales, while Roxanne soaked the back of the barn. Slowly, the flames retreated, dying down to nothing more than wet charcoal by the time Roxanne was done.

With the hay bales scattered across the dirt, they burned down to ashes without lighting anything else on fire.

Roxanne stared at the charred barn, heartsick.

"It could be worse." Pierce slipped an arm around her waist and relieved her of the hose.

"Sheba could have died." Her voice didn't sound like her own, all gravelly and hoarse. She leaned into Pierce's side, pressing her face against his naked chest.

Pierce dropped the hose and held her close. "*You* could have died."

"But I didn't." She coughed, her lungs hurting, her throat scratchy and raw.

"You could have." Pierce led her around to the front of the barn.

Jim limped forward, his face pale and anxious. "You okay, Miss Roxy?" He hugged her carefully, his movements awkward with the cast.

Roxanne smiled at the older man. "I'm okay, just a little smoke-filled."

"Speaking of which." Pierce grabbed her elbow. "We

need to get you to the hospital. You don't take chances with smoke inhalation. I should call for an ambulance."

"No. Don't. Really, I'm fine," she insisted, her heart warming at Pierce's concern. "Just a little sore throat."

"You're at least going to the clinic in Medora. If the doc says you're okay, then you're okay. Until then, you're not."

She frowned. "I have cattle—"

"That can wait," Jim said, siding with Pierce. "Your health is more important than a few strays."

"You don't understand." Roxanne glanced from Jim to Pierce. Both had those stubborn looks, and she really didn't feel much like arguing. She could lose her ranch to the bank and they'd still stand firm on her seeing a doctor. "Fine. As long as Dante has to go, too. He looks worse than I do."

Dante had a hand pressed to the nape of his neck.

"Yeah, what happened to you?" Pierce turned his brother around and parted the hair at the back of his head.

Roxanne whistled, her stomach rolling. "You've got a lump the size of a goose egg."

"Yeah, and it hurts like hell." Dante rubbed the back of his head. "I was going to the ranch house to make a call when someone hit me from behind with what felt like a tire iron. I must have passed out."

All the blood rushed from Roxanne's head and she staggered. "Someone hit you?"

"Apparently whoever hit Dante probably wasn't trying to kill him. Otherwise, it would have been easy enough to take him out while he was unconscious. No, they just wanted him out of the way, so he wouldn't interfere." Pierce's frown deepened, his dark eyes icy. "This was a deliberate attempt on Roxanne's life."

The pounding of horses' hooves made Roxanne's head jerk up and she looked out across the pasture.

The four ranch hands raced toward them.

Toby arrived first, followed by Abe and Fred and finally Ethan.

"We saw smoke and came as quickly as we could." Toby dropped down out of his saddle and hurried up to Roxanne, stopping when he saw the destroyed barn door. "Holy smokes, are you all right?"

Roxanne smiled at the young man. "I'll be okay."

"What happened?" Abe dismounted, a frown creasing his forehead.

Roxanne sighed, not really feeling like going into it all. She just wanted to take a deep breath and have it feel good, instead of burning and making her chest ache.

Jim took over. "Someone started a fire in the stack of hay behind the barn."

Pierce gave a narrow-eyed look at the four ranch hands. "When I get back from taking Roxanne to the clinic, I'll want a full accounting of where each of you were, down to the minute and GPS coordinate. Got it?"

Three of the four men nodded. Ethan glared, a sneer pulling his lip up.

Feeling she was letting her men down, Roxanne made the call to back off the roundup in the canyon. "I don't want you all out in the canyon until I get back and can ride with you. Someone's causing problems, and until we figure out who it is, I don't consider any of you safe." She turned to Jim. "Can you handle things here?"

"Yes, ma'am. Don't you worry about a thing." He patted her arm with his good hand.

Roxanne swallowed hard on the lump in her sore throat. "I'll be back as soon as possible." She stared at the ranch hands. "Work on getting this mess cleaned up and don't give Jim a hard time. He needs to put his foot up as much as possible."

With her final instructions issued, there wasn't much more she could do there. Roxanne turned to Pierce. "Let's get your brother to a doctor."

PIERCE HELD OPEN THE DOOR to the borrowed car for Roxanne. His brother climbed into the backseat, still holding a hand to the back of his head.

As he drove into town, Pierce's gut clenched. Who the hell was behind all the trouble on the Carmichael Ranch? And just how many of the "accidents" were related? Had the same man sabotaged his car and attacked his brother just to keep them from protecting Roxanne?

"Whose car is this?" Roxanne sat up straight. "I hate to get it all smoky."

"It belongs to Rita from the diner in Medora."

Roxanne frowned. "Where's your truck?"

"Had a problem with the wheel on the way back from Bismarck."

"Sorry to hear that."

Dante leaned forward. "Did you get a chance to talk to Tuck in Bismarck?"

Pierce nodded. "No prints on the bullet casings or wrapper."

"That's too bad," Roxanne said, her eyes closed and her head tipped to one side.

Pierce reached out and touched her arm. "Are you okay?"

Roxanne opened her eyes and gave Pierce a lopsided smile. "Yes, I'm just resting my eyes. They're still burning from all the smoke."

Pierce's eyes still stung from the little time he'd spent going in to retrieve the horse. He could only imagine

Roxanne's discomfort. "We'll have the doc check you over good."

Roxanne shrugged and closed her eyes again. "Did Tuck find anything else?"

Pierce glanced her way. "I had him run a background check on your employees."

Roxanne's eyes opened and she frowned. "And you didn't ask me?"

"It's routine in a case like this. You always look to the people closest to the victim."

"I would think I could tell you what you need to know about the men who work for me."

"Sometimes employers only know what the employees want them to."

"I'd trust every one of them."

"With your life?" Dante asked from the backseat.

Pierce could tell she wanted to say yes, but for once, Roxanne hesitated. "Usually."

"Did he find anything?" Dante prompted.

Again Pierce glanced at Roxanne as he said, "Ethan Mitchell has a prior arrest record."

Roxanne gasped. "He does? He didn't mention it when I hired him."

"The charges were minor. He paid a fine, and that was the end of it."

"Then why is there a problem?" she asked.

Pierce's gaze met hers for an instant. "It was for disturbing the peace during one hell of a fight with his girlfriend. Looks to me like he's got a problem with his temper."

Pierce didn't like breaking it to Roxanne. She'd always been so trusting and open with the people who worked with and for her.

"He's never yelled at me." Roxanne's voice was nothing more than rough croak.

"Are you sure you haven't been the victim of his temper in other ways?" Pierce gave her a penetrating stare before returning his attention to the road. "An angry man can find a lot of ways to hurt someone, as you should be very familiar with by now."

Roxanne sat silently in her seat the remainder of the ride into Medora.

The clinic had already closed. Determined to get medical attention for both Roxanne and Dante, Pierce said, "We're going to Bismarck."

"No." Both Roxanne and Dante said in unison.

"Take us to where they house the ambulances," Dante suggested. "There should be EMTs there on call."

"Yeah," Roxanne agreed. "They should be able to help. It will give them something to do."

"They've had plenty here lately." Pierce frowned, not sure he liked the solution. He was outvoted, though, so he drove directly to where the ambulances were housed, calling on the expertise of the emergency medical technicians on duty.

After a thorough exam and observing Roxanne and Dante for a full hour, the EMTs pronounced them fit enough to return home.

Pierce insisted on grabbing dinner at the diner since he had to return the borrowed car to the waitress who was due to get off work by then.

As they entered the diner Roxanne headed for the bar. "I'll call one of the hands to come get me and take me back to the ranch."

Pierce cut her off. "You and Dante sit. I'll take care of the call. Order me a steak and baked potato."

She frowned. "Bossy much?"

"Tired. And you have to be just as worn out with all that's happened in the past couple days." He motioned toward a booth. "Please. Let me handle it."

She sighed. "I don't want to get used to anyone organizing my life for me, but you're right. I'm tired." Roxanne gave him a little smile. "Medium rare, like usual?"

Pierce grinned. "That's my girl." He chucked her under her chin just like old times, when they'd been a couple and nothing could have separated them. Or so they thought.

The death of her brother had proved that theory wrong. He froze a little when he realized what he'd done, how he'd fallen back into old habits with her... but he pointedly didn't apologize before walking away.

While Dante and Roxanne slid into a booth, Pierce made arrangements he was sure would make Roxanne mad. He was through backing down when it came to her protection. If she wanted to yell at him for it, he'd deal with it. But he'd take the hit on a full stomach. Not before.

Much to Roxanne's chagrin and relief, Pierce paid the bill at the diner. By the time she'd finished a heaping helping of Ma Clements's famous chicken and dumplings, Roxanne didn't have the energy to argue. The smooth dumplings had slid right past her sore throat and hit bottom on her empty gut, filling her up and warming her inside and out. Sleepy and ready to call it a day, Roxanne left the diner, hoping whoever was coming for her from the ranch would be sliding up to the curb right about then.

A truck did pull up to the curb, but Maddox Thunder Horse was driving it.

Dante got in the front passenger seat and closed the door.

Roxanne stared down the street, hoping to see one of her men soon. She could barely hold her head up, much less stand for long. Sleep called to her and, despite the weight of the world resting on her shoulders, Roxanne was ready to give in. Tomorrow was another day. The cattle they'd rounded up already would have to do. Maybe the beef prices would be up on the day of the sale. She could always hope.

Pierce greeted his brother and opened the back door to the king-cab pickup. "Hop in, Roxanne."

"That's okay. I can wait here on the curb for my ride."

"This is your ride," Pierce said.

Roxanne frowned. "You have done more than enough for me. I can't keep relying on you and your family. Besides I'm sure my ride will be here momentarily."

"I called Jim and let him know that you won't be coming home tonight."

"You did what?" Anger beat out exhaustion as heat rose into Roxanne's cheeks. "I have to go back tonight."

"Jim said he had everything under control. They patched up the barn and made sure all the fires were out. He agreed you weren't safe there and that you should stay the night at the Thunder Horse Ranch."

Roxanne breathed in and out several times before she could speak in a normal tone. "You have no right to make that decision for me…."

"You've been shot at twice, almost run over and today someone tried to burn your barn down with you in it. You're safer at the Thunder Horse Ranch, Roxanne."

"But my ranch hands—"

"Right." Pierce pressed a finger to her lips to stem

her next argument. "Jim made another really good point. With you off the ranch, your men are safer, as well."

"But what about everyone at the Thunder Horse Ranch? What about Julia? Lily? Katya? Your mother? Wouldn't I put them all in danger by staying there?"

"Julia's decided to stay at Tuck's place in Bismarck for now—with all the time he's spending at the office, it's the best way to see him, anyway. She and Lily will be safe there. Maddox won't let anything happen to Katya. And you know my mother too well to think that any amount of danger would keep her from helping a friend. It was her idea for you to come and stay with us."

Roxanne crossed her arms over her chest, hating that he made sense. "Seems you and Jim thought of everything."

"We tried," he said, grinning, "knowing you wouldn't like it."

She huffed. "Got that right."

"Can you two wrap it up?" Dante leaned out of the front passenger seat window. "I have a giant-size headache and it isn't getting better."

Pierce tipped his head to the side. "Now, are you going to keep Dante waiting?"

Outnumbered, outmaneuvered and overwhelmed, Roxanne stepped up into the pickup and slid as far across the backseat as she could get. Sitting too close to Pierce would be a bad idea, even without her emotions on the edge and her heart hammering inside her chest. In her current state, Roxanne didn't trust herself, much less Pierce.

As they drove out to the Thunder Horse Ranch, the past few days' events crashed in around her. The danger to herself, and to others, reminded her how fragile life could be.

Despite the threats and attacks, the danger that scared her the most was the one to her heart, being near Pierce again. How was she supposed to remember that she couldn't rely on him if he kept being there for her every time she needed him?

Roxanne leaned her head against the cool window, closing her scratchy eyes. What a wreck she must be. She couldn't even summon enough anger to be mad at Pierce anymore. As far as she was concerned that was the most dangerous position she could be in. If she had a lick of sense and an ounce of energy, she'd make the Thunder Horse brothers take her home.

But Jim's insistence that her presence might put her men in danger hit too close to home—especially when she thought of how the danger had already gotten Jim hurt. Suddenly, she felt very alone, even in the truck with the Lakota brothers.

By the time the truck pulled into the driveway at the Thunder Horse Ranch house, Roxanne had sunk into a blue funk of colossal proportions.

All she wanted to do was shower and go straight to bed.

Pierce helped her climb down from the truck and insisted on taking her arm, leading her into the house.

Amelia met them at the door, clucking like a mother hen worried about her brood.

"Dante, sit," she ordered. "I want a look at the bump." She reached up and tried to part his hair.

"Mom, the EMTs said I'd be just fine." Dante waved his mother's hands away. "I want a shower before I touch anything. I reek of smoke."

Pierce chuckled. "She needs to mother someone, Dante. Let her."

"It's my job to worry. I'm your mother."

"Then worry about Roxanne," Dante insisted. "She's had the worst of it."

Roxanne shook her head. Though she loved Amelia Thunder Horse, she didn't want her to fuss around her. Pierce and his brothers would come and go, but Amelia was Roxanne's closest neighbor and the member of the Thunder Horse clan she interacted with the most. She didn't want the woman to see her as an object of pity. "I should go back home. I don't want to be a bother to you."

"Nonsense, dear. I'll find clothes you can wear." Amelia glanced at Pierce. "She can have my bedroom for the night."

"No, Mom, no need to give up your room," Pierce said. "She'll sleep in mine."

Roxanne's cheeks burned and she opened her mouth to protest.

Pierce cut her off before she could blast him. "Don't worry, I'll sleep on the couch."

"If you'll excuse me, I'll only be a few minutes in the shower." Dante hurried down the hallway.

"Oh, dear, you look like you've all had a rough day." Amelia led her down the hallway to the room that had always been Pierce's.

The room held too many memories for Roxanne. She'd hung out in his room on a number of occasions during their courtship. They'd lain together on his bed, kissing and touching each other, like teenagers. Out of respect for Pierce's mother, they saved the more intimate encounters for Roxanne's house where she was chaperone-free, but for her brother.

As Amelia pushed through the door, a flood of sadness threatened to overwhelm Roxanne. She stood in the center of the floor, unable to move, to speak or react lest she burst into tears.

Amelia flitted in and out, depositing a nightgown, clothes for the next day and a fresh towel on the end of the bed. The bed Pierce slept in, covered in a quilt his mother had hand stitched with pictures of wolves, buffalo, horses and other animals filling the big squares.

Everything about the room was masculine, from the rough-hewn cedar four-poster bed, down to the brown-and-black braided rug covering the hardwood floors.

"Dante is done in the shower if you'd like to go next." Amelia hugged Roxanne. "I'm so sorry you've had such a time of it. You're safe here. Let me know if you need anything else."

She backed out of the room, leaving Roxanne more alone than she'd felt since she'd called off her engagement to Pierce.

Things had been so good between them—and had then gone so terribly wrong. She'd told herself over and over again that she was fine on her own, that she didn't need anyone else, but now she was starting to wonder if that was true. Much as she hated to admit it, she'd needed Pierce over and over again during the past few days. And it wasn't just "need"—there was "want" to be considered, too. She'd never wanted any man like she'd wanted Pierce—like she wanted him, still.

But all of that was over between them…wasn't it? After the way he'd shut her out, and the way she'd vented her pain and anger on him, she didn't see how they could ever truly reconcile. And if they did, could she truly let herself trust him? Was there any way they could be fixed, or would she have to feel this alone for the rest of her life?

Chapter Twelve

The rest of the family settled in for the night. Maddox and Katya held hands all the way to their bedroom, and Dante suffered his mother's attention as she applied antibiotic ointment to his scalp wounds.

If all was well in the Thunder Horse house, then why the hell couldn't Pierce go to sleep?

Because Roxanne lay in his bed.

Images of her dark red curls feathering across his pillow kept him wide awake and aching.

When she'd skipped down the hallway after her shower, wearing the short filmy nightgown Katya had loaned her, Pierce thought he would come undone.

Now, as he paced the living room, he went over the events of the day, hoping the danger and turbulence would quell his desires and remind him what was important:

Keeping Roxanne safe.

He wanted to believe that nothing bad would happen to her while she stayed at the Thunder Horse Ranch. That Pierce could go to sleep without worrying that someone was outside waiting to throw a firebomb through the window.

But could he? Who was to say that whoever had been

responsible for the attacks on Roxanne hadn't followed her here to Pierce's home?

He suspected the wheel and tire problem he'd had on the road had been a setup to get him out of the way and keep him away from Roxanne for the day, just as knocking Dante on the back of the head had disposed of him.

His pulse thrumming faster than usual, Pierce slipped on his boots and stepped outside. One last pass around the house should help to ease his mind.

The cool night air felt good against his skin. He hadn't bothered with a shirt, normally preferring to sleep naked. In deference to the females in the house, he'd slipped on a pair of boxers to sleep in. They covered what was necessary to appease his family's sense of propriety.

As he walked around the house in boxers and boots, he could imagine the spectacle he made. A chuckle rose up his chest that caught in his throat when he passed his room.

The French door leading out of his bedroom stood open. A rush of fear for Roxanne spiked in his blood, sending his heart racing.

He spotted a dark silhouette outside, moving in the shadows, easing slowly along the porch toward his open door.

In three giant steps, he'd closed the distance to the house. Bracing his hands on the porch rail, he vaulted over the edge and grabbed the intruder from behind, trapping the stranger's arms against his sides.

A feminine squeak caught Pierce off guard. The person in his grasp fought and kicked. Beneath a bulky robe, Pierce could feel the curve of breasts and hips.

"Roxy?" he whispered, and spun her in his arms.

Her hair hung down in her face, her soft, silky curls

slipping free of the robe's collar, brushing against his hands.

She stared up into his eyes, her breathing ragged, her body tense. "Pierce?"

"Yeah, baby, it's me." His grip relaxed.

"Why the hell did you grab me?" Roxanne pressed a hand to her throat and leaned her head into his chest. "You scared me half to death." A shaky laugh barely dispelled the fear in her voice.

After a steadying moment, she pushed away from him, backed up to the porch rail and sat against a thick wooden beam. Drawing her knees up to her chin, she wrapped her arms around her legs. The robe fell open, exposing the flimsy nightgown and a generous portion of her thighs.

Pierce cleared his throat to keep from groaning. "Can't sleep?"

"I'm so tired, I could tip over this rail." She shook her head. "But I couldn't fall to sleep."

"Too much to think about?"

She shrugged. "Too much of everything."

He stood beside her and leaned against the same beam, staring up at the stars, wanting more than anything to draw her into his arms but afraid she'd push him away again. "The stars sure are bright."

"Yes, they are." Her voice caught and she sniffled.

Pierce's heart skipped several beats and he turned to face her, capturing her arms in his hands. "Are you crying?"

"I've told you before, cowgirls don't cry." Her head dipped and she sniffed again.

"Liar." He tipped her chin up. Moonlight glistened off the moisture on her face. "Come here."

He drew her to her feet and into his arms, resting his cheek against her hair. "What's wrong?"

"It's your room," she whispered against his bare chest.

His room? He tipped her chin up. "What about my room? Aren't the sheets clean? Is it too warm?"

"No, no, everything's perfect…except…the last time I was in your room…we made love."

His hand slipped beneath the robe, which he recognized now as his, and he pulled her close. "And why does that bother you?" He held his breath, afraid of her response but needing to hear it nonetheless.

"I feel tense, alone…sad." Her hands slid up over his chest, circled around his neck and pulled his head lower, until his lips hovered over hers. "Damn you, Pierce Thunder Horse, I miss you," she said so softly he almost didn't catch her words.

But he did hear and his body stiffened. "You called off our wedding."

She nodded. "I was angry, grieving. And you wouldn't talk to me, wouldn't share with me what you were feeling. You wouldn't even tell me what had happened, other than to say it was your fault."

Pierce wanted to hold her in his arms and make love to her more than he wanted to breathe, but he couldn't. "That's because it *was* my fault your brother died. I shouldn't have taken him on that raid. I should have done better by him—and by you. You need to marry someone who can be there for you. Not someone whose life is at the mercy of the bureau."

"The bureau." She leaned her forehead against his chest, trapping their hands between them. "How much do you have to give to your country?"

"I love my work."

"And I love mine, when I'm not being shot at, run over or trapped in a burning barn." A shiver shook her body.

Pierce knew how scared she'd been. Hell he'd been as scared for her.

She pulled her hands free and wrapped them around Pierce's waist. "For now, all I want is for you to hold me. No strings, no commitment, just hold me until I go to sleep."

When she put it like that, Pierce couldn't say no. His determination to let go of Roxanne and allow her to live her life free of him and the bureau was pushed to the back of his mind.

His arms slipped beneath the robe, and he lifted her up and carried her back inside to his bed. There he laid her against the pillows, her fiery red hair dark against the white pillowcases, moonlight casting a soft blue glow over her pale skin.

His groin tightened. The night would be hard on him, but he couldn't turn his back on her. He lay on the bed beside her and gathered her into his arms.

Roxanne laid her cheek on his chest, her hand resting low on his belly, one leg draped over his thigh.

Pressing a kiss to her forehead, he tightened his arm around her. "Go to sleep, Roxy."

Her face tipped up to him, her lips parted.

He bent to kiss her lightly. "Just sleep."

She deserves more became his mantra through the long, heartbreaking night of lying so close to Roxanne, knowing he couldn't hold her forever. Understanding that their time together was limited to the time it took to determine who was after her.

He held her, without moving, long into the wee hours of the morning. Near sunrise, he kissed her forehead and slipped out of the bed. After a quick shower, he stepped into the kitchen.

His mother was already up and cooking breakfast for the family.

"Morning, Mom." He dropped a kiss on her hair. "Tuck left a message on my phone about a lead on Roxanne's case, so I'll be headed to Bismarck today to follow up."

"What about Roxanne?" his mother asked.

"Keep her here. It's too dangerous for her to go out on her own."

His mother frowned. "I can't hold her hostage."

"Don't offer her a ride and don't let her take a horse."

"Honey, you know Roxanne better than any of us. You can't keep her from doing whatever she pleases."

"Should I be involved in this discussion?" a quiet voice said from just outside the door to the kitchen as Roxanne entered.

Pierce spun to face her.

She wore his robe, her curly hair was rumpled, and she blinked sleepily. "Are you going somewhere?"

"Bismarck," he said.

She bit on her bottom lip then stated, "I need to get back to my ranch."

Before she finished her sentence, Pierce was already shaking his head. "You're not going anywhere."

Her brows rose, her lips tightening.

Pierce's mother clucked her tongue. "Told you." She went back to the stove to stir the scrambled eggs in the pan.

Pierce decided on another tactic. "I have business in Bismarck at the bureau. Can you be ready to leave in five minutes?"

Her hand rose to smooth her hair back. "I'm not going. The cattle—"

"Will survive without you. And your men can get them ready for loading."

"I need to be the one to cull the breeders."

"Jim will be able to watch from the sidelines. If you're not going with me, you need to stay here where you're safe."

She opened her mouth to protest, but Pierce pressed a finger to her lips. "Where you go, trouble follows. I worry about you. You worry about your employees. If you go back to the ranch, which of your employees will be the next in collateral damage? If you won't stay because I want you to be safe, stay here to keep the others from being harmed. Nothing's happened since you've been here so I think whoever's after you doesn't know where to find you. But even if he figures it out, I'd feel a lot better knowing you were here with Dante and Maddox."

Roxanne sucked in a deep breath, her gaze locked with his. Then her chin dipped and she nodded. "Okay, I'll stay, but hurry back. I need to be there. The Carmichael Ranch has too much at stake for me to run scared."

Pierce wanted to trust her, but she'd given up too easily. "Promise you'll stay safe?" He gripped her shoulders, forcing her to look back into his eyes.

"I promise to stay safe."

He frowned, not totally convinced, but he let it go. "I'll be back as soon as possible." He hated to leave. Something in his gut told him that Roxanne would only be safe if he was by her side. But this new lead of Tuck's could be the answer to finding the guy behind all of this. He had to leave Roxanne in order to protect her.

So why did it feel so wrong?

ROXANNE WATCHED THROUGH the living room window as Pierce pulled out of the yard and disappeared down the gravel driveway.

"Don't worry, he'll be back soon." Amelia patted her back. "Pierce can't stay away long knowing you're in danger. He loves you so much."

"I doubt that." Roxanne glanced down at the shorter woman. "How can you be so nice to me when I dumped your son? I don't think I could be as gracious."

Amelia smiled and patted Roxanne's cheek. "Grief has a way of making a person a little crazy. You know, first there's the denial, then there's the anger." Amelia shrugged and moved away to gather magazines from the coffee table. "I think you were so heartbroken by your brother's death that you lashed out at the only person you could at the time. Unfortunately, it was Pierce."

Roxanne's gaze shifted back to the window. Had she pushed Pierce away in her grief? Did she still love him? "He told me it was his fault that Mason died."

Amelia nodded. "I'm sure he believes that. But he'd probably say the fire at your house was his fault, too. Do you agree with him?" Amelia held the magazines to her chest, her eyes sad.

"No, of course not. Why would he think it was his fault?"

"Because he didn't stop it from happening. I imagine he blames himself for Mason's death in the same way—thinking it's his fault because he was responsible for Mason and yet he couldn't protect him."

Was that true? Roxanne knew that Pierce was never one to pass the buck—he always accepted blame when he thought he'd been in the wrong. But was he blaming himself for things that weren't his fault, things that had never been in his control? She'd been so angry when Mason died that she'd never thought to question whether Pierce really had been to blame. Was there a chance that his mother was right?

"He wouldn't talk to me about the explosion," Roxanne hedged. "I still don't know what happened."

"Neither do I, dear. I was never able to get him to open up, either. But I do think he needs to talk about it, if someone's stubborn enough to get through to him." Amelia excused herself to go see to things in the kitchen, leaving Roxanne alone in the living room. She lifted a pillow from the floor and arranged it on the couch, at a loss for what to do with herself. Wishing she was out on a horse, the wind in her hair.

On an end table next to her was a photograph of Lily. Roxanne picked it up, staring at the image of the small child who looked so much like a little Lakota papoose, her face pale, her pitch-black, straight hair pulled into a tiny tuft held by a pink bow-shaped clip on top of her little head.

Roxanne settled in a rocker-recliner, touching her toe on the floor to set the chair in motion as she stared at the photograph.

Looking at the image of the baby who so closely resembled her father, Pierce's brother, Roxanne couldn't help thinking *what if.* What if she hadn't called off her wedding to Pierce? She could be pregnant now. What would their baby have looked like? Would she be dark like Lily or would she have red hair like her mother? Would he be strong, with high cheekbones and dark skin like Pierce? Would he like riding horses or playing football?

The list of possibilities seemed endless and…useless.

A tear slipped from the corner of Roxanne's eyes as she rocked back and forth, the chair's gentle sway only reminding her of everything she'd given up. She still loved Pierce, but she didn't know what kind of future they could have. He'd more or less told her he didn't want her back. What kind of crap had he said? She deserved someone better?

Pierce was a man of character, a man who stood by his family and friends. Did that really go with the idea she'd clung to—that somehow Pierce had let Mason down, leading to his death?

Roxanne closed her eyes to the image of her brother's battered body lying in the coffin at his funeral.

"Are you okay, honey?" Amelia Thunder Horse appeared before her.

"I'm fine." She set the photograph back in place.

Amelia settled on the couch and took up a crochet hook and a half-finished afghan, her fingers twisting around the yarn as she poked the needle in and out of loops. "It sure has cheered up the house, having the baby here," she commented. "I have to say, I worried about my special agent sons—especially Tuck—wondering if they'd ever settle down enough to give me grandbabies."

"Why Tuck, in particular? Pierce is certainly very dedicated to his job. He loves being an FBI agent."

"True, but he knows there's more to life than that. You know Pierce tried to talk Mason out of joining the FBI."

Roxanne's head jerked up and she stared across at Amelia. "No, I didn't know."

Amelia's lips twisted. "You can't tell young people anything. They have to make their own decisions, find their own way."

Brushing away a stray tear, Roxanne nodded, unable to speak, her heart hurting, the pain of her loss still fresh.

"Mason came over practically every evening for a week after he got accepted into the academy. He could barely wait." The older woman's lips lifted in the hint of a smile. "I remember trying to talk Pierce and Tuck out of joining the FBI. Lot of good it did. I heard them telling Mason the same things I told them—mostly that they needed to stay and run the ranch."

"That's what I tried to tell Mason."

Amelia glanced across at Roxanne. "Don't get me wrong, my boys all love this place. It's their home. But Pierce, Dante and Tuck wanted to follow their own dreams—they wanted to make a difference for others. I couldn't hold them back, even if I had wanted to, and I did want to. They had to live their own lives."

"And the ranch didn't fit in with their plans...or Mason's."

She'd blamed Pierce for so many things—was it just because she hadn't been able to accept the truth? She fought so hard to defend her right to choose her own life on the ranch. Had she held Mason back by not giving him the right to make that choice for himself?

"You might not have known that Pierce was the one to find Mason after that warehouse explosion."

Roxanne shook her head, the tears falling faster.

"He held Mason until the medical folks arrived. But Mason died in his arms." Amelia Thunder Horse brushed a tear from her cheek. "He never said anything. Tuck told me."

Roxanne's heart broke all over again, but in a strange way she felt healed. The anger and blame that had taken over, ruining her relationship with Pierce, had finally begun to lift. She could forgive him for everything that had happened…and maybe she'd be able to help him forgive himself. Amelia had said he needed someone stubborn to help him see the truth—and no one was better at out-stubborning Pierce Thunder Horse than her.

As soon as he entered the FBI building in Bismarck, Pierce went straight to his office. Tuck popped in while Pierce was booting up his computer.

"Remember that lead I said I was looking into?"

"Yeah." Tuck had Pierce's full attention. "Who is it?"

"The neighbor who filed the report that got Ethan Mitchell arrested."

"Ever get the name of the woman Mitchell was arguing with?"

"No, but I got the name of the police officer who arrested him. He might know more about what happened."

"Let's pay the man a visit."

"I'm a step ahead of you, brother." Tuck grinned. "Got an appointment to have coffee with the man in fifteen. Grab your keys and let's hit the road."

Pierce led the way out of the building and climbed into the truck, Tuck sliding into the passenger seat.

Ten minutes later they pulled into a diner that had seen better days but had an impressive number of cars gathered in the parking lot.

"Must have good food," Tuck observed.

"Have to—the place looks like a dump." Pierce climbed down and entered the establishment, his gaze panning the busy restaurant for a uniform.

"He said he was off duty," Tuck informed Pierce.

A man sitting alone at a table waved at them as a waitress plunked a plate full of pancakes in front of him.

Pierce strode across the room and pulled out a seat

in front of the off-duty police officer. "Pierce Thunder Horse." He stuck out his hand and shook the policeman's.

The man didn't apologize for eating in front of them; he just lifted his fork and knife and dug into the stack. "What can I do for you two?"

Tuck unfolded a printout of Ethan Mitchell's mug shot. "Remember this guy?"

The man nodded, chewing on a gooey bite of pancake. He swallowed. "Arrested him a couple months ago for disturbing the peace. From the looks of it, if I'd been about ten minutes later, I could have gotten him on assault, too. I got there just in time to keep him from getting violent."

"Why wasn't the girl's name listed in the arrest report?"

"She refused to give a statement. And we couldn't file any charges against her—she wasn't the one making all the ruckus."

Pierce leaned forward. "Did you ask the neighbors who she was?"

"They said she was his girlfriend, but they didn't know her name. She was always coming and going."

Pierce hid his disappointment. The cop hadn't been able to tell them much more than what was already in the report. "Sorry to interrupt your breakfast."

"I didn't know her name at the time of the arrest, but I think I know who she is. Saw a picture of her that same week in the obituaries."

Tuck glanced across at Pierce then turned to the officer. "You say it was the same week?"

"Yeah. It's been a couple months so I don't remember her name anymore. But I bet if you look through the obits for that week, you'll find her."

Pierce wasn't sure that knowing the name of Ethan's

dead girlfriend would help, but he didn't have anything else to go on. "Thanks for your time." He passed on shaking the man's hand, preferring to let him finish his breakfast.

Back in the truck, Pierce sighed. "I feel like we're chasing our tails."

"You said to dig deep on Mitchell. That's what we're doing. You know your gut is your best investigation tool. If your gut tells you to look into Ethan Mitchell, that's what we've gotta do." Tuck clapped a hand on Pierce's shoulder. "Let's go to the newspaper office and see if we can access the obituaries for that week. They might find things faster than we can."

Pierce headed for the local newspaper office. Once there they waited ten minutes for someone to free up to help them dig through the files for the week Ethan Mitchell was arrested.

It had been a busy week of deaths.

Going through the newspaper stories for that week, Tuck sat back. "I remember that week. We were here in Bismarck." He looked up at Pierce.

At the same time, Pierce ran across the article reporting an explosion at a local warehouse. The blood drained from Pierce's face. "That was the same week as the raid."

He didn't have to say which raid. His brother knew... he'd been there. "The one where Mason died," Tuck finished.

Pierce sat back in his chair, the air knocked out of his lungs just as if he'd been punched in the belly.

"It wasn't your fault Mason died," Tuck said. "It could have been you or me in that warehouse. He just happened to get there first."

"I know that. We lost a number of good agents that day." And Pierce had lost his fiancée, as well.

"Look, Pierce, if this is too much to go through, I can finish."

"No." Pierce leaned forward and pressed on. "I'm fine."

"You don't look so fine."

"It's been a bad week."

"I'm sorry about you and Roxy. I never thought she'd blame you for Mason's death."

"It was my fault. I should have stopped him." Pierce shook his head. "It's just as well. We could never have made it work between us."

"How so?"

"She has the ranch. I have the bureau. What kind of life is that for a couple?"

"If you love each other enough, you can make it work."

"How?" Pierce shot a straight look at his brother. "She'd be in the corner of Nowhere, North Dakota. Who knows where I'd be if she needed me?"

"It's a chance you take on each other. And there would be family close by if she needed help."

"She deserves someone who will stick around and be satisfied with ranching."

"What if she doesn't want to keep up the ranch?"

"It's her home. She's the last Carmichael. I would never ask her to give it up to follow me. She has dreams of her own."

Tuck nodded. "You have a point. Besides, she dumped you. It's not like the issue will ever come up again. She doesn't strike me as a woman who will come crawling back on her hands and knees."

"I wouldn't want her to," Pierce said.

"Do you want Julia to talk to her? She wasn't keen on marrying a special agent, but she came around."

"No." Pierce shook his head. "Just leave it. It's over between Roxanne and me."

"Doesn't look too over to me," Tuck muttered.

Pierce ignored him, flipping through the computer screen to the next day's paper and scrolling down to the obituaries. That's when he found a picture of a woman in her mid-twenties. He glanced at the name, Leah Jennings. "Tuck, why does this name ring a bell?"

"I don't know, but it does." Tuck leaned over and stared at the picture. "I don't recall her face, just the name." Pierce hit Print and pulled the photograph and write-up off the printer. "We got what we came for here. Let's go back to the office and see what we find on Ms. Jennings."

Chapter Thirteen

Roxanne paced the living room and kitchen of the Thunder Horse ranch house, becoming more agitated with each hour that passed. Several times she'd called the Carmichael Ranch trying to get through to Jim, and each time she'd hung up frustrated when she'd gotten no answer.

Her foreman had just survived a significant fall with multiple fractures. He shouldn't be up and running so soon. And yet, if he wasn't, the work might not be getting done.

Guilt burned like bile in Roxanne's already scratchy throat. Standing on the porch, staring out over the pastures, wishing she could see all the way to her place, she had just about had enough of the waiting.

Maddox had made a run to town for feed, taking Katya with him. Dante had stayed behind, claiming he had reports to catch up on for his work with the U.S. Customs and Border Protection. Yet instead of holing up in the office, he'd gone out to the barn.

Roxanne suspected he only stayed because of her.

She hated being watched over like a child. And she hated even more that Dante had already been the recipient of her attacker's violence.

Roxanne gripped the porch railing, her fingernails

digging into the wood. Inactivity made her crazier than not knowing who was after her. She needed to talk to her men and find out where things stood with getting the cattle ready for sale. In the bright light of day, it seemed crazy to think that she wouldn't be safe with her men—or that they'd be in danger just from having her there, especially if they all stayed together. Surely they could protect each other.

She'd trust Abe, Fred and Jim with her life. Toby and Ethan were newcomers to the ranch, but they'd been there for the past three months before the incidents started so she was sure they couldn't have been involved.

Not being there to keep an eye on the people and place that meant so much to her was killing her.

Amelia joined Roxanne on the porch and laid a hand on her arm. "They'll call if something happens that shouldn't. Why don't you come have a cup of hot tea with me? Or I could make up some lemonade, if you'd like that better."

She stuck her hands in the back pockets of the jeans that Mrs. Thunder Horse had laundered. Her clothes no longer had the acrid scent of smoke, but Roxanne couldn't get the smell out of her senses—a constant reminder of everything that had happened and of how easily her home could be taken away from her if she wasn't vigilant in protecting it. "No thanks. I really need to get home."

"Honey, you're not safe there right now. And you promised Pierce you'd be safe."

Roxanne closed her eyes. She had promised him that. But surely she'd be safe as long as she took precautions and stuck close to the men. They needed her out there with them.

If she didn't get the cattle to the sale, she wouldn't be able to pay her ranch hands. They'd leave for paying work and she'd be left to run the ranch on her own. She couldn't manage all the work by herself to earn enough money to pay the mortgage. All strikes against her.

She stood to lose her home and the ranch that had been in her family almost as far back as when Theodore Roosevelt had lived in the badlands. The cattle sale was her only hope, and she couldn't help with the roundup, all because someone was playing her.

Roxanne smacked the porch railing with her palm. "Horsefeathers!"

"Excuse me?" Amelia stared at Roxanne, her brows wrinkled. "Did you say horsefeathers?"

"I did. I'll be damned if I let my ranch be taken back by the bank or anyone else."

"Is the bank giving you troubles, dear?"

Already regretting opening her mouth, Roxanne scuffed her boot on the wooden deck. "Not yet. But they will if I don't make my mortgage payment. I need to be out helping with the roundup."

Roxanne grabbed Amelia's hands. "Please. I just need a ride over to my place. Or I could borrow a horse and bring it back tomorrow. Please, Mrs. T." She stared into the woman's eyes.

Amelia squeezed her hands. "Honey, you know I can't keep you here. You are not a prisoner. I only ask that you reconsider. Maybe Dante could go with you, to keep an eye out for you."

"Dante already took a hit for me. I can't ask him to take me."

"Maddox will be back shortly, I'm sure of it." In her concern, the older woman gripped her hands hard enough to hurt. "Can you wait at least until then? Perhaps Pierce will be back from Bismarck by that time, and he can take you himself."

More guilt washed over Roxanne. She'd already put two of Amelia's sons in danger watching over her. She didn't want anything else to happen to the Thunder Horses. With a sigh, she hugged Amelia. "Okay, I'll wait until Maddox comes back, or Pierce—whoever gets here first. Then I really must go home."

"Thank you, dear." Amelia hugged her back, her arms strong, reassuring. "I'd be so worried if you left without someone to watch out over you."

"I'm just not used to standing around, doing nothing. It's making me crazy."

"You could help me with lunch," Amelia offered. "Or maybe you'd rather help Dante out in the barn. At least you'd have something to keep you busy while you wait."

A shiver trailed across Roxanne's skin as she thought about the day before, being trapped inside the burning barn. If she hoped to get over the trauma of the fire, she could start in the Thunder Horse barn, where burning was less likely. "I'll find Dante. Maybe I could be of some use to him. No offense, Mrs. T."

"None taken, dear. Go."

Roxanne hurried down to the barn, ready to do something physical, anything to pass the time until Maddox or Pierce returned and took her back to her ranch.

Dante was bent over the unshod hoof of a black stallion, scraping it clean with a hook.

"Need a hand?" she asked.

"Not really."

"Okay, let me put it this way...." Roxanne took a deep breath and released it slowly. "Is there anything I can help with, to keep me busy before I blow a gasket? Please?"

Dante chuckled. "Bored?"

"More frustrated than bored. But yes."

"Then you can bring the bay mare in from the pen and tie her up to the next stall. Her hooves are in bad shape. I'm pulling shoes and cleaning. The farrier will be by later."

"I can do that." She grabbed a lead rope from a nail and hurried outside.

The next thirty minutes was spent in silence as the two pulled old metal horseshoes off the stallion and mare and cleaned the accumulated gunk out of their hooves.

"Dante!" Amelia Thunder Horse's shout made Roxanne drop the mare's last hoof halfway through cleaning.

Dante had just settled the stallion in a stall and given him a bucket of feed and a couple sections of hay. He stepped out of the stall and hurried to meet his mother outside the barn, pulling her into his arms. "What's wrong, Mom?"

Amelia Thunder Horse's hand shook as she spoke. "I just got a call from the sheriff's department. Maddox and Katya have been involved in a wreck. They're being sent to the hospital in Bismarck."

Her heart thumping hard against her ribs, Roxanne emerged from the barn, wiping her hands on her jeans. "How bad was it?"

"They didn't say, just that they were being taken by ambulance to St. Alexius in Bismarck. We should go at once."

"Come on, I'll drive." Dante led his mother toward the house, then stopped and turned toward Roxanne, frowning. "You'll have to come with us."

"No." Roxanne remained standing beside the barn.

"You'll need room in the truck to bring Maddox and Katya back, if they release them immediately. And I want to be here in case Jim needs to reach me for anything. You two go. I'll stay here."

"But that leaves you alone." Dante shook his head. "No, you'll have to come."

"If anything happens, I know how to shoot a gun and I can call the sheriff." When Dante opened his mouth to protest, Roxanne held up her hand. "Go. You need to check on your brother and his fiancée. I'll be fine."

Dante's frown deepened. "You wouldn't try to go home, would you?"

Roxanne waved them on. "I'll just finish up on the mare's hoof and get her settled. You two should hit the road. It's a long drive to Bismarck."

Amelia's brows knit. "I don't like leaving you."

"I don't like knowing Maddox and Katya are hurt. Please, go." Roxanne turned back to the barn, ending her side of the argument. By the time she'd finished scraping the mare's hoof, she heard the crunch of gravel in the driveway as Dante and his mother left for Bismarck. Roxanne wondered if Maddox and Katya's accident was caused by the same person who'd been gunning for her. More guilt piled into her already churning gut.

As she led the mare into a stall and fed her grain and hay, she couldn't stop thinking about what had happened in the past few days and how it didn't make any sense.

The shooting that had started it all made the least sense of all. Who had it out for her and why? Other than the land she owned, she couldn't come up with a single reason someone would want to kill her.

Was it the land? No one had approached her about

purchasing the Carmichael Ranch. With times as tough as they were, not many people were stupid enough to invest in a small-time cattle operation that barely paid the bills.

Not many people except for her. Because it was all she had left of the family she'd loved.

A lump rose in her throat and she swallowed hard to clear it. She'd done enough moaning and crying over the loss of her family. And she'd let recrimination and bitterness lead her to pushing away Pierce, and her best chance to start a new family.

Now that she looked back over the past couple months, she recognized her actions for what they were. Anger over the loss of her brother and fear of investing her love in yet another person who stood a good chance of dying and breaking her heart.

Not that she was the only one to blame—Pierce had pushed her away, too. But if they were both willing to let go of the past, was there still a chance that they could build a future together?

A shadow passed over the door to the barn, blocking the sunlight.

Roxanne glanced up to see the silhouette of a man astride a horse.

She froze, unable to see the rider's face and whether or not he carried a gun.

"Ms. Carmichael?"

Roxanne let go of the breath she'd been holding and stepped forward at the familiar voice. "Toby?"

"Yes, Ms. Carmichael, it's me." He leaned over his saddle horn.

"What's wrong?" She emerged from the shadows of the barn and blinked in the bright light of day. Ethan sat on a horse a few paces behind Toby, his cowboy hat pulled down, shading his eyes. "Is Jim hurt? Are the others okay?"

"They're fine. Ethan and I were sent over to get you because one of the wild horses is down. We thought you should know, being that you're the representative to the Bureau of Land Management and all."

Roxanne stiffened. "Which one?"

"I'm not sure. Ethan saw her. He thinks it's Sweet Jessie, the one injured the other day when that man shot her."

Roxanne glanced at Ethan. "Was she down…dead… or still alive?"

"Still alive," he answered, his words terse.

"Where?"

Ethan touched the brim of his hat, tipping it lower, the shadow all but hiding his face. "Not far from the watering hole near the canyon rim."

"Ethan and I can try to doctor her, or—" Toby paused "—put her out of her misery, but we thought you'd want to call it."

A weight as heavy as lead settled in Roxanne's chest. Sweet Jessie had been one of her favorites. When they'd spotted her a day ago, she'd been up and running, as if the gunshot wound hadn't fazed her a bit. It must have been worse than they'd thought for infection to set in that quickly and take her down.

"I'm coming." Roxanne glanced around. "Can one of you saddle a horse for me? I need to run in and call Pierce to tell him where I'm going."

Ethan leaned forward. "No time. If you want to help her, we need to go now."

Roxanne frowned at Ethan's sharp words. "By the time you have a horse saddled, I'll be ready." She stared across at the younger man, her early thoughts resurfacing. But she pushed them aside, the horse's welfare more important than her own safety. "Find a horse in the pen over there. Don't saddle one from the stalls, they need shoes. I'll be back before you're done."

Toby dropped down out of his saddle and hurried toward the pen Roxanne had indicated. Ethan dismounted and strode into the barn.

Taking off at a run, Roxanne raced to the house and up the porch steps. She found the kitchen phone and tried calling Pierce's cell phone, but the call went straight to voice mail. Frustrated, she hung up and tried Tuck's cell, hoping that he'd be with Pierce and could pass the phone over to him. When she got his voice mail, too, she went ahead and left a message. Then she grabbed a pad of paper and a pen and quickly scribbled a note to Amelia explaining what had happened, in case she got home first.

Then she ran back to the barn.

Ethan was slipping the bridle over a mare's head while Toby cinched the saddle's girth around her belly.

Instead of mounting immediately, Roxanne ran into the barn, found the large-animal medical supplies and filled a saddlebag with items she might need. Pierce's family was just as involved with the care and concern for the wild horses of the badlands as she was. They wouldn't mind her taking supplies, especially in as big a hurry as she was. She'd pay the Thunder Horse family back when she could.

When she emerged from the barn, she tossed the saddlebag over the horse's hind quarters and tied it to the saddle with the leather straps. All in all it had taken less than eight minutes to run to the house and gear up.

She mounted and reined the horse around, aiming in the direction of the canyon. "Let's go."

They took off at a gallop, Roxanne in the lead. The ride seemed to take forever, with Sweet Jessie's fate in the balance. When they finally neared the border to the Carmichael Ranch, Ethan pulled up next to Roxanne. "We might need help holding her down."

Roxanne slowed to a stop, her gaze panning the landscape.

"Ethan, go get Abe and Fred. Toby and I will find Jessie and assess the situation."

"I saw her. I know exactly where she is. Toby can get the others and bring them back."

"Fine. Toby, go." Her thoughts were half a mile ahead on Sweet Jessie, hoping it wasn't too late to save the mare.

"Where should we look for you?" Toby asked.

"Around the watering hole near the rim of the canyon," Ethan answered.

Toby galloped away, leaning low over his horse.

As Ethan and Roxanne neared the watering hole, Sweet Jessie was nowhere to be seen.

"I thought you said Sweet Jessie was here."

"She was. She might have gotten up and moved down into the canyon to hide. Maybe she's trying to find a place to die. We'd better hurry."

Roxanne's throat tightened. Not Sweet Jessie, the filly she and Pierce had nursed through a storm. It would be like breaking the last link to their shared past. She nudged her horse, sending her to the canyon rim.

As they neared the edge, Roxanne glanced down the trail they'd used when Jim had been injured. "I don't know how we're going to get down in there. This trail is a mess from the landslide."

Ethan reined his horse to the north. "I know another way down." He followed the rim for several hundred yards before he nodded toward a rocky outcropping. "There's a trail on the other side of those boulders." He started down.

Roxanne had never seen this trail before, hidden as it was in a maze of brush and boulders. She was surprised that it was wide enough for horses to climb in and out of the canyon easily.

As they descended, Roxanne glanced around, keeping a watch out for men with guns. "You know, Ethan, I think it might be better if we wait until Pierce can ride down with us. I'd hate for one of us to get hurt."

Ethan shot a frown over his shoulder. "Jessie was really bad off. If we wait, she might not make it."

Roxanne looked above her at the canyon rim, wishing she'd waited on Pierce. But if Jessie was as bad off as Ethan was making her out to be, every minute counted. "Okay. Go." But she'd keep an eye on Ethan all the way, still unsure of him. Without a gun to protect herself, she could be riding into a trap. But then Ethan didn't have a gun on him, either.

She rode silently down the trail, working through all the incidents in her mind. Each time she'd been attacked, her ranch hands had been out in the field rounding up cattle—as far as she knew. Rounding up cattle on a large spread meant splitting up to find those animals hiding in the bushes. The ranch hands could have been scattered and busy enough they wouldn't see if one of them had slipped away.

The time she'd almost been run over by the motorcycle, Ethan had claimed the four-wheeler had broken down. Had he swapped the four-wheeler for a dirt bike to terrorize her?

As the trail leveled out onto the canyon floor, Roxanne pulled her horse to a stop and she stared across at Ethan. "Ethan, have I ever done anything to make you mad?"

He turned to face her. "No."

"Have I treated you unfairly?"

With a shake of his head, he nudged his horse. "Nope. These tracks might lead to the horse. Come on."

Roxanne moved out a little slower, letting the distance between her and Ethan lengthen, her gut telling her that being alone in a canyon with Ethan wasn't one of her brightest decisions. Either he was telling the truth, and he wouldn't be much protection for her, unarmed as he was, or he was working against her and she could be in danger. She reined in her horse. "I'm heading back to the Thunder Horse Ranch to wait for Pierce. It doesn't feel right down here."

Ethan pointed ahead. "There! I think I see her." He dug his heels into his horse and raced ahead.

Adrenaline shot through Roxanne's veins. As Ethan's horse took off, her own horse couldn't stand being left behind. She tossed her head, trying to loosen Roxanne's tight grip.

"Okay, fine. We'll check it out. But if she's not there, we're heading back." Roxanne gave the horse her head.

The animal leaped forward, galloping along the rocky ground.

Ethan and his mount disappeared over a rise.

Roxanne tempered her horse's headlong rush to catch up, afraid she'd slip on the loose rocks and hurt herself.

As she topped the knoll, she spotted Ethan's horse standing still, its sides heaving, the saddle empty. The animal stood at a narrow choke point in the canyon, the walls pocked with an array of caves, some mere overhangs, others gaping entrances. Roxanne had spent many summers exploring the canyons with their father and Mason, but she didn't remember this place.

She eased her horse forward. "Ethan?"

"In here! She's in here!" His voice echoed off a cave's walls.

The sound bounced around the cliffs towering over Roxanne's head. "Where are you?" she called out.

"Follow my voice."

Roxanne dismounted and walked toward one particular cave. She led her horse by the reins.

The horses occasionally entered the caves to avoid the bitter winter winds in North Dakota, but it was summer. Sweet Jessie wasn't making sense, unless, like Ethan had intimated, she was looking for a place to die. "Ethan, come out so I can see where you are."

As she waited for him to appear, she glanced at the ground, searching for hoofprints of an unshod wild horse. Instead, she found narrow tire tracks.

Her breath lodged in her throat. "Ethan! Get out here."

She backed away from the cave's entrance, her pulse hammering through her veins. "Ethan. Please. We need to leave, right now."

Ethan stepped out of one of the larger caves, his right arm by his side, aligning with his right leg. "We're not going anywhere."

The tone of his voice sent chills along Roxanne's spine. "We need to go, it's not safe here."

He lifted a rifle in his arms and aimed it at her chest. "Correction…it's not safe for *you*."

Chapter Fourteen

Pierce sat in front of his computer, poring through the criminal databases, trying to find a match on Leah Jennings. So far, nothing. Ready to call it a bust and head back to the ranch, he tried searching the internet for the name in Bismarck.

His fingers tapped against the surface of his desk as he waited. Finally a string of hits popped up on his screen. The first was a high school yearbook photo of Leah Jennings from the local Bismarck high school, dated several years back. In the photo, she was a fresh-faced young woman with long sandy-blond hair who smiled back at him from the screen.

He clicked on another photo of a woman in a mug shot, her hair dirty and streaked purple and pink, piercings on her eyebrow, nose and ears. What made a young person go from girl next door to that? Probably drugs.

Farther down the list was a string of news headlines from a couple months back. He clicked on one and a picture popped up on the screen with a caption that knocked the air from his lungs.

Explosion Claims Lives of Four Feds.

He recognized the picture from one that had been plastered over all the newspapers and newscasts. It showed the night they'd raided the warehouse in Bismarck that had been used to store stolen and illegal weapons. The FBI and ATF had conducted a joint operation to expose and disarm a radical militia rumored to be preparing for an attack on government buildings across North Dakota, Montana and Minnesota.

Pierce had been the one who'd received a tip from a concerned citizen that the militia group would be meeting at a certain time to distribute weapons to their counterparts, using a warehouse in the southern part of Bismarck.

Because the tip had come to Pierce, he, Tuck and Mason had been assigned to assist the ATF in capturing members of the militia and seizing the weapons. At first, everything had gone according to plan. The ATF had lead on the bust, and Mason had insisted on volunteering to go in with them. Pierce and Tuck had set up a communications outpost on the outside. It should all have gone down smoothly.

What they hadn't counted on was the explosives hardwired throughout the building, set to go off if the warehouse was raided. It had all been a setup. Pierce had led the team into a trap. He'd received the tip and he hadn't questioned the validity or the possibility that it wasn't what it seemed. It had been his fault that Mason and the three ATF agents had died in that explosion.

Pierce's fingers curled into a tight fist, his eyes burning. Mason had lived long enough to die in his arms, his final request for Pierce to look out for his sister.

The memories washed over him like a black, murky wave of swamp water, dragging him down into the well of despair he'd experienced, knowing it was his fault and that he had to be the one to break the news to Roxanne.

The kicker of the entire event was that not all the

arms the militia had amassed had been stored in that location. An entire arsenal of deadly weapons had been relocated only hours before the raid. Pierce's team had moved in faster than the militia had expected, otherwise there would have been no weapons or militia members in the building at the time of the explosion. But the bulk of the inventory—and the militia membership—was still at large, and no one knew where…at least, no one who was willing to talk.

"Anything?" Tuck leaned in the door to Pierce's office. "I checked criminal databases and didn't have a match.

His brother's voice yanked Pierce out of the past and back to the article in front of him. "I'm reviewing old newspaper articles."

Tuck entered the office and leaned over Pierce's shoulder. "Damn. Isn't that—"

Pierce nodded, his empty stomach roiling. "The warehouse explosion."

"Why are you revisiting it?"

"I did a search on Leah Jennings in Bismarck and this was one of the articles that came up."

"Holy smokes." Tuck poked a finger at the screen farther down the page. "Says Leah Jennings was one of the members of the militia who died in the explosion. What kind of coincidence is that?"

The air left Pierce's lungs in a whoosh. "Leah died in the explosion?"

"You think Ethan has anything to do with the militia?"

"I don't know." Pierce opened another tab on the browser and keyed in "North Dakota Militia" and "Ethan Mitchell" and waited for the search engine to do its thing.

A moment later, several articles and images popped up on the screen, all of which had something to do with the militia but held no mention of Ethan Mitchell in particular.

Pierce pulled up photographs taken of a demonstration at the capitol of North Dakota by the local militia six months ago. He blew up the photograph and studied the blurred images.

"There." He pointed to the screen. "Isn't that Leah? The one with the purple streaks?"

"Could be. Who is that next to her?"

A young man in dark cargo pants and a slouchy jacket could have been Ethan, but his face was turned too far away to be certain.

"Move the picture to the left." Tuck's brows pulled together. "See what I'm seeing?"

Pierce tried to adjust the focus on the image, but it didn't get much better. "Looks kinda like…"

"Shorty Duncan." Tuck let out a long low whistle.

"What the hell was he doing at the rally?"

Pierce stood so fast his chair rolled back and hit the file cabinets. "When did the sheriff bring him on?"

"I don't know, but Mom or Maddox would."

"I have to get back to the ranch." Pierce grabbed his keys from the desktop.

"But we might find more information while we're here."

"Something doesn't feel right. I need to get to Roxanne." Pierce skipped by the elevator and took the steps down to the ground level, Tuck on his heels.

They climbed into the truck and pulled out of the parking lot, Pierce driving, Tuck pressing buttons on his cell phone.

Before he could hit Send to place a call to the ranch

house, his phone buzzed, indicating a couple of voice mails had come in while Tuck's phone had been in a pocket of bad reception.

Pierce strained to hear the message while negotiating the traffic.

Tuck hung up the phone with a muttered curse and stared across at Pierce. "Bad news."

His pulse shot blood and adrenaline through his arteries. "Give it to me."

"The first call was from Mom, letting us know that she got a call from the sheriff's department saying Maddox and Katya had been involved in an accident and were on their way to St. Alexius hospital here in Bismarck."

Pierce's heart jumped into his throat. "A car accident? Was their car tampered with, too?"

"Mom didn't say. She didn't seem to think it sounded too serious, but she did say that she and Dante were going to drive out and see what was going on. The second message I got is the one you're really not going to like. It was from Roxanne."

"Tell me Roxanne went with Dante and Mom," Pierce said through gritted teeth.

Tuck's mouth formed a thin line as he shook his head. "Wish I could, but she didn't."

Pierce's stomach plummeted. "Where is she?"

"She called to say that two of her men showed up claiming Sweet Jessie was down and needed immediate attention. She called to let us know that she'd be leaving with them."

Pierce drew in a shaky breath. "Did she say which two of Roxanne's men?"

"Toby and Ethan."

Could it get worse? Pierce forced himself to think.

"Call the sheriff's dispatcher and see what they know of Maddox's accident."

Already dialing, Tuck held the phone to his ear and waited, then asked the dispatcher what was going on. A moment later his face looked even more grim. "They never called Mom."

"See if you can get Maddox on the phone."

"You know cell phones have little to no reception out that far."

"Try."

Tuck hit speed dial for Maddox's cell phone with no luck, then Dante's.

"We have to get there faster than driving." Pierce jerked the steering wheel to the right, sending them south.

Tuck held on to the armrest. "Where are you going?"

"The airport."

"We won't get a plane out that fast."

"We're not going by plane, if we can help it. Dial your friend Rick Knoell, tell him it's an FBI emergency."

"We don't have clearance from our supervisor," Tuck said even as he glanced down at his phone.

"If it was Julia, would you question it?"

Tuck searched his contacts list and selected one, holding the phone to his ear. "Rick, I need another favor. I know, we've been making it a habit. This is important. We need to get out near Medora ASAP."

Pierce listened to the one-sided conversation, holding his breath.

"Can you be ready in ten minutes? Thanks." Tuck shook his head and hit a number on his speed dial, glancing across at Pierce. "I should make you place this one."

"Who are you calling now?"

Tuck sighed. "Our boss. He's not going to be happy."

"Give it to me." Pierce took the phone from Tuck as their supervisor answered.

"Radcliff speaking."

"Pierce Thunder Horse, sir. We've made a command decision to appropriate the use of a helicopter to get us to the badlands in a hurry."

"Better have a damn good reason," Radcliff barked.

"Sir, I believe we may have narrowed down the Nor-Dak Militia weapons stash we lost track of on the raid two months ago. We might need backup should things go south."

"Then you should wait until I can call in the ATF."

"Sir, no sir. There's a possible hostage situation that won't wait. I believe we can get in and lock down the location before the militia catches wind that we're coming." He paused. "With your permission, sir."

A long pause ensued as Pierce pulled off the highway at the airport exit and sped toward Rick Knoell's hangar. If he had to, he'd pay Rick out of his pocket for the use of the helicopter.

But if his gut had this right, this was a bigger can of worms than even he had originally anticipated.

"If you're wrong…" Radcliff started.

"I know, it'll come out of my pocket." Pierce maneuvered the truck into a parking space and shifted to Park.

"That's not all that you'll lose."

"I'll risk it, sir. I have a gut feeling." Pierce shifted the phone to his other ear and switched off the truck.

"We need more than a gut feeling."

"Sir, given the last operation, I think we have a better chance of rounding up the weapons without fanfare and joint ops." Pierce held his breath. He'd go without permission, but having it would help.

"If I didn't trust you, I'd say you're risking a helluva lot." Radcliff snorted. "Hell, I trust you and I *still* think you're risking a lot."

Pierce opened his door and climbed out, still holding the phone.

"Do it," Radcliff commanded. "Keep me informed."

"Yes, sir." Pierce hit the off button before Radcliff could change his mind, and he tossed the phone to Tuck.

Tuck shook his head. "Why did you just tell the boss you'd found the weapons?"

"Because I think we have." Pierce jogged toward the hangar, Tuck keeping pace. "Think about it. Someone shot at Roxanne when she got near to the canyon. When she tried to go down into the canyon with Jim, they were stopped with a landslide."

"What about when you two were in the canyon that night it rained?"

"Maybe there were too many people around to get away with anything at the time. We had cover as we descended to the canyon floor. The rain kept us from exploring too far."

"What about the fire in the barn?"

"I'm not sure, but I have a hunch." Before he could elaborate, they were pulling out their FBI credentials and showing it to the lady at the desk of the helicopter courier service run by pilot Rick Knoell. Rick was out on the tarmac finishing up his preflight check.

"Ready?" he asked, sliding into the pilot's seat.

"Let's go." Pierce climbed into the front seat and settled the headset over his ears.

"Where exactly are we going?" he asked.

"The badlands north of Medora." Pierce closed his

door and settled back. "Can you hurry? It could mean the difference between life and death."

ETHAN JERKED THE RIFLE to the left. "Get in the cave."

"Why?" Roxanne stalled.

"Just do it." The young man's lip lifted in a sneer. "Just because you own a ranch doesn't make you better than anyone."

"I didn't say it did."

"People like you lord it over regular folk, making our lives miserable enough until we want to do something about it."

"When did I make your life miserable?" Roxanne walked slowly up the incline to the cave's entrance. Oddly enough, now that she was faced with the man who might have been responsible for the attacks against her, she felt calmer than she had the entire week. Maybe it had to do with finally having someone in front of her that she could deal with directly, not having to wait and worry about when danger would strike. Maybe it was just that Ethan was someone she knew—someone she might be able to talk down from whatever crazy plan he'd formed.

"I hired you to do work on a ranch. You said you'd done ranch work before. Did I ask you to do anything I wouldn't have done?"

"You're like the rest of them," Ethan muttered, his eyes wide, his hands shaking.

Roxanne stopped in front of him, wondering how she'd get through to him when he looked so unstable. "Who is 'them'?"

"Shut up!" He poked her in the belly with the end of the rifle. "Just get inside."

"I'd like to know what I've done that warrants being yelled at and prodded with a rifle."

"You poked around where you shouldn't have."

"And where was that?"

"Here in the canyon, damn it!" He grabbed her arm and jerked her into the cave.

Roxanne stumbled and righted herself. "It's part of my ranch—why wouldn't I go into the canyon?"

"Because that's where we keep this…" He waved his free hand at the stacks of boxes lining the cave walls. On top of and beside the boxes were military rifles, grenade launchers and machine guns, all shiny and new.

Roxanne's stomach flipped over as she stared around the interior of the cave, lit by a single gas lantern. "Good Lord, how'd you get all this in here?"

Ethan smiled. "The badlands can hide a lot, if you know where to go."

She shook her head, stunned by the amount of equipment. "I don't get it. I live on this land, and I don't remember seeing anyone coming in and out of the canyon."

"Because we didn't want you to. We moved it at night."

"But why do you need it? What's the purpose?" Her gaze landed on a long fat tube that looked like a World War II bazooka. She wasn't sure exactly what it was, but knew it could probably inflict a lot of damage. "You could supply an army with this much stuff."

"Exactly. It's the beginning of the end of a government that is no longer run by the upper-class minority."

"What are you talking about?" She faced Ethan, trying to make sense of what she saw and what he was saying.

"The silent majority, the working-class people are

taking back our government from people like you who think you own everything."

Roxanne laughed, in spite of the tension of the situation. "I don't own everything, I'm struggling to make payments on what I have. What does this have to do with you holding a gun on me?"

"My job was to keep anyone from discovering the cache." He shook his head. "But you just couldn't stay away from the canyon."

She tore her gaze from the stockpile. "You were the one that shot at me. I should have known. You disappeared often enough, when you should have been working." She nodded at a dirt bike leaning against the wall in the corner. "You're pretty good on a dirt bike, but thankfully a lousy shot. So why bring me here if you didn't want me to find this cache?"

"To kill you." Ethan's words rang out against the cool stone walls, his eyes a colder gray, the gun leveled on her.

Now she was starting to get scared. The air left Roxanne's lungs and she struggled to keep it together in the face of imminent danger. "Kill me? Why? What have I done to you?"

"Other than poking around in the canyon, not anything worth dying for."

"Then why me? Why now?"

"It's not so much what *you've* done, it's what your *boyfriend* did." His voice dropped low, echoing in a low hum off the cave walls. "And I didn't know who your boyfriend was until yesterday."

"What are you talking about? I don't have a boyfriend."

Ethan waved the rifle wildly. "Bull! I saw you two practically crawling into each other's skins."

Roxanne stood with her hands planted on her hips, facing Ethan, refusing to show her fear in the face of his threat. If he was going to shoot her, he'd have to shoot her face-to-face. "That doesn't mean we're together. We split up two months ago, after my brother died."

"Yeah, after he killed my girlfriend."

"What?"

"You heard me. Your boyfriend was responsible for killing my Leah."

"How?"

"His raid on that warehouse set off the explosion. He got there too early. Leah was inside. She shouldn't have been in there when it went off. The feds were supposed to come later, after our people got out. But no, your boyfriend ordered them in earlier. It's his fault. Pierce Thunder Horse killed Leah just as if he'd stuck a gun to her head and pulled the trigger." His body shook, his voice cracking as tears filled his eyes.

"Oh, Ethan. I lost someone I loved in that raid, too." Roxanne stepped toward him.

"Stay back."

"Listen. You don't have to do this." Roxanne reached out. "Please, Ethan, let me have that gun before it goes off."

"That's the idea." He shoved the gun at her hard, the barrel hitting her in the rib, making a snapping sound.

Pain lanced through her where metal smacked against bone. Roxanne doubled over, clutching her rib cage. "Ethan, hurting me won't bring Leah back." She pushed her words through gritted teeth, fighting to hide the pain.

"I know that." He swiped his empty hand across his face, brushing aside his tears. "What do you think I am, stupid?"

"No, I don't. I think you're grieving and lashing out at anyone you can, because you're still hurting." Like she had.

"Shut up." Ethan fired off a round.

The bullet missed Roxanne, tearing into a wooden crate.

"Ethan, you're not a killer." Roxanne struggled to keep the fear out of her tone, to be firm yet gentle. "Put the weapon down and let me help you."

"No. It's over. I'm tired of hiding, tired of guarding this stuff, tired of being told what to do. I just want Leah back."

"Ethan, she's not coming back." Roxanne shook her head, turning sideways to provide the narrowest target she could if he decided to shoot again.

"It hurts. Missing Leah hurts so bad." His tears spilled over and ran down his cheeks, the rifle shaking in his hands. "Your boyfriend needs to know what it feels like to lose the woman he loves."

"You'd hurt me to punish Pierce?" She straightened, though it hurt to. "Pierce didn't send Leah into that building. She went in there on her own."

"They weren't supposed to move on the building until Leah got out, but they did, because of Pierce."

"What happened is done, Ethan." Roxanne inched toward the man as his tears continued. If she could get close enough, she might be able to grab for the gun. "Don't make it worse."

"It wasn't supposed to happen that way. Leah wasn't supposed to be there, or stay that long. She was supposed to get out before…"

"Before the explosives went off?" Roxanne whispered, recalling her own anguish over losing her brother, Mason.

"Yes!" Ethan jerked the gun. "They weren't supposed to get there that soon. Not until she got out. Not until it was time."

"What time was that?"

"The specific time I tipped them off with, damn it! The ATF and FBI agents were getting close to the truth. I wanted them to raid the empty warehouse, to set off the rigged explosives and get rid of them. It wasn't supposed to happen like it did. Leah wasn't supposed to die, and because she did, you will, too."

"Ethan—" Roxanne started.

"Shut up and turn around." Ethan demanded, jabbing her again with the barrel of the rifle. "I'm going to kill you and when Pierce comes to find you, I'll kill him, too."

No. Roxanne couldn't let that happen. No matter what happened to her, Ethan couldn't go after Pierce. And, she realized, she couldn't die without letting Pierce know how much she still cared for him. She had to tell him that she didn't blame him anymore, and that he shouldn't blame himself. No matter what had happened during that raid at the warehouse, Pierce hadn't been responsible for Mason's death. She'd known that all along, even though she'd refused to admit it, wanting to have someone to blame.

But what had happened over the past couple days had made her realize life was short. She could die in a car wreck or be thrown by a horse. When your number was up, it was up, no matter how you went out. The most you could hope for was to love someone with all your heart for as long as you could and be thankful you had that time together.

She refused to believe her time with Pierce had come to an end.

A surge of adrenaline and determination shot through Roxanne and she made a grab for Ethan's rifle, knocking the barrel to the side.

The gun went off, the bullet pinging against the wall of the cave, ricocheting back at them.

Roxanne dropped to the dirt.

The bullet hit Ethan in the shoulder, knocking him backward so hard that he hit the cave wall and crumpled to the ground, the rifle falling to the ground in front of him.

Tears welled in Roxanne's eyes as she staggered to her hands and knees and scrambled across the floor, reaching for the rifle.

As her hand closed over the stock a black boot landed in the middle of her hand, pinning it.

"Leave it," a heavy voice said.

Roxanne shrieked and jerked her hand free, sitting down hard on the cave floor as she turned to stare up into the barrel of a semiautomatic pistol.

Chapter Fifteen

"Can this thing go any faster?" Pierce leaned forward as they skimmed across the plains heading west.

"I'm giving it everything I can," Rick's voice crackled over the headset into Pierce's ears. "Look down. That should be the Thunder Horse Ranch we're passing over now. Where to from here?"

"Head for the canyon." Pierce pointed toward the wide, scarred swath of broken earth.

As they neared the edge of the canyon, Pierce leaned over, peering down at the land below. "See that pond?"

"At one o'clock?" Rick nodded. "Yup."

Disappointment washed over him as he stared at the deserted ground around the pond. No sign of Roxanne, Ethan or Toby anywhere to be seen. That didn't deter him. Pierce would use the tracking skills his father had taught him to find them. "Put us down close to the canyon rim."

As the chopper lowered over the land, Pierce could see a cloud of dust rising from the east and another in the west. Riders, heading their way. If they'd gotten his messages then it was probably his brothers from the east and Roxanne's men from the west. They wouldn't get there for several more minutes. Minutes he couldn't waste waiting for backup. He had Tuck. His brother was a trained agent and they both carried their guns. It would have to be enough to start with.

He prayed to *Wakan Tanka* that they didn't run into the entire militia in their efforts to bring Roxanne home alive.

As the helicopter skids brushed the ground, Pierce threw open the door, jumped out and ran toward the watering hole, Tuck racing to catch up.

Fresh tracks led away from the pond toward the edge of the canyon, veering to the north, instead of descending at the old trail.

Tuck caught up with Pierce. "Only two horses. Julia said Roxanne left with Toby and Ethan."

His chest tightened. "We have to assume she's with Ethan, and that he's dangerous."

Pierce followed the tracks to an outcropping of rocks and boulders where they vanished. The ground was rough, made of plate rock swept clean of dust and dirt. Horses wouldn't make tracks on solid rock. He'd lost the trail.

ROXANNE HELD UP A HAND as if that would stop a bullet from killing her. As her focus shifted from the gun's barrel to the man holding it, she gasped. "Deputy Duncan? Oh, thank God you're here. Ethan tried to kill me."

The deputy didn't reposition the weapon. "He'd have saved me the effort."

"What?" Roxanne had trouble wrapping her mind around the deputy's words. "What do you mean?"

"If Ethan had done his job right in the first place, no one would have found this cave."

"I don't understand. You're an officer of the law."

"Yeah, and I'm tired of crap for pay and the government taking a huge chunk of what little I make in taxes. Taxes that go to building bridges to nowhere and investing in companies that take jobs out of the United States. We plan on retaking our country."

"By force?"

"It's the only way."

"And you're going to use this stuff to do it?" Roxanne waved her hand around the cavern. "I assume you're part of the militia Ethan was talking about."

"Damn right I am." Shorty glanced around at the stacks of weapons. "Ethan really screwed up. He should never have shot at you in the first place. It only brought more attention to this canyon. Now we can't get the weapons out without drawing even more scrutiny from the Thunder Horses. The FBI will get involved and, if they put the pieces together, the ATF will be back in the mix. It'll be a damned warehouse fiasco all over again. Had I known Ethan was responsible for tipping off the FBI about the warehouse, I'd have killed him sooner."

Roxanne shook her head. She'd heard the warehouse raid hadn't netted the number of weapons anticipated. "Were these the weapons moved before the warehouse raid in Bismarck?"

"Yeah, and now, because of you and Ethan, we're back to square one. I'll have to bury the weapons to keep the feds from finding them and discovering my part in it."

Roxanne knew that his plan to keep his link to the militia a secret meant he'd have to get rid of her. She scooted backward, trying to get as far away from his gun as possible.

"Yeah." Shorty's eyes narrowed. "You and the idiot will be buried with the weapons." He raised his arm, pointing the gun at Roxanne's face.

She grabbed the only thing she could find in reach,

a loose stone, and flung it at Shorty's hand. It missed, glancing off his cheekbone, but it was enough to distract him from shooting as a trickle of blood ran down his neck.

"Damn you!" Clutching a hand to the wound, his lip curled into a snarl and he aimed at her again.

Roxanne's life passed before her eyes as she waited for the bullet. The one thought that stood out above all others was an image of Pierce on horseback, his cowboy hat shading his eyes, a smile across his face as he rode toward her. Back when they couldn't be apart for long, when their love had been untainted, fresh and new.

She wanted it back. Wanted Pierce's love. Wanted to tell him that she loved him and had never really stopped loving him, even when she'd called off their wedding.

Now she sat on the floor of a cave, staring death in the face, wishing she had one more chance to tell Pierce how she really felt.

A loud click echoed against the cave's walls, but the bullet didn't come.

Roxanne scooted back farther, bunching her knees beneath her.

"You're not getting away from me." Shorty pulled the trigger again. Click.

Roxanne jumped to her feet and flew at Shorty, hoping to startle him into dropping the weapon altogether, giving her time to escape.

Just before Roxanne collided with Shorty, he raised his pistol and slammed it down on her head.

Pain bolted through her skull, clouding her vision as her body crashed into Shorty's chest, knocking them both to the ground.

Roxanne rolled to the side and tried to rise, but blood ran into her eyes, blinding her.

Another blow to the side of her head and she was done, collapsing face-first into the dirt, swallowed by the black void of unconsciousness.

"THEY CAN'T HAVE DISAPPEARED." Pierce dropped to his haunches and scanned the ground, hoping to find a horsehair, droppings…something…anything that would lead him to Roxanne. "Their trail is somewhere close by. It has to be." He rose and rounded the outcropping of boulders protruding up and spilling over the edge of a rocky cliff. The boulders formed a maze of giant obstacles, with gaps around and between. Desperate for some sign, some indication as to where the horses had gone, Pierce entered the maze and wound his way through a corridor wide enough for a horse or an ATV.

As he emerged on the other side, he discovered a trail leading down into a part of the canyon he had never explored. As he descended a few feet down the stony path, the ground grew more dusty and he could make out tracks of horse hooves…and a dirt bike. "Tuck, down here!"

"Down where? Where are you?" His brother's voice sounded muted and distant, the boulders muffling his words.

Pierce hurried back through the maze to where Tuck stood. "Come on. There's a trail wide enough for horses. And I found the tracks of a dirt bike."

"What about the others on their way? How will they find us in this?"

Pierce yanked his shirt over his head and draped it on the boulder most visible from the pond, in case the others looked that way. Rick Knoell had seen the direction they'd headed, so he'd point the others in the right direction. Once they reached the boulders, they'd find the trail he'd leave on the stones. Pierce dug in his pocket for change. As he led the way through the maze, he dropped quarters, dimes and nickels to indicate the correct path.

As they emerged on the crooked trail leading down into the canyon, Pierce drew his gun, holding it at the ready.

The trail wound up and over ridges, in and out of boulders that had fallen halfway down the sides of the cliffs, leading them deeper into nature-carved valleys, ravines and crevices.

When they emerged on the canyon floor, Pierce hugged the walls, weaving in and out of giant boulders that had once been a part of the cliffs above. Pierce could understand why they hadn't discovered this area before. The horses and cattle would find little or no food in the rocky ravines. But someone wanting to hide would find plenty of places in the caves dotting the cliffs, especially the ones closest to the ground.

He stopped beside a giant stone the size of a house and looked up at the dark holes in the cliff walls, some high up, others near the canyon floor.

Tuck moved abreast of Pierce, who was peering over his shoulder. "Which one do you think they're in?"

Pierce scanned the darkened entrances. "I don't know, but they have to be inside one of them." He nodded to the other end of the deep crevasse. "They wouldn't have ridden out that way. Too steep."

Again the ground turned stony and tracks were hard to follow. Once he left the shelter of the boulder, he would be exposed to anyone holding a gun. "Stay here and cover me," he said to Tuck, and took off running toward the cave with the largest entrance of those on his left.

No shots rang out as he climbed up the slope toward the gaping maw.

The first cave proved to be no more than an overhang, barely large enough to hide a man and a horse, much less two horses. As he slipped down the slope and moved on to the next cave, he heard a voice. He inched toward the entrance. The voice continued muttering and the scuffling of shoes across loose gravel carried to Pierce.

Someone was inside.

Adrenaline kicked in, sending him up the slope faster. As he neared the entrance, he scooted to the side, plastering himself to the wall, scanning the ridges and cliffs around him, searching for sharpshooters or sentries to warn those inside of intruders.

Nothing moved, no sun glinting off metal or field glasses. Pierce waved for Tuck to join him. Backup would be important if he hoped to get to Roxanne, especially going into a dark cave after being in the bright sunlight. He closed one eye, preparing for his move into the darkness. He prayed he wouldn't be too late.

He gave Tuck a thumbs up and covered for his brother as he headed his way.

PAIN RICOCHETED OFF THE inside of Roxanne's head, forcing her back to the world of the living. She blinked once, then twice, willing her eyelids to remain open.

The darkness that greeted her made her think she was still asleep. As her vision came into focus she realized she was lying on her side next to a wooden crate. She wasn't in her nice soft bed, but on the cool stone floor of a cave.

The events that led her there rushed in on her and she tried to sit up. She couldn't move. Her hands and feet were duct-taped together in front of her. Another piece kept her lips from moving. Near the mouth of the cave, Shorty Duncan, the deputy with a dark secret, reached as high as he could, pushing claylike lumps against the rocks.

It had to be some kind of plastic explosive material.

Roxanne didn't have much time. If she wanted to get out of the cave alive, she couldn't lie there all trussed up.

She wiggled her way to the corner of one of the crates and rubbed the tape binding her wrists against the coarse wood. A strand at a time, the tape broke free. She kept an eye on Shorty during the process.

When he glanced her way, Roxanne played dead, her body going limp, her efforts ceasing until Shorty went back to his work preparing to bury her alive. He pressed wires and something metal into the malleable substance, stringing them together.

When Roxanne had her hands free, she hurried to pull the tape free from her ankles and mouth, timing her movements with Shorty's to mask the sound.

A groan rose from nearby where Ethan lay against the wall. His hand moved to the wound on his shoulder and he groaned again.

Roxanne held her breath, hoping Shorty wouldn't hear him and come to investigate. At least until she could climb to her feet and run.

Ethan beat her to it. He lurched to a standing position. "What are you doing?"

Shorty turned to face Ethan. "I'm burying the cache, thanks to your stupidity."

Ethan staggered forward a step. "And you were planning to bury me with it?"

His lip curling into a snarl, Shorty glared at Ethan.

"I wouldn't have to sacrifice our hard work if it hadn't been for you going on some revenge kick."

"I loved Leah. Those Thunder Horse brothers killed her."

"No, you did that yourself, by tipping them off."

Ethan opened his mouth.

Shorty jabbed a finger at him. "And don't try to deny it. You were the one who told the FBI where to find us and got our people inside the warehouse killed. If you want to blame anyone, blame yourself for Leah's death."

Ethan's face darkened, his breathing growing more erratic. He threw back his head and roared, charging at Shorty like a drunken bull.

Shorty braced himself, but it wasn't enough.

When Ethan hit him, he slammed against the wall of the cave, his head hitting hard.

The two men fell to the ground.

With Shorty and Ethan occupied, Roxanne pushed to her feet and scrambled for freedom. As she neared the entrance, she could see the sunshine and practically feel it on her skin.

A hand snaked out and locked on to her ankle.

She tipped forward, her momentum slamming her into the cave floor. Her vision blurred, a gray haze closing in around her. Roxanne refused to give in, refused to pass out and die in the cave. She pushed against the floor, rolling over as Ethan flung himself at her.

Barely avoiding him, she rolled out of reach and shoved to her feet, only a few steps away from escape.

Ethan leaped up, grabbed her hair and jerked her to a stop, his arm clamping around her neck.

Roxanne kicked and struggled, but Ethan's hold remained firm, cutting off her air.

"I want Pierce to know how it feels to lose the one he loves," Ethan said.

With the little air she could squeeze past his hold, she said, "Pierce doesn't love me." Her heart broke at her own words.

"Yes, I do, Roxanne." A silhouette filled the cave entrance. "Ethan Mitchell, let go of her, or I swear on the Great Spirit, I'll rip you apart."

"Pierce?" Roxanne cried out, the sound cut off as the arm around her neck tightened, lifting her until her feet no longer touched the ground.

She dug her fingers into the arm, scratching and clawing for oxygen to refill her starving lungs. Her chest hurt, her vision started to blur as her arms weakened. It was over—she didn't have the strength to fight anymore. But Pierce had said he loved her. Pierce Thunder Horse had said he loved her. She had everything to live for. Dying was not an option.

A surge of hope filled her body and sent a flash of adrenaline through her system. She let herself go limp, playing dead, letting the full weight of her body land on Ethan's arm—the arm still injured from the shot he'd taken to the shoulder.

Ethan staggered back, his grip loosening.

Roxanne jabbed her elbow into his gut as hard as she could.

He released his hold and Roxanne dropped to the ground.

Pierce charged across the floor in a linebacker stance, plowed into Ethan, and sent him flying into the stack of wooden crates.

The impact knocked the wind out of the injured man and he crumpled to the floor, his hands clutched around his ribs. "Damn you, Thunder Horse. Damn you to hell." He rolled to his side, reaching for his rifle.

Pierce kicked it away from his hands. "Enough. You've caused enough problems. Give it up." He jerked Ethan to his feet and twisted his arm up behind him. Leaning close to the other man's ear, Pierce spoke in a clear, intense tone. "I'd have killed you for what you did to Roxanne, but that would have made me no better than you."

"You killed Leah," Ethan cried.

"No." Roxanne pushed to her feet. "*You* did by leaking the information to the FBI. You knew the warehouse was wired to blow. It was your call that killed Leah and my brother, Mason."

Pierce shoved Ethan forward. "I'm sure there's a prison cell with your name on it."

"Don't be so sure he'll make it that far."

Roxanne spun to face Shorty Duncan.

The man held a metal box in his hand. He blinked the blood out of his eyes and staggered backward toward the entrance, his hand reaching for a toggle jutting out of the top of the box.

"He's got the detonator!" Roxanne yelled, diving for the man, knowing she'd never reach him in time.

Another form appeared behind Duncan, yanking the box from his grip before the deputy could flip the switch.

Shorty rounded on the man behind him, reaching for the detonator. "Give me that."

Tuck Thunder Horse pistol-whipped Shorty against the side of his head, sending the deputy flying backward. The older man tripped over a boulder and landed flat on his back. When he tried to get to his feet, Tuck pointed his gun at the man. "Stay where you are. I've lost all patience for the local law enforcement, so don't try me."

Roxanne found the duct tape and bound Ethan's wrists behind his back while Pierce held him steady. Then, with a great sense of justice, she bound the deputy's wrists behind his back, as well. She wanted to slap a piece across his mouth, but resisted the payback urge and tossed the roll to the ground.

She led the way out of the cave, letting the sunlight warm her face and her insides. So much had happened, everything spun inside her head.

Maddox and Dante had just crested the ridge overlooking the crevasse where the caves were hidden. As they dropped down to the canyon floor smiles spread across their faces.

Mattox chuckled. "I see you didn't need our assistance after all."

Tuck emerged from the cave dragging Shorty Duncan behind him.

Dante's eyes rounded. "Well, well. What have you got there?"

"One of the leaders of the NorDak Militia and an entire cave full of weaponry." Tuck tossed the detonator to Dante.

Roxanne ducked, her body tensing, anticipating the explosion.

Tuck chuckled. "Don't worry, Roxanne. I pulled the wires loose from the explosives.

Roxanne let go of the breath caught in her throat and laughed shakily. "Don't scare me like that."

Maddox dropped down out of his saddle. "Need a hand there, brother?"

Pierce pushed Ethan Mitchell into Maddox's grip.

"Take him, will you? I need to get Roxanne home. She's been through a lot."

"Take my horse. I'll catch a ride in the helicopter."

Roxanne's heart skipped a couple beats as Pierce hooked her arm. Suddenly shy, she pulled back, avoiding the showdown with Pierce Thunder Horse, afraid it would be their last. More afraid that what he'd said wasn't true. He really didn't love her.

Tears welled in her eyes, her head pounded where the deputy had hit her and she didn't have the strength left to keep from telling this man just how much she loved him. "Leave me alone, Pierce," she said, then turned to walk away.

"Damn you, woman." Pierce caught up with her and scooped her legs out from under her, crushing her to his chest. "You will stop running from me and listen to what I have to say. After that, if you still want to leave, I'll let you go."

Tears slipped from the corners of her eyes. "I don't want to hear it."

"You damn well better." Pierce shook his head, his own eyes glazing. "Why are you crying? You know I can't stand it when you cry."

"Because…because…oh, hell, because I love you and I was stupid and…well…now you know. And you're not in any way obligated to love me back. Even though you said you did in the cave when you thought I was going to die. I love you, Pierce Thunder Horse, and I'd just as soon die if you don't love me back—"

Pierce's lips closed over hers, stemming the gush of words spewing from her mouth.

Chapter Sixteen

A round of applause erupted behind Pierce as his tongue slid past Roxanne's lips, between her teeth to connect with her tongue.

Her arms circled his neck, drawing him closer.

Wakan Tanka had to be smiling down on him. Roxanne was alive and in his arms. He'd found all the happiness he needed in this kiss. If he could freeze a moment in time, it would be this one.

As his head lifted, reason returned with the air filling his lungs.

"Why did you kiss me?" she asked, her tears glistening on her cheeks.

"To shut you up." Tuck chuckled as he led Shorty Duncan past the pair. "Never heard a woman say so little with so many words."

Roxanne swung a hand at Tuck. "I can still whip your butt, Tuck Thunder Horse."

"You'll have to get in line behind Julia. She has full rights as my fiancée."

Pierce glared at Tuck.

"What?" Tuck looked all innocent.

"Stop flirting. You're practically a married man."

"Then do something about her." Tuck pointed at Roxanne. "She's trouble."

Pierce's gaze captured Roxanne's. "I know. More than you can imagine."

Roxanne looked down first. "You can put me down, you know."

"What if I don't want to?" He held her tighter.

She inhaled and let the air out in a short burst. "Why, Pierce? Why won't you let me go?"

"Because I almost lost you. I'm afraid if I put you down, I might lose you all over again."

Roxanne waved at the men climbing up over the ridge, leaving them alone in the canyon. "No one's shooting at us. You and Tuck took care of the bad guys."

"They aren't the ones I'm afraid of." Pierce let her feet fall to the ground.

Roxanne didn't move out of his arms. She stood close, her hands resting against his chest. "You're afraid? Of what?"

He gripped her arms, staring down at her, his body tense, his heart pounding. "That I should let go of you… but that I won't be able to."

Her hand cupped his cheek and she shook her head. "You don't make sense."

Pierce let go of one of her arms and captured her fingers with his. "I'm not the right man for you, Roxanne."

Her lush, full lips thinned into a straight line. "Then who is? And don't give me that crap about someone who will be around for me. I can take care of myself."

He started to shake his head, but she jumped in before he could say anything.

"Okay, so I needed a little help when I had someone gunning for me. But that's not something that happens every day. I've been running the Carmichael Ranch for four years, and up to this point, I've had no problems. I can do it again."

"But—"

"But what? You don't trust me since I was the one who called off the wedding?"

"No, I understand why you did that. Believe me, I blame myself for Mason's death as much as you do."

"Stop." Roxanne held up a hand. "You said it your-self—the one to blame for the explosion is Ethan. He's the one who set the explosives and sent your team in. You need to stop blaming yourself."

"I got the tip. I should have seen it as a setup."

"None of the agents did—why should you? I don't blame you for Mason's death."

Pierce smoothed a strand of hair out of her face. "Mason asked me to protect you. How can I do that when I know that an FBI agent's wife is never safe from waiting and worrying if her husband is going to come home?"

Roxanne frowned at him. "Is it that you've had time to think about us and realized you couldn't live with a sometimes long-distance relationship?" She pulled out of his arms. "I can understand and accept that." She turned and started to walk away. "Don't worry about hurting my feelings—I'm a tough girl. Besides, I have to get back to work. I have a ranch to save from the bank."

"Roxanne Carmichael, sometimes you talk too much." Pierce caught her before she got two steps and spun her to face him. "My problem is that I love you *too* much."

"You sure have a way of showing a girl." She reached up to wipe the tears from her face.

He captured her hand before she could brush away a single tear and thumbed the moisture from her cheek. "It's not fair to ask you to wait for me, to be alone so often. Like you said…you have a ranch to run. I go where and when the bureau sends me. We'll always be going in different directions."

"So, you're letting me go. Fine. Let go." She glanced pointedly at his hands.

Pierce shook his head. "I can't." He pulled her into his arms and rested his cheek on her head. "You're so much a part of me, I can't function without you. I'll give up the FBI, if that's what it takes to be with you."

She pushed against his chest. "You'd give up the FBI for me?" Her lip trembled and she sucked it between her teeth. "No way."

"Yeah, I would. I'll turn in my resignation as soon as I get back to the office."

She shook her head. "You can't."

"Why?"

"Because I love you." Roxanne stood on her toes and pressed a kiss to his lips.

Pierce held her at arm's length. "Now you're not making sense."

"I couldn't live with myself knowing you gave up a job you love for me." She smiled up at him. "I'll sell the ranch. I could follow you wherever the FBI sends you, or be waiting when you get back." Her brows furrowed. "If you want me to."

Pierce hugged her to him, his heart full of his love for this woman. "We'll figure it out, sweetheart. Somehow, we will."

"Does that mean we'll be together at least some of the time?" she said into his chest, her fingers curling into his shirt. "Please say it does," she whispered.

"It does." His arms tightened around her.

Roxanne's hands circled the back of his neck and she tipped her head up to stare into his eyes. "Will you marry me, Pierce Thunder Horse, even though I canceled on you before? I promise I won't this time."

A chuckle rose up his throat. "Yes, I'll marry you. But shouldn't I be the one asking?"

"Does it matter?" She leaned into him, pressing her lips to his.

No, Pierce thought. It didn't matter as long as they were together.

"HERE LET ME HELP YOU with that." Mrs. T. took the veil from Roxanne's hands and slipped it over her head, anchoring the comb in her hair. "There."

Roxanne stared at herself in the mirror, amazed at her own transformation. She smiled, her eyes filling with tears. "My mother would have loved being here. She always wanted to see me in a dress."

"What?" Julia slid up beside her and stared into the mirror, patting her own veil. "Didn't think you had it in yourself to get all dolled up in a wedding dress?"

Her cheeks burned. That's exactly what she'd been thinking. "I'm just surprised I can still fit into it."

"Like you were going to gain any weight rounding up a couple hundred head of cattle and loading them onto trucks. That's about as likely as you finding time to eat while dealing with the bank, making a couple trips back and forth to Bismarck and giving statements to the FBI and ATF, and—in your spare time—planning a wedding over just a couple of days." Julia dragged in a deep breath. "Whew! I'm tired just listing it."

Roxanne laughed. "You make it sound…chaotic?"

"It was." Julia hugged her, grinning.

"I'm just glad the bank decided to renew my mortgage. When I get the check from the cattle sale, I'll be okay."

"What a relief after all you've gone through." Julia hugged her again. "I'm so glad you agreed on this double wedding."

"Me, too." Roxanne liked Tuck's fiancée and was glad she'd be around at family gatherings.

"And to think I didn't want to marry Tuck because he was an FBI agent." Julia shook her head. "And here I am, about to do just that."

Roxanne tucked a strand of her red hair into the bunch of curls secured to the top of her head. "What changed your mind?"

Julia smiled. "I thought I couldn't live with him, knowing he could die at any minute. But I realized I couldn't live without him, and would rather have as much time with him as I could get. And Lily deserves to know what a wonderful father she has." Julia stared across at Roxanne. "What changed your mind?"

"Pretty much the same reasons." Roxanne chuckled. "Even when I was being pigheaded, I never stopped loving the man."

Amelia laughed. "My boys can be pretty pigheaded, too."

Katya entered the room, a smile lighting her eyes. "You two look so lovely." She pressed her hands together. "I cannot wait for my own wedding to Maddox."

"It's too bad you couldn't join us." Julia crossed the room to hug Katya.

Roxanne smiled. "Julia, you're going to run out of hugs at this rate."

She laughed. "I'm delighted to be a part of such a big family. If not for Tuck and the Thunder Horse clan, it would be just me and Lily." Her smile faded. "I miss my sister so much."

Roxanne fought the ready tears that had been bubbling to the surface since she'd woken up that morning. "I miss my brother, too."

Katya sighed. "I would have loved a simple wedding, here on the Thunder Horse Ranch. But that is not to be. My brother insists we marry in my country."

Roxanne grimaced, imagining the crowds and required decorum. "Sounds like a lot of pomp and circumstance."

"Of which you will all partake." Katya stood tall and commanding in a way only royalty can pull off without looking arrogant. "I insist that the entire family come to Trejikistan for the wedding."

Roxanne hugged Katya. "I'd love to. I'll have to clear it with my husband, though." She grinned, almost pinching herself over the use of the word *husband*.

"I'm sure he'll agree." Amelia and Julia took turns hugging Katya.

"Hmm, someone's missing." Roxanne glanced around the room. "If all the women are in here, who has Lily?"

Julia's lips turned up on the corners. "Tuck volunteered to take over diaper duty while we got ready. I wonder how he's holding up?"

"I CAN'T GET THIS BOW tie to look right." Tuck yanked it loose yet again.

"What's wrong, brother, getting cold feet?" Dante lounged in a chair across the room.

"Shut up, Dante. You'll be next at the altar, after Maddox." Pierce held Lily carefully so that she didn't spit up on his tuxedo.

Dante shook his head. "Not if I can help it. I like being a bachelor. Kinda like the last man standing. Footloose and fancy free."

"You just haven't met the right woman," Tuck said. "I give up." His hands dropped to his sides.

"Here, let me." Maddox took over, and in a few quick movements had Tuck's tie perfect.

"How is it that the cowboy knows how to tie a bow tie and the fed doesn't?" Dante teased. "You'd think with the undercover activities you guys participate in, it would be a requirement to know how to tie a bow tie."

"Guess I missed that training session at Quantico." Tuck smiled. "Thanks, Maddox. You doing okay over there with the little one, Pierce?"

Pierce nodded. "She's an angel." He liked the way Lily snuggled against him and how warm and soft she was. His heart squeezed in his chest as he wondered what his and Roxanne's babies would look like. Would they have red hair like Roxanne or the dark straight hair of their Lakota ancestors?

"It's about time. You two ready?" Maddox crossed to the door and held it open.

"You bet." Pierce's pulse quickened. He handed Lily over to Tuck. "I believe this sweetheart belongs to you."

"Hey, Lily. Let's say you and me go to a wedding." Tuck straightened his little girl's pretty white dress, dropped a kiss on her cheek and stepped through the door. No hesitation.

Maddox clapped a hand onto Pierce's back. "Any second thoughts, little brother?"

Pierce shook his head. "Not one." He'd loved Roxanne for so long, marrying her would only make his world complete. Still, he couldn't believe it was actually going to happen.

Maddox's brows dipped. "You look a little nervous."

Pierce's lips twisted. "Until I get a ring on her finger, I won't believe she's really going to marry me."

"Kinda the way I feel about Katya." Maddox sighed.

"And you have to go all the way to Trejikistan to tie the knot." Pierce clapped a hand on his brother's back. "I'm glad the ladies decided on home for this shindig."

"Shall we?" Maddox held the door.

"I'm ready." Pierce led the way, emerging into the great room of the Thunder Horse Ranch house. The space had been transformed into a garden with flowers and greenery strategically draped over the mantel, wooden beams and walls. The huge leather couch had been moved to one of the bedrooms, replaced by a couple rows of white wooden chairs, decorated with cheerful white daisies, ribbons and yellow roses.

All of Roxanne's ranch hands were present, except Ethan, who had spent the past couple days in jail in Bismarck with Shorty Duncan. A contrite Toby stood with his cowboy hat in his hand, still mentally kicking himself for being played the fool by Ethan.

Pierce chuckled at how uncomfortable the cowboys looked all duded up in freshly pressed jeans, crisp white shirts and neckties. Every one of them tugged at the constriction, probably counting the minutes until the ceremony was over and they could lose the ties while digging into the catered barbecue brisket and cases of beer.

Pierce's stomach rumbled as the rich aroma of smoked brisket and roasted corn drifted to him from the kitchen, reminding him that he hadn't eaten breakfast.

He took his place beside Tuck and Lily in front of the fireplace, tugging his jacket and checking the placement of the single white rose on his lapel. At least he had on his black cowboy boots, instead of the patent leather dress shoes the tuxedo shop had tried to rent to him. Thank goodness Tuck had been in agreement with him and chosen to wear the same.

Music filled the room from the piano their mother had tried unsuccessfully to get all the boys to play at one time or other. She'd arranged for one of the young men from the Medora Musical to play for the ceremony.

As the music swelled then faded, Pierce shifted beside Tuck, starting to worry that Roxanne would get cold feet and regret her decision.

Then the wedding march filled the air and Julia emerged from the hallway and floated toward them, smiling.

Tuck adjusted Lily in his arms and stepped forward to take Julia's hand. "You're so beautiful," he whispered as he turned toward Hal Jorgensen, the local justice of the peace, who'd come out to perform the ceremony.

Pierce held his breath, his gaze riveted to the hallway, his hands clenched at his side.

Then she stepped from the shadows, her deep red curls piled high on her head, her long, slim neck bare all the way down to the dip of her cleavage into the strapless wedding gown that hugged her figure like a glove.

Pierce froze, his heart stopping as her gaze met his. He'd never seen a more beautiful woman, and she was about to become his wife.

As she moved toward him, his chest tightened and his heart kicked in, shooting adrenaline throughout his body. He let go of the breath he'd been holding and hurried forward to take her hands in his. "*Cante waste nape ciyuzapo.*" He pressed one hand to his chest. "I greet you with my heart."

Roxanne's smile lit the entire room. "Did you think I wasn't coming?" She took his elbow and squeezed. "Didn't you know?" She stared into his eyes and took a deep breath. "I'm going to mess this up, but here goes... *Mitawa cante itawa niye.*" She looked up, hopefully. "Did I get that right?"

Pierce grinned, his chest swelling so full he thought it might explode. "Yes, if you were trying to say, 'You got intoxicated on the way to the market.'"

Roxanne's eyes widened and she pressed a hand to her mouth. "Is that what I said?" She laughed. "I was trying to say my heart belongs to you."

"Pierce." His mother's voice reminded him he was standing in a room full of people, waiting for the wedding to begin.

"You said it right, and..." he brought Roxanne's hand to his chest "...*mitawa cante itawa niye.* Forever."

She blinked back tears.

Pierce inhaled and let out a steadying breath. "*Wakan Tanka yuha yuwakape miye.*" His hand slipped around Roxanne's waist and he pulled her to him as they stepped toward their destiny. "The Great Spirit has blessed me."

* * * * *